King Street Run

King Street Run

V. R. Ling

Elsewhen Press

Contents

For Nick

Chapter 1: The Palaeolithic Phase

Five words. That's all it took. Just five words to sow the first, far away thought that somehow, something was horribly wrong. The kind of inexplicable nagging that digs a crevice into the pit of your stomach and takes root. The kind of realisation that, like it or not, something is heading straight for you. Like a cricket ball. Ignore it as he tried, and he really did try, that cricket ball was making a beeline for Thomas.

— ∞ —

Thomas H. Wharton was a student of King's College, Cambridge. Prior to winning a scholarship to study for a Masters in archaeology he completed a degree at King Ethelred's College in Winchester and much like its namesake, Thomas had been unready for life in academia. He was the first person in his family to attend university and despite his scholastic greenery – indeed, perhaps because of it – he had a pragmatic approach to tackling life's pitfalls; useful training for the metaphorical sinkholes not far ahead.

Time had been feasting upon Michaelmas Term for nearly a month and for Thomas, who was as awed by the surroundings as he was daunted by his course, there could not have been a more glorious, more cheery October morning. Buttoned up from knees to nose in a padded green parka, the young man was in characteristically chirpy form as he made his way to the Student Facilitation Building in Mill Lane; on a mission to submit a request for a supervision room. Now that he was a graduate, Thomas was determined to seize every opportunity to push himself academically and so he had signed up to supervise undergraduates in the Archaeology Tripos.

His tall, lanky frame bounded along the narrow road, occasionally pausing to crunch through piles of windswept leaves or admire the neo-Gothic architecture. The pretty terraced buildings had once been home to an array of subject-specific lecture halls, but were now used as administrative offices. There remained but one lecture hall in Mill Lane, huddled uncomfortably at the far end like a bus passenger edging away from the malodorous drunk that had plonked down next to them.

Externally, the buildings were tidy and dignified with an enigmatic air. Each one sported a shiny black door with brass letterbox and hexagonal door knob, and as Thomas turned the one belonging to the Student Facilitation Building a spacious hallway fanned out before him. The sound of keyboards being tapped and fragments of faint conversations wafted out from half open office doors and he stood motionless, glancing around the dim entrance. There were white painted dado rails set against stark white walls, brass wall lamps radiating cool white light, and each white door led to a separate University office, painted white.

To his right was a wide stone staircase. The turned oak spindles of the balustrade were, in deference to the wider design solution, embalmed with a thick coat of white gloss. The paint was flaking off here and there, leaving behind a spatter of jagged, round wooden wounds. It looked as if the past had carried out a drive-by shooting. The paint didn't suit them. It was like the time Thomas had gone through a punk phase and dyed his brown hair blond. It looked awkward and wrong. Somehow, the chunky handrail had escaped the decorator's brush and its polished wooden surface gleamed with stately dignity as it swept up the staircase.

The coir mat on the foyer floor was scattered with leaves blown in from a large elm tree overhanging the building and noticing one poking out from the sole of his boot, Thomas tapped his foot against the bottom step to dislodge it. Walking up the stairs he smiled at the broad, grey steps, smooth depressions worn into their centre by several hundred years of footfall. There are many such staircases in the older buildings of the University and its

Colleges, and it was Thomas' custom to walk directly in the indentations because, in his own quirky way, he felt he was walking through history. As his foot left the first step he noticed something unusual. Just for a moment he thought he saw a ripple around his boot, as if he had trodden in water.

He stopped, blinked, placed his hand on the balustrade to steady himself, and lowered his head for a closer inspection. Nothing.

He tapped his boot on the step several times more but no water droplets fell from it. He then looked behind to the foyer floor to see if it was wet, perhaps a puddle from last night's rain that had leaked under the door, but it was bone dry.

"I must have imagined it," he muttered as he curved his hand over the banister and trotted on.

Thomas arrived at a small half-landing and paused to read a brass sign on the wall. The shiny metal square resembled a memorial plaque of the type one might find inside a church and it lamented the occupants of each room as it would the incumbents of a tomb. He scanned down the list until 'Mr T. Pyrone. Rm 13' presented itself. No one knew what the 'T' stood for and no one wanted to engage its owner in conversation for long enough to find out. Unfortunately for Thomas, Mr T. Pyrone was the Room Clerk and all requests for room bookings had to pass through his talon-like fingers for approval.

The walls on the first floor were also painted sepulchral white, but these ones were replete with an ornate picture rail, albeit devoid of pictures. Thomas walked slowly along the corridor assessing the condition of the rail, eventually stopping to run his hand over its bumpy surface.

"There's so much paint on that it feels like woodchip wallpaper," he said to himself. "Still, nothing a decent sanding couldn't cure. It'd come up a treat." He cast an eye behind him, curious if one of the doors might conceal a caretaker, "I wonder if I could volunteer to do it."

Thomas loathed to see an old building in want of repair and being of a practical nature he was invariably keen to help fix their maladies.

Further white painted doors lined the corridor, each with a black plastic number plate screwed to the front. Thomas continued walking until he spied '13' at the far end. It was nestled next to a tall, arched window and as his eyes glanced across the glass they caught the reflection of a man standing behind him. He turned around, expecting to find one of the administrators he had come to see, but there was no one there. He paused, a little surprised.

"Trick of the light," he shrugged, continuing along the hallway.

The door of number 13 was wedged ajar with a pile of tatty books and Thomas knocked twice before entering with his best smile, a smart-casual little number with sheepish undertones.

The air inside was thick and stale, and there was an uncomfortable melancholy that seemed to part out of the way as he walked in. Two people were interred within: Mr T. Pyrone who sat at a large desk that ran parallel with the wall opposite the windows, and his assistant Mr A.C. Edy. Both men raised their heads but neither spoke. Despite it being a sunny day and the office boasting two large windows, the room felt unnaturally sombre, as if the light were reluctant to enter. At the top of the high walls the lining paper was peeling, heavy with dust upon its upturned edges, and the ceiling was patterned with cracks running without order this way and that. This, Thomas was repressing the suspicion, is where cheery moods are laid to rest.

Noting the shiny name plaque at the front of his desk, Thomas turned his attention towards the larger man and the chap at the smaller desk whipped his stare back to the computer. Behind the large, chunky table, sat the large, chunky figure of Mr T. Pyrone. Half concealed by shadow, he looked down his wide, flaring nose scanning a dog-eared pile of papers on the desk before him. He had one elbow on the table, rotating a cheap plastic pen between his long fingers, whilst the other hand flipped to and fro through the sheets, as if picking over a carcase. To the side of his large name plate sat a bowl filled with ornamental acorns, dry and discoloured, peppered with bent paperclips and expended sticky tape reels. Mr T. Pyrone secreted the same sense of hollow superiority so expertly mastered by investment bankers, right down to the perfectly pressed, almost concrete texture of his dark grey suit.

"Hello!" chimed Thomas, trying to inject as much friendliness into the encounter as possible.

The man raised his head.

"Room booking?" he asked, a sulphur hexafluoride voice leaking into the air.

"Yes, absolutely, I'm a new archaeology grad and these are my first students. Starting to think I've taken on too many to start with but you know how it is, thought it best to get stuck in."

Disinterested in Thomas' existence, the man turned back to his carrion.

"Mr Edy." He gestured with his pen towards the equally smart, equally grey chap at the other desk who upon hearing his name craned his neck around the monitor, hair like patent leather and two beady eyes darting in Thomas' direction. He walked over to Mr Edy and placed the room request form in a green wire tray marked 'In'. The desk showed signs of rampant woodworm and the metal accessories upon it were weak with rust. Thomas nodded in friendly acknowledgment and was about to retreat when, "Copies?"

A single word thrown out by Mr Edy which lassoed Thomas backwards.

"Copies?" queried Thomas.

Mr Edy picked up the wrinkled green form with an exaggerated huff and turned it over to reveal a swathe of small black writing which he now scanned with a profound sense of purpose.

"Point 5C," with an emphasis on the 'C'. "Each form

should be submitted to the Room Clerk's Office along with *two copies*," he snapped triumphantly. Mr Edy didn't show any obvious signs of the Black Death but it would have suited him.

"Oh okay. Sorry, I didn't see that," apologised Thomas. "May I use your photocopier?" He gestured to the large machine in the corner of the room as he moved towards it.

"Have you been manually trained to use one?"

Thomas paused in his tracks, suspecting the wispy little man *might* have a sense of humour after all and he let out the kind of chuckle one gives when not finding something funny, but wishing to express gratitude for the attempt, "Ha! I think I can manage it, thank you."

Only, it wasn't a joke.

"No! Not if you haven't been manually trained." Mr Edy waved his hands at Thomas with all the gusto of a castaway hailing a passing ship.

"You'll need to request a place on the appropriate course as delivered by the Manual Handling and Operation of Essential Equipment team. You can find their office by looking it up on the SIS:TUM."

Thomas stared at him in un-thrilled bewilderment.

"SIS:TUM?" repeated Mr Edy, "Student Integration System: Technology, Uptrading, Management." He tutted. "It's what makes uptrading *possible*. This should have been explained as a priority when you matriculated. If the answer isn't on the SIS:TUM then you don't need to know it."

"What's uptrading?" enquired Thomas, who immediately regretted asking and wished life came with an 'Undo' button.

Mr Edy tutted again, shaking his head in bitter disappointment; it was quite some time since he'd been burdened with a double tut-ee.

"Archaeology?" he asked, leaning back in the chair whilst sagely plaiting his fingers.

"Yes," responded Thomas, feeling he should apologise.

"Anyone can dig a hole," the man waved his hand

dismissively. "But what you *really* need is the training to select the project management software that will keep you task-focused, adhering to a risk-managed efficiency model, and always..." he paused for emphasis before continuing, "*always* keep your value chain analysis at the forefront of your mind."

"I wouldn't dream of keeping it anywhere else," simpered Thomas, unable to animate his expression.

Deciding he would pop around the corner and make a couple of copies in the newsagents, Thomas retrieved the green paper that Mr Edy had by now flung into his 'Out' tray, folded it up, and left the room with a polite yet bewildered "Thank you."

What?! said Thomas inside his head as he left the room and retraced his footsteps along the corridor. *What?!* he repeated with duelling eyebrows as he slouched down the wide stone steps and back into earshot of the tapping keyboards on the ground floor. This time, the tapping keyboards gave him an idea and rather than trudge to the newsagents he decided to enquire if there was another, less dangerous breed of photocopier he could use elsewhere in the building. He walked back into the foyer and knocked twice on the first door he came to, stepping back to read the sign on the front as he did so: Office of Data Service Transmission and Inter-Communication for Alumni Smelting and External Opportunity Quantification.

No one answered and so Thomas tentatively slunk in. It was a large office and looking at the ridge that ran up either side of the walls he guessed it had at some point been two smaller rooms knocked into one. Two dozen desks were arranged in neat rows that ran parallel with the walls and four bright fluorescent tubes buzzed loudly overhead. Thomas' pockets didn't jangle loudly enough to elicit a reaction and so he looked around for someone to approach. To the right of the door sat the immaculate Miss Harbinger, Assistant to the Secretary of the Office Clerk's Support Administrator, and being the closest desk to the door, he sidled over to it.

"Ah, hello," he began.

Without looking up, Miss Harbinger raised the index finger of her right hand which signalled the young man should wait. There was no coming back from this; she had granted Thomas the latitude to hate her. He sighed quietly and looked around the desk while she tapped with unfettered leisure on her keyboard. Stuck to the wall behind her was a flimsy, pine-framed pin board, its flaking cork filled to capacity with dozens of smiling photographs. Men in dinner suits, smart and cheerful, women in black rimmed spectacles and ball gowns, their arms draped over each other's shoulders as if each were carrying a dying soldier, but amongst them all, the focus was always upon her own disproportionately large face. It may not have been immediately obvious, but Ms Harbinger was at her most vivacious in team meetings, of which there were many, where she specialised in overusing the word 'literally'.

After waiting a minute or so, Thomas defiantly spoke again.

"I really am sorry to trouble you. My name is Thomas Wharton, I'm an Archaeology grad and I have a room request form to hand in." He glanced down at the folded paper in his hands, shifting nervously on his feet.

Miss Harbinger sniffed.

Trying to be affable, he continued with small talk.

"Lots of supervisions planned for Michaelmas. I don't know where the time goes. I've been emailing the undergrads and they all seem incredibly eager. I hope they aren't disappointed to have supervisions with me rather than with one of the professors." He looked up, anticipating a response.

Miss Harbinger picked up a small tube of hand cream from the side of her laptop, squeezed a pea-sized amount onto the back of her hand and rubbed it against the back of her other hand.

"You need the Room Clerk's office. You can literally find the location of their office by looking it up on the SIS:TUM." And with that she cast her eyes back to the screen.

"Yes, yes I know," said Thomas breathlessly, "but I didn't know I needed two copies of the form and they won't let me use their photocopier, so I was wondering if I could use yours?"

"Have you been manually trained to use one?"

Just as Thomas was about to pinch himself to see if he were awake or had been transposed into a Monty Python sketch, a soft middle eastern accent appeared, like an oasis, to his rescue.

"You wish to book a room for supervisions?"

She was tall, with short, dark hair tied into a neat braid and a strong, carved face. According to the ID badge hanging from a lanyard around her neck, the woman's name was Petra Jordan. She wore a long woven linen dress, a pair of delicate rose-shaped earrings, and was accompanied by the spice-like aroma of incense. As she spoke she had risen from her desk on the opposite side of the room and traced a route to where Thomas was standing. She had impeccable posture and a perfectly balanced gait that looked as if she were carrying a dozen invisible books upon her head.

"Hand this to me, I will make copies and deliver it upstairs," she said assertively.

Taken aback by the relief, Thomas happily surrendered the paper.

"Thank you! Thank you very much. Are you sure you don't mind? I'm happy to make the copies, I just need to find a photocopier that won't set off any nuclear warheads."

"This is not a problem…" she studied the name on the form, "…Thomas. As the saying tells us, time is made of gold, and I'm sure you have better ways of spending yours."

"If you're absolutely sure you don't mind then that would be great, thank you. It's very kind of you."

He grabbed the strap of his rucksack and pulled it further up his shoulder.

"I really appreciate it, thank you," he repeated.

Petra inclined her head politely before walking off with

the form to the other end of the office, disappearing through a door marked *Private*.

Drained by all the facilitation he had received, Thomas drifted out of the building.

"All things considered, it's probably for the best that I didn't offer to sand the picture rail," he mumbled to himself, rearranging the scarf inside his coat. "The perceived body count would have been horrendous."

Thomas was starting to consider that *nothing* on Earth could be more curious than university bureaucracy. In about fifteen minutes time however, he would discover that whilst nothing on Earth *is* quite as curious as university bureaucracy, there are a few things on the periphery of Earth that give it a run for its money. He had no lectures for the remainder of the week and so he elected to return to College to read through some papers.

As he wandered through the busy streets, admiring architecture and soaking in the atmosphere, Thomas was soon again in fine fettle and he stopped at the bakery to inspect the vegan options. He had been vegetarian since he was 17 and over the past few years had evolved that one step further. Just as his eyes met with the sausage rolls, his attention was snared by the reflection of a man standing very close behind him, looking over his shoulder. Thinking how outrageously impolite it was to stand so close when there was plenty of room for them both to look in the window coveting savouries at a civil distance, Thomas turned around with "Do you mind!" cued on his lips, but there was no one there.

He paused, then spun to look over his other shoulder but still there was no one standing anywhere close to him. In fact, there wasn't anyone within at least several metres of him. He looked one way down the street then the other but it happened so fast that he hadn't caught sufficient sight of the man to identify him and so he brushed it off, thinking he must have been mistaken.

He reached into the pockets of his jeans and pulled out all the change he could find, counting it in his hand outside the bakery doorway: £1.59. As expected, he didn't possess the required funds to splash out on a sausage roll, so he continued on his way, using the time to mentally place his supervision schedule in order.

Thomas was born into a typical working class home in the typical Essex town of Baulkwall and so encountering a financial shortfall alongside a rumbling stomach was just part of life's ever darkening black humour. He was raised in a 1950s-built, ex-local authority property that sat at the end of a row of four houses in the middle of Cairnstone Avenue. Across the road and on either side of it was another identical row of four houses and next to those another set, then another set, and so the pattern continued along the entire length of the street as it seeped its way through the eastern edge of the town. The surrounding houses, though structurally identical, contained a quaint mix of the dispirited and the plain odd. There was the occasional broken pram poking out from Amazon-length overgrowth, no doubt an unconscious yet bold surrealist statement on the travesty of lost youth in modern Britain, and then there were the concrete lawns; former gardens buried mafia style in order to make space for a third pile of car-shaped rust. And like every such street, Cairnstone Avenue had that *one* particular house that went the extra mile to flaunt its urban flair. The fixer-upper imprisoned behind a chain-link fence with no gate. The house that should you, for some unfathomable reason, wish to enter, you would first have to negotiate the Tate-like installations of its garden decor; an abandoned sofa, a double mattress, and several small piles of red bricks that appeared to have hurled themselves from the walls in despair.

Local ambience aside, ever since a door-to-door salesman sold his father an illustrated book of Greek archaeology, Thomas had been gripped by a fascination for all things ancient. As a matter of self-preservation, door-to-door salesmen did not commonly tread the potholed asphalt of Cairnstone Avenue, but when one brave soul arrived on a bitterly cold and rainy night, Mr Wharton Senior felt such pity for the drenched wretch that he made a kind gesture by purchasing the cheapest book from his tatty portmanteau. After closing the front door his father glanced down at the small black book with its swirly gold-coloured writing 'Ancient Greece in Pictures' and placed it in front of a six-year old Thomas.

"Something for you to scribble in," he said as he affectionately ruffled the child's head of thick brown curls.

When Thomas' bright green eyes caught sight of the book, his little fingers reached for the cover and began slowly turning the pages, each photo pulling him further and further into a new and larger world. For the record, he never scribbled in the book, except to proudly inscribe his name 'Thomas Wharton age 6' on the frontispiece. He didn't realise it at the time, but that little black book was the first domino to fall; the more pictures of ancient artefacts he looked at, the more he wanted to find out what they were. When he knew what they were he wanted to know what they meant. When he knew what they meant he wanted to understand the connection between the objects and the people that made them. And when he had reached the end of these archaeological whodunnits, he wanted to know how the objects were discovered in the first place. To Thomas, archaeology was time travel. He was bewitched by the notion of holding an object that had last been held hundreds, perhaps thousands, of years ago. He considered there to be something especially venerable about archaeologists, those brilliant minds building upon knowledge for the sake of knowledge, but it never occurred to him, at least not then, that he might become one.

With hands in pockets, Thomas strolled casually through the College Gatehouse. At King's the last building before the river is Bodley's Court, a striking nineteenth century affair with beige stone walls and Gothic ambitions. It is largely laid to lawn with a path carved through the middle and an old quince tree just off-centre. The tree is surrounded by a neatly dug circle of earth, its gnarly trunk and branches reaching out from the ground like a wrinkled hand. Life may rush on about it, students come and go, but the elderly quince has seen it all before and takes time in its stride, fruiting every 40 years or so if the mood takes it. To the west, facing the river, sits a small patio area with a faded wooden bench; inviting enough to remind students to take time out to enjoy their surroundings but liberal enough in its dispensing of splinters to send them back to work. It is here that Thomas would huddle every morning, feeding the ducks with grain that he bought from a stall in the market.

Bodley's is chiefly utilised to provide accommodation for Fellows and students, and when Thomas discovered he had been allocated rooms on the ground floor, he was ready to burst with excitement.

— ∞ —

"Bodley's Court! I don't believe it! Alan Turing had rooms in Bodley's Court!" Thomas had exclaimed to his mother and aunt at one long ago breakfast as he read the letter detailing his accommodation.

"Who?" asked his mother.

"Alan Turing!"

"Well I hope he's gone before you move in."

"No-no mum, I mean that Alan Turing *used* to have rooms there."

"Who?" asked his aunt.

"*Alan Turing,*" stressed Thomas, "he once had rooms in Bodley's Court."

"Is he the one that did the programme with the woman about the murders?" asked his aunt. "You know, they solved all those mystery murders in locked rooms."

"I suspect you're thinking of Alan Davies and no that's not who I mean," said Thomas, "I mean *Alan Turing*, the mathematician."

Blank stares.

Thomas elaborated, "Cryptographer, founder of computer science, his work was critical in breaking the Enigma codes during the Second World War?"

His mother looked to his aunt and laughed, "We've always said that Thomas looks like a young Alan whatsisname. It's the hair."

— ∞ —

One of the things Thomas particularly liked about Bodley's was that its heavy wooden doors, stone staircases, latch windows, and even much of the ironmongery were not only original, but largely untroubled by the passing of time. Whenever he opened a window he couldn't help but wonder who, a hundred years ago, may have grasped that same fixture and pushed open that same window. He had never felt so at home as he did living in his set of two rooms, and they were very much rooms with a view. There was a bedroom and a study area connected by a small vestibule, and both enjoyed quaint leaded windows that overlooked the Back Lawn.

As he approached the gate to Bodley's Thomas noticed a tall, thin woman standing behind it, fumbling with the latch and he stopped to greet her. This was no ordinary woman, or so she implied to anyone that would listen; no, this was Ms de Midden, the Critical Success Factor Liaison to graduate Supervisors, their eyes and ears in the wider key performance landscape. She was in her mid-fifties, mondaine, and with luxurious shoulder length black hair. Her wide brown eyes, though the fated hook of at least three husbands, were sometimes so overwhelmingly dark and so unnaturally large, that she appeared not to have any at all, just cold, empty sockets. She had a particular liking for things that did nothing; chiffon scarves to drape around her shoulders, too thin to be of any warmth; diamanté hair clips that held back one part of her thick hair, whilst long, strategically combed down strands hung limply in front of her eyes; and an array of different sized pockets down the sides of her pressed trousers, all sewn shut. She clasped her clipboard to her chest like a crucifix as Thomas approached.

"Hello," he chirped. "That gate gets stuck all the time. I

think it's where people let it bang shut and the keep plate has become crooked over the years. May I help you with it?"

Ms de Midden eyed him sourly.

"I doubt it," she replied, still trying to brute force it open. Thomas nodded and was about to walk on when a thought occurred to him and he swivelled back to face her.

"While you're here," he said, fishing out an envelope from his pocket and removing the contents so she could see. "I've been invited to the Supervisors' dinner next week and I was wondering if there's a dress code or if it's just a casual do?"

Ms de Midden paused her disagreement with the latch.

"If you feel it's appropriate for you to attend the *dinner,*" she began waspishly, looking at Thomas like a disappointing hire car, "then, as per the instructions on the invitation you should follow the SIS:TUM. Log in, verify your identity – your pass code will remain active for five hours – navigate to your actionable items, request the appropriate attendance form, fill it out, and email it to me along with the reference number on the back of your letter."

"Could I not just tell you I'd like to come?"

"The instructions *are* on the letter," she repeated.

He glanced down at the missive and bobbed his head. Unbeknownst to Thomas, Appendix D of the invitation made it quite clear that his own Supervisor, Professor Thanatosis, would not be in attendance. The beleaguered Fellow was last sighted entering his rooms a month prior – after deciding to clear the pre-term admin from his desk – and hadn't been glimpsed since.

Thomas was about to thank Ms de Midden for her time when he noticed someone staring out of one of Bodley's first floor windows. Maybe it was a trick of the light but the person appeared unnaturally faint, almost transparent, and they were looking directly at *him*. Although he couldn't see clearly, Thomas felt sure it was the same reflection he had observed at the bakery. A chill plunged down his spine and for a few moments he couldn't focus on anything other than the figure. He was mesmerised by it. But it wasn't fear that he felt, it was familiarity. But familiarity of what?

"Well?!" Ms de Midden had continued talking while Thomas was preoccupied with the window and her impatient tone pulled him from the trance.

"Okay… yes, um thank you," he replied with a polite half-smile and no idea at all what she had been saying. He immediately looked back to the window but the figure, if indeed it had been there at all, was now gone. He sighed, nodding in a gesture of goodbye and leaving Ms de Midden to rekindle her disagreement with the ironmongery.

Thomas had already decided to stroll a little further to the bridge, but he peered over his shoulder at the window a few times before once again dismissing the occurrence. As he approached the camber, a large rhododendron to his right issued him with a friendly "Ay up Thomas."

The thick green vegetation shook side to side and stepping out from its full and leafy embrace came Rangemen, the College's Head Gardener. Rangemen was one of those people whose natural kindness made them shine with beauty. He was a tall, stocky man with a slightly stooped stature, a head of thin, wavy white hair, and a lilting Derbyshire accent.

"Mr Rangemen!" greeted Thomas, "Afternoon to you too. I was about to head to the river but looking at that sky I think I might just head back to my rooms instead. Looks like it's gonna pour down."

"Nowt wrong with taking a break, Thomas," asserted Rangemen. "Afternoon's not too grim an' I reckon you've got a good half hour before rain comes. Get yourself some air while weather's with you. I would."

Thomas pondered the suggestion. He didn't usually mind Thursdays but this had been the kind of day that would eat the last biscuit in the tin and put the lid back on. He had spent much of the morning inside offices and it would feel good to brush away the crumbs.

"Yeah, why not, you're right," he said, turning his attention to the portly rhododendron. "This looks incredible, what on Earth are you feeding it?!"

Rangemen pressed his lips tightly together, casting a look to the buildings beyond the lawn before answering, "They can be spectacular providing you're diligent in removing dead wood." A small spider ran down his arm and he gently coaxed it onto his hand, then placed it onto the shrub, into which it hurried away.

"But for rhododendron the trick is to use pungent fertiliser," he continued, brushing his hand over the top of the plant. "They grow fast to get away from it."

Thomas laughed and was about to respond when there came a loud metallic *bang* from behind them. He turned to see Ms de Midden sauntering off in the other direction, the gate snapping angrily behind her. His eyes couldn't help but find, then linger upon the window where he had seen the figure. There was something about it that he was struggling to ignore.

"Owt up, Thomas?" asked Rangemen, noticing the distracted gaze.

"No, no I'm fine," replied Thomas. "It's silly, but I thought I saw someone at a window. Someone staring at me. But… no."

"Someone waiting for inspiration to arrive."

"Yes, yes you're right, Mr Rangemen. I do the same thing. Staring out of my windows when I've been reading a lot. It's just…"

"Aye?"

"Oh nothing. I couldn't really see who it was but I had the strangest feeling that I knew them. Daft I know."

"Windows are peculiar that way," said Rangemen, tapping a worn but sturdy spade on the grass to remove the mud. "Look through clearest glass an' things'll be turned round, one way or t'other."

"I'm just being silly. It was a ridiculous thought," sighed Thomas as he glanced back at the sky. "Look at those clouds! If ever one looked like a bad mood, there it is!"

Rangemen nodded and responded with a wry smile.

"Wildflowers have appeared on riverbank; *Asphodeline lutea, Hypericum perforatum, Viola tricolour*. You could do worse with yer time than take a walk to see 'em."

"Again, you're right," nodded Thomas. "I'll have a potter by the river, freshen up the old grey matter, *then* return to my reading."

"A good idea," assured Rangemen, now using a hand fork to scrape the mud from a trowel.

Thomas took in a long, deep breath, "Right then, I best be off." He took another look at the impressive rhododendron and began to walk away.

"No doubt I'll see you tomorrow." He smiled and added over his shoulder, "Have a nice evening, Mr Rangemen."

"Same to you." Rangemen raised a hand in goodbye as Thomas disappeared over the bridge, his thin frame absorbed by festoons of rich and vibrant Autumn vegetation. The elderly gardener's attention was then immediately hijacked by an impatient *tic-tic-tic*; a robin had landed on top of the rhododendron and with one eye fixed upon the tall figure, was hopping about the bush most impatiently. Rangemen nodded intuitively and began to pat his pockets, searching for something. After a few moments he pulled out a small pyramid of sunflower hearts and held them in his outstretched palm. The robin flew to his hand, selected a suitably plump offering and fluttered off. He smiled as the little bird zig-zagged away then set about gathering up his spade and smaller tools that lay scattered about the path. He placed them into a wheelbarrow and squeaked off towards the Gatehouse. As he reached Bodley's gate he paused to look up at the window that had so occupied Thomas and softly shook his head.

"Tomorrow's a little further away than usual," he muttered.

By now, Thomas had reached the centre of the bridge and, as was his custom, paused to look over the side. This was partly because of the picturesque view and partly to check if anyone was on the Member's Only area of the bank. It was a glorious landscape and in his short time at Cambridge this little stretch of river had become his favourite place to think. Looking from the bridge, the fabled Chapel sits resplendent in its Gothic charm and beside it, keeping watch over the river, is the Gibbs Building, a classic Georgian construction with a large, central archway. Thomas couldn't look at the Gibbs Building without thinking of M.R. James.

— ∞ —

"M.R. James used to have rooms in the Gibbs Building." Thomas had told his brother excitedly as he prepared to leave for Cambridge. "That's at King's College." Thomas was sitting on his suitcase, trying to compress it adequately for the zip to work.

"Who?" His brother glared through the bedroom doorway.

"Monty James."

"Meh."

"He wrote ghost stories," explained Thomas, falling sideways off the suitcase.

Blank stare.

"Well," he climbed back up, "that is, he was a Mediaevalist but he's, grrrrr —" he pushed down with all his might on the top of the case, "—famous for his ghost stories, grrrrr." At last the zip cooperated.

Zzzzzzzzzzip

"Meh… I'm having your bedroom when you leave."

— ∞ —

Thomas had read M.R. James' complete works and relished the thought that he now walked the very same staircases. He particularly delighted in how James wrote his stories as entertainment for friends and students, reading them aloud on Christmas Eve. That was one of many things about Cambridge that both inspired and petrified Thomas; people so clever in the clogs department that even their side hustles are impressive.

"If I pass my Masters, get a PhD and end up back

here," Thomas sometimes fantasised, "I'll write ghost stories for *my* students." Of course, he didn't believe he would 'end up back here'; from where he was standing a PhD required a terrifying level of confidence that he felt wholly incapable of, but he hoped, and he would try his very best anyway. As he always did.

Leaning nonchalantly against the moss patterned stone, Thomas observed three people by the river; a woman standing, looking into the water, and two men sitting on the grass further back, one with dark hair and one with light. If Thomas had been anywhere else in the world he might have thought there was something odd about the trio, but as this was Cambridge he didn't think too much of it. The oddness came partly from the way the people were dressed, as if they had fallen from the pages of a Victorian science fiction novel, and to a lesser extent an unusual atmosphere that surrounded them, which at the time he excused as the mind fog created by a challenging day. There was also something familiar about them. Something Thomas couldn't quite put his finger on. He looked at each of them in turn but could not remember where he had seen them before.

Perhaps, he mused, *they had been on television.*

The woman was slim, a little over 1.8 metres in height and she had light brown hair rolled into a neat French pleat. Her long coat was cut away at the front into a tunic, fastened with a row of black buttons. The fabric was dark blue with a similar plush lining, but on the back there was a single red line down the centre and a thinner, parallel yellow line extending from each shoulder. An attached hood lay dormant across her back and as she moved the bottom of the coat rippled as it brushed the top of the grass. The tunic had a high collar and there was what appeared to be a brass whistle fastened where the breast pocket would otherwise have been, a long chain looping through the top button hole. Her costume was finished with tight fitting black trousers, like jodhpurs, and a pair of low-heeled black boots, each with a bronze buckle at the top near the knee.

"You have to give it to the Victorians," said Thomas under his breath, "they had style."

He raised his forehead in contemplation. "They also had appalling levels of social injustice, poverty, corruption, and colonialism, which lacks commendation, but style, *yes*. By the cart load."

Of the two men seated on the grass, the dark-haired man, who was strikingly pale and with well-defined sideburns, was a commanding figure. He wore black trousers, a grey waistcoat, a white shirt with long sleeves that reached his knuckles, and black boots with four square clasps up the sides. A black tailcoat with an unusual side pocket – navy in colour with a light blue stripe at the centre edged with red – completed his outfit. The man was focused intently on a blade of grass held between his fingers, lazily stripping it apart as he lay on the bank, but despite his distracted air, the three people were deep in conversation. All of a sudden he threw the grass aside and stood up, turning from the river, hands on his hips, staring down and shaking his head.

The man on the left, who had a classic angular face, sandy coloured hair, and wire-rimmed spectacles, had also stood up and it struck Thomas that the three people were exactly the same height. If given maximum wiggle room on the fashion front, the sandy-haired gentleman was passable as Victorian but erred more towards the 1930s. His light brown suit jacket had a subtle herringbone pattern and there were dark brown patches over the elbows. The remainder of his attire was stylishly neutral; beige trousers, a checked shirt, brown tie beneath a tweed waistcoat, and well-shined brown brogues. A brass chain looped from a lower buttonhole in the waistcoat to a side pocket, and now and again the man would pull out a full hunter brass pocket watch, flip open the cover, stare at the face for a few seconds, then shake his head as he replaced it. Thomas screwed up his brow and stared hard at him. Of the three figures, the sandy-haired man was the most familiar.

Deciding to give the people a few moments to,

hopefully, finish up and move along, Thomas looked about him at the delightful setting, and his mind began to wander.

— ∞ —

It had never been his intention to go to university. Although he revered the idea of further education – engrossing one's self in the study of a subject and contributing to collective knowledge – it had been a pipe dream so far removed from where his path was heading that he dared not look in its direction. For him, university had been the aspirational equivalent of staring directly into the sun. He had performed poorly in school exams. He hadn't tried to pass them. He hadn't even revised for them. If someone had asked Thomas at the time why he hadn't prepared for his exams, he would have looked at them with bemusement. What a ridiculous question. He simply didn't come from *that* sort of background. After leaving school he worked in a range of different jobs, each one just a little worse than the one before, until eventually he found himself working as a Sales Clerk for a hardware wholesalers. At five minutes to five o'clock every evening the other clerks in the office would declare, "It's five to five!" and this would be followed by a low, apathetic cheer around the room. The torture of this commonplace ritual had not registered with Thomas until one day, after joining in with the cheer, he looked up at the clock, watching the second hand tick inexorably towards the top, and he was overcome with dread. It suddenly occurred to him that he did not want to spend the rest of life waiting for five to five.

When an idea entered Thomas' head he tended to run with it at near superhuman speed, and the need to change his life by simply *doing* something with it was the strongest pull he had ever felt. He spent that entire Saturday rooted inside a small internet café on the outskirts of town. His impecunious situation meant that he did not possess a laptop of his own and given that Baulkwall Council had long since closed the local library, his need for internet speed was satisfied by Lewisham Café, vegetarian and vegan hot and cold meals served all day.

The café opened at 8:00am on Saturdays but by 7:30am Thomas was already standing eagerly outside. It was a drizzly, cold morning and he had retreated as far as possible into his dark green parka, a slightly over-sized hand-me-down from his brother. His worn white trainers were already letting in water and he could feel his socks squish against the sides as he moved his toes. With one hand he held the coat hood tight around his face and from the other dangled an orange plastic carrier bag containing a few essentials; pen, pencil, an A5 notepad with only 12 remaining pages, and all the spare change he could find down the side of his bed. And so, with £3.14 burning a hole in his pocket, it was time to paint the café beige.

It was 7:40am when a tall, heavily built man with a short, simple afro walked past the interior door carrying a tray of salt cellars. No sooner did he see the bedraggled Thomas, shaggy brown hair stuck to his face with the rain, than he put down the tray and sprang to the door. With a *clink, clink, thud* of locks and a long *creeeeeak* he beckoned the soggy figure inside.

"Thomas!" exclaimed the shop owner with a strong east London accent. He was wearing a neat light blue uniform with matching bow tie, immaculately ironed and mostly covered by a crisp white apron with *Lewisham Café* embroidered at the top. He held out both arms and moved in to give Thomas a hug before stopping abruptly as he realised the extent of the saturation.

"Stone me! Look at the state of it! You need a shower to dry off!" he laughed.

"I feel like an otter's bath mat," chuckled Thomas, tactfully removing his coat in such a manner that would create the smallest puddle on the floor. "Alright if I 'ang this up?"

"Yeah, yeah, waddle out back, there's a towel on the hook."

Thomas pushed through the *Staff Only* door and headed

to an enclave opposite the kitchen. At the centre was a wall-mounted, cream-coloured telephone and beneath that, a series of aluminium hooks holding several wire coat hangers and a towel hung in readiness for days such as this. He took one of the hangers and threaded it through the arms of his sodden coat, its dark green fabric made a shade darker from the rain. Even the plastic buttons managed to look wet through. He then picked up the towel and dried his face.

Not so long ago, when Thomas was finishing secondary school, he had worked part-time at George's café every other weekend. He mostly washed dishes, swept the floor and unpacked deliveries, but when they were really busy he would make the odd toastie or two. And he was very good at it. Even when he had moved onto bigger and not better jobs, he and George had remained firm friends.

George was a widower of 20 years, he had distinguished flashes of white hair shooting through his sideburns and an oval face that housed two of the largest brown eyes this side of the human-tarsier divide. When Thomas re-entered the café George threw him a broad smile and gestured towards the corner table, a bright silver laptop at its centre. It was the best seating in the house, sandwiched between a window on one side and a long black radiator on the other.

"And take those flippers off and bung 'em on the radiator," shouted George as he pulled open a door behind the counter, immediately ascending the steep staircase that led to his private flat.

The café was a cosy little space with good food, mismatched furniture, and vintage crockery. There were a dozen or so tables, a motley crew acquired from junk shops and tips; square ones, round ones, an oval one, some light wood, some dark wood, all of different sizes and of a slightly different height. The seating was reclaimed church chairs, solid and sturdy, made of beech wood with ladder backs and bible pockets on the reverse. George was happy to distribute pamphlets from local musicians, artists, and theatres, with one copy being neatly pinned to a large cork board on the left hand wall, and the remainder divvied up between the bible pockets. The latest advertisement was for a series of Ken Loach films showing at the town's Arts Centre and George had given the poster a prestigious central placement on the board. There were two large windows either side of the front door, each with *Lewisham Café* written in white, swirly letters arranged in a circle.

When George returned, Thomas was nesting at the table; removing the items from his carrier bag and studiously placing them on the surface next to the laptop.

"Try these on," said George as he laid down a pair of thick white socks on the table. "Can't have your trotters scaring off me customers."

"Awh, cheers mate!"

"Tea and a toastie, sir?" George joked in the most well-spoken accent he could muster, standing like a fancy waiter with one arm bent neatly behind his back.

"Awwww yeah please, I'm starvin'!"

"And it's on the house." The lines on George's elderly face deepened as he smiled. His was an earnest smile and it brightened up the café even on a miserable grey day like this.

"I wanna go to university George," declared Thomas, his excitement spring wound so tight he could no longer suppress it and the words blundered out of him in a semi-coherent mind-dump.

"You know all that talking we used to do about the Neolithic mines in Hangman's Wood? And the Roman burial site next to the quarry? And those times we went metal detecting in Baker's Field, which by the way I wouldn't do now because, well, I read how it might destroy context…"

Thomas was never one for ending a sentence simply because his thought process had changed course, "and, yeah… but even then we never found much. Well, except that *one* Roman coin, but anyway – it hit me; I wanna *do* somefing wiv me life. I wanna go to university to study archaeology. I don't s'pose I'll be much good at it but it's worth a try. The subject that is. I've applied for a grant – that's money to pay some of the fees – and if I do alright I'll be able to get a better job than being a sales clerk for the rest of me life." He paused, thought, and quickly added, "Not that there's anyfing wrong with being a sales clerk. It's just, I don't wanna be one. And there's nuffin' wrong with that either."

An even wider smile spread across George's face, like someone drawing up the blind on a sunny day.

"Belting news Thomas! You know, I *knew* you'd end up doing something like this. I *knew it*! Absolutely flippin' fantastic!" and he leant over the table to give the damp Thomas a hearty hug.

Thomas spent all that day sitting in the small café, his eyes fixed on the screen searching for a university that would accept a 'mature' student which, at the grand old age of 23, is how he was classified. Given his poor exam results he was also in need of an institution that had flexible entry requirements. It was a tall order. Thomas had received no formal tuition in archaeology; he was entirely self-educated on the subject. Since the age of six he had read voraciously, mostly out of date books picked up from charity shops, and by his early teens he was a volunteer on the occasional local digs run by the town's ever diminishing museum. His mind started to fill with small, niggling doubts; his humble efforts couldn't compete with applicants who had an official qualification to support them. He would probably say the wrong thing at interview, he had a knack for that. His reading material wasn't reliable; permitting the charity shops of Baulkwall to dictate his learning curve was at best, experimental. With every uncertainty that infested his thoughts it spurred two more and just when he was feeling like the whole thing was a ludicrous notion and about to give up, he felt the presence of someone standing next to the table.

"This is for you," said George pulling out a chair and sitting down. He extended his hand and his fingers uncurled to reveal a small charm. It was a silver coin set inside a round metal disc, with a sturdy lobster clasp at the top so that it could be clipped onto a belt. Thomas instantly recognised it as the coin that he and George had dug up while metal detecting in Baker's Field. The *only* coin they ever found.

"Is this *the* coin?" asked Thomas laughing, fondly remembering the evenings he traipsed home covered up to his knees in mud after digging holes in deeply ploughed fields.

"We never found much, did we, but it was fun looking," replied George. "I always said I'd set it into some sort of keyring for ya and you must be psychic 'cos I finally got round to it last week. Bought the clasp and setting from one of those door-to-door salesmen. Poor bloke was soaked."

George leant back in the chair. "Something to remember me by when you're on the telly presenting the next big archaeology programme." He turned the coin over, rubbing it with his thumb as if remembering days long past and a different emotion took over his face, sad and regretful.

"Before me and Ethel opened this place," George raised his eyes to imply the café, "I had two happy weeks working as an engineer in the power plant." He sighed and shook his head. "I worked in that place for 23 years." He held the coin in his upturned palm, as if it were sand, fearful of it slipping through his fingers. "Twenty-three years," he repeated slowly. "So you go to university," he continued in a suddenly upbeat tone, "and you dig up the biggest mosaic this side of Rome!" He patted Thomas on the arm and stood up, leaving the coin on his notepad, and after tucking the chair neatly back under the table, returned to his place behind the counter.

Thomas sat quietly for a few moments, considering both the coin and George's words. Then, with renewed energy he set back to work, tapping furiously on the keys, making notes, crossing them through and tapping furiously again. The hours slipped away but Thomas did not budge from his seat. Customers came and went, vegan toasties were prepared and eaten, plates were collected and washed, and outside a small line of trees swallowed the remnants of a deep red sun. Thomas was oblivious to it all. He sat wide-eyed on the edge of his seat, reading the screen with all the anticipation of someone who had picked five winning numbers in the lottery and was waiting to see if he had the sixth.

"That's it," he declared at last, staring at the screen. "That's it!"

St. Ethelred's in Winchester was inviting mature applicants to apply for a place on their BA archaeology course via a written essay. His poor exam results could, he hoped, be ameliorated by an essay assessment detailing why he wanted to do the course. Appointments for interview had to be requested by 5pm on Saturday.

That Saturday.

A bolt of panic ran through him. He looked at his watch: 4:55pm. He scribbled down the phone number, jumped up, knocked over the chair, bumped into the next table which was thankfully uninhabited, and slammed through the *Staff Only* door to the phone. Holding the scrap of paper in the same hand as the receiver, his fingers dialled the number, pressing hard on the large beige buttons. A ringing tone sounded on the other end of the line. Thomas held his breath and closed his eyes.

"Please answer, please answer, please answer."

"Hello, St. Ethelred's Winchester, Department of Archaeology, how can I help you?"

Thomas had never been so relieved to hear a voice in his entire life. He spent the next few minutes speaking with the course co-ordinator and was invited to interview the next day. With little time to prepare, he spent the tail-end of Saturday writing his essay. The resulting manuscript was good. Not blow-your-big-white-socks-off incredible, but for someone who had never written an essay before it was insightful, perceptive, and expressed just enough earnest desperation for the Admissions Tutor to stamp the front of it with 'ACCEPTED'. From that point on, Thomas did not look back. On the following

Monday he handed in his notice at the hardware wholesalers, took his last look at that miserable clock, and two weeks after that he moved to Winchester. His final pay cheque would cover him just long enough until the grant kicked in.

Hanging from his belt, he wore the coin.

— ∞ —

With a deep breath, Thomas cleared his thoughts and peered over the bridge again. The unusual characters were still there. He paused, puzzled at what they were doing. *Maybe it's for something at the theatre*, he contemplated. A much respected venue for student productions, the ADC Theatre is just a few minutes walk from King's and it was not unusual to find students and their associates practicing their roles in secluded nooks of College grounds. He stepped back for a moment, looking down at his faded War of The Worlds t-shirt depicting a Martian tripod discharging a heat ray; "Maybe I should make an effort to dress with a little more *élan*," he pondered. He rested his elbows back on the stone bridge, leaning his head to one side in his hand and quickly amended the decision, "But I'm keeping the t-shirt."

The three people did not appear to be arguing but judging by their body language they were either rehearsing a rather intense play or discussing some eclectic subject. Thomas had no desire to interrupt them but similarly he was keen to sit by the river and gather his thoughts, so he decided to approach, greet the strangers, and continue walking further up the bank so as not to encroach on their space. Or them on his.

The stone steps leading down to the river have a small metal gate at the top and Thomas paused before it, admiring the narrow trail as he fumbled in his pocket for the key. Some of the overhanging trees have grown so large that their giant roots twist and turn in and out of the risers creating impromptu half-steps. Thomas adored it. Having finally switched to the correct pocket and feeling the cold metal at his fingertips, he pulled out the key, passed through the gate, and as requested by the sign on the front, secured it behind him. It was approaching ten minutes past 1pm and with clouds gathering, the remaining daylight was already fading to grey.

"Afternoon," greeted Thomas as he reached the bottom of the steps.

The two men turned to face him. The woman gave a brief, scrutinising glance but quickly looked back to the river. Upon seeing the people up close, Thomas had a revelation. *They're steampunks!* he thought. Back home, Thomas had lived near the town's Arts Centre, a funny little lozenge of a building with a neglected, slightly domed roof covered in self-seeded wispy brown vegetation, scruffy white stucco walls, and – courtesy of its leaky guttering – a prominent green line at one side of its wide double doors. It looked like an old boiled sweet covered in pocket fluff. One of the most popular events it hosted was a bi-yearly steampunk festival. Thomas never partook, but he used to sit on the wall at the top of his street and watch the neo-Victorians arrive in their homemade finery: elaborate outfits that embraced 19th-century aesthetics and the spirit of industrial machinery, all tastefully garnished with elements of classic science fiction. He had always found it an inexplicably hopeful sight. Without thinking, as is so often the wont of his species, this is precisely what he concluded the three people were dressed for and he couldn't help but comment.

"Terrific outfits!"

The sandy-haired man was the first of the three to smile and the first to offer a hand outstretched in friendly welcome, the other hand tucked casually into his trouser pocket.

"Welcome Thomas, welcome. Delighted to see you," was his opening gambit. "I'm Nick."

Confused at how the man knew his name and subsequently worried he may have missed some kind of tutorial, Thomas responded with a crack in his voice.

"Oh, sorry, am I late? I didn't realise." He had attended

such a large number of introductory seminars, formal dinners, casual lunches, and preliminary meetings that his first instinct was to doubt himself and consider if he had indeed forgotten one.

"That is, no one told me. Maybe the SIS:TUM isn't working." As he spoke, his mind raced through the pile of paperwork on his bedroom desk and very gradually, as he mentally sifted through the envelopes and invites, he became increasingly certain he hadn't overlooked anything.

"Actually, I wonder if you may have me confused with someone else. I was just taking a stroll. I don't think I'm *meant* to be here."

"One has to admire your existential approach," grinned the dark-haired man, also offering a hand. He appeared slightly younger than Nick, with prominent cheekbones and a strong, square jaw.

"I'm John," he said. "And the maudlin water baby over there is Trinity."

At that moment, the woman turned towards them, a weighty expression in tow, and she uttered the five words that would turn Thomas' life inside out.

"The river is flowing backwards."

As the words left her lips, Thomas had taken a step forward and the air seemed to thicken around him. He continued to look at Trinity, trying to focus, but her movements slowed to an unnatural speed. A strand of stray hair blown in front of her pale face was moving as if he were watching the scene in slow motion. He turned his head to the steps and stared in disbelief as the remaining daylight faded over the grass, evaporating like water in burning heat, shadows retreating as if running from his sight, and the sounds around him shrank gradually to an unsynchronised dub. With the exception of a few surreal reds and greens clinging on here and there, the colours of his surroundings turned monochrome. The vista took on the appearance of an artificially coloured 1950s photograph, the type commonly used on birthday cards depicting happy, smiley people wearing swimming suits at Clacton beach. A sharp chill entered through the back of his neck and shook every nerve as it rattled down his limbs. He began to feel light headed, but still he tried to keep his focus, walking towards Trinity and to observe the river for himself.

"It's not running backwards," slurred Thomas as he staggered forwards. "I saw it from the bridge and it looks normal."

He stepped back, wobbling as if three sheets to the wind.

"It's normal," he repeated, looking around at the bizarre change in his surroundings. "It's everything else that's wrong."

Trinity stepped forward to stop him from falling, placing a hand on his shoulder. She looked squarely into his eyes.

"Not *that* river," she responded calmly. "The one behind it."

Her serene demeanour was the last thing he remembered before waking up on his bed in Bodley's Court.

— ∞ —

Thomas sat bolt upright, his eyes wide open. He snapped his head to look at the grey plastic alarm clock on the bedside table: 1:10pm.

"What?" he declared, wiping a hand down the front of his face.

"What?!" he repeated, swinging his legs round the side of the bed and planting his feet firmly on the thin blue carpet.

"No! *What*!?"

He stood up, ruffling his hair and turning this way and that.

"*What*?!"

It was safe to say that Thomas had reached the 'What' stage of trying to make sense of things. According to his watch he had been at the river no fewer than two minutes ago, conversing with a few steampunks about the water flowing like it shouldn't or some such nonsense. He had no memory of the intervening time, but he *did* have a churning sensation in the pit of his stomach telling him that he needed to be somewhere else. Urgently. He had to get somewhere for something. But what?!

"Okay. Okay." He stopped still and closed his eyes, taking a long breath and exhaling slowly. He looked down at his clothes. He was fully dressed, ostensibly in the same outfit he had on at the river, right down to his damp shoes.

"I'm wearing the same clothes," he rationalised as he stretched his t-shirt out in front of him to better examine the belligerent Martian. But what was that? He bent down while pulling the bottom of the t-shirt up. There was a small tear in the fabric at the centre of his stomach.

"That wasn't there before!" he exclaimed, poking his finger through the hole in dismay. "Oh no, not my t-shirt, what have I done!?" It looked as if it were pierced by something small and sharp. He sighed, "I *should* be able to mend it. I'll get a patch."

With a sulky pout he let go of the t-shirt and continued searching for an explanation. He angled his left shoe to one side, and his right to the other. He then lifted a foot slightly and wiggled it, "Same shoes."

He patted his trousers, "Same jeans."

He reached a hand to his belt and felt his lucky coin. "Still there," he confirmed to himself.

Everything he was wearing was the same, so it would logically follow that it was the same day, a hypothesis corroborated by the bedside clock. But how had that hole appeared in his beloved t-shirt? It wasn't there earlier in the day or he'd have noticed.

"Think rationally. What's the last thing I remember?" He held his arms out in front of him as if grasping the steering wheel of an invisible car, turning them slightly as he looked for clues.

"I was talking to those people at the river. The lady… Trinity. She said something about the river. Th-that it was flowing backwards. But I saw it from the bridge and it was fine."

He rubbed his forehead.

"Then…" he looked to the ceiling as if hoping the answer might be written there.

"Then… Then… arggggghhhhh, I can't remember."

Thomas walked around and around his rooms, and his last memory – Trinity's words – ran around and around his head. He did not remember walking away from the river, nor picking his way up the narrow stone steps, and he most certainly did not recall opening the door to his staircase which required the hinged equivalent of a Masonic handshake before it would consider letting anyone in; a precisely timed push against the handle whilst turning the key. No, even in one of his more absent-minded moments Thomas would have remembered unlocking that door.

He pondered the alternatives: had he been drugged? Unlikely. As salty as the food occasionally seemed in the College canteen he was reasonably confident it wasn't the culprit.

Except, he considered, *maybe the fruit salad. That often has a suspicious aftertaste to it.*

He paused, dismissing the thought.

"No. No. Ridiculous, I haven't had a chance to get to the canteen today."

Suddenly his eyes widened, "That's it!" He pointed his finger upwards in a eureka moment.

"Maybe it's *because* I haven't eaten. I'm hallucinating because of lack of sustenance." The moment he said it, he knew he was grasping at straws.

"No, that wasn't the product of an empty stomach." He tousled his hair, "No one hallucinates steampunks on an empty stomach."

He looked back up at the ceiling, resting his hands on his hips, "I need a list!"

Thomas sprinted into the other room, headed for a pile of clothes in the corner and started throwing them on a small sofa, gradually excavating a freestanding whiteboard.

'Drugged' he wrote at the top and immediately struck a line through it.

'Malnutrition' he wrote next and similarly struck it through.

"Oh!" he exclaimed, "what's it called when you share a delusion?" He tapped his head with the board marker. "Folie à deux!"

He wrote it on the board but scratched it through straight after. "First of all that'd be quatre wouldn't it? Folie à quatre? And second I haven't imagined anything as such, I just can't remember how I got back to my room."

He let out an exhausted sigh. "No, there has to be something else." He placed his hands over his ears then ruffled his hair again.

"Did…" his hand paused as it reached his chin, "…I divide by zero at any point?" His arm fell despondently to his side and, as if the confusion had filled his whole body with lead weights, he sank onto the sofa, his head falling back on the cushion.

"What nonsense," he told himself. He rubbed his eyes and let his head drop sideways. His gaze drifted from ceiling to floor to sofa, until eventually it landed upon some light reading he had picked up from the University Library. Poking out from beneath the pile of clothes was the corner of *A Stamp Collector's Guide To Physics*. He suddenly perked up, standing as he grasped the book. As he stared at the cover his mind surrendered a half-remembered conversation with a physics undergraduate about quantum tunnelling – a phenomenon, so he scrambled to recall, whereby sub-atomic particles are able to pass through a physical entity. Had his atoms overcome the energy barrier presented by the wall and permitted him to walk straight through it, thus negating the careful precision required to open the staircase door?

'Quantum tunnelling' he wrote on the white board, deciding not to immediately put a line through it. He stood back and contemplated the suspects.

"Quantum tunnelling?!" he repeated as if horrified by his own desperation.

"Quantum *flippin'* tunnelling?!" He threw the pen on

the sofa and mumbled as he leant his forehead against the board.

"Yes, thank you very much Niels Bohr, I *am* shocked by it."

The 'how' however, was soon of little consequence because as Thomas rotated his forehead against the board to glance over the Back Lawn he caught sight of Nick, the sandy-haired man, walking bold as brass past his window. Thomas dropped the pen, fell over the whiteboard and could barely get his own feet to move fast enough as he clambered out of the room. He swung open the door and burst into the daylight of Bodley's Court with all the grace of a stuffed toy strapped to a bucking bronco. His shoes churned up the gravel as he turned an almost perfect 90-degree angle towards the gate, but he had no need to rush. Nick had just walked through the gate and stood there in front of him.

"May we talk?" he asked calmly.

Chapter 2: The Mesolithic Phase

Without waiting for a response Nick ambled over to the riverside bench and sat down. He crossed his legs and rested an elbow casually on the wide wooden arm. The Court had taken on a singularly relaxed atmosphere and the air was unusually mild for the time of year. Two collared doves landed in one of the large oak trees lining the bank and their soft *coo-COO-coo* echoed pleasantly around the buildings.

Nick exuded intelligence. He was charismatic, avuncular, and his voice was mellifluous without being overly posh. He was gently spoken, but his words were deliberate and confident. Without knowing him, Thomas liked him. Without knowing him, Thomas couldn't help but feel that he *did* actually know him.

"How are you feeling?"

Thomas stared at the reclining figure, blinking rapidly as if it might refresh his memory, "What?"

Nick gave a soft laugh, not a trace of mockery, but genial and reassuring, meant to put Thomas at ease, and the odd thing is, it did.

"We have a lot to discuss," he said, gesturing at Thomas to be seated. "A lot that might be challenging to accept, but I shall do my utmost to be plain with you."

Thomas sat down heavily at the other end of the bench, a defeated look washing over his face as he glared into the river. He couldn't think what question to ask first, so he asked them all at once.

"Who are you and what happened at the riverbank? And how did you know my name when I hadn't introduced myself?"

He ruffled his hair as if trying to shake an answer out, then leant sideways against the arm.

"I don't remember how I got back to my rooms. According to my watch only a few minutes passed but that can't be possible. And what was wrong with the river? It looked fine to me."

The smile tugging Nick's lips gave way to another gentle chuckle and had Thomas been facing in the opposite direction, towards the buildings, he would have seen all of the lights in all of the rooms of Bodley's Court flicker on and brighten as Nick laughed. The lights then slowly dimmed and went out.

"Thomas, what is the name of this College?"

"What?"

"Please consider the question," Nick requested politely.

Thomas shrugged, "It's King's College."

"Its *full* name."

"Ah." Thomas had to drag up the information from a box marked 'Lost Property' at the very back of his mind. "Yes, it's ah, the King's College of our Lady and Saint Nicholas."

"Yes."

"What does that have to do with the price of lemonade?" implored Thomas.

"I'm Nick."

"Yes, I know, you said."

"No. I'm *Nick*."

"Yes. I *know*."

"Nick, as in short for Nicholas."

Thomas hung his head in frustration, preparing to echo the words 'Yes. I. Know' but as he turned to look at Nick there was something so bright in the depth of those blue eyes and something so familiar in his calm, gentle countenance that Thomas couldn't bring himself to respond.

"They call me Nick because 'King' would be unthinkably pretentious." He turned his attention to a collection of stone plant pots neatly arranged to the side of the bench, then briefly to the velvety lawn behind them, "I do appreciate what Rangemen has done with the gardens. He really is the quintessential artisan."

Thomas thought he understood what Nick was implying, but just for a short spell he needed to sit quietly and marinate in the idea. So, the two men sat in silence while the non-human residents of Bodley's got on with making a living; the sound of the collared doves continued to play in the background, *coo-COO-coo coo-COO-coo*, a couple of wood pigeons squared off over a discarded bread crust, and a lone mallard bobbed about in the river reeds. In one of the towering oaks a grey squirrel hurled himself from one branch to the next, winding his way around the trunk then hopping, tail flinching all the way, to a bird feeder in the quince. He cast a locksmith's eye over the contraption, pulled a peanut through the wire mesh and scampered off to bury it beneath a pile of leaves.

Back in the primordial soup of Thomas' mind, understanding was forming, but it was still not ready to make its way onto land.

"I am King's College," clarified Nick. "I appreciate this isn't an easy concept to grasp but I hope all will become clear."

Thomas had calmed down considerably since first settling on the bench, he hadn't said 'what' for several minutes and although in his logical mind he thought what Nick was telling him must surely be a ruse, there was something about his matter-of-fact tone that was so very believable.

"Every College has a personification," continued Nick, "a manifestation of its character if you will."

He paused, allowing a few seconds for the information to be absorbed before pouring more on.

"We are guardians of a kind, muses at times. We observe from a distance. Not interfering enough to change a natural outcome, but not so passive that we permit a critical opportunity to pass by."

He paused again, watching with a smile as the squirrel ran back for another peanut.

"We offer a nudge to a brilliant mind who might otherwise have missed a paper that has ramifications for their research, and other times we may simply provide an atmosphere conducive to a good evening's discussion."

Thomas sighed and Nick moved only his eyes to assess the tailspin.

From the moment Trinity had uttered those five words, Thomas seemed to know that something, somewhere was wrong and that he, somehow, was a part of it. As a begrudging acceptance crept upon him, a well-spoken voice broke the silence.

"Hello Thomas, good to see you again."

The black-haired man had arrived and he delivered Thomas a friendly slap on the back as he squeezed himself onto the arm of the bench.

"Permit me to re-introduce John," said Nick, nodding in welcome. He then looked to Thomas with a smile wholly sympathetic to the situation and added softly, "Yes, St. John's."

John craned his neck to look along the river, following the others' gaze. "What are we studying chaps?" He had a cheerful, glass-half-full enthusiasm about him that not only created an air of instant affability but it also put Thomas further at ease.

"You don't appear quite so chirpy old boy," said John, casting a frown at the dazed student.

"I'm abstaining from chirpiness for the time-being," replied Thomas, trying to force his stunned expression into something that looked a little less like he'd been electrocuted.

John gave a solicitous nod, "Understood." He sat silent for a few seconds, drumming his fingers on the back of the bench before his tightly pressed smile curved gradually into a more playful grin. "I presume Nick has unwoven the not-so-pathetic fallacy?"

Nick interposed, "John, thank you for joining us." He shifted position to face him. "Your punctuality is welcome but may I request curbing the humour while Thomas recalibrates."

John pushed himself up, straightening his coat as he did so, "Apologies old boy, consider it curbed."

"I blame Douglas Adams," came a female voice from behind them.

Thomas turned, and Nick and John acknowledged Trinity's arrival with a nod.

"John is unsuitably jocular at times," she raised an eyebrow at the man in black, who accepted the comment in good form and politely moved aside as she rounded the bench.

"Good afternoon Thomas, I'm glad to see you looking so well. In case you have yet to recall, my name is Trinity." She held out a hand.

"You were there earlier, too," answered Thomas, acknowledging the connotation of her name with a slow, thoughtful handshake. "I don't remember anything after you spoke. It's gone. Like someone erased the time from my mind."

Trinity looked at him kindly. She had a narrow face with bright, round eyes pushed in like deep-set buttons.

"Can you…," she began cordially, "… call to mind anything of what happened?" She too took a moment to look along the river. "We were attacked. Do you remember?"

He stared at the paving slabs at his feet, blinking as if trying to wake up. But he did not remember and he did not wake up.

"Attacked? No. All I recall," he muttered, the information and its implications piling upon him, "Is talking with the three of you very briefly but then-then, after I moved towards the river…" He rubbed his forehead. In a flash, a few hazy visions returned to his mind's eye. He started to recall the conversation that had taken place when the shadows retreated and the riverbank drained of colour but he wasn't able to focus long enough to see them sufficiently. He stood up as if hypnotised, lifting a hand to his shoulder, "You stopped me from falling."

At this, Nick also rose from the bench, lightly resting a hand on Thomas' shoulder to guide him back down. A faint purple glow appeared beneath his palm and Thomas flinched. Suddenly the lost memory flooded back. But the events did not form an orderly queue and filter back politely, rather, they surged into his mind like a crowd of bargain hunters waiting for the doors to open at a 50% off sale. He slumped backwards, eyes wide and brow furrowed as he was reunited with the missing time.

— ∞ —

Flummoxed, Thomas looked around at the near monochrome vista with its unusual tints of colour, the imposing sight of the Chapel set against a burgundy sky, the grey, grey grass beneath his feet, and the surreal stillness.

"It's everything else that's wrong," he had responded to Trinity.

Thomas wobbled on his feet and she placed one hand on his shoulder to steady him, looking squarely into his eyes.

"Not *that* river," she corrected. "The one behind it."

He inched closer to the water, stared hard into it, and just for a moment made out what looked like a second river running beneath it. It was as if there were two rivers with a sheet of glass between them. One flowing in one direction, and one in the other.

"Here, sit on the grass," said Trinity as she and John lowered him to the ground before he fell upon it. The Colleges then stood like a triptych before him.

"We appreciate this is a lot to process," began Nick, the centre panel, "but we've been waiting a considerable time for your arrival and thought it advisable to commence introductions post-haste."

Thomas could hear what was being said but he felt woozy, the kind of disorientation one experiences in the first few seconds of being injected with a general anaesthetic, and so he sat holding his head, trying to stop it from spinning. He couldn't quite make sense of what he was being told, but he knew it was important that he listened, even if it were just to help focus his senses.

Trinity smiled down at the groggy student, his eyes shut fast. "We are," she held out her hands to include Nick and John, "the Colleges. Or at least three of them. Nick – King's. John – St. John's. And I am Trinity."

Thomas clenched his eyes tighter, seemingly in hope that it might morph her words into something more believable.

"It's a symbiotic relationship," explained Nick, pushing his hands into his pockets. "We are ideas created by the many minds of each College, but we also feed back into their character." He cast an eye to the Chapel then back to Thomas. "For these past 30 years we have been in decline, not in number but in strength. Each of us has a Keeper; a very particular person who works at each College and provides support should it be required, but even *they* are at a loss to identify the root cause."

Trinity took a few steps towards the river, looked along it for a moment then turned back, "Our world – the Keepers call it grey time – exists just a moment out of sync with yours. Not in some form of parallel universe, but in the slipstream of time behind your own. That is the reason you feel a little out of sorts right now. Think of it like jet lag – it is disagreeable but the feeling should soon subside."

By now Thomas had opened his eyes and was attempting to steady himself with both arms outstretched behind him.

"Something has gone amiss," added John. "In civilised circumstances we take corporeal form in *your* time every All Hallows' Eve – the only day of the year when time passes in our world as it does here – but every year it's a little more difficult to remain for sustained periods and that goes double if we leave our own grounds. Of course in grey time we can move around as we please, but it's become so dashed difficult in *your* time that the Keepers have obtained *these* to assist us." He reached into the top of his shirt and from around his neck removed a small, irregular shaped object threaded on a silver chain which he then lowered to Thomas.

"A stone?" his power of speech had returned and he reached up to take the chain, turning the fragment one way and the other before handing it back.

"It's chipped from my foundation stone," said John,

slipping the chain back around his neck. "Nick has one from the foundation stone of King's and Trin has one from her old place."

The others simultaneously pulled out the stones around their necks to show Thomas, then tucked them discreetly away.

Nick elaborated, "For Colleges who do not possess a foundation stone, we discovered that a fragment chipped from their earliest building suffices just as well. Possessing this small piece strengthens the connection between ourselves and *your* time, a temporary fix that increases the duration we can remain and facilitating movement beyond our own grounds. This is part of the reason we require your assistance."

"Are you saying you want me to find the other Colleges' foundation stones?" asked Thomas, still not entirely compos mentis.

Sensible of his student's disorientation – both physical and philosophical – Nick knelt down and spoke with a reassuring inclination, "No, no, certainly not. Our Keepers have excelled themselves in retrieving the ones you've seen here and as we speak they're collaborating with other Keepers to truffle out the full set, as it were."

Thomas stared at the monochrome grass, his eyes ricocheting about the slate-grey blades as he brushed the tops with his palm. "Is this world a copy of mine?" he digressed, picking up a small stone and rolling it between his fingers, testing its texture. By this point he couldn't help but think that, compared to any type of sense, blood might be a breeze to extract from it.

"In a way," answered Nick. "Even though we live out of sync with your time, it *is* the same world with the same structures and geographical features."

He then slowly stood up, looking over the roofline of the Chapel as if something distant had caught his eye, but when nothing appeared he quickly returned his attention to Thomas, "But grey time does not contain the same accessories as yours. For example, you could enter a public house in our time but there would be no beer glasses, there are no cars on the streets, no litter bins. You follow the idea?"

"Er, yes, I think so," responded Thomas.

Nick gave an understanding smile, elaborating as he took a few paces towards the river.

"The temporal span between our time and yours has been gradually stretching over the past 30 years. This is, we suspect, why it is increasingly bothersome for us to move outside of our own grounds when in *your* time. You see, once we occupied the fragments of seconds just after your own. Now it is full seconds, but soon it could be minutes. If the temporal gap expands too much further we risk losing the connection entirely."

Thomas shook his head. Perhaps it was the steampunk aesthetic that gave the whole situation an air of verisimilitude, or maybe it was the absence of a more pedestrian explanation to account for what he felt deep in his gut, but against his better judgement he couldn't help but consider what they were telling him with anything other than serious contemplation.

"Who would do this?" he asked, his common sense feverishly patching its punctures.

"You put your finger on the bullseye of a particularly sticky wicket," answered John. "We have reason to believe that person or persons unknown are, in way or ways unknown, pushing our time further and further from your own. Imagine a line." He walked to the water and knelt down, rummaging through the vegetation. After a brief but attentive search he plucked a long piece of grass from the bank and wandered back with it, pulling off a few side leaves. From his pocket he produced two round black buttons, threading one onto the stalk and spinning it around in front of Thomas' face. As the perplexed young man looked up, he momentarily raised a hand to shield his eyes from the grey sunlight reflecting off John's waistcoat buttons. After moving his head from the direction of the glare, he noticed the waistcoat had an odd combination of three large, exceptionally shiny brass buttons and three smaller ones of duller pewter.

"There's *your* world, your time," said John as the button span around on the thick blade of grass. "And here's *our* time." He threaded the other button onto the grass, to the left of the first, holding the blade taut.

"And that someone," joined Nick, "is pushing our time away from yours." And with that he pushed the second button along the blade of grass, away from the first.

"What do they want?" queried Thomas. "It seems like a damn lot of effort to go to for something that isn't immediately obvious. What could they hope to gain?"

Nick sighed heavily, "At this stage one can only speculate, but in all likelihood?" He shook his head slowly then looked up. "Not only to erase our positive influence but to actively encourage apathetic thinking that will harvest an intellectual recession; a decline in critical thinking, the subsequent closure of university departments, and ultimately the erosion of everything we stand for." He placed his hands in his pockets and looked out over the Back Lawn. "Someone who has a vested interest in corrupting the very essence of academia."

"You mean… Tories?" Thomas asked earnestly.

John rolled his eyes and opened his mouth to speak but then paused, as if contemplating.

Nick continued, "In the wider scheme of things, I am unable to disagree, but insofar as our more immediate buttons-on-a-blade-of-grass are concerned, we are not sure *who* it is. But whoever this *does* trace back to, we believe they are located geographically close to College."

Thomas, whose mind had been waving a white flag for some time now, finally surrendered to intrigue, and he wriggled into a more comfortable cross-legged position, staring up at Nick with an enthralled, wide-eyed stare.

"Why do you think that?"

"Because it is here that the river first started to run backwards. Now it has spread the entire length of the Cam as it flows along The Backs."

Thomas fell silent, taking the information in but not entirely sure what to do with it.

"John?" he asked.

"Yes old boy?"

"Why does your waistcoat have such odd buttons?"

"Buttons are great. They do things up," replied John, flicking one of the loose buttons from the blade of grass into the air and catching it with his other hand.

Feeling John had supplied the most succinct answer he could hope to receive and lacking the mental gusto to pursue the matter, Thomas tried a different route of questioning.

"Why me? I'm nothing special, I don't see what I can do to help," was his initial response. "I think maybe you're telling all this to the wrong person, probably mixed me up with a physics grad or something and I'm probably hallucinating or drunk, or both." He rubbed his head, perhaps hoping to scratch the ineffable itch of confusion by throwing out all the explanations he could think of and hoping one came up trumps. "But if you think I can help, then I will, but I know I probably can't."

The Colleges exchanged a look of quiet satisfaction, whilst Thomas, only just beginning to regain his equanimity, clumsily manoeuvred himself to stand. It was like watching a rag doll animate itself. Nick and John each took a hand and pulled him up, though it would prove a short excursion.

"Really old boy, good show," retorted John. "We knew you'd come through." And with that he gave the lad a firm slap on the back. "As your College, Nick is best placed to diabolise the detail."

Nick didn't respond.

"Nick?" repeated John.

Nick was looking up, the neatly combed fringe of his sandy hair fell forward and he flicked it back without averting his gaze. His eyes were trained on the roofline of the Gibbs building. In unison, John and Trinity spotted the focus of his attention and without a word spoken, their hands moved swiftly to their hips, each one pulling a short baton from a brass clip. Save for a different College crest engraved at the top, the batons were identical; dark wood, around 20cm in length and with the last few centimetres of one end noticeably darker than the rest.

At first, Thomas had difficulty discerning what they were looking at. He craned his neck one way and the other, but as the small grey shape grew closer he had no trouble making out a pair of bat-shaped wings and a round, frog-like body. Only this wasn't a bat, or a frog, or any combination thereof.

Nick, who had drawn his baton first, held it vertically to one side. Eyes still fastened on the incoming figure, he cast the dark end down and it met the grass with an incongruous sound of metal striking metal then leapt back up, still vertical, where it hung in the air for a split second before telescoping out equally from both ends. Thomas could barely believe what he witnessed; not only was the little stick now around two metres in length but its composition had morphed into a smooth metallic purple with a white stripe on each half. Nick caught the baton at its centre, turning it 90-degrees and holding it horizontally before him.

"Let's see what our storm petrel has to say," remarked John as he too threw his baton to the ground, followed in quick succession by Trinity. The sound of metal on metal, a rush of air, and John's baton was dark blue fading to light blue edged with red. Trinity's was dark blue, with a red stripe on one side and a yellow one on the other.

As the grey bat-frog came into sharper view Thomas could make out every grim detail. The creature, for it was a creature, had a body the size and approximate shape of a medium sized dog, stocky like a hyena but with a grey, concrete texture. Its stumpy limbs looked powerful and its thick, webbed wings beat down with such strength that even from a distance of what was now 30 meters overhead, it created a vigorous downdraft that blew the Autumn leaves into the air. Its head was round with a gorilla-like jaw and either side, poking out at a 45-degree angle, was a large, shell-like ear. The forehead, with three deep set wrinkles running side to side, had two small horns protruding from the top while the mouth, which hung slightly open, boasted four large fangs; two at the lower back and two in the upper jaw where one would otherwise expect a mammal's canines to reside. Its stumpy back limbs supported equally stumpy back paws, but the front ones were more like human hands, with thick grey fingers and an opposable thumb, each finished off with a long, pointed claw.

"Gargoyle," said Nick in a composed, measured tone. "Remember what we agreed."

Immediately, John and Trinity walked to either side of Thomas, placing him at the centre of a triangle formed with Nick.

"Whatever you do," said Nick throwing a quick glance over his shoulder to Thomas. "Don't do anything."

"What?!"

"Sit down," instructed John.

Thomas, still looking up at the rogue architecture circling the sky above them, slowly lowered himself into an awkward sitting position on the grass. In order to assume this posture he moved in much the same way as a cat trying to avoid a fight with another cat, whereby the subordinate attempts to move away from the dominant with exceedingly slow, but precise steps. It was comical, but one had to admire its meticulous execution.

"Good. Stay like that," approved Nick.

Suddenly, the grey mass dived towards them. John and Trinity crossed their batons to form a protective cross over Thomas, while Nick jumped a clear two metres into the air and took a swipe at the creature; not to make contact but to ward it off, at least for now. The gargoyle pulled up at the last moment, narrowly missing the side of Nick's baton and as it screeched away Thomas could hear its heavy wings beat with a sound like two concrete slabs sliding over one another. The force tore what was left of the leaves from nearby trees and almost ripped Thomas' breath away with it too.

Nick looked searchingly as the creature ascended, "I need a glance at its other side to be sure," he said firmly. "One more pass should suffice."

"It's trying to kill us!" shouted Thomas, peeking through his raised hands to get a lock on the gargoyle's location.

"It's not trying to kill us," corrected Nick, manoeuvring his position to match the creature's trajectory.

"It's trying to *distract* us," clarified Trinity.

The gargoyle flew in circles over the four figures, occasionally hovering on the spot to survey the scene. Its large, cumbersome head moved from side-to-side and all the while its expressionless eyes stared intently towards the ground, assessing the best opening for its next attack. Then, without warning, it found it. It swooped in from the left of the group, coming down at a steeper angle this time.

"Wait," directed Nick calmly.

The gargoyle let out a piercing wail as it hurtled towards them, its figure growing larger and larger as it approached closer and closer, its mouth opening wider as it raised its front paws, pushing out its razor-edged claws and baring its fangs.

"Wait," repeated Nick.

The creature was within ten metres and as soon as it reached shoulder height Nick cast his baton towards it. With another fearsome screech it ducked out of the way and climbed sharply into the air.

"Jumped up drain pipe," muttered John as he watched it pass overhead.

Nick turned to follow the direction of the gargoyle and without looking, stretched out a hand to catch the baton as it plummeted back to Earth. The projectile seemed to have a boomerang-like way of returning to its master.

"It's one of St. Edward's'," remarked Nick, his gaze still shadowing the creature. "Definitely from the church. No doubt about it."

"Now we're clear on *that*," began Trinity, "Let's get this over with." She broke the triangle, walking forwards whilst twisting her baton into a vertical position then thrust it to the ground for a second time. When it bounced back to her waiting hand its outer edge had acquired a luminescent appearance, as if charged with energy. She gave a nod to John then raised the baton to her shoulder as an athlete would a javelin, launching it skywards before the gargoyle could make another turn. It sliced through the air, grazing the creature's left shoulder and knocking it like a cricket ball from the sky.

Thomas flattened himself to the ground and once again placed his hands over his head, certain the falling masonry would smash into them. John grasped his baton at one end, as if holding a large bat, turned to face the spinning creature and prepared to strike.

"Not the bridge!" shouted Nick, suddenly noting John's stance. "NOT the bridge!"

But it was too late.

John's baton struck the gargoyle with a tumultuous bang. It was the kind of sound one would expect to hear if playing tennis with two industrial forklifts and a wrecking ball. The impact sent the gargoyle spinning towards King's bridge and with an ungodly explosion it smashed into the centre, obliterating both itself and the structure, save for a few remnants of the arch. A cloud of puffy, grey dust rose into the air like a soufflé before deflating in the same dejected manner.

In Thomas's time, two collared doves who had been sitting atop the bridge, minding their own business, started up in surprise. They retreated to a nearby oak tree and stared down as if expecting something to happen. But nothing did.

"1819," brooded Nick, closing his eyes and raising his face to the sky. "That bridge was built – at least in this location – in 1819."

Trinity turned her baton upside down then threw it to the ground. With a characteristic *swoosh* it shrank in mid-air, returning to life as an inconspicuous truncheon. Placing it back in her belt clip she paused to give Nick a consoling pat on the arm before heading off to inspect the gargoyle crumbs. Nick rubbed his eyes and pinched the bridge of his nose as one would at the onset of a bad headache.

Aside from Nick's annoyance over the damage to the bridge, the three Colleges seemed unperturbed.

Thomas, who by the second swoop had resolved to lying face down on the grass and observing the scene only intermittently from between his fingers, slowly lifted his hands from his head and looked up. Feeling something sharp at his stomach, he rolled over to investigate. It was a small, angular piece of masonry. He held the fragment between his thumb and forefinger, examining it with all the scrutiny of a jeweller assessing the worth of a diamond. By connecting with this simple piece of stone he had somehow hoped to either wake up, realise he was in the middle of a dream, or in some other way bring this curious reality into perspective. However, the piece of stone refused to comply and Thomas was left with very little choice but to get up, dust himself down and see what had become of the gargoyle.

Life can be like that sometimes.

Nick let out a quiet sigh, brushed the arms of his jacket, straightened his tie and walked towards the rubble. The dust had nearly cleared, revealing a mountain of debris in the middle of the river which the water now passed with indifference on either side. Nick knelt down at a pile of coal black stones that lay scattered amidst the grey masonry of the fallen bridge.

"At least we know where they're coming from," he said, picking up a small piece of the black stone, examining it closely, then throwing it back.

"They're getting stronger," remarked Trinity.

"Uglier," noted John, putting a commiserating hand on Nick's shoulder. "Genuinely. Mortified. Apologies old chap," he added, surveying the destruction before him whilst simultaneously patting the dust from his coat. "Gargoyle soot. It gets everywhere."

"It will mend," Nick assured himself, looking at the bridge as another piece of masonry plopped unceremoniously into the water. He put both hands in his pockets and stared forlornly at the rubble.

Curious, Thomas bent down to pick up a piece of the black stone.

"No, leave it," urged Nick, and Thomas pulled his hand away.

"The black stone is gargoyle," he explained. "It'll give you a nasty sting if it evaporates in your hand." Just as Thomas was about to reply, the inky deposits started to disappear, shrivelling to specks until not a trace was left.

Nick then gestured at the bridge, "Physical damage in this time is not mirrored in yours. At least, not to the same extent. If you look at the bridge in *your* time, superficially it will look the same as it ever has."

"Only superficially?" pressed Thomas.

"On a sub-atomic level the integrity of the bridge *will* be affected but not to the extent you see here." He sighed, slowly shaking his head at the scene. "Imagine a bridge behind the bridge, but in the same place. An echo. Because of that, damage sustained here repairs itself which in turn repairs any hitherto unobservable effect in *your* world." Nick straightened his tie again. "Regardless, it's a sobering…" He paused and looked sideways at John, a clear tone of disapproval in his voice. "It's a thoroughly uncouth thing to demolish a Fellow's bridge."

John grimaced and furrowed his brow remorsefully, "Mortified, old man. *Really*."

"It's simply not cricket," continued Nick, still shaking his head. Then, as if suddenly figuring out the answer to a tricky crossword puzzle, an oddly impressed look leapt into his face, "Although, that was a rather splendid cover drive…" he added reluctantly, referring to John's terminal shot, "…under the circumstances."

With an involuntary grin of pride, John nodded, "I didn't think anyone would notice that."

"It was a nice touch."

"Why thank you."

"If damage sustained here repairs itself," began Thomas, ignoring the diversion, "then what's going to happen to the gargoyle that just attacked us? Did you kill it?"

"Our world and everything in it, is merely a ripple of

yours," replied Trinity. "One can break the gargoyles into pieces but they will reform in their original place eventually. We've been doing this on and off for the past 30 years."

"Wait." Thomas shut his eyes and screwed up his forehead. "Are you saying you've been getting attacked by gargoyles for the last 30 years and it's only just occurred to you to *do* something about it?!"

"This is not a situation to rush into," replied John.

"Or out of," added Trinity.

"And to be clear, aside from data gathering we *have* taken practical steps," corrected Nick. "Corpus installed a chronophage to consume the excess time but it wasn't enough."

Thomas was incredulous.

"A chronophage?" repeated Nick. "It's a sort of temporal dehumidifier."

"Yes," began Thomas, his mouth hanging open. "I know the clock but —"

"There were additional contingency measures to put in place too," mumbled John. "And not *all* of us have been attacked. Peter hasn't seen hide nor spiky hair of a gargoyle."

"Peterhouse," clarified Trinity.

For a long moment Thomas stared blankly at what remained of the bridge, before another question occurred to him, "Can *you*... be hurt?"

"You can't kill an idea," replied Trinity, crossing her arms as she surveyed the damage. "And ultimately, that's what we are. But we can be stifled, which is what the temporal gap is doing."

"You can't kill an idea but you *can* dilute and corrupt it," amended Nick. "But in terms of physical damage we cannot be harmed in the same sense as a person can be harmed in your time. We can be injured and it would weaken us, but we'd regain our strength after a short while. Probably."

"The only thing," added John, kicking over a piece of stone at his feet, "that could potentially deal more long-term damage would be if something of our own turned against us. For example, let's say the scoundrel directing these gargoyles could control one of our own statues and that statue were to clobber one of us over the head."

"What would happen?" asked Thomas, his eyes wide with suspense.

John chortled, "I really don't know old boy. It's never happened. And I can't imagine it ever would. It's a speculative hypothesis." He coughed and assumed a more serious tone, "But anyway, it's one thing for the gargoyles of St. Edward's to run amok and quite another for us to inflict architectural self-harm." He straightened his waistcoat with a single, proud tug. "We might be eccentric at times but we draw the line at hitting ourselves over the heads with masonry."

Thomas looked about at the rubble strewn across the bank and nodded slowly, still struggling to take everything on board, "How long will it take for that gargoyle to… to repair?"

"Long enough," answered Nick. "It'll reform in its rightful place atop St. Edward's church and by the time *that* happens," he took out his pocket watch, flicked open the cover and examined the face, "we should be on the cusp of a solution. With any luck."

Now that Thomas was closer, he could see the cover of the pocket watch featured three finely carved flowers, two at the top and one centred below. Oddly, on the top were two winding crowns as opposed to the usual one, and Thomas would come to notice that Nick always pressed the one on the right to spring open the cover.

"Right," answered Thomas, "Of course."

When John batted the gargoyle into the bridge, shattering both the creature and the structure, Thomas had felt his reality explode along with them, and since that moment his sensibilities had been scrambling around on the grass bank attempting to gather up what was left, his mind frantically trying to put the pieces back together. And in that time, another question had been forming amidst the wreckage. Thomas contemplated the remains of the bridge before turning to the Colleges, looking from baton to baton to baton that hung from their waists.

"What are they *for*?"

"They save the students from getting their feet wet," answered John, also sizing up the bridge.

"No, no, the batons," replied Thomas.

"John knows perfectly well what you mean," tutted Trinity.

"Do all the Colleges have one of those? A weapon?" clarified Thomas.

Trinity buried her attention in the rubble and did not answer. John gave the baton a fleeting glance then looked away, as if uneasy at having one at all. Nick, his eyes having found distraction in a remote area of the Back Lawn, reluctantly answered.

"Royal Colleges," he said, shaking his head as if dismissing it as an embarrassment. "Only the royal Colleges possessed them and of those, these are the last."

"I see," nodded Thomas.

Nick turned away from the lawn and towards Thomas. When he spoke, it was with such composure and consideration that it was difficult to imagine anyone more ill-suited to violence than he, and by the remorseful look on his face, Thomas suspected he felt the same. In a surprise about turn however, Nick took the baton from its clip and tossed it playfully into the air, catching it with one hand and staring down at the seemingly harmless wooden stick.

"A symbol of repression. A hangover of social inequality brought about by the application of violence and manipulation, an insidious establishment that continues to this day through the feeding of rapacious greed at the expense of the oppressed."

John and Trinity stood silent.

"But they did save your lives," stressed Thomas, attempting to lighten their spirits – help them see their actions had been self-defence, not aggression. "You didn't have a choice. That gargoyle might have killed you. Okay, well, not *killed* you, you said you can't be killed in that way, but it might have killed *me*, so you saved *my* life. So, you know, don't feel bad about carrying those weapons." He looked around at the Colleges, hoping to see a small chink of relief in their guilt-ridden expressions.

"I wasn't referring to the sticks," said Nick, baffled by the suggestion.

"And you, our dear Thomas, appear to have grasped the wrong end of one entirely," added John. "The next gargoyle to creep up on us like that will have its Gothic spout ceremoniously batted into the architrave."

"And now we know where the devils are coming from, any further attackers will be summarily dispatched," proclaimed Trinity, tapping her baton with confident appreciation.

"But, I thought… oh."

Thomas, suddenly light-headed, stepped backwards as he lost his balance.

Swiftly caught by Nick, he and John each slung one of Thomas' arms over their shoulders and walked him back toward the narrow steps, whereupon the richness of colour and a non-smithereened bridge signalled they were once again in Thomas' time. There, at the top of the steps they were greeted by Rangemen. With all the ease of picking up a skinny sack of potatoes, the Head Gardener heaved Thomas over his shoulder and marched across the bridge, pass the gate into Bodley's Court, through the temperamental door with its Masonic leanings, into his already open set, and laid him upon his bed.

— ∞ —

"I feel like someone removed my brain, held it under the cold water tap for half an hour and plonked it back in my skull," remarked Thomas, staring into the river in acquiescence. His missing memories had zoomed into focus like a stereogram illusion. "How —"

"Did you get into our time?" pre-empted Trinity. "The coin hanging from your belt. It isn't a coin, it's a key." She paused, "That is, it *is* a coin but it is also a key."

"Evolution likes to co-opt adaptations for one purpose and use them for another," explained Nick, still seated comfortably upon the bench, "we like to do the same."

Thomas looked down at the inconspicuous little coin.

"A key?"

Nick sat forward, clasping his hands together.

"Colleges can move between times at will but Keepers require specific entryways." He checked Thomas' status with a covert sideways glance. "These – let's call them doorways for now – are scattered throughout the Colleges, their grounds, and the city, and providing a Keeper has a key about their person they can pass into our time the same as if they were walking through any other type of doorway." He bobbed his head side to side, "More or less."

A swan floated nonchalantly by on the river and Thomas took comfort in its serene demeanour, watching peacefully as the current slowly carried it away, half wishing he could go with it.

Nick made another tactful pause but after consulting his pocket watch soon perked up again, "The keys change every 30 years or so just to add a pinch more security. A specific Roman coin now, but they were vintage Beatles badges last time and Edwardian thimbles before that."

John, who had long since opted to lie on the lawn behind them, suddenly jumped up to rejoin the discussion. "Oh I *loved* the badges," he said, starting to hum 'Hey Jude' under his breath. "We should go back to the badges."

Trinity smiled at the suggestion. "Many Keepers sew the key into the lining of their coats. Given the nature of some of the keys, it's often more discreet."

"But I didn't see a doorway at the river," said Thomas.

"They're not actual doorways," answered Nick. "They're allocated locations. Although most *do* happen to coincide with a physical delineation. It makes it easier for the Keepers."

"Like portals?" asked Thomas, his mind awash with

memories from his teen years spent reading and listening to vintage science fiction.

"In many ways, yes. The key triggers a response in space-time, bridging the temporal gap between this world and ours. Effectively bending time in a defined area so the key wearer can walk through. A portal," nodded Nick.

Thomas turned directly to Nick, frowning, "Does that mean I could pass through one of these portals without knowing it, or without meaning to?"

"Most unlikely. I situated the portal at the river specifically for you to pass through, but it was returned to its traditional location after you departed. It was necessary to reveal our time to you, but I apologise for the graceless manner in which it was done."

Nick meant what he said. He was clearly uncomfortable placing Thomas in this sink-or-swim situation and that is perhaps what signalled just how severe the predicament was.

"Like regular doors that require a nudge, a kick, or a specific way of turning the key," Nick elaborated, "most of the portals have a quirk to them; it provides another level of security. One cannot simply fall through accidentally should you somehow manage to obtain a key. At some point in the near future this might be something we have to demonstrate to you."

"But if that's the case and this…" Thomas lowered his hand to his belt and unclipped the coin, holding it in the palm of his hand, "…is a key, what are the odds that I should have it? My friend George – George Lewisham – gave it to me, he runs the veggie café back home and surely he's not a Keeper." He continued staring at the coin. "I mean, he's a really nice person and … no, he's a fantastic person, he's been like family to me, but surely he isn't. Is he? Is *George* in on this?"

"No," replied Trinity softly. "He's not." She patted his shoulder gently and wandered to the back of the bench, leaning against it with both hands.

"But even so, it's too much of a coincidence. Really, what are the chances of me having this?"

There was protracted silence and after a flurry of uneasy looks, it once again fell to Nick to respond.

"Do you remember where you found the coin?"

"In Baker's Field, in Essex, where I'm from." Thomas rubbed the face of the coin. He would never forget the days that he and George hiked through fields of grazing cattle with the metal detector to reach the recently ploughed field beyond, full of hopes of finding Anglo Saxon treasure.

"Was anyone else there that day? The day you found the coin," asked Nick, as if he already knew the answer.

"No," replied Thomas. "Just George and me. Aside from this one coin, all we ever found were old bits of pipe and rusty nails."

"No one else was there?"

"No." A distant, seemingly unimportant memory then raised its hand at the back of Thomas' mind. "Oh, hang on. There was someone else but only for a bit. It was nothing. Just another metal detectorist that passed us by."

Trinity looked at Nick and smiled knowingly.

"Did this other chap…" Nick raised his eyes and rocked his head side to side in anticipation of the answer "…say anything to you?"

"Er, no. Not really, he just said that he'd been getting a lot of response at the south of the field and that we should try looking in that area. Load of old pony though. All we found was —"

"Old bits of pipe and rusty nails," finished Nick. "But you also found *that*," he nodded at the coin.

Thomas sat forward, as if hit by a thought driving a bus.

"Was that *you*!? Was the other metal detectorist *you*!?" he asked, the pitch of his voice rising with every word. "Did you have something to do with sending me on that wild goose chase traipsing the length and breadth of what must be the only field in England without a coin in it?! And that was a *big* field!"

"Compose yourself Thomas," responded Nick, straightening his already straight tie. "And no, it wasn't. I have no time for such fancies. And there *was* a coin in the field." He coughed, "Albeit just the one. Your being here is *not* a fait accompli."

There was a momentary pause as Nick looked in the opposite direction and added quietly, "Although there may have been a gentle nudge of a few variables."

Thomas didn't appear to have heard; he took a deep breath then clipped the coin back onto his belt.

"I don't know why I thought that," he laughed, a nervous shake running through the middle of it. "That was a ridiculous idea. It just all seems so unbelievable. I can't make sense of it."

The four people fell quiet. Thomas, his constitution soothed by the cool Autumn air, rested his elbows on his legs and placed his head in his hands. A few silent seconds passed when suddenly his head jerked back up.

"Wait! Am I —"

"No," pre-empted Trinity, again. "You are not a Keeper, Thomas."

"You sound like my ex-girlfriend."

"And in case you were wondering," she continued, "the reason you could see us from the bridge is because when you looked over the side and came down the steps we were indeed standing in *your* time, but as you reached the bottom and walked further towards the river you passed through the portal."

Thomas closed his eyes, attempting to digest what his ears were busy disbelieving.

"And all we had to do..." she gestured with outstretched hands to imply herself and the others, "...was phase into grey time to meet you."

"I almost went back to my rooms," ruminated Thomas. "Instead of going to the river I almost went back to my rooms. Mr Rangemen encouraged me to–to enjoy the afternoon, to take a walk by the river."

"Sometimes chance rolls the dice and they comes up snake eyes," smiled John. "Rangemen is the Keeper for King's. In fact, now I come to think of it, quite a few of the Keepers are Head Gardeners."

"Rangemen is a one-of-a-kind," added Nick proudly. "Rangemen is *the* gardener."

"And what's *phasing*?" asked Thomas, who was starting to think that all he had done for the past hour was to ask questions.

"The Keepers gave it that name," answered Nick. "It's what they call it when we slip from one time into another, that is, between this time and grey time."

"We sort of *phase* out of sight," clarified John. "Like the picture on a television screen flickering on or off. Or so they tell us. Do television screens still flicker? Not keen on it myself. Clever invention but terribly poor application."

Thomas nodded although his expression remained blank, as if he were waking up from the worst night sleep of his life.

"Why me?" he continued, waving his hand at the river. "And what do I have to do with this...this... whatever this is."

"Pithily put," said Nick. He jumped up, took in a breath, and rocked forward and backward on the balls of his feet several times. He then took a few, deliberate steps towards the river before turning abruptly.

"You are one of those rare, wonderful people with enough strength of character that, simply put, makes you the right person, at the right time."

Overwrought, Thomas responded offhandedly, "In other words, I'm a fitting candidate for a cat's paw."

"Good grief, Thomas!" Nick pulled off his spectacles and began rubbing them with his pocket square – purple with two equally spaced, vertical white lines. Behind the seated Thomas, the lights of Bodley's flared up, then quickly dimmed down. Even after battling an airborne gargoyle, this was the most animated Thomas had so far seen Nick.

"Quite the opposite, Thomas, quite the opposite." He re-folded the handkerchief and pushed it back into his pocket.

"Brace yourselves," exclaimed John with a grin. "He's

going in." And with that he took two comical sideways strides in order to lean on the back of the bench with Trinity and watch Nick's explanation.

"In 1800," began Nick, "at a time when scientists across the disciplines were grappling with the antiquity of our species, John Frere published a seminal paper in which he described two stone handaxes as 'man-made'. In doing that and in also noting the artefacts were associated with ancient animal bones, he challenged perceived wisdom regarding the time-depth of life on Earth. Granted, the significance of his work was not acknowledged until almost 60 years later but the point remains; he was the *right* person at the *right* time." Nick was like a ship in full sail and gathering speed.

"In 1859, when Charles Darwin published his theory of evolution by natural selection, it is not an exaggeration to say that it unified biology by providing an explanation for the mechanisms behind the diversity of life. He was the *right* person at the *right* time. If he had not done so then we'd be discussing Wallace's theory instead, but we aren't." Nick placed both hands in his trouser pockets and stared into the distance.

"I refer you to Dorothy Hodgkin whose work on vitamin B12 led to her being awarded the Nobel Prize in 1964. Had chemistry not so thoroughly absorbed her childhood energy then she may well have become an archaeologist. But it did and she didn't; she followed her own path and developed the area of protein crystallography. She was the *right* person at the *right* time."

Nick turned back to Thomas. He took a deep breath, as if repressing further examples, exhaled slowly and with a soft smile spreading over his face he continued.

"Everything we achieve is half chance, as are our failures, but being the right person at the right time means having the determination to seize that moment, grab it with both hands and sprint to the finish line – *that* is the test of greatness."

In a flash of muddled memories, both good and bad, his

many part-time jobs and false starts in life, disappointments and directionless wandering, Thomas realised that he had not been wasting time; he had been waiting. The continental plates of his life were breaking up and drifting apart, and every turn and twist it had taken to arrive here, at *this* moment, suddenly looked like a straight path. He felt more awake, more alert, and more utterly baffled by the world than he thought possible. And it felt incredible.

"Tell me what I need to do," was his resolute reply.

Chapter 3: The Neolithic Phase

It had been a long day. By the time Nick snapped his pocket watch closed for the last time that evening, dozens of people had passed the bench where the four figures talked; lively students and sprightly Fellows had walked along the central path and disappeared through various wooden doors, up twisting staircases, and flicked on the lights which now shone warmly through the leaded windows and onto the Court below. Thomas, despite his eagerness to learn more and help formulate a plan, was overwhelmed by the revelations of the past few hours and was struggling to hide the fatigue in his eyes. Nick had suggested that Thomas retire to his rooms and they would reconvene at the Porter's Lodge at 9.30am the following morning.

Thomas slept deeply, his dreams woefully mundane compared to recent events. The first rays of morning light crept impishly into his bedroom, slipping through the panes of glass, sneaking over the window sill, and tip-toeing their way up the bed before coming to rest upon his closed eyelids. He woke with a start, his mind immediately flooded with thoughts of the previous day and he jumped out of bed with an alacrity of spirit. His bedside clock flickered out the time: 8:25am. He skipped to the white ceramic basin in the corner of the room, completing his morning ablutions in record time. By 8:40am all that was left of Thomas in Bodley's Court was the echo of his bedroom door clicking shut.

Front Court of King's College is a complementary mix of Mediaeval and Georgian architecture and the Hall, the destination to which Thomas was now heading for breakfast, was built during the College's neo-Gothic period of the 1820s; like moody teenagers, all the old Colleges went through a goth phase. Large enough to comfortably seat around 300 people, the Hall is one of the most majestic of its era. Its oak panelled walls are peppered with the gold gilt framed portraits of former

Fellows, above which sit large stained glass windows, and the ceiling, which is nearly 14 metres in height, climbs to a visual crescendo of ornate arches.

Thomas pushed open the heavy oak door and strode through the bar to the canteen. He glimpsed Rangemen exiting through a side door ahead of him but was too far away to bid him good morning. Picking up one of the wooden trays, he moved stealthily around the array of hot and cold counters, selecting three large tomato and mushroom pancakes and a blackcurrant compote. After scanning his dining card he passed into the Hall and took a seat at one of the long wooden tables. He placed his blue rucksack on the chair beside him, draped his coat over the back and, in one of his little rituals, turned to see which portrait was behind him. Staring back was a grumpy demeanour wrapped up in a white-haired Victorian gentleman. "This morning," he declared under his breath, "I shall breakfast with Stratford Canning."

He was just about to demolish the first of the pancakes when an enthusiastic greeting froze his fork mid-shovel.

"I know you! Thomas isn't it?!"

The voice belonged to a dishevelled, windswept woman with a wide grin and a pair of sparkling blue eyes. She stopped on the other side of the table, "We met at your Matriculation. I'm Helena Troi, PhD in Zoology, predatory behaviour." The woman had a very distinct voice, high pitched with a black belt in exuberance.

"Yes, I'm Thomas Wharton." He stood up, leaning forward to shake her hand but then realised she was carrying a tray and slowly withdrew.

"How's your research eating… I mean, going… How's your research going?" he asked, desperately wanting to be polite but thinking of pancakes.

"I've been bird watching on the fens with some of the undergrads, hence this stylish mud ensemble." Helena turned in a circle, jovially showing off her filthy bright red dungarees.

"The joys of fieldwork!" laughed Thomas.

"It never occurred to me that fieldwork would actually

require me to be in a field, but them's the breaks!" she giggled then drifted off piste thinking about it. "Actually, I almost missed the trip altogether. I wish they'd put lectures and field trips on the SIS:TUM."

Thomas was about to respond with one of his own field-related anecdotes but she quickly moved on. "Thomas," she repeated his name with a pronounced gravity, seemingly to stress the importance of what was to come. "I'm organising a grad trip to London – dinner and a show – for our new grads, are you up for coming?"

Helena had an approachable, friendly disposition and voluntarily championed the social side of College life with unrivalled gusto. She delighted in zoology and produced solid research but enjoyed it in the same way she enjoyed playing Solitaire on her phone; it was something to do.

"Oh, ah," Thomas stumbled. He was indeed in possession of a scholarship, but after covering tuition fees and accommodation, there wasn't much left for life's frilly bits. As much as he yearned to accept the offer, pragmatism shook its head.

"Thanks Helena, it sounds great but I don't think I can afford it right now."

"We're all penniless students aren't we? I know how you feel," she replied, nodding empathetically. "I'm off skiing with my folks next week – seriously, who goes skiing with their folks? It's embarrassing." She shook her head, aggrieved. "Look, give me your number and I'll send you a text if someone pulls out at the last moment – which *always* happens – and you can take their place. The theatre doesn't give last minute refunds so it's a shame to waste a ticket."

Thomas was genuinely moved by her consideration but given his new and peculiar circumstances, he was hesitant to make any unnecessary commitments.

"That's really kind of you, but honestly, I've got a lot on at the moment; I've taken on a big project and it's rather unpredictable right now, so best let someone else have the chance if that happens."

"It's fine Thomas, I'll give you first refusal. What's your number?"

Thomas shuffled uncomfortably, "I-I don't know, I don't really use a mobile. The one I have is very old."

Helena looked baffled.

"Give me your number, then I'll phone you and we can save each other's."

Reluctantly, Thomas reached into his bag and pulled out a very old but immaculate little phone with a small screen at the top and the number neatly taped onto the back.

"I said it was old," smiled Thomas. "I prized this from the hand of a Neanderthal."

Helena laughed.

"Thomas, you are *so grunge*," she said, leaning forward to marvel at the – quite nearly vintage – phone.

"We're all too commercial these days," she added shaking her head, "more of us should make a stand by refusing to buy the latest gizmos. Good on you!"

Thomas' brow knitted, "Er, right. Well, it's not really by choice," he confessed, not knowing when to stop. "I can't afford a decent one and there's no credit on this old thing. I keep it just in case, for incoming calls. Silly really."

He was embarrassed and it compelled him to explain further, "It's just an expense I can't manage right now. I don't get much left over each month so I try to put a little bit aside for an emergency. You know?"

She did *not* know.

Helena refused to experience emergencies. She viewed life from a high wire with a very bouncy, well-connected safety net. She understood the *definition* of poverty but couldn't comprehend how that translated into not being able to afford things. She preferred conversations where everyone's life experience tallied with her own and when they did not, she modified them into something more agreeable.

She stared at him for a few seconds and a look of admiration swept over her face.

"So, *so* grunge!"

Cradling her tray on one arm, she reached into her pocket and tugged out a very thin, top of the range mobile. The edges were battered and there was a long crack like a lightning strike extending from top to bottom of the screen. As far as Thomas was concerned, she may as well have produced a gold bar.

"So, what's your number?"

He was about to answer but Helena spied another new graduate enter the Hall and she quickly concluded, "I'll leave a message in your pigeonhole if a place becomes available. It was *so* nice chatting with you! Keep on socking it to the man!"

She promenaded off through the Hall and a few seconds later Thomas flinched when her high-pitched voice called out to the other student, "I know you!" and she proceeded with a similar narrative.

When Thomas won a scholarship to King's he became caught between two worlds. Being from a working class background he initially had the devil of a time fitting in, not because his peers were unpleasant to him, quite the reverse, but because unlike most of *them*, Thomas was already life-weary by the time he arrived. He grew up without expectations, had already worked in a series of soul-eating jobs, and was accustomed to walking life's tightrope without the financial harness. More than that, he lacked social collateral, the protein of middle class success; opportunities that spilled over for his peers had never been within his grasp, there was an absence of professional connections to offer advice, and a lack of encouragement to become anything more than what was expected of someone 'like him'. Whatever that meant. The playing field he traversed wasn't only uneven, it was a sheer cliff, and Thomas had climbed it in flip-flops.

If Thomas was an outsider to the typical Cambridge student's life, then going to university made him every bit as much an outsider to his family; they did not ask about his work and he did not force it upon them. It was sometimes alluded to with raised eyebrows, but overall his academic leaning was treated as an embarrassing taboo. Had he dodged university and remained at home, regaling his brother with Saturday night stories about getting plastered at the local pub and throwing up in the neighbour's rose bushes, *then* he would receive his brother's unconditional respect. But as it was, Thomas occupied an awkward cultural purgatory; racked with guilt for being clever and saddled with inconvenience for being poor.

His accent changed too. If he had been confronted on the subject Thomas would have denied it, but the truth is that he was ashamed of being ashamed that he had an Essex accent, and the more he learned and the more brilliant he became, the more necessary he felt it to lose the Essex twang and sound like he came from the sort of background where he knew what the different types of pasta are called. Even the shell-like one. Thomas wasn't a snob, not by any means; he simply didn't want his accent to taint people's opinions of his ideas. He had reluctantly observed that if one says something with enough confidence and in the right accent, even the messiest mental jetsam can be passed off as intellectual prowess. With the notable exception of a decent, jam-making chap in Islington North, the brass-balled sophistry of politicians relies upon it, but to see it in action about him had been entirely novel. In times of duress however, it wasn't unknown for Essex to perch upon the tip of his tongue, spaghettifying vowels or throwing out strikingly candid metaphors, almost without his realising.

Back in the Hall, it did not take long for Thomas to inhale his breakfast, washing it down with a glass of water poured from one of the dimpled grey pitchers that sat at the end of each table. Such was his sense of urgency that no sooner had he placed the glass on the tray than he pushed back his chair, scooped up his belongings, and hurried from the Hall. With a passing "Thank you Mrs Willendorf," to the elderly lady sitting at the till, he flew back through the Bar and out the door that leads into Front Court. From there, the Porter's Lodge is merely half a minute's walk.

"Steady on there!" a man declared in surprise as Thomas, head down, stepped onto the path, narrowly missing bumping into him.

"Graham!" he responded looking up, "I'm so sorry. Too much speed and not enough direction."

"You sound like my Supervisor," joked the man. "But I know how you feel. I took some sleeping pills and didn't wake up until eight! I'm not entirely convinced that I'm not dreaming you." He rubbed his eyes and smiled.

This was Graham Wakes, a first year archaeology PhD student who was not only graced with a sharp mind and unflappable manner, but who also shared Thomas' love of vintage science fiction. He was wrapped tightly inside his College scarf – Christ's – with a small, round nose poking over the top and a pair of gnome-like red cheeks.

"What's all the rush?" asked Graham.

"Oh, I've got to meet a few guests at the Porter's Lodge. Didn't want to be late."

"Fair enough, I won't keep you but as you're here, may I take a minute of your time?"

Thomas glanced at the Gatehouse but, knowing he had a few minutes to spare, was happy to oblige.

"Of course. What's up?"

"How d'you feel about co-chairing the Retro Science Fiction Group with me? Co-pilot if you will."

Thomas had taken up College rooms several months prior to the start of term – there no longer being room at home for him – and this portico of time had not only been used to set about his reading, but to force himself to ferret out a number of clubs and societies to join. His knowledge and seemingly endless delight for niche subjects that had so alienated him from his brother, had made him well-liked in everything from the Archaeology Society to Master Barrington's Cat, a book club for Victorian gothic.

"Co-chair?!" Thomas was very fond of the Retro Science Fiction Group in all its heavenly geekdom; being offered the position of *co-chair* was a true honour.

"Can't think of anyone better, and your help in

selecting books and themes would be second to none. What d'you say?"

"Yes! Tremendous!" Thomas glanced nervously at the Gatehouse again, but nevertheless he beamed from ear to ear.

"Great! Dr Wotton said we can use the Council Room – the white one – at Christ's for the next meeting. The history club who usually use it have gone on a field trip to London to see a windmill or something."

"How about if we work out a plan next week?" suggested Thomas, enthusiastic but unable to dress up the fact that he was, uncharacteristically, in a hurry. "There are some radio programmes I'd like to suggest too."

"Sounds good!" replied Graham, who tipped his head to one side, peering over Thomas' shoulder in an attempt to see what he was so concerned about.

In normal circumstances, Thomas could easily have lost the next few hours discussing potential subjects, themes, books, radio programmes and other sci-fi related ideas, but he felt compelled to keep checking the Gatehouse and it was obvious to Graham that his friend was anxious to depart.

"I hope these guests of yours are bringing you a confirmed offer of a PhD scholarship tied up with a big red bow, because the only other time I've seen you this keen to get somewhere is when the bakery were flogging half price sausage rolls."

They both laughed.

"Well, off you fly then!" chuckled Graham as he started to walk away, shaking his head in amusement. "I bet it *is* all about sausage rolls," he mumbled to himself.

Thomas took a few steps backwards, "Thanks mate and I'll see you next week."

"Good stuff!" Without turning around Graham raised a hand in goodbye and Thomas set off at double speed towards the Gatehouse.

Every College has a Porter's Lodge staffed around the clock by a team of the eponymous Porters. Their many and varied duties set them at the interface between the world outside of College and the academic one within. Thomas, like most students, knew all his College Porters on a first name basis, but more impressively, the Porters knew the first and last name of every Fellow, student, and visitor from at least the past thirty years. Perhaps longer. Even before Thomas had introduced himself on his first day, James, the Head Porter, had greeted him with a friendly, "Hello Thomas, got your room sorted out?"

Porters have a special way of looking at the world, and perhaps other worlds. They are the dignity and decorum that sits with a warm smile and a nice cup of tea at the heart of every College.

The Porter's Lodge of King's is located inside the neo-Gothic Gatehouse facing King's Parade. As you enter from the street, the Porter's Lodge is on the left and the North Lodge, which houses student pigeonholes, is on the right. The Gatehouse is quietly dramatic, with a vaulted ceiling well-known for playing host to a dozen swallow nests every Spring. Visitors are inclined to stand beneath the nests, marvelling at the birds' agile antics, but for the same reason that it is never a good idea to look directly up at a coconut tree, the sagely Porters advise fair-weather twitchers to observe from the side-lines; there isn't always enough kitchen roll to leave folk to their own devices.

It had just turned 9:27am and Thomas stood inside the Gatehouse, rucksack over his shoulder, glimpsing through one side then the other as he looked for any sign of Nick, John, and Trinity. Impatiently, he pushed up his coat sleeve to check the time on his watch; an ill-fitting article with a wide black strap and a large analogue dial, the type that likes to stop working now and again just to inject a little temporal peril into one's life. It was unreliable and uncomfortable, but it was also a long-ago birthday present from his brother and somehow Thomas couldn't bear to part with it.

"Good morning Thomas," came a baritone voice from the now open door of the North Lodge. It was James, the Head Porter. "That's the morning post distributed, and what a fine morning it is." He nodded towards the sunny sky framed by the arch of the Gatehouse.

"Morning James," replied Thomas, tucking his sleeve back over the watch. "Yes, it's glorious. The type of morning where you feel that anything is possible."

James locked the North Lodge and headed to the door opposite, pausing as his hand touched the round, brass door knob. "Never a truer word spoken," he agreed. "Are you waiting for someone?"

"Yes-yes I am, just meeting a few people, they should be here soon, thank you."

James nodded and carried on inside, "Have a very possible morning." And with a passing smile he disappeared through the doorway. "Such a polite young man," he added directly the door had closed.

Thomas stared thoughtfully over the lawn, wondering what on Earth, or off it, he was getting himself into when all of a sudden a familiar voice struck his ears, "Penny for them."

He swung around to see John and Trinity standing behind him.

"I'd have to find you some change," chuckled Thomas. "I'm *so* glad to see you." Excitedly, he heaved his rucksack higher onto his shoulder and walked to join them at the centre of the Gatehouse. "I didn't notice you arrive. I've been thinking about the gargoyles —"

John held up a hand for Thomas to slow down, "Top marks for industry old boy, really, but all in good time. Let's wait for Nick and we'll head up."

At that moment something caught Thomas' eye, something odd in the corner of the Gatehouse. A long, vertical section of the wall had started to ripple. It was as if the stone were nothing more than a thin layer of wallpaper and something had wriggled its way underneath and was now undulating inside the fabric of the building. He jumped back, his eyes following the shape as it moved along. It had a fluid-like quality, gliding seamlessly from the corner of Front Court to the moulding just before the North Lodge door. At that point the strange form began to bulge out from the wall and the further it protruded, the clearer he could make it out; it was the figure of a man, but before Thomas could ask what was happening, the stone and mortar on the surface of the distortion was replaced with the visage of Nick. He stepped out from the wall and immediately pulled the pocket watch from his waistcoat.

"Good, good," he said, smiling at the dial.

Thomas gawked, open-mouthed, first at Nick, then at the wall, then back to Nick. He gave a quick glance through the arches either side of the Gatehouse, checking to see if anyone else had witnessed the unorthodox arrival. There was the usual tourist footfall wandering by in the street and a few groups of students were making their way around Front Court, but it would appear no one else had observed Nick's appearance.

"H– how…" began Thomas.

"Good morning, Thomas," replied Nick, exchanging nods with John and Trinity, yet seemingly unaware of the young man's shock.

"All ready?"

"I-I suppose I am, but how…" Thomas was a portrait of confusion, albeit one with a distinctly cubist edge; his screwed up eyes and furrowed brow broke his face into a series of heavy lines with an uncomfortable, fractured expression. As for his mind, recent events had turned it into a repository for the impossible and he felt there was little to be done other than to accept the situation and limp on.

"Yes, yes, I'm ready," Thomas affirmed, waving a hand as if attempting to brush away what he had just seen, whilst the other rubbed his forehead consolingly.

If there were such a thing as a friendly creak, then the door to King's Porter's Lodge has it. A short wooden yawn that welcomes and bids goodbye to every visitor. And it was as Nick clicked shut his pocket watch, spot on 9:30am, that the familiar sound beckoned and James reappeared in the doorway.

"Everything is ready, sir." His face gleamed with pride

as he addressed Nick, stepping backwards into the Lodge to make way for the company. "Nice pot of hot tea waiting upstairs, just as you like it."

"James, you are a god among men. Thank you," replied Nick in earnest appreciation.

The small group funnelled towards the door but Thomas hung back. "My uncle Erasmus used to talk to plants." He was speaking quietly, partly addressing himself, partly Nick, and partly the universal void. "I don't mean just flowers to get them to grow, but anything." He looked over his shoulder at the North Lodge wall and shook his head. "Used to stand in his potting shed for hours just chatting with them; flowers, vegetables, fruit, he didn't discriminate."

Nick listened in a preoccupied fashion then gave an amused but sympathetic smile. "Good, good," he said, shepherding the student towards the door.

Thomas gave the wall a parting glance as he shuffled away. "What I mean is," he looked directly at Nick, "I hope this isn't the start of some sort of hereditary inclination manifesting." He nodded resolutely, "The first turnip to make small talk and I'm out."

John, Trinity, and a sluggish Thomas followed Nick into the Lodge, its panelled walls and soft lighting created a warm, homely feel. On the left, a tall reception desk stretched from wall to wall. Upon its surface sat the Porters' most vital accessories, two metal racks; one containing maps of the town and the other maps of College. At the start of the academic year, when new students flooded to the Lodge with questions about the location of their Supervisor, department, lecture hall, room, or pub, the Porters would invariably pull out one of the maps and with unerring patience, circle the whereabouts of each one, though not frequently in that order of request.

James lifted a panel in the centre of the counter, passed through and purposefully placed it back down as he turned. He stood regimental but at ease, one hand resting on the surface and his other cradled over it. Behind him, two additional Porters, all wearing the same smart black suits with white and purple ties, stood in quiet acknowledgment.

"May I say sir," said James to Nick, "it is good to *see* you again."

Nick smiled and as he did the Lodge lights grew a little brighter, the faint wrinkles aside his eyes falling into place like the fan vaulting of the Chapel ceiling.

"A sentiment returned, James. I thank you." He gave a nod of acknowledgment to the Porters standing behind, then turned in the direction of a narrow, darker wooden door in the far corner. Without Nick touching the handle, the door opened slowly before him and he sprinted up the tight stone staircase that was revealed beyond. John and Trinity followed closely behind and Thomas, still coming to terms with Nick's mode of arrival, raised his hand to the Porters in a silent gesture of thanks as he ascended.

Thomas did not touch the door, but it closed gently behind him nonetheless and he followed the twisting staircase until it delivered him to a small landing. The area was around four metres in length and barely two in width, with a single, slightly crooked door at the far end. The dark panelling was reminiscent of the Hall and there was a small brass wall lamp on either side radiating soft, yellow light. Each had a short, curved neck that hung onto an exquisite cut glass shade in the shape of an acorn. Against the centre of the left wall sat a thin, oak occasional table with four cabriole legs that curved elegantly to the wide wooden floorboards. Gracing the wall to the right of the door sat a heavily carved hall chair with a high, shield-shaped back and thick octagonal legs.

The crooked door was open and it was through here that Nick and the others had settled.

Thomas walked slowly along the landing, the floorboards creaking with his every step and gingerly entered the room. It was a small, cramped study with a single square leaded window at the centre of the opposite wall that overlooked the street. With the exception of the space behind the door which housed a slim hall stand, the walls were fitted with shelves from floor to ceiling, each one packed with antiquarian hardbacks that ran almost seamlessly from one side to the other, stopping only intermittently to navigate the occasional objet d'art strewn amidst them; an ornate metal hour glass, a cast of a *Homo heidelbergensis* skull, a green ceramic pot full of shiny brown acorns, a dark wooden metronome with a brass plaque on the front, an antique Jelly Baby box, and other such curios.

A small oak desk was pushed up to the window sill and to its side was a scruffy umbrella stand stuffed with rolled up maps, their oxidised edges curled and brown. To the other side of the desk was a full-sized model of a human skeleton wearing a deer stalker hat, and facing each other in the centre of the room were four mis-matched armchairs. It was the most divine work space that Thomas had ever set eyes upon.

Set between the chairs was a low wooden coffee table and on top of that was a mahogany tray containing a silver tea service and four China cups and saucers adorned with the College crest. Nick and Trinity were seated in the armchairs and John was browsing the bookshelves. Thomas lifted off his rucksack, dropped it on the floor by the door and slipped into a mustard coloured armchair with a striped throw and threadbare arms.

"First of all," commenced Nick, "I'd like to thank you *all* for your company. These are unprecedented times and we have a lot to work through." He picked up the tea pot, a little puff of steam rising from the spout, and poured generously into each cup.

"We are particularly grateful to Thomas, who has shown remarkable fortitude. There aren't many people who can believe as many as six impossible things before breakfast…" he switched to the silver milk jug and began the same circuit around the tea tray, "…but Thomas has excelled himself."

Thomas was perched on the very edge of his chair, not in suspense, but in an attempt to avoid being impaled upon one of its many commendably lively springs.

"No milk for me thanks," he said quickly.

Nick lifted the milk jug, intuitive of his concern.

"It's soya milk, Thomas."

"We're not barbarians," added John, briefly turning from the array of books. He then plucked a large encyclopaedia from the shelf above his head and started flicking through it.

"Unless scientific and technological developments are mirrored with advances in ethics, society will *never* see progress." He slotted the book back into place and cast an approving eye along the rest of the shelf. "And goodness knows it's in need of progress."

"Pilgrim's or March of?" retorted Trinity.

"Most certainly the latter," laughed John.

"Yes. Yes that's it exactly," enthused Thomas, responding to John's initial remark. "Actually, I'm surprised you drink tea at all. I mean, you don't *need* to, do you? Do you have to eat too?"

"We don't *need* to eat," replied Nick, "We don't *need* to drink tea. We *like* to drink tea. In regular circumstances we are presented with the opportunity but once a year, so as we're here we might as well partake. Sugar anyone?"

John tapped the glass of a small, hexagonal-shaped barometer hanging at the centre of one of the shelves and its measuring hand climbed to 'Change'.

"I shall do no such thing," laughed John as he turned away and made his way to the chairs.

Trinity leant forward and whispered to Thomas.

"Contrary to popular understanding, not all barometers dispense pressure related forecasts."

"Really? No? I thought that was the point of them. What do they dispense then?"

She smiled, "Advice."

John squeezed into the bundle of armchairs, lifting his cup in thanks as he sat down.

Nick used a pair of silver sugar tongs to drop a single lump into his own cup then leant back in the chair and took a sip.

"To summarise," he began. "For the past thirty years John, Trinity, myself and the other Colleges, have found ourselves drifting further away from this time. An act of wanton temporal vandalism inflicted upon us by person or persons unknown." He took another sip and the cup made a gentle *clink* as he returned it to the saucer.

"The past few weeks have witnessed a development. In that time we have been subjected to increased and intensified gargoyle attacks. We now know those gargoyles belong to St. Edward's church."

Trinity stirred her tea then gently laying the little spoon in the saucer, cast a shrewd look about the group. "The gargoyles cannot *kill* us and we have to assume that anyone capable of manipulating them would *know* that, so a reasonable hypothesis is that they are trying to *distract* us. If that is correct then the more interesting question is: from *what* are they trying to distract us?"

"It's a rum business," frowned John, strumming his fingers on the arm of his chair.

Thomas shifted from side to side a few times then edged back a little on the seat. "Do you have any enemies?" he asked, holding his cup and saucer in one hand as he attempted to plump up the cushion with the other.

"If we were talking philosophically then yes, existentially then absolutely, but within the somewhat less metaphysical parameters before us? No," replied John, his cut-glass diction making his response all the more definitive.

"What about…" Thomas paused and continued in a quieter tone of voice "…the *other* place."

"Hell?" responded John being wilfully obtuse. "My dear Thomas we are not in the habit of wrapping our minds in fairy tales. You may as well ask if Father Christmas has put us on the naughty list."

"No, not hell… Oxford."

"Same thing."

"If it is quite convenient!" interrupted Nick, holding one hand in the air to curtail the diversion.

"One cannot deny that place has spawned an inordinate number of questionable politicians but we can rule them out of this."

"And what about Oxford?" quipped John.

Trinity rolled her eyes. "We can rule out Oxford," she clarified.

"I certainly did," blurted out Thomas, turning his cup in its saucer. "You should see the length of the application form."

There was an appreciable pause, the Colleges eyeing the young man with owlish displeasure; Nick looked up in quiet surprise, John momentarily refrained from strumming his fingers, and Trinity froze with her cup half way between the saucer and her lips.

Suddenly self-conscious, Thomas absolved himself as best he could, "I never had any intention of going." He smiled awkwardly.

Nick leant forward to top up his cup. "Moving on," he coughed, raising the pot in a silent offer to the others.

Trinity nodded in acceptance and he dutifully obliged. She gave the brew a long, thoughtful stir. "*How* are the gargoyles being manipulated?" she pondered aloud. "We must investigate the church."

Thomas, unable to stop himself from reflecting more widely upon the morning was compelled to ask another question, "Do the Porters know who you are?"

"Of course," replied all three laconically, as if any other answer were inconceivable.

"There seems to be very little option," declared Nick, staring into his tea cup. "We must consult Dr Watt."

John and Trinity glanced at each other, then chorused, "Agreed."

"Who?" asked Thomas.

"No, Watt," corrected Nick.

"Dr Watt?"

"Yes."

"I haven't heard of him, what does he teach?"

"He doesn't. He's retired…of sorts. He holds a non-teaching Research Fellowship at Emmanuel," said Nick.

"What's his subject?" persisted Thomas, still attempting to push back on several bony springs in the back of the yellow chair.

"Hm, well, one could say he takes a holistic approach to quantum anthropology."

Trinity placed her now empty cup and saucer back on the tray. "One could *say* that," she smiled.

"Quantum anthropology? What's that?" asked Thomas.

"We don't know. He's still working on it," replied Nick. "Now, to return our attention to the matter at hand; Thomas, are you amenable to calling upon Dr Watt? That would enable John and Trinity to investigate St. Edward's church, and I to visit Peter."

John leant back, crossing his arms in the air and tucking them casually behind his head. "A reconnaissance mission!" he declared mirthfully. "Perfect, ay Trin? You're *at least* five times the spy I am so I shall be keen to observe a master in action."

Trinity shot him a contemptuous glance.

"Yes, no problem for me," replied Thomas. "Is this Dr Watt a bit, you know, *difficult*? Is that why you want me to go?" he queried, trying to be diplomatic and thinking of a particularly highly strung molecular biologist he once sat next to at Formal Hall.

"Not at all," opined Nick. "He's an anthropologist!"

"Quite so," seconded Trinity. "Dr Watt is the height of affability but he prefers not to be disturbed and we try to respect that. Also, as we mentioned previously, it would be advantageous for us to preserve as much of our energy as possible for the time being."

She proceeded to pour a second full cup, "Anyone for seconds?"

Realising the ambiguity of her statement she swiftly clarified, "That is, a second cup of tea? I think *more* seconds are the last thing we require right now."

Thomas chuckled. There was an incongruity between Trinity's grand, almost austere appearance and her reassuring, warm character, so much so that her dry humour could easily go undetected.

"Yes please, Trin." John leant forward, pushing his cup towards her.

"Not for me, thank you," answered Thomas. "I'm quite keen to get going and speak with this Dr Watt. Where do I find him?"

With a polite shake of his hand, Nick also declined another cup of tea.

"Emma," he replied, referring to Emmanuel College. "Go to the Porter's Lodge at Emma and tell them I sent you."

"Okay, is that all? Shouldn't I explain anything else?"

"Unnecessary. The Porter will tell you where to find Emma and she will tell you where to find Dr Watt," clarified Nick.

"Surely one of the Porters could just look him up on the room sheet?" queried Thomas.

"No, no," insisted Nick. "Dr Watt moves his rooms too frequently to keep track of. It will be necessary to enquire with Emma."

"Frequently moves his rooms? I bet the Porters *love* that," grimaced Thomas. "It was trouble enough shifting all my things into my rooms just once without moving an entire office full of books and belongings on a regular basis."

Nick reached into his waistcoat pocket and removed the fob watch, glancing briefly at the dial. "Oh, he doesn't trouble the Porters with it."

"Right. Well, okay, no problem," responded Thomas with a resigned bewilderment. *Perhaps*, he thought, Dr Watt bucked the typical Cambridge trend and kept a minimalist office. Maybe he stored all his research and reading material on a computer, which would certainly make it easier to move rooms on a regular basis. It was extraordinary to contemplate, but minimalism among academics is not unheard of; as an undergrad Thomas had once visited the office of a geneticist who dabbled in minimalism. The only item on her shelves was an A to Z of Rickmansworth. It was an unnerving experience.

Nick placed his cup and saucer on the tray then moved

forward in his chair, clasping one hand inside the other as he addressed the room.

"The game, as they say, is afoot!"

With that he stood up, edged his way out between the chairs, and walked to the window, surveying the street.

"You ready Trin?" asked John as he too finished his tea and returned the crockery to the tray.

"There's no time like the fraction of a second behind the present," she responded gleefully.

As Trinity rose she leant forward, placing a hand on Thomas' shoulder, "To paraphrase one of my finest: The incompetent are full of certainty, whilst the capable are full of doubts." She smiled. "Your doubts are many but they are not to be ashamed of, Thomas. It is a strength and we are most appreciative of your help."

John concurred with a nod.

"I'll relent just this once Trin, I'd have accepted old Bertie as one of my own."

She inclined her head graciously at the comment.

Adding under his breath, "After all, he *was* up for grabs at one point."

Thomas was stoic by nature and had so seldom encountered gratitude that now he was in the possession of some he wasn't at all sure what to do with it, so he merely reflected the smile.

"Nick," continued Trinity, gliding towards the door. "May I suggest we reconvene here at 1pm?"

"By all means, yes." He then turned to his student, "Thomas? What say you?"

The young man shuffled forward in his chair, nodding.

"One o'clock. Back here. No problem."

John shoehorned himself out of the tightly packed seating, landing a slap on Thomas' back as he passed. "Top drawer," he declared with a grin.

Thomas smiled, raising a hand in goodbye as John and Trinity departed. The hallway lamps provided just enough dim light to illuminate their outlines and he watched as they flowed through the crooked landing.

"I do hope you realise *The March of Progress* is an

overly simplified and misleading depiction of evolution," remarked Trinity as they neared the steps.

John turned to answer but their figures and voices started to fade before Thomas could hear the response, and by the time they descended the stone stairwell they had disappeared altogether. Not even the echo of a footstep remained.

"Phasing," said Nick, observing Thomas' surprise.

"I'd do the same if I could," he responded, still looking down the corridor in awe. "In the 9am lecture rush it'd save a lot of bruises and bike damage."

Nick smiled. "Come on," he declared with a sudden zeal. "Time, as it has made itself blatantly clear, is *not* on our side and we have much to do."

Thomas hauled himself out of the armchair and picked up his bag by the door.

"Oh!" he said, remembering the tea tray and turning en pointe to retrieve it.

Nick and Thomas then descended the staircase, the tea cups rattling in their saucers all the way, like teeth chattering in fearful expectation of being dropped. Upon reaching the Porters' Lodge Nick headed immediately for the door, giving a wave to the Porters as he strode out.

Thomas headed for the reception desk and slipped the tray onto its surface. "Thank you," he grinned.

"We're very pleased to have you here," said James with a nod of thanks for returning the tray.

Thomas smiled, "I'm glad to be here." And he paused when he reached the door. "And I appreciate the tea, it was really nice to have proper cups."

Back home, they never used proper cups. It was always mugs. And that was fine; there's nothing wrong with a big, comforting mug of tea, but now and again it was nice to have a *proper* cup of tea.

"What a polite young man," said the Porter standing behind James as the Lodge door clicked shut.

Outside, the Autumn sun had retreated behind a swathe of billowing grey cloud and a cold wind whipped at Thomas' neck. He fastened his coat and pulled the hood over his ears. With his distinctive stance of hands in pockets, Nick was standing at the opening of the Gatehouse, looking over Front Court. Rangemen had recently given the lawn its last cut of the year, leaving the lush green grass patterned with the vertical stripes of an expertly manoeuvred mower. Dark green, medium green, dark green, medium green and so on, and there was not a leaf to be seen upon its immaculate surface.

"It's tidier than my bedroom," said Thomas, standing beside him to share the view.

Nick nodded, "Of course, next year the leaves won't be swept. It's part of Rangemen's plan to encourage biodiversity. Leaf litter is terribly important for birds and other critters. I admit it will be a trial in terms of the aesthetic but Rangemen is quite correct. We should and must play our part." Nick gave a satisfied nod then turned his gaze to the back of the Court.

At the centre of Front Court is a striking stone fountain featuring a statue of Henry VI, the founder of King's College, but that isn't what interested Nick. Beyond the fountain, on the other side of the Court is the Gibbs Building. Its large central archway houses racks for Fellows' bicycles and it was to this general area that he cast his attention. He stepped firmly to the left, thus avoiding the fountain hampering his outlook, raised two fingers to his mouth and emitted a loud, two tone whistle. The resulting sound echoed around the Court and if Thomas hadn't known any better he would have sworn the whistle split itself in half, each note taking a separate route around the Court until they collided into one again beneath the bicycle arch. As the sound dissipated, there appeared at the centre of the arch an oval-shaped distortion. Thomas could still see the distant image of the Back Lawn, trees, and other vague details as he looked through it, but they were grey and blurred, as if obscured by a sheet of incredibly slow running water. In terms of size, the anomaly was more than ample for a person to walk through, but it wasn't a person that emerged, it was a bicycle.

To be clear, it was *only* a bicycle. No rider. And yet this two-wheeled stallion quickened over the grass, its pedals rotating steadily, past the fountain and over the path until eventually it squeaked to a halt at Nick's side. Even when not in motion the bicycle remained standing upright. It had a charming vintage look to it and bicycle aficionados would have had no trouble identifying it as a 1930s *All-Black Royal Sunbeam For Gentlemen*. It had an immaculate black frame, 28 inch wheels, silver bell, and on the back, a handy rack for books.

"The fountain was completed in 1879," said Nick as he took hold of the bicycle's handlebars, wheeling it in a wide semi-circle to face the exit. He was oblivious of the need to account for the appearance of his bicycle, or indeed for arriving at their meeting via the stone wall express, but reeling off the dates of College attributes was a conversational must-do.

"You are at ease with the assignment?" checked Nick.

Thomas reached out a single finger and touched the handlebar with a quick prodding motion, as if fearing it might give off an electric shock.

"Y-yes, yes," he belatedly replied, still regarding the bicycle with curiosity. There was no electric shock and so the prod turned into a pat, which was enough to assure him that it was indeed a real bike and he elaborated, "I mean, yes, absolutely. Off to Emma, ask for Dr Watt, and back here at 1pm."

"Good good," remarked Nick. He put one foot on the left pedal and pushed off with the other. After a few metres and gaining speed, he slung his other leg over the top of the frame and sat down, his coat blowing gently behind him. He raised one hand in the air in a gesture of goodbye and like John and Trinity before him, gradually faded into the air, the remnants of his outline blowing away with the wind.

"Right," said Thomas to himself. "Emmanuel College here I come."

And with that Thomas grasped the strap of his rucksack and headed purposefully out of the Gatehouse and into the street.

Chapter 4: The Bronze Age Phase

Although it was only the beginning of his time at Cambridge, Thomas had so quickly acquainted himself with the city that as he commenced the short walk to Emmanuel his body fell into automatic while his mind raced with recent events. It was a mercifully bright, dry morning but the busy streets stymied his progress with a barrage of mobile chicanes; chattering schoolboys clumped around bicycles, intermittent pausing to navigate dithering shoppers, and long periods of reduced speed courtesy of the slow meander of hand-holding couples. But none of this could dampen Thomas' unflagging enthusiasm. His body took the strain while his mind kicked back, running through the extraordinary revelations and the incredible things he had seen. Without realising how far he had walked or how quickly he had walked it, there stood the imposing edifice of Emmanuel, rising like an iceberg – the frozen water variety, not the vegetable – from the bustling metropolitan sea.

The lights at the pedestrian crossing were green and Thomas bolted over the road, making his way directly into the forecourt. He paused briefly, looking up at the Gatehouse with apprehension. Swallowing his doubts, he heaved his rucksack higher onto his shoulder and pushed through the half-glass door. Inside, a crescent-shaped reception desk shone in the corner, bathed in sun from a tall arched window on the adjacent wall, sharp points of light twinkling on its laminate surface. A second door at the other side of the Lodge led into a large, stately looking Court.

"Hello?" said Thomas timidly, looking around the room.

The Lodge appeared to be unmanned and he turned to see if he had missed any of the Porters standing outside when, "Hello!" came a cheery voice. The head it belonged to appeared promptly afterwards, popping up from behind the desk. "Putting away some parcels. Didn't see you there."

The man, who wore a smart black suit, had a friendly face that peered out from behind a pair of large, silver framed spectacles. He had the look of a young Charles Darwin but with wilder hair and, if such a thing can be imagined, more dramatic whiskers.

"Oh hello," replied Thomas, suddenly self-conscious and approaching the desk with his least shifty gait.

Now that he was actually standing there, face to face with another person, the sheer unbelievability of the situation hit Thomas squarely between the eyes. There was no way to approach the conversation without appearing utterly ridiculous, or perhaps giving the impression he was attempting to play a student prank on someone. But he had to keep a level head. He reminded himself of the importance of complying with Nick's instructions and so, pushing back on his misgivings, he proceeded.

"My name is Thomas Wharton, I'm an archaeology grad at King's —"

"Nice to meet you, Thomas."

"Oh yes, you too." He fiddled with his bag strap, nervously pulling the padding up and down his shoulder.

"I was sent here by Nick."

"Ohhhh," reacted the Porter, "*That* Thomas."

"I'm not sure," he replied, not feeling privy to enough information to evaluate whether he was indeed *that* Thomas.

"I need to speak with…" he paused, stealing a quick breath and hoping desperately the request would make sense, "…Emma."

The Porter cast him a look of quiet understanding, the light glinting off the frames of his spectacles as he pushed them further back on his nose.

"Of course," he nodded, conferring with his wristwatch. He then gazed upwards, puckering his brow, his lips moving ever so faintly as he appeared to run through a schedule in his mind. Then, returning his attention to Thomas he gestured to the door with the large, open Court behind it, "You'll find Emma in St. Cedd's Court."

For just a few seconds Thomas stood perfectly still, a mixture of surprise and relief beating in his chest. "Thank you!" he finally forced out. With a grateful nod he proceeded to the door, grasped the handle, pushing when it needed to be pulled, and finally hurtled through with as much dignity as he could muster upon realising his mistake.

St. Cedd's is the first and largest court of Emmanuel College, its springy green mattress of a lawn framed by a befittingly quaint flagstone path. The east range is formed by a cloister and chapel, one of Christopher Wren's early projects.

"Well, he had to practice somewhere," Thomas would later recall one of John's flippant remarks.

The rest of the Court consists of distinguished seventeenth century buildings with jolly leaded windows that take in the sun and wink it to visitors. They are predominantly given over to the accommodation of Fellows and students, and as Thomas cast a cursory eye along them he was very much hoping Dr Watt's rooms were among them. In Autumn, the southern buildings are ablaze with the red and orange leaves of a Virginia Creeper and it is here, tucked in a shady corner, that Thomas located a petite, delicate looking woman tending creeping thyme in a collection of mismatched terracotta pots.

He walked around the path until reaching what he regarded to be a polite distance, then spoke, "Excuse me madam."

The lady did not desist from her green figured pursuit, cutting a stem in one place and pulling off a dead leaf in another, but her movements slowed upon hearing Thomas' voice and she tilted her head to one side as if listening. She stood about 1.4 metres in height and had a slender frame that looked so light and fragile that one strong gust of wind would surely carry her away. She was wearing a 1940s style dress that reached half way down her calves, navy with rose pink specks in the pattern, long sleeves finished with a broad line of lace, and a thin blue belt around her tiny waist.

Thomas edged forward, now just a few metres from the slight figure. There was a moment's hesitation before he spoke again.

"Good morning."

He coughed politely. "My name is Thomas Wharton. Nick sent me. I-I hope I've come at a convenient time."

The lady placed her secateurs on top of an upturned flower pot and swivelled around to face him, her dress swishing gently as she did so. She appeared to be in her mid-sixties, with a round face and a small pointed nose. Her thick hair flowed back in a soft perm that was clipped either side with silver hairpins and Thomas was struck by how its rich auburn tones matched the colours of the Virginia Creeper. She had wide, inquisitive eyes and her thin lips were drawn into a gracious smile. It was the kind of face that you want to talk to. She stood with one hand clasping the other and her head on one side, contemplating.

"May I ask, are you Emma?"

"I am, young Thomas, I am." She stretched out a hand. "And I always have time for my fellow Essex countrymen."

If handshakes were bonds then Thomas would think himself tethered to Emmanuel for life. So firm was Emma's greeting that as the handshake continued it reminded Thomas of the time he accidentally clamped his fingers into the large vice in his father's workshop. After drawing back his hand, he discreetly clenched and released his fist behind his back in order to restore the blood flow.

"Look at this." Emma turned to the Virginia Creeper and pulled aside the foliage of the potted plants to reveal a section of bare vine on the lower part of the wall.

"Nothing wrong with it. Healthy leaves all over but bare patches appearing willy nilly." She raised her arm, allowing the plants to drape back down.

"When the Virginia Creeper has trouble creeping, I do

not require Nick to tell me that something is rotten in the state of Cambridge." She picked up the secateurs and clipped a woody stem from one of the potted plants. "But I do thank him nonetheless."

"I was wondering," Thomas picked up the thread of his original point. "That is, Nick asked me to find someone called Dr Watt. He said he has rooms here and you would know where to find him."

"Dr Watt?" she let out a staccato chuckle at the mention. "Oh, he is a fascinating conversationalist, absolutely fascinating."

"He's here then?"

"Yes. Yes he is."

"Would you mind telling me where I can find him please?"

Emma brushed her hands together, a few flakes of soil falling from her fingertips. She took two steps closer to the verdant lawn, put her hands on her hips and scanned the Court from left to right.

"You're in luck!" she said with a tone of surprise. "The second door to the left of the Chapel entrance."

"Thank you!" exclaimed Thomas.

"Better be quick though," she added. "Before he changes rooms again!"

Emma let out another delightful chuckle and Thomas couldn't help but laugh with her.

"I can't imagine how the Porters keep track of him!" he remarked.

"Oh they don't. He doesn't take up any space. We leave him to his own resources. Well, they're the best kind aren't they." She turned back to the potted plants, picked up the secateurs and began clipping here and there amidst the greenery.

"Better dash Thomas. Be off, before he is!" she said over her shoulder.

"Yes, yes. You're right. Thank you!" exclaimed Thomas as he began to walk away, eyeing up the archways of the cloister as he headed towards it, "and it was very nice to meet you!"

Emma turned her head, watching as the young man approached the Chapel, whispering to herself, "An acorn, which, when it becomes an oak, God alone knows what will be the fruit thereof." She put down the secateurs, frowned, then brushed her hand over the Virginia Creeper a few times before pausing in thought. "Of course, I'd always assumed it would be more acorns." And she chuckled, once again busying her fingers amidst the leaves.

— ∞ —

The air rippled with the shape of two human-like forms and seconds later John and Trinity phased into view, walking through the mogshade of a large yew tree overhanging the cobbled path and heading towards the chunky, black-studded door of St. Edward's. The church is a small yet imposing thirteenth century stone building chiefly located within the Y-shaped embrace of a charming little lane called St. Edward's Passage. The narrow thoroughfare has been on the run from developers since the sixteenth century but remains happily intact, its riven-stone pavement serving as a walk-through from King's Parade, which houses King's College, to Peas Hill which adjoins the Market Square. The church is notable for the quantity and quality of intricately carved gargoyles lining the perimeter of its roof, all of which are nineteenth century additions. The majority are medium sized installations, around three quarters of a metre in height, displaying various wide-eyed glares and mid-screech grimaces, but there is one small gargoyle, with beady eyes and a particularly toothy grin, that sits just above the entrance.

Trinity took hold of the iron latch and lifted it cautiously. The door creaked as she pushed it open and the pair stepped into the surprisingly spacious, yet dimly lit interior. Stretching out before them were two impressive rows of slender stone arches. The aisles, along with four lines of dark wooden pews reach all the way to the east side, whereupon the altar was covered in a white cloth with two gold candlesticks at either side. John and Trinity stood side by side, scrutinising the darkest nooks and the smallest crannies. They listened intently for any sound that might evince the untoward but, for the moment, the untoward remained incognito.

There are neutron stars less densely packed than a College's nod and as Trinity made the gesture to John, she walked into the north aisle and he into the south. They swept up the gangways, their footfall echoing around the columns and arches, and with every other step they blurred out of focus, phasing rapidly between one time and the other. They were comparing the appearance of the church in both times, searching for structural differences, unusual movement, or anything at all that seemed out of place. They walked to the centre of the chancel, facing each other and took solid form.

"Nothing," said John.

"How very unobliging," remarked Trinity.

Nothing that is, aside from a pair of small blue eyes observing their every movement from the corner of a window in the south chapel. The air around the eyes rippled in a similar fashion to when a College phases in and out of time, only this was accompanied by a distinct dark blue tint. Given the Colleges' acute observation skills it may seem unusual that they were oblivious to the presence of the eyes, but oblivious they remained. With a furtive jitter, the eyes disappeared before re-emerging seconds later at a smaller side window, peering towards them like a curtain-twitching neighbour. John and Trinity scanned the chancel and walked around the altar, lifting up the candlesticks and white cloth lest they conceal a hidden clue.

"Clear," said John, leaning on the altar with one hand and placing the other in his trouser pocket. "Confound it! This is all tediously uninformative."

"Organ loft," instructed Trinity as she walked to an arch-top doorway in the north chapel.

A set of sharply turning wooden steps led up to the organ gallery and John and Trinity once again phased back and forth between times as they ascended. When they reached the top they were greeted by a modest but handsome pipe organ. Sitting proudly at the heart of the gallery, it had three keyboards and two tilting pedals. At some point over the last 50 years or so the pedals had been covered with a piece of crudely cut tapestry carpet which was now worn to grey at the centre with pieces of fraying material sprouting like potato roots from the edges.

"You'd think someone would replace that," tutted John as he cast a downward eye at the pedals. He then immediately set about skimming a hand along the bottom of the wall.

After a few minutes of searching, "Over here!" he announced, turning corporeal and pointing towards an unobtrusive patch. A single word was carved into a stone on the lowest line: 'nosniboR'.

"Robinson," said Trinity with a look of intrigue. "But why spell it backwards?"

"Why spell it at all?" countered John. "And why can't I touch it?"

To demonstrate the problem he attempted to tap the stone but his finger could only reach to a fraction above the face, the surface rippling like water as he tried.

Trinity phased out of view and in the grey light of the monochrome world, she too tried to touch the stone but was met with the same resistance.

"Impossible," she declared, phasing back into form. "It's as if the stone is there, but not there, and it's the same for both times."

"Here's another one!" hollered John from the other side of the pipe organ. This time he was on one knee, attempting to touch a stone further up from the gallery floor.

'llihcruhC' read the inscription.

"Churchill," said John, running his hand over the water-like surface of the name, similarly unable to touch it.

"It's you!" added Trinity, standing on tip toe at the left of the pipe organ and pointing upwards. "St. John's."

"If I might be so bold," responded John, "what in the nuclear name of Cockcroft is occurring *here*!" He pointed to a large stone located around half a metre above their heads. Upon it were the letters 'esu' and what appeared to be half an 'o' in the process of being carved extremely slowly by an unseen hand.

Trinity immediately phased into grey time and back.

"Nothing. There's no one there!" she huffed.

"Find all the stones with an inscription," suggested John as he hurled himself to the floor and began running his hand along the lowest line. "Whatever this means, we need to examine every centimetre of this wall."

John and Trinity began inspecting the wall for further engravings, starting where the lowest stones met the heavily scratched wooden floorboards and moving up row by row, their eyes not missing a single dent or fleck in the masonry. When the stones were so high as to be out of reach, the two levitated like spectres to peruse them. At the bottom of the stairs, still unbeknownst to the floating duo, the pair of diminutive blue eyes appeared in a corner of the chancel window, looking up at the gallery before vanishing in a blur of dark blue ripples.

The arches of Emmanuel's cloister are wide and stout, with chevron detailing following the curves and mock Doric columns standing proudly either side. The ceiling is surprisingly low but it accommodates the broad span of the arches with an effortless grace. It has the look of a once tall vaulted ceiling that was pressed down by a giant hand, squashing it into a dumpy version of its former self. Thomas found the combination grand yet tranquil and he paused for a brief moment, looking up and down the cloister to appreciate the effect. Morning sun flooded through the openings, creating little domes of light on the flagstone floor and he trod through them one by one as he walked towards the second door to the left of the Chapel entrance. There was no name plaque beside the dark wooden door and unlike others along the cloister which were set into striking Gothic surrounds, this one sat within a humble, undecorated square frame.

"It looks like the broom cupboard," muttered Thomas as he knocked with a determined *thud thud*.

No answer.

He knocked again.

Thud thud thud.

This time he heard a faint sound emanating from within. He cocked his head to one side and placed his ear closer to the door, holding his breath to better decipher the noise. It was the sound of someone walking from far away, footsteps echoing from the furthest end of what sounded like a long, metal corridor. Surely, he thought, those footsteps were approaching from much further away than the outside of the room would suggest is possible.

He took a step back.

Judging by the distance from this doorway to the ones on either side of it, Dr Watt's office couldn't be much larger than his own study area at King's. He rationalised; sometimes doors can be deceiving, especially in old buildings. For example, if two smaller rooms are knocked through to create a single larger room, the external doors are often left in place and simply covered over on the inside. Thus, the room behind the door could be at least twice the width it appeared from the outside. But even that was inadequate to account for the perceived distance of the echoing footsteps. The strides in question became louder as they approached the door, eventually turning into the clear and distinct shuffle of someone standing directly on the opposite side. With the sudden scrape of a metal latch, the door flung open with such a *whoosh* that it blew back the fringe from Thomas' face.

"Hello, yes?"

The man, half visible as he peered out from the behind the door, had fair blond hair with a thick side-swept fringe. He wore a three piece brown suit with matching tie and gold-framed pince-nez, behind which sat a pair of slightly irritated but genial green eyes. He appeared to be no older than his mid forties, certainly nowhere near old enough to be dallying with retirement, but yet, as with the Colleges, there was something ancient in his countenance.

"Dr Watt?" asked Thomas.

"Yes," replied the man with restrained curiosity. He moved in front of the door, propping it open behind him and removed his spectacles, sliding them into his breast pocket. In his other hand was a thick, very old-looking book with two large brass clasps holding the cover shut and what appeared to be a French latch key dangling from a piece of ribbon tied to one of them. He tucked the book under his arm and reached the other forward to shake Thomas' hand.

"Yes. That is correct," he repeated with a nod, a sudden flash of realisation upon him.

"Well, come on in, I'm almost finished." Dr Watt pulled the door open, standing aside so his visitor could pass.

After shuffling through a small, beige vestibule Thomas entered Dr Watt's study. The room was commodious, although not quite on a scale to account for the sound of those distant, echoing footsteps, which, given that it was carpeted wall-to-wall with tapestry rugs made even less sense. Thomas looked down and wiggled a foot gently side-to-side, testing for his own peace of mind that it *was* a rug and not for example, an elaborate painting. As the material puckered, he began to question whether he really heard what he thought he heard.

The light wood panelling was barely visible behind a series of chunky bookcases that extended three quarters of the way up the high walls, each one crammed with books of various sizes, which in turn had more lying horizontally atop them. The bookcases lined both sides of the room and after every two stacks another was placed perpendicular to the wall, effectively dividing the space into three reading sections on each side. It looked more like a College library than a Fellow's office. To his right, tucked behind the door, was a freestanding Edwardian coat stand with serpentine hooks curving out from a central finial. Its beech wood had a rich patina with russet hues and a fine grain, and Thomas was so taken admiring the piece that he almost tripped over a tatty portmanteau on the floor beside it. At the far end, surveying the room with suitable grandeur, was a twin pedestal desk with panelled sides, ornate brass handles, and a green faux leather top. Directly behind that sat a large Victorian armchair, its thick green velvet surface held onto the frame with brass studs along the front and wing facings. It had an inviting curved back and a slightly bowed front seat, and the whole sumptuous creation rested upon a four leg base with a set of shiny brass casters.

Thomas, ever mindful of providing thorough and correct details, commenced to give a brief account of himself.

"My name is Thomas Wharton, I'm an archaeology grad at King's —"

"Masters student?" interrupted Dr Watt as he removed the book from under his arm and began searching for a gap in the nearest bookcase to house it. Thomas followed slowly behind as the Doctor moved along the bookshelves, his head bobbing up and down as he scanned the shelves, high and low.

"Yes, yes I am."

"Staying on to read for the PhD?"

Thomas grinned shyly, "Well, I'd like to. It all depends how I do with the Masters I suppose."

Dr Watt paused, gazing dreamily at the ceiling, as if reminiscing.

"Ah, a PhD in the social sciences ay? It's all about learning more and more about less and less, and if you're doing it right you'll never be certain of anything." He gave Thomas a quick smile then resumed scanning the bookshelves.

"Nick asked me to come here to speak with you," explained Thomas shuffling along behind the Doctor. "I spoke to Emma in the Court and she directed me here."

Dr Watt removed four smaller books from the bottom

shelf of a bookcase and held them in one hand as he pushed the large tome into the opening. He then clutched the four smaller books to his side and resumed searching for spaces to re-home them.

"I was not without warning you would be visiting," he replied. "Something, somewhere must be very out of sorts if Nick has sent you to speak with *me*. They usually deal with these issues in-house, so to speak." He walked along to the next bookcase and pushed one of the four books into a slim opening.

"What seems to be the problem, Masters student Thomas?"

"This is going to sound a bit strange."

"Oh good!" replied Dr Watt in delight.

Thomas sighed as he ran through all the potential starting points in his head and yet, as with the Porter previously, not a single reasonable introduction was prepared to raise its head above the parapet.

"Do you…" he let the strap of his rucksack fall along the length of his arm and flop onto the floor beside a bookcase, "…do you *know* who Nick is?" he asked.

Dr Watt was still scanning the shelves, searching for another gap but he paused briefly and spoke over his shoulder.

"If you mean am I aware of Nick's, and the other's, existential disposition then yes. It's not unheard of for buildings to acquire personalities, especially not places of learning."

A wave of relief washed over Thomas; establishing a common understanding, or even a shared delusion, bolstered his confidence.

"They have a problem," Thomas went on.

"Who are *they* exactly?"

"The Colleges."

"Not just Nick?"

"No, all of them."

"Continue."

"I was with Nick… and John and Trinity, and a gargoyle attacked us by the riverside at King's. They were able to destroy it – well, at least, to send it back to the church that it came from, but they say they've been getting attacked by gargoyles intermittently for the last 30 years."

"The past 30 years? You're certain of the time frame?"

Dr Watt's measured responses seemed to fence more with Thomas' understanding of the questions than the veracity of his answers, the latter of which he accepted with polite tedium.

"Yes, I remember clearly, Nick was specific in saying this has been happening for the past 30 years."

Dr Watt carried on scouring the bookcases for gaps and managed to clamp open a space between two large almanacs and squeeze the smaller of the remaining books into it.

Thomas pressed on.

"But perhaps just as worrying is that Nick says something, and they don't know what that something is at the moment, is pushing them away from *our* time. Whatever it is has reduced the amount of time they can remain here, especially when outside of their own grounds, diminishing their influence, and they're concerned they might soon… well, fade away."

Dr Watt, his interest now very much piqued, turned to Thomas.

"How much further?"

"Seconds."

"Tell me again, how long has this been going on?"

"About 30 years, the same amount of time the gargoyle attacks have been taking place. They think the two things are connected."

"They are Thomas, they most *certainly are*."

"Here's another gap," declared Thomas pointing towards a space on the nearest shelf.

"Tremendous." And with that the Doctor slid in the penultimate book.

He then strode off purposefully towards the other end of the room.

"Come!" he bellowed without turning his head.

As he approached the desk, Dr Watt gently dropped the last book onto the edge of its cluttered surface and jumped like a spring lamb over a pile of books to access the chair. The volumes in question were stacked like a neat, low brick wall on either side of the desk. Book after book, from the profound to the transformative, one after the other lying flat on their backs. Thomas craned his neck to scan another, smaller pile of books dumped behind the desk in a manner out of keeping with the organised placement of those at the sides. These ones looked as if they had been thrown, rather than set down on the floor; *The Benefits of Work Houses* by Lyka Tory, *Heavy Machinery & Its Use in Negotiations* by L. Prosser, *The Jolly Side of War: How to Get Rich as an Arms Trader* by Gavin Meant. Thomas raised a disapproving eyebrow which did not go unnoticed by Dr Watt.

"Thomas," he said in a firm but understanding tone, "Dispossess your mind of the notion that one should avoid reading books written by those with opposing views to your own." He waved his hand dismissively at the books in question. "Admittedly, it may involve holding one's ethical nose but nevertheless, one has to understand what one disagrees with, otherwise, how would you know you disagree with it? Because someone else told you to? No, no, that will never do."

He paused.

"It's all about *understanding*. Understand the psychology of any life form, especially those with whom you disagree," he gave another disapproving wave of his hand at the books behind the desk, "and you have the power to build bridges, expand the frontiers of knowledge, and unleash collaborative potential." He paused once more, his face blanched with despondency. "Of course, there *are* a few – fortunately rare – instances where one is presented with such a regrettable mix of attributes that one has no other option than to pour a water and brandy, accept nothing can be done, and press on with other matters."

He shook his head regretfully.

"Take Earth for example, where human psychology is so deeply pock-marked with cognitive biases that it is dull to predict and easy to exploit. Add to that but a passing acquaintance with morality and you find that potential is instead used to create a series of predatory systems that manufacture heinous circumstances – war, famine, disease and so forth – as investment opportunities. Send your fellow beings to hell in a handcart as it were, but never mind, you're only human, what you lack in ethics you make up for in sneakiness."

Dr Watt sighed regretfully then, in a misjudged attempt to lighten the mood, perked up as if closing an after dinner speech.

"Of course, there *are* parts of the universe that classify humans as poisonous fungi."

Thomas stared, nonplussed but smiling respectfully.

"Probably," mumbled Dr Watt, suddenly conscious of it being construed as a slight, which it was. "Probably… *might* classify that way. Nothing personal, of course, I admit there *are* exceptions," added the Doctor with a quick nod to Thomas. "Sadly, very, *very* few exceptions." He shook his head again.

"It's a species level observation. Or," he contemplated with an absentminded stare, "it could be the whole genus that's rotten."

Thomas, who felt as if something important had just been explained to him but had yet to realise what, ran his eyes over the desk and lying at the edge, the last book that Dr Watt had dropped onto its surface, was the familiar cover of a little black book with scrolls of gold writing, *Ancient Greece in Pictures*. He smiled and before he could comment upon having the same book he noticed something on the floor. Just visible between the twin pedestals of the desk was the outline of two shoes set into a thin layer of dust, like footprints set in concrete. It looked as if someone had sat in that very spot for years without moving.

"Do they know where the gargoyle came from?" asked

Dr Watt, turning in his chair and pulling out a large flat book from beneath a pile of rolled up papers.

"St. Edward's church," replied Thomas. "The one on Peas Hill," he added for accuracy.

Dr Watt swirled around in the chair and jumped up from the opposite side to which he had just sat down. He skipped over the wall of books and headed towards a rolling library ladder, leaping onto the bottom rung. The ladder immediately zipped sideways, stopping abruptly at the second bookcase along and he ascended to the very top.

"From where did the gargoyle come?"

"St. Edward's church," repeated Thomas, "On Peas Hill."

"I can't hear you," shouted Dr Watt from atop the ladder, and he pulled out his glasses from his breast pocket and slipped them on.

"That's better. What did you say?"

"St. Edward's church on Peas Hill."

"Ah·yes. S, S, St…" He ran his hand along the top row of books until arriving at a small, unassuming brown spine. "Ah-ha!" he exclaimed.

Dr Watt blew a layer of light dust from its surface and fanned through the pages. Then, confident it was the correct book, he snapped it shut and held onto the ladder as it flew back to the other end of the bookstack, sliding down the rungs like a fireman when it stopped.

"Here we go! Permit me a moment to triple check one small detail."

His energy was electric and it was difficult for Thomas to comprehend how someone so naturally animated managed to repress such exuberance beneath an otherwise self-possessed exterior. Dr Watt sprung back over the pile of books and landed in the chair, swinging around to face the desk and opening the book before him. Without looking up or saying a word, he pointed in the direction behind Thomas and the latter dutifully turned to observe what the point intended. Backed up against the last bookcase were two rickety wooden chairs, the type one sees outside bric-a-brac shops with worn varnish and missing back spindles, the type with a Russian roulette approach to structural integrity, usually reserved solely for propping up the 'Open' sign. With little regard for gravity, one of the chairs held upon its seat a neatly stacked pile of journals that ascended with a slant to over a metre in height. The other chair was untenanted and Thomas lifted it carefully, placing it in front of the desk. He gave the seat a gentle wiggle from side to side to assure himself it wouldn't collapse upon contact, then sat down, cautiously.

Dr Watt rolled his chair tight to the desk and began leafing through the pages of the little brown book.

"Yes. Yes," he mumbled as he read.

"A-ha."

Another page turned.

"Yes."

He returned to the first page.

"Hmmm."

Three pages were flicked forward.

"As I suspected."

Thomas watched with bewilderment as the good Doctor proceeded in this fashion of thumbing to and fro for at least ten minutes before finally removing the pince-nez and placing them back into his breast pocket.

"Time lice."

"Time lice?"

"Yeeessssss," replied Dr Watt as he stretched out his arms then placed them behind his head.

"Time lice are the balancing of an equation, and not a particularly pleasant one. Not too particularly unpleasant either, but terribly inconvenient if they get out of control." He leant forward, sitting up straight and folding his arms on the desk like a Victorian schoolmaster.

"I don't follow," Thomas responded with a frown.

"No, you don't. It's a venerable trait."

"I'm sorry?"

"Don't be, Masters student Thomas. Don't be."

Dr Watt paused as if processing multiple complex

equations. "Where were we? Oh, yes. Now you see, you have the Colleges. Fine and decent ideas, one and all. Not a single one I wouldn't welcome onto my side for a game of cricket. *But*," he emphasised raising both index fingers then dropping his hands to the desk, "all things in time and space have balance. Like it or not, and many do not, cold, simple balance. To quote the Third, for every action, there is an equal and opposite reaction. You have 900 years of positive thinking so you have 900 years of *negative* thinking. Yes?"

"Er, yes," replied Thomas, uncertain of the meaning of the question.

"No."

"No?"

"No. The universe is highly nuanced Thomas, highly nuanced. Unlike positive thinking which requires imagination and contemplation, structure and perspicacity, and so forth, et cetera, negative thinking is fragmented and impulsive, it is disorganised and messy, and this means the equation is usually balanced through many small, usually harmless expressions; time lice."

"Time lice? Are they animals?" questioned Thomas.

"No. They're ideas. Similar to the way that Nick and the other Colleges are ideas. But unlike *them*, time lice are *small* ideas. Very, very small ideas. Twi-thoughts. In fact, they're more like mind itches. Tiny impulses seeping through from one time into the other; usually resulting in little more than a fleeting suspicion that your paper isn't long enough, or you have the wrong time for an exam, or your theory has been proposed before. Small. Passing. Doubts. Nothing more, nothing lasting. Time lice do not exist for long enough to make coherent sense. *Usually*."

Thomas nodded, "They sound familiar. Could these… time lice have found a way to stick around for longer or could they have grown into something bigger, something more structural, more meaningful?"

Dr Watt took a deep breath and leant back in the soft plump chair, pleased with the question.

"Very perceptive Thomas, but not quite. They would not have *found* a way to stick around in the sense that they had the *idea* to stick around for longer, but there's a high probability these little rascals became stuck and developed into something more cohesive through no intention of their own. Not to begin with."

Dr Watt picked up the small brown book and flicked to the end, running a finger down both sides of the page before closing it softly.

"My guess, and that's rock-solid confidence by anyone else's reckoning, is that they've caused a blockage and the temporal flow has backed up because of it."

Thomas frowned and momentarily closed his eyes, trying to cast out images of a backed-up sewage system or an overflowing basin.

"A blockage? You make it sound like a plumbing problem," he laughed, trying to make light.

Dr Watt shrugged, "Similar principle. Think of the flow of time like the flow of water running through a pipe."

"Okay."

"Crudely put, time lice are detritus inside the pipe, tiny pieces of matter that would usually pass through the sluice, disintegrate and fade back into the ether. But when detritus builds up in a pipe it eventually causes a blockage, resulting in an ever larger accumulation of unpleasantness, which for the Colleges means an ever larger mass of time lice; ever more conscious, ever more logical, ever more cohesive as an idea. I have little doubt that it's time lice..." he paused as if rearranging the thought, "...an *accumulated mass* of time lice, that has seized control of the gargoyles, but as to *how* it is conducting this coup d'état, well, that's another question, one that based upon the information supplied to me, is not immediately within my capability to answer."

Thomas shook his head thoughtfully, "How could this have happened? I mean, what could have caused the time lice to accumulate in the first place?"

Dr Watt smiled.

"Another most pertinent question, but perhaps the one

thing you and I are powerless to remedy." He drew a long breath.

"The Colleges pass from one time to the other. They are positive, but they have a negative balance – the time lice. This unobservable residue would usually dissipate with minimal efficacy, balancing the universal equation. But," he paused again.

"But what?" pressed Thomas.

Dr Watt, suddenly uneasy, loosened his tie. He held his chin in his hand then grimaced ever so slightly.

"The Colleges *do* have a tendency to turn a blind eye to the mundane details of life, so if they've been too busy being brilliant and not balanced it with enough housekeeping, then it's possible the time lice started to linger and built up quicker than they could dissipate. The metaphorical cooking oil."

"Housekeeping?" said Thomas quizzically.

"Yes," replied Dr Watt, staring into space. "The Colleges are pretty poor at housekeeping, but ironically they can be terribly good at sweeping things under the carpet."

"I still don't follow."

"Simply put," began Dr Watt, "If you don't question something that is jumping up and down waving its arms in the air demanding to be questioned, then you will inevitably end up with a problem. The Colleges have a tendency to focus almost entirely on academic pursuits and pay very little attention to *how* things are run. Of course, it's not a failing as such, it's what they are; academic personifications, but if they don't put a *little* effort into overhauling the system now and again – a system which is as much a part of them as any academic paper – then the system, so to speak, will overhaul *them*. And that, in a globule, is what appears to be happening."

Thomas stared vacantly at first, but slowly Dr Watt's words began to resonate; that he had been required to jump through administrative hoops upon entering the University was inaccurate; it was more a case of being handed a hoop at the door with the instructions to hula or perish.

"I'll explain this to them, surely they can make a few easy changes for the long term. It's *so mundane*!"

Dr Watt frowned, "Thomas, you are well meaning and earnest, but my suggestion would be not to broach the subject with the Colleges. It is one of few taboos for them. They dislike being told they need to pay attention to things that bore them."

"But I can try."

"Oh yes, you can *try*. But do not be discouraged if they respond by playing *Symphony to Denial* with full orchestral accompaniment. Trust me, I've witnessed it before. They are most effective in treating the symptoms but rarely the cause."

"Well, I'll try anyway," responded Thomas, quietly confident that his good rapport with Nick, John, and Trinity would yield success.

"Be aware Thomas, the Colleges are wonderful," he flung his arms up in the air to emphasise the point, "truly magical and I would not be here myself if I had anything less than absolute respect for each and every one of them, *but,*" he let out a deep sigh, "a warning to the curious, they can be obstinate when it comes to matters that cannot be brushed off with a few lines of Latin and a quote from Wordsworth."

"It's Words-*worth* me trying though," rejoined Thomas with a grin, feeling optimistic and demonstrating he had every confidence in Nick to listen. "If there's something I can say to help in the long term then I should try to explain."

Dr Watt smiled and let the matter go.

Thomas didn't notice the smile, and even if he had noticed he probably wouldn't have recognised the sadness in it, not yet. As incredible as the scenario sounded, it made increasing sense to Thomas who jumped to his feet, running a hand through his hair in contemplation.

"I've got to get back. I must get to College and explain this to Nick."

Dr Watt remained seated at the desk, calm as the eye of

a storm. He reached for the small brown book again, "Please, do not depart just yet. There is more to tell."

Still doubting the seriousness with which the chair took its load-bearing responsibilities, Thomas returned to perch awkwardly upon it, drumming his fingers restlessly on the underneath of the seat as he repressed the urge to run as fast as he could back to College.

"There is no panacea but the situation is not without precedent, and it is certainly not without a solution." The Doctor's relaxed tone and constructive approach were a tonic.

"Okay, that sounds good, how do we fix it?" Distracted by the thought of there actually being options, Thomas forgot his caution and slid more fully onto the chair.

Dr Watt reached to his left, picked up the top book from the pile on the floor, glanced briefly at the page where it fell open, then placed it back. "When a pipe becomes blocked and one needs to isolate the problem, what is the first thing you do?"

"Turn off the tap?" replied Thomas.

"Second thing?"

"Shut off the stopcock?"

"Bingo! A valve that regulates the flow of water, or in our case, the flow of time. And just for fun, let's pretend that time is always linear."

Dr Watt leapt up from his chair, jumped the low wall of books and rummaged around in the heap of journals sitting atop the other wooden chair. Upon pulling out a well-thumbed manuscript from near the top of the pile, he trotted back to the desk and opened it in front of Thomas, tapping the page as he did so.

"Et voilà, your stopcock," he announced, pointing to a series of photographs on the open page then retiring with a look of satisfaction to the other side of the desk.

Thomas studied the photographs in disbelief, "No. No." He picked up the journal and slunk back with the photos held close to his face, studying the page. Before him was a row of coloured images showing different angles of three misshapen pieces of bronze. The largest piece featured a gear with four central spokes, its surface coloured green with corrosion.

"This is the Antikythera mechanism!" he exclaimed.

"Or, for your purposes, a stopcock," repeated Dr Watt, indifferent to the item's archaeological status.

"It's 2000 years old! It was made to predict the position of astronomical bodies, not for shutting off water pipes!"

"A *fancy* stopcock," conceded Dr Watt.

"*This*," declared Thomas, his voice a cocktail of frustration and scepticism, "is a stopcock?"

Dr Watt leant forward in his chair, folding his arms neatly on the desk.

"It wasn't *made* to be a stopcock. In the same way that coin hanging from your belt wasn't *made* to be a key. But it just so happens that it can *operate* as a stopcock. It was discovered, the last time anyway, underwater wasn't it?"

Thomas leant forward and placed the journal, still open, on the desk. He sat quietly for a few moments, collecting his thoughts.

"Even if this is true – and I'm sure it is Dr Watt, it's just a lot, *really* a lot to take in – then we're still in as much trouble as we were before I came here because there's no way we can get hold of the Antikythera mechanism. It's in the National Archaeological Museum of Athens. And even if I *could* magically find the money to fly me to Greece, and they *did* let me take it out of its protective case to look at it, they're certainly *not* going to let me take it away. I'm not Lord Elgin."

Dr Watt raised an eyebrow, as if baffled by Thomas' lack of grasp on the logistics, but then, he *was* privy to background information that the young man was not.

"The stopcock —" he read the look on Thomas' daunted face, acknowledged his veneration for its archaeological prestige and began again. "The Antikythera mechanism will, in a few days' time go on display here, in the Museum of General and Local Archaeology, as part of its exhibition on astronomical science in ancient Greece, on *loan* from the National Archaeological Museum of Athens. The very 'Surprise feature exhibit' touted by those garish posters plastered about town."

Thomas' state of mind refused description but judging by his expression a Venn diagram would place it at the intersection of *I really must take up drinking* and *Whatever I do I must never take up drinking*.

"My dear fellow," continued Dr Watt. "You didn't think I would be so frivolous, so contrary of mind, as to consult my very best resources," and he waved his hands around at the floor and at the walls, "just to suggest that your only option is to acquire the unobtainable from the impenetrable? That simply wouldn't be research well done now, would it?"

Suddenly, an incredible possibility coalesced in Thomas' mind. Turning in his seat, his eyes glided over bookcase after bookcase, taking in the rows of tightly packed volumes on every shelf: small books, medium books, large tomes, manuscripts, and journals. He then looked at the two piles of books sitting either side of the desk, neatly discarded and purposefully placed, and to the dust between the pedestals. He then raised his eyes to the knowing smile of Dr Watt and had no choice but to infer what his gut already suspected; that Dr Watt had spent years reading, cocooned from time, just to arrive at *this* moment and provide, so very calmly, the fruit of that ridiculous oak.

"Answers are easy," said Dr Watt. "But encouraging people to ask the right questions." He shook his head slowly, "Now *that* is the tricky part."

— ∞ —

Peterhouse is the oldest of the Cambridge Colleges, but it doesn't like to flaunt it. It sits back from the busy road with a quiet dignity, like an elderly gentleman surveying life from the comfort of a bistro table, sipping a glass of port as the world rushes by. The black iron railings that run along the street have two large gates at either side that are usually open for visitors, but today they were closed while repairs to the Hall floor were carried out.

For this reason, aside from a few stray students rushing off to lectures, the forecourt was relatively empty and there was no one to witness the fast-moving outline of a man riding a bicycle take shape in the air. The form quickly passed the Chapel and disappeared beneath a small archway, swallowed by cobwebs and shadows. Seconds later it emerged, charging over the grass of Old Court, a tyre-width line spreading across the newly mowed lawn like a crack in a champagne glass. As the line reached the edge of the lawn, the distinct metal frame of a Royal Sunbeam stormed into corporeal glory, conveying Nick to within a centimetre of the buildings that make up the west side of the Court.

Swinging a leg over the bike, Nick dismounted and stood with one hand on the handlebars as he looked up at the building. Thin shards of sunlight were slicing through the large, grey clouds and the distant chattering of busy streets had long since given way to the occasional *tchup tchup tchup tchup tchuuuuup* from blackbirds scouring the grass for a meal.

"That's a splendid little runner," commented a youthful but shaky voice from behind. The man it belonged to was on his hands and knees, head lowered to the grass, his slight frame shuffling along in a crab-like fashion as he searched the edge of the lawn where it met the path.

Nick smiled and patted the handlebars. "Any luck?" he enquired, crossing his ankles as he leant casually against the seat of the bicycle, unperturbed by the man's behaviour.

The crouching figure raised a pair of cobalt eyes. He had thick brown hair and a learned, thin face.

"Still looking," came the reply.

He crept along the edge of the grass until he was level with the back wheel of Nick's bicycle.

"You know, I'm certain it was *Xestobium rufovillosum*," he said, lifting his head with a look of defeat. Giving a few final glimpses around the grass, he slowly rose into a kneeling position.

"As clear as glass, I'm certain of it, but to observe such

a beetle in October? No, no, no, this is most extraordinary." He shrugged. "Still, that's what one gets for being liberal with certainty."

Peterhouse, for this is who the nimble beetle had eluded, gave up the search with a sigh and manoeuvred again in order to sit more comfortably on the grass, leaning backwards on one outstretched arm, although a closer inspection would have revealed him to be hovering just above it.

"Peter," began Nick, "the situation is forcing our hand."

Peter raised an arm to cover his eyes from the sunshine then, paying due deference to Nick's words, slowly stood up. He was casually dressed; a pair of navy linen trousers with matching blazer, white shirt with no tie, and a thick, blue scarf wound loosely around his neck.

"You've consulted Dr Watt I presume?" he asked, adjusting the scarf.

"Thomas is there now, and John and Trinity are investigating St. Edward's church. We'll have more information after we reconvene. But Peter, look," Nick stood up from the bicycle, pushed back his spectacles and placed both hands into his trouser pockets, "something is going to have to happen. I don't know what just yet and I don't know when, but could you, please, get the word out to the others to stand by?"

"Consider it done." Peter pulled up the collar of his blazer and cast his eyes along the tops of the buildings, as if looking for a distraction to take his thoughts away from the unseemly subject.

"Do we have any idea who, if anyone, is paying the gargoyles' piper?"

"No, not yet."

Peter nodded.

"A dash over 700 years and I haven't been assailed by the architecture yet. I must be clear in my desire for it to remain that way. I'm too old for that kind of excitement. I wonder. Is that short term luck or long term complacency?"

Nick smiled, "Let's hope it's neither."

"My Keeper obtained this last night." Peter reached into the top of his shirt and pulled out a small stone hanging from a silver chain. It was a piece of masonry chipped from one of the lower courses of his Dining Hall. He continued, "As we speak, they're in the final stages of resetting the floor. They powered through the night like a jet engine."

Pleased at the sight of the little stone, Nick took in a deep breath of Autumn air, "How are the other Keepers faring with the stones?"

"Oh pretty well. Mostly all found," replied Peter with an optimistic tone of achievement. He nodded encouragingly as he folded his arms.

"Well, there was a slight delay at Queens'," he added. "They couldn't find the blasted thing. It was eventually unearthed in the south-east corner of the Chapel. Always the way isn't it? You leave something in a safe place and 600 odd years later when you need it, you can't remember where you put it." He rolled his eyes and gave an empathetic tut.

"Then of course we had the unfortunate incident at …" he hesitated, "Well, propriety prevents me, but it involved a large trench, an overlooked spade, and a delegate attending one of those workshop affairs held by the Department for Student Uptrading." He sniffed unsympathetically. "Gravity was not kind. Still, he shouldn't have been walking on the grass."

"If gravity didn't see fit to spare him then nor shall my sympathies," laughed Nick. He frowned, "Were any students involved?"

"Oh heavens, no. The Department for Student Uptrading operates a strict no student policy at all its events." He scratched his head. "And its offices."

"A workshop in term time?" puzzled Nick.

"Yes, yes. The students were placed into alternative accommodation in order to make way for the workshop delegation." He sighed, then smoothed the corners off his statement, "But of course, if that is the Department's policy then it is certainly not *our* place to question it.”

“Quite so,” replied Nick.

The two Colleges stood in quiet, slightly uncomfortable contemplation for a few moments until Peter rallied his enthusiasm. “Well! I shall personally find the other Colleges. Make sure we’re all identifying beetles from the same taxonomic crib sheet, so to speak.”

“Even Edmund?” enquired Nick with a smile.

“*Even* Edmund, the young whipper snapper!” laughed Peter.

— ∞ —

Dr Watt sat quietly, flicking through the small brown book and occasionally denoting interest with a low “Hmm.” In his own subtle way, he thought it prudent to give Thomas a few moments to brood upon, consider, reject, take in again, reconsider, and ultimately resign himself to the inevitable.

“If,” Thomas broke the silence, “I can get the Antikythera mechanism —”

“When,” corrected Dr Watt.

“When?”

“Not *if*. When.”

“Okay. *When* I get the Antikythera mechanism – and let’s assume I don’t get sent down for doing so – *when* I get it, what do I do with it? And isn’t it divided into lots of tiny pieces? Do I need all the parts?”

Dr Watt put down the small book and leant into his chair, arching his back in a casual stretch.

“82 pieces to be precise but you only need the largest of those, referred to as Fragment A. The piece with four spokes. As to what you do with it, well, that’s a little more involved.”

He crossed his legs and shuffled in his seat, “The when and the how.” Another repositioning and he leant forward, hands folded on the desk.

“The When? All Hallows’ Eve. No doubt you are familiar with the notion that the veil between the world of the dead and the world of the living is, the folks of

Mediaeval Europe inform us, at its thinnest on All Hallows' Eve?"

"Y-yes," replied Thomas with a slight hesitancy. "Although I was under the impression that was more of an 18th or 19th century trope."

Dr Watt smiled, "As far as the written record goes, yes, but the written record, even when dancing arm-in-arm with archaeology, offers but a narrow spy hole into the everyday lives of everyday people." He nodded as if agreeing with himself. "A brief chat with your average Mediaeval European is quite the eye-opener." He paused, glanced ever so briefly at Thomas and corrected himself, "Would be. Probably." And he waved his hand as if dismissing his own comment.

Just as Thomas was about to ask how that spy hole could possibly be enlarged, Dr Watt took off again at his usual speed.

"Chronological receipts aside, they *did* hit upon a universal truism, because on a theoretical level the concept stands firm for *all* worlds; bubble universes, parallel universes, temporal separation, the whole jolly lot."

Thomas sat forwards, attempting to adopt a less precarious position on the wooden chair.

"Nick and John made reference to that. They said the Colleges usually only appear in corporeal form on All Hallows' Eve."

"Indeed. Whatever is to be done will have to take place at *midnight* on All Hallows' Eve, when time is at its most pliable."

Thomas pulled up the sleeve of his coat and stared at the watch dial, double-checking the date, "That's tomorrow night!"

"I cannot fault your assertion."

Dr Watt crossed his arms.

"Now to the *how*." He ran a finger around the inside of his collar, tugging it gently. "They won't like this. They won't like this one little bit."

Thomas, whose face over the past few hours had flip-flopped between bemusement and abject horror, now closed his eyes and braced himself for whatever unobtainable, far-fetched task was placed before him.

"They need to call Michael."

He opened one eye and perused the Doctor's face with it.

"Is that it? They just need to call someone?"

Dr Watt wrinkled his forehead and nodded slowly, giving a response that took Thomas' words at no more than their face value.

"Yes, they *just* need to call Michael. And be careful to make that clear to them when they sulk about it. As they inevitably will. They won't like to admit they require his assistance. You'll have to give the stopcock to Michael. He'll know what to do with it."

"And what *will* he do with it?" queried Thomas.

"A stopcock is only effective when it is in the right location and the Antikythera mechanism is no different. Imagine two connecting pipes, this time and their time." He picked up a couple of pencils from the desk and held them between two fingers, horizontal and tip to tip in front of him.

"The stopcock has to be placed outside of both worlds in order to stop the flow and permit the Colleges' time to drift back to where it should be." With his other hand he picked up a small metal pencil sharpener and held it above the pencil tips to represent the stopcock.

"There is only one place that can be done and that is where Michael resides." Dr Watt stood up, placed a hand either side of his lower back, stretched, then walked around to lean over the back of the chair.

"When deployed correctly it will halt the flow just long enough to permit their time to bob back to where it should be; a fraction out of sync with yours." He gazed into space again as if exasperated by the entire mess.

"Like a tug boat pulling an aircraft carrier."

Thomas hung on Dr Watt's every word. It may have been with all the agitation of a burglar holding on by the fingertips to a third-floor windowsill, but he hung on nonetheless.

"Okay," began Thomas, said more in an attempt to calm himself than acknowledge what had just been proposed.

"Okay," he repeated as he jumped up. "Hang on a minute." And he hurried to where his rucksack lay on the floor. Kneeling down he un-zipped the front pocket and pulled out a small lined notebook and a pencil bearing the name and crest of King's College, a memento from his first day in Cambridge. Standing up, he flipped back the cover with a sharp flick of his wrist and began writing as he drifted back to the other end of the room.

"Housekeeping," he mumbled under his breath as he sat back down, "Call Michael."

"And let us not forget," Dr Watt recommenced, "stopping the flow is likely to be the last piece in the puzzle. Before that, and continuing with our plumbing metaphor, the blockage will need to be cleared. That means dealing with whatever form the time lice have taken, and given the co-ordinated attacks that have been carried out on the Colleges thus far, not to mention the very act of controlling the gargoyles, we can be confident they *will* have taken form."

"Why can't the Colleges *see* whatever it is, whatever form the time lice have taken?" asked Thomas, still frantically scribbling.

"Two reasons. One is because time lice are negative, they dwell in the dark places, hiding from the light, both literal and philosophical. Whatever it is, it will have to be drawn out. They'll need a drain rod of an idea and the means to deal with the mess once they have it."

He sighed. "And the second is because people are rarely prepared to see what they most dislike in themselves."

The whole situation rotated in Thomas' mind, his head awash with thoughts and his common sense drowning in them. He couldn't think of anything to ask or anything to contribute. He felt dumbstruck. It was like sitting in his first job interview. And the second one. And the third. Thomas really wasn't very good at interviews.

"Dr Watt?"

"Yes?"

"Thank you. Thank you for your help." Thomas looked up from his notepad, laying the pencil at the centre.

"I'll probably never understand how all of this has happened, how I've seen the things I have or how I've come to be sitting here with you having the most surreal conversation of my life – and if you'd ever held a discussion with my uncle Erasmus about how celery can look irked, and you probably haven't – then you'd appreciate how the situation presents something of a credibility hurdle."

Dr Watt raised an eyebrow but did not interrupt.

"There are so many things that don't make sense and I still half think I'm dreaming, even though these are things I never *dreamed* were possible. But even with all that, putting all those doubts to one side, and maybe that's the wrong thing to do, but if I *do* put them to one side then there is at least one thing I recognise."

Intrigued, Dr Watt placed one hand on the top of the chair and leant against it.

"What would that be, Masters student Thomas?"

"Kindness," he replied matter-of-factly, and he carefully closed the little notepad, placing the pencil on top which disobediently rolled off and onto the rug without him noticing.

He swept his eyes over the trove of books flanking the desk.

"I don't know how you know what you do, and again, chances are I never will, but I reckon it took you a long time to know it, and my friend George – he runs the veggie café in my home town, you'd like him – he always says the most valuable thing you can give anyone is your time. So thank you. Thank you for your time."

Dr Watt did not move. It was almost as if, just for a moment, he couldn't. The raw humility of Thomas' appreciation had taken him entirely by surprise.

"For the right person, at the right time, it is an absolute pleasure," he responded, a smile lighting up his face. "Your friend George is a wise counsel."

"He is," answered Thomas. "We used to go metal detecting together looking for Roman coins. That's where this came from," he gestured to the coin hanging from his belt.

"Where did you go metal detecting?" enquired Dr Watt as if suddenly remembering a detail of great importance.

"Baker's Field in Baulkwall, that's my hometown, it's quite well known for Roman coins, only, like I tell everyone, we never found much except bits of old junk and this one coin."

"Baker's Field?" repeated Dr Watt, manoeuvring to the desk and scribbling on the underside of a map.

"Yes, do you know it?"

"I will do," replied the Doctor, and he moved on before Thomas could respond. "You understand what you need to tell Nick and the others?"

"Yes. Yes I do. Is there anything else I should pass on to them?" he asked, rising from his seat.

Now leaning at an angle with one hand on the desk, Dr Watt took the question seriously, raising his eyes as he considered an answer.

"Well," he mused. "If they could *all* refrain from pollarding their old buildings, *that* would be good spherical advice." He threw a glance to Thomas, "Good advice regardless of how one looks at it."

But quickly he settled on another thought, pushing himself upright and crossing his arms.

"The Keynes building. Now, I don't know if it was Nick's intention to embody in architecture the idiom 'a face like a bulldog chewing a wasp' but by jove he nailed it. Ask him to be a good sport and put a façade on it – something pleasingly neo-Gothic." He smiled, casually sitting back on the desk, arms still folded. "But transforming the Back Lawn into a wildflower meadow was inspired. Rangemen is both engineer and artisan, Nick was right to trust him."

Thomas nodded in agreement, "I'm confident he'll be pleased with the meadow compliment. As for the other bit..." he laughed, "... I'll do my best."

The two men walked slowly back through the library, the sound of their footsteps muffled by the tapestry carpets. Thomas' head turned one way and the other, his eyes roving around the room, admiring the Victorian elegance of it all. He picked up his rucksack and kept his fingers clutched tightly around the notepad. Dr Watt stood to one side and politely opened the outer door for him.

"Good luck Thomas, bowl a yorker."

"Thank you," he replied as he exited the room. "Thank you very much," and he waved the notepad in the air as he turned away.

With a gentle *click* of its latch, the wooden door closed behind him and taking a second step into the cloister he found himself on the receiving end of a curious look from a passing student. She curved out of his way and looked back as if finding his exit from the room to be somehow odd. Thomas thought nothing of it and headed off in the direction of the Porter's Lodge. He opened the notepad to peruse his scribbles but then stopped. He tapped his left trouser pocket, then the right, then twisted his bag to his front and unzipped the pocket.

"Ahhh my pencil," he said, rolling his eyes to the vaulting as he turned on the spot. He approached Dr Watt's door and knocked twice, very gingerly, embarrassed at having to return so soon.

Thud thud.

No response.

Thud thud thud.

Still no response, but unlike the last time there was no noise emanating from within. No distant footsteps. No tell-tale echo.

Another student walked past, giving him the same bemused look as the one before.

"I don't think you have to knock," she said, clearly trying to be helpful.

Thomas gave a nod of appreciation for the advice whilst at the same time thinking how very rude it would be to walk into someone's office without knocking. He waited until the student had passed out of sight before moving forward, cautiously placing his fingers on the handle. He waited a few more seconds just in case Dr Watt answered the door, but when only silence remained, he timidly pushed down and stepped inside. If, at that moment, any further students had been walking by the second door to the left of the Chapel entrance, they would have heard a bewildered cry.

"A broom cupboard! It's a broom cupboard!" he repeated, just in case he hadn't heard himself the first time. The large, stately room in which Thomas had not moments before spent several hours adrift in conversation, was not where he had left it.

He stepped backwards, reversing until he reached the edge of the cloister, scanning the line of doors to make sure he had approached the correct one.

He had.

He walked back to the door and grasping the notepad to his chest, stared forlornly inside. The room was approximately the size of a standard box bedroom, with five long shelves on the righthand side that harboured an array of housekeeping products; window cleaner, disinfectant, a large furniture polish with the lid missing, a plastic spray bottle, a pile of black sacks, and other domestic essentials. To the left, a series of clips held to order three different sized brooms, a rake, a dustpan and brush with a large chip in the corner of the pan, and a wooden window pole with a brass hook. A black and red Henry vacuum cleaner stared back at him from the far corner, its hose coiled neatly around the base and its long stainless steel extension tubes leaning casually against the shelving. He ran his eyes over the little room once more; along the left wall, over the ceiling, down the shelves, and up the narrow centre until his gaze reunited with the chirpy white smile of the Henry.

"I suppose you think this is funny?" quipped Thomas.

He stepped out of the broom cupboard, closed the door softly behind him and leant against it. Searching for a few moments of calm, his eyes traced the flow of the cloister arches, along to a column with its ball-flower carvings, then down the rippled grey stone to the floor. He gave a short chuckle as he resigned himself to the inevitable; the good ship *Logical* had long since sailed and it was now time to strap in, hold on, and assume the crash position.

So engrossed in thought was Thomas that he barely noticed his journey back to King's. His deft manoeuvres around dithering shoppers and his skilful into the road, onto the path, into the road weave through groups of camera-happy tourists went largely unchecked by his conscious mind. Had he been slightly more lucid as he left St. Cedd's Court he might have noticed the friendly Porter pulling the ropes that sent the flag of Emmanuel flying to the top of its pole, waving in the wind from the College's highest roof. And if he had been particularly observant, he would have noticed the flag was upside down.

It had started with Peterhouse. After speaking with Nick, Peter had given a nod to his Head Porter who raised the capsized College flag. It was seen by neighbouring Pembroke and St. Catharine's who immediately followed suit, and those in turn were noted by Queens', Darwin, Corpus Christi, and Emmanuel, a silent declaration of distress that spread across the city until, not five minutes later, 31 flags flew upside down. In Cambridge, this meant war. But before that, tea.

When Thomas reached the Market Square he accelerated into a sprint towards St. Edward's Passage, speeding past the church with such focus on his destination that there was a third thing he did not notice: a pair of small blue eyes looking out from the Gothic arch window of the bell tower. But these eyes most certainly noticed Thomas. They narrowed with interest as they followed his movement along the busy alleyway, skulked along the stone frame and held still behind the glass panel nearest the cornice to better see the direction he took, and as he disappeared from view and into King's Parade, they rippled out of sight.

Thomas paused as he reached the curb. The pavement was pulsing with shoppers and the road was awash with bicycles, the occasional *ting ting* reminding shoppers to refrain from walking in the road, and the more frequent 'oi!' reminding cyclists to stay off the pavement. He was briefly distracted by the smell of freshly cooked pastries drifting from a nearby café and although usually a slave to his stomach, even this aromatic siren could not seduce him from the task at hand. He jogged across the road and into King's Gatehouse.

Standing before the Porter's Lodge, he leant forward and rested his hands on his knees, taking a few seconds to regain his composure. His freckled cheeks were flushed pink and his green eyes watered from the cold. With a sharp intake of breath he straightened up, pulled open the Lodge door and made a beeline to the smaller door in the corner of the room.

"Hello James!" he called out, the door sighing shut behind him. Although attempting to be discreet, Thomas' raspy voice hadn't thought twice about betraying his exhausted state.

James was standing at the centre of the reception desk, an island of calm, tending to administrative duties. He did not need to look up to know it was Thomas who had entered the Lodge and with a flicker of a smile he responded just as the young man disappeared around the first curve of the inner wall.

"Afternoon Thomas. Tea upstairs if that makes you feel any better!"

A husky "Thank you!" floated down the stairwell, followed by an audible intake of breath. Taking the small stone steps two at a time, Thomas puffed upwards and upon reaching the crooked landing he could hear a spirited discourse emanating from within Nick's study. He checked his watch: 12:45. Life upturned, reality re-evaluated, and *still* 15 minutes to spare. What a day.

"Thomas! Good to see you," welcomed Nick as the wheezing lad appeared at the doorway. Trinity gave a courteous nod and John picked up the teapot from the tray and poured for him.

"I don't know where to start," opened Thomas, still mentally digesting his conversation with Dr Watt. He dropped his rucksack by the door as he walked in, then squeezed between the chairs, sinking into the mustard one with the striped throw. Previously, the lumpy seat had been akin to resting on the inner door of an iron maiden, but it now seemed marginally more amenable to helping a fellow out.

"First, eat," instructed Nick. "We appreciate your sense of urgency but you must provide fuel for the machine." He placed his tea cup into the saucer and held it in one hand as he pushed a plate across the table with the other. On top was a folded, white paper bag with the words *The Multi-Coloured Cafe* in grey letters at the centre. Thomas opened the envelope and the sweet aroma of a vegetable pasty greeted his nostrils.

"Awh, thank you!" he smiled, breathing it in.

With eyes like organ stops, he pulled out the golden semi-circle and began to eat.

The Colleges reignited their conversation.

"Whether you have an archaeological site that's 500 thousand years old or one that's clocked up over a million has, for too long, ceased to be the issue," asserted Nick. "We know they're there, and it's all very interesting, but it's the *permanency* of colonisation that needs to be addressed more rigorously. Short lived excursions do not equal colonisation."

"Quite so," agreed Trinity. "Humans first landed on the Moon in 1969, but it falls far short of being what one might describe as *colonised*."

And so, to Thomas' temporary relief, the conversation proceeded without him, permitting a few relaxed moments to forget his thoughts while he fed his churning stomach. He ate heartily, China plate balanced upon his knees, munching his way through the large pasty and conscientiously, if not entirely successfully, attempting to keep the flakes on the plate.

The little room remained every bit as charming as it was on his first encounter; its bulging book shelves still bulged, the creaky floorboards still creaked, and the quirky curios were still wonderfully curious. The minutes passed leisurely and soon the pasty was little more than crumbs.

"That was the best meal I've ever had," declared Thomas, screwing up the paper bag and placing the crumpled ball onto the plate. "Thank you very much. I thought of stopping for one before I ran back here but I didn't want to waste any time."

Nick smiled knowingly and gestured towards the tray, "More tea?"

He nodded eagerly, "Yes please," now mulling over his conversation with Dr Watt again.

"You have James to thank for the opulent repast," smiled Nick. "We can't have you wasting away now can we. The Department of Student Facilitation would not be impressed."

"I doubt they'd notice," replied Thomas with a distant stare. "Unless my wasting away required a form filling out in triplicate and someone only filled out two." He picked up his brimming tea cup and held it carefully over the saucer, drinking so deeply that he almost gulped the contents down in one.

"Are we correct to presume that you succeeded in consulting Dr Watt?" enquired Trinity as Thomas placed the cup back in its saucer.

Clink.

"Yes, yes I did, and he really is out of this world."

"Upon that we cannot disagree," remarked John.

"I could listen to him talk all day, you were completely right Trinity, and he was incredibly helpful. I've got so much to tell you." He scratched his head, "Ah, now, where do I start?"

With a *clink* and a *clink clink*, Thomas slid the cup and saucer onto the tray and pulled out the notepad from his trouser pocket. He began flicking through its pages, running his eyes over the scratchy writing as he assessed the best place to commence. Finally deciding upon the beginning, Thomas spent the next two hours recounting every aspect of his meeting with Dr Watt, leaving no detail unpacked and fielding the Colleges' every question. He explained about the time lice, which the Colleges appeared to be familiar with, he detailed the plumbing analogy, which they appeared less familiar with, and he explained about the Antikythera mechanism with which they seemed quietly impressed. Then, he mentioned the need to call Michael.

"Michael?!" was the unanimous response. The Colleges looked at each other with Trinity appearing notably ruffled.

"Yes, Dr Watt was very clear. He said the mechanism has to be given to Michael because he's in the only place where it can work and he'll know what to do with it. Why? Is that bad?"

Nick immediately poured himself another cup of tea and sat forward in his chair.

"This is quite a three cup problem."

He took a sip.

"Michaelhouse is a former College. Founded in 1323 it existed for a little over 220 years before…" he paused, sharing a sympathetic look with Trinity, "…being carefully and thoughtfully recycled. However, that was more than enough time for Michael to come into existence, but his premature dissolution left him bitter and something of a misanthrope." Nick tutted, mourning the loss.

John filled out more of the detail as he topped up his tea cup, "Michael exists in a separate timeline. More of a bubble really, one that bounces along parallel to our own."

"So how do we call him?" asked Thomas. "I'm guessing he doesn't have a telephone."

"It's not that kind of call," clarified Nick. "It's something we've only done once before. It's fairly simple but it *does* extend our to-do list to the very bottom of the page."

"How *do* you call Michael then?" enquired Thomas.

Nick furrowed his brow.

"It's a little convoluted," he began. "The Colleges – all 31 – gather on Midsummer Common. As a representation of time we form a circle, with the oldest College at the

North. The youngest College, Robinson, opens the circle by calling his name, then Clare Hall, and after her Lucy Cavendish and so on. By calling our names in this configuration we turn back through our collective history until we reach the beginning, Peterhouse."

"Michael, if he is in the mood of course, will then come out to play," interjected John. "It's like a temporal knock down ginger, only we don't get to run away; the circle cannot be broken." He inclined his head, "If he takes a liking to you he'll be more amenable to helping. Mind you, I'm not entirely confident that Michael is quite Putney to Mortlake."

"John!" chided Trinity.

Thomas looked at him quizzically.

"The full course," he clarified.

Trinity shot John a glare before adding, "It's a gamble in the sense that Michael has always been somewhat unpredictable, but it seems we have little choice."

Thomas nodded, replaying the extraordinary conversation in his head, "Dr Watt said that whatever we do, it would have to take place on All Hallows' Eve."

"Yes, indeed," remarked Nick, the others nodding in agreement. "All Hallows Eve is the easiest time to, in a temporal sense, move from one place to another."

John sat forward in his chair, "I'm sure I speak for all of us when I say the timeline is considerably more economic in length than we had been hoping for. Timescales and deadlines," he tutted. "The twin assassins of good research."

"There was something else that Dr Watt said," began Thomas sheepishly. The mundane topic he had previously been so confident in raising now seemed a heavy weight to lift.

"Yes?" replied Nick.

"Well, it seemed important but it – it —"

"Thomas, please, you need hold nothing back *here*," encouraged Nick.

"Well, it's just that Dr Watt was very complimentary of *all* the Colleges, but he said the time lice might have accumulated as a result of – and this is the phrase he used – poor housekeeping.”

The room fell silent. John and Trinity exchanged an indignant look and all three shuffled uncomfortably in their seats. Nick seemed almost lost for words. They appeared collectively stung by Dr Watt’s observation.

“I think…” Thomas proceeded cautiously, as if the ground might give way beneath him, “…he was referring to a culture of intellectual vanity fair.”

Nick pulled out his pocket watch. He did *not* press the winding crown and subsequently he did *not* look at the dial. He simply flipped the object to and fro in his hand then pushed it back into his pocket. Not only was Thomas failing to read the room, he hadn’t even taken the book off the shelf.

“I *think*,” repeated Thomas, trudging forth in his well-meaning innocence, “that Dr Watt might have been referring to the way the Colleges – and he made it very clear that he holds each of you in the highest regard – don’t always like to look at the duller details of how things run. You see, I don’t know if you are aware of what the SIS:TUM is and in particular a thing called uptrading, but it’s growing out of control and the paperwork —”

John was the first to comment and he cut Thomas off half way through his sentence.

“Paperwork, paperwork!” He waved his hands in the air as he spoke. “Thomas old boy, we cannot be held responsible for the running of the entire place, we are not administrators. That is why we *have* administrators.”

“Yes of course,” replied Thomas. “And you do have an awful lot of them.”

Nick, clearly uneasy, shifted sideways in his seat.

“Let us reacquaint ourselves with the subject at hand shall we? This is a deuce of a mess and we have *a lot* of ground to cover in very little time.”

“Dr Watt seemed to think it was *extremely* important and I said I would try to explain,” persisted Thomas. “I’m sure he didn’t mean to rattle you with subtext, it’s just I think I see what he means, for example, when I tried to book a room for my supervisions —"

"We really must press on," hurried Trinity.

"I know," agreed Thomas. "And I appreciate that it's prosaic, but you see, my Supervisor, so the rumour goes, hasn't been able to do any research for over six months because —"

"We are not impugning your efforts," clarified Nick.

"Just the content," retorted Thomas, frustrated and somewhat confused by the subject's reception.

"There is no benefit to be had from tilting at *that* particular windmill," he responded with a reassuring smile. From their first encounter Nick was kind, open, and perceptive and so it was with much surprise that Thomas observed his unwillingness to discuss the issue.

The conversational brick wall that Thomas had run so optimistically into is what he later came to recognise as the politest, most passive form of a Cambridge upbraiding. Slightly taken aback and now doubting his former conviction on the subject, he did not pursue the matter. It was a plucky attempt but he had to accept that no doubt the Colleges knew best. In fact, after winding his neck back in, his inner thoughts were entirely focused upon chastising himself for raising the subject in the first place. The exchange left him feeling socially gauche.

To Thomas' relief, the discussion quickly moved on and continued into the early evening. Street noise drifting in through the little window slowly morphed from peak shopping din to the scramble of bicycles hurrying to early dinners and late seminars. By the time the first signs of dusk were settling into the corners of the tiny room, John and Trinity had only just introduced their discovery from St. Edward's church, explaining how they found the names of each College, barring one, written backwards on individual stones in the organ loft.

"Which one was missing?" asked Thomas, pushed to the edge of his seat with curiosity.

"In light of your revelation that we are urged to call

Michael, it will come as little surprise that the missing College is Peter," answered Trinity.

"Why is that no surprise?"

"Because the necessity to call Michael has exposed the fact that whoever is doing this appears to be using the same premise for another purpose." Her expression evidenced deep unease.

"The names of the youngest Colleges are written on the lowest stones, rising chronologically. Except for Peter, who was only partly engraved." Trinity stood up, pushed the tea tray into the middle of the table and sailed through the gap between chairs. She headed to a wrought iron floor lamp nestled at the side of the window, a striking piece of craftsmanship standing over a metre in height. The base resembled three tree roots that arched to the floor and the stem, which took the form of a tree trunk, twisted its way upwards, resplendent with art nouveau branches and stylised leaves. The large, cone-shaped shade was a piece of art in its own right, comprising dozens of segments of stained glass neatly soldered into a scalloped dome, a harmony of vibrant reds, orange and yellows pieced together to form oak trees whose roots looped elegantly into each curve along the rim. Hanging from beneath the shade were two pull chains, one either side of the stem, each with a decorative silver acorn on the end. Trinity pulled one of the chains and the lamp sprung into life with a warm Autumnal light that spread itself generously around the room.

"And you are *positive* Peterhouse wasn't written anywhere else?" checked Nick.

"As a proton, old boy," confirmed John. "The names of 30 Colleges are concentrated in the organ loft, each one carved into a separate stone, each one spelt backwards, and each one completely out of our grasp." He placed both hands behind his head and locked his fingers, leaning his head to one side, "Except Peter." He shook his head in annoyance then hunched forward. "Trin phased directly in front of the perishing stone and there was no sign of the engraver. Right under our noses. Impudent jackanape."

Placing a hand on each of the mustard-coloured arms, Thomas quietly wrenched himself from its jaundiced embrace. He slipped through the narrow gap between chairs and leant on the desk that jutted up against the window sill. A vague, clumsy thought had seeded in his mind and he cocked his head to one side, trying to make sense of it.

Trinity returned to her chair, sitting down heavily and tapping her fingers impatiently on the arm. "30 years of gargoyle attacks, 30 names written backwards on stone," she ruminated.

"All Colleges except Peter, the only fellow without a fully inscribed stone," added John. "By the notepad of William Gregor, I'll be the first to agree that correlation does not imply causation but at the very least we have a titanium link between the act of inverting a College name in stone and subsequent gargoyle attacks."

Nick cast him an enquiring eye, "One name written on the wall of St. Edward's church every year for the past 30 years, perhaps." He looked about the room, gauging opinion. "Let us suppose, every All Hallows' Eve."

"If that were correct," posited John, "it would mean by tomorrow night Peter's name could stand complete within the wall."

Maybe it was the metronome-like reasoning of the Colleges that ticked so solidly along, or perhaps it was the mention of All Hallows' Eve that blew upon the tinder of a distant memory and gradually ignited, but Thomas' clumsy thought was starting to look a little less ragged.

"Could it be?" he said quietly to himself, looking fixedly at the floor, almost as if looking elsewhere would break the spell.

"Could it be?" he repeated slightly louder as he pushed himself up from the desk.

"Could it be…" he turned his head to face the group, "…witchcraft?" The penny had dropped so suddenly that he was sure it must have fallen from his brain and spun around the room.

The Colleges looked at him with curiosity.

"That is, not witchcraft in and of itself," elaborated

Thomas, rubbing his jaw, "but could it be something from Wiccan folklore?" He hammered his hand in the air before him as if beating an invisible drum. "Bear with me."

Chasing the thought, he made a few short laps of the Lilliputian space in front of the desk, then turned back to the seated group. "I'm not saying it's witchcraft in the sense of magic being real and someone issuing a curse or something like that, but could whoever's doing this be using a *premise*? The *idea* behind one of the oldest tricks in the Wiccan book?"

Nick, John, and Trinity stared at him, silent and without so much as raising a tea cup. Thomas rested against the desk and as the thought developed he slowly slid himself back to sit on it. He looked at the others, expecting a spark of recognition as to where his mind was racing to, or for the notion to be instantly dismissed out of hand, but the collective light blue touch paper remained unlit.

"You don't know about this?" asked Thomas, surprised.

"Please," said Nick earnestly. "Enlighten us."

"Well, this might be silly and it might not be the answer, but it *is* something so at the very least we can rule it out." He looked to the ceiling then to the floor, once again searching for a place to start.

"When I was a child, my family and I went on holiday to Cornwall, to Boscastle."

Thomas was dredging up a memory so deep that he never conceived it would be useful. This was the lichen-covered shopping trolley of memories.

"We went to a witchcraft museum there. It was really interesting and they had a whole section on witchcraft in East Anglia, you know Black Shuck, the green children of Woolpit, the Fenstanton Witch and the like, but anyway, after that visit I got quite interested in Wiccan folklore – from a historical point of view, I mean." After much gesticulating his hands paused in mid-air, as if grasping a large crystal ball, and he checked the room.

The Colleges were listening with polite attention but their interest remained decidedly unsparked.

Unfazed, he persevered.

"I know it's been heavily commercialised, but Wiccan folklore *does* have valuable archaeological and historical significance. For example, from at least the sixteenth century symbols like witches' marks and all manner of ritual objects were a common part of life in Europe, it's a window into how our forebears made sense of the world, their *ideas*. At one time these were hard-held beliefs." He stopped momentarily but was met with the same blank expressions. He shook his head with a hint of disbelief.

"Apotropaic magic?"

"Apologies old boy, fairies aren't a strong starter for ten for us," retorted John. His eagerness to disagree with what he perceived a fanciful subject may have come with a side order of ribbing, but John always treated Thomas as an equal. "Trin's more your mathematics and natural sciences type, Nick's a general all-rounder with a speciality in arch and anth—"

"And John prefers the picture rounds," interrupted Trinity.

John let out a strident laugh.

Nick did not react; he was deep in thought. He gave a glance to John which suggested he suspected where Thomas was heading and suddenly the atmosphere changed, "Thomas, forgive our facetious mood, it helps lighten the spirit. Please do continue, you were speaking of folklore."

"Yes, um." Thomas reconvened, blown off course but quick to recover. "It's standard rhetoric in Wiccan folklore that writing something backwards denotes negative intent. For example, you write someone's name backwards and place it along with a curse to bring them bad luck or you read a good spell backwards to reverse its effects. It's all about reversing intent. Or in other words, it's about *reversing the meaning of an idea.*"

There was a heavily pregnant silence, something in the region of a 24-pounder, three weeks overdue and in a complete change of tone.

"Give the man a distinction!" exclaimed John, shuffling forward in his chair so that he now sat on the very edge, his hands clasped in front of him. Hanging from the bookshelf, the little hexagonal barometer looked rather pleased with itself.

Nick started up, holding a hand to his forehead.

"That's it!" he proclaimed, taking up position behind his armchair, resting his elbows on the high winged back and cradling his chin in his hands.

"And if you *really* mean something, if you *really* want an idea to stick. What do you do?" questioned Nick with a victorious grin.

"You write it in stone!" answered Trinity.

A series of successive sighs and triumphant smiles made their way around the room as piece by piece the jigsaw fell into place and a positive charge permeated the air.

"Oh well done Thomas, well done indeed!" remarked Nick, his mind racing forward.

John rose from his seat and side-stepped through the gap to deliver Thomas a hearty slap on the back, "Not bad old boy, not bad at all, you've prised the lid off it." He continued towards the bookshelves and looked up, stretching his arms then moving his neck one way and the other, as if limbering up for a marathon.

"But the question remains, *why* couldn't John or I touch the stones that bear the inscriptions?" pondered Trinity.

"In light of these revelations, I rather imagine it's because those stones are negative inscriptions that harbour negative intent from a negative idea and they are so imbedded in that negative residue that *we* can't get anywhere near them," responded Nick. "Think of those inscriptions like insects trapped in amber."

Nick then solely addressed Thomas, "Do you know *why* it's called Peas Hill?"

"Because the good people of East Anglia have an eccentric sense of humour?" he answered, thinking of how flat the ground is in that area of the city.

"Yes they do, but no it's not." Nick smiled to himself, the extent of the revelation still unravelling. "It's because

Peas is a corruption of the Latin *Pisces*. Peas Hill used to be the location of the cities' main fish market."

"Okay," replied Thomas, his eyes darting around beneath his straggly hair. "And Pisces is a constellation, the twelfth sign of the zodiac. It's also a *water* sign. That's another connection to the river."

"Yes, yes, and yes," enthused Nick. "It's also what's called a *negative* polarity sign. But more than that, much, much *more* than that, the ground in that area slopes very gradually towards the river. So gradual that you don't notice it as you walk."

Nick and Trinity rose slowly and simultaneously from their respective positions, turning towards John, a shared look of recognition between them.

Nick addressed Thomas again.

"That makes St. Edward's church the perfect location from which to contaminate the river with negative intent. To turn the tide, so to speak. That's why *our* river is running backwards. And of course…" He shut his eyes and slowly shook his head, as if chiding himself for not making the connection earlier. "…All Hallows Eve is the only day of the year when time passes in our world as it does here, so with every name that was added to the church wall we received another push. It's the only day it could have that effect."

Nick's face was poised, but his eyes were glinting with unrest.

"We should have seen it." He pinched his forehead. "We *should* have seen it."

"Slowly but surely, time backing up," said John, the severity of the implication tumbling about his mind.

Trinity raised a hand to the brass whistle clipped to her tunic and Thomas was almost certain he saw a flash of dark blue light beneath her fingers as she touched it, but swept up in the moment, he didn't consider it to be anything more than a reflection.

"And the gargoyles," observed Thomas, "in folklore they have grimacing faces and fierce poses to ward off evil intent, but with the intent reversed and with *your* names carved into the fabric of the very building they were made to protect, they've been coming after *you*."

"We cannot, under any circumstance, permit Peter's name to be added to the wall. It could spell the end of us," asserted Nick.

"What would happen? Would you all disappear?" asked Thomas, wishing the situation came with a summary he could have read first.

"Worse than that," answered Trinity. "That is, one can only hypothesise." She looked at Nick, and he looked back, acknowledging the same concern.

"Apathy," she said. "We would be… nothing. At least, effectively nothing."

"Apathy," remarked John. "The apex predator of critical thinking." He leant back against the bookshelves, letting his arms fall to his sides and slamming a palm against the edge of the nearest shelf in frustration.

"Thomas," began Nick, "as we explained when we first met, we cannot be killed in the sense that one can exsanguinate life from a being in your world, but if you remove the guts from academia, if you corrupt its very essence, then you are left with a series of empty systems that do little more than pander to target figures. For all intents and purposes, we would slip away."

Thomas jumped up from the desk, the floorboards beneath him releasing a series of musical creaks.

"Yes! Yes! You *do* know! This is the point Dr Watt was making!" He looked eagerly around the room but his observation garnered no response and so, not wishing to repeat his conversational faux pas, he skipped to his next thought.

"Let's get going *now*," he enthused. "I'm going to get the Antikythera mechanism *now*." And with that he started to make his way towards the door, but as he reached the bookshelves John put a hand on his shoulder to stop him, "On the morrow, old boy."

Thomas glanced at his watch: 6:55pm.

"What?! Where did the time go!" he exclaimed. "Look, you can open the Museum for me, I can get in there.

Better still, can't one of you phase into the Museum to take the mechanism?"

"Thomas, it's okay. At this stage, haste brings us no advantage," said Nick double checking the time against his pocket watch.

"First, with the exception of the small fragments from our oldest buildings, we are unable to transport objects when we phase. Second, do please recall we need to conserve as much of our energy as possible; being outside of our own grounds is a considerable drain. This is why we require *you* to get the mechanism, but regardless, let us leave the Museum for tomorrow. There is something more pressing we must show you and it would be judicious to do it while the town is quiescent."

Nick looked at John and John looked at Trinity, and between them they exchanged an understanding that temporarily eluded Thomas.

"It's a lot sooner than we intended," remarked John to Nick.

"My students know how to hit the ground running," he answered confidently.

"I think he has a touch of the mubble-fubbles," returned John.

"Understandable, but not in itself a problem," countered Trinity.

"But do we think the hair would slow us down?" queried John with a wry smile.

By this stage the Colleges were, of course, making game of Thomas, but *he* was deadly serious, hanging on their every word. It was as if he were watching a tennis match, his head moving right and left throughout the entire volley.

"Thomas!" exclaimed Nick suddenly, breaking the moment and manoeuvring around the chairs to where the befuddled young man stood. He placed a friendly hand upon Thomas' shoulder, a benevolent smile with just a hint of mischief upon his face.

"We are going to take you on the King Street Run."

Chapter 6: The Roman Phase

King Street is an inconspicuous thoroughfare in the heart of the city. At one time a distinguished road lined on both sides with ornate eighteenth and nineteenth century buildings, Corinthian pilasters and balustraded parapets in abundance, the ravages of time have not been kind to the wizened old street. Twentieth century development flogged it to within an inch of its architectural life and most of the historic buildings are now gone, executed by the blight of aesthetic emptiness and complacent planning. When passing through, Thomas always opted for the pavement on the south side because it harboured the lion's share of those surviving old buildings and he liked to think of the gesture as an act of solidarity.

It was into these insipid surroundings that he found himself walking at just gone 8pm. The night air was cold and he was grateful for the hood on his coat which he pulled up to shield his ears from the snapping wind.

The evenly spaced street lamps threw down orange pyramids of light, softening the square concrete slabs that make up the pavement. The road was much quieter than it would be during the day, but even now an intermittent but regular trickle of lone cyclists whizzed along then curved out of sight as they reached the large roundabout at the top of the road. Small groups of students chatted as they left or entered one of the street's public houses, the clatter of glasses amplifying as they opened the door, then fading just as quickly as it closed behind them. It is a street in decay, but it has an irrepressible will to live that continues to draw people to it.

Upon concluding their discussion in the little study, Nick had insisted that Thomas take time to dine in Hall before they reconvened in King Street. After all, even the world's finest pasty can only sustain man for so long. Thomas had reluctantly agreed and after leaving the Porter's Lodge he made a brief diversion to Bodley's to drop off his bag, then headed directly to the Hall. Three portions of nut roast with mushroom gravy and a mango sorbet later, and Thomas was refuelled, re-energised, and really confused over what the King Street Run could be. Of course, he had *heard* of the King Street Run, which is precisely why he was confused. To the student body of Cambridge it is the name of a pub crawl that involves drinking a pint of beer in every pub on King Street, but Thomas was quietly confident that was not what the Colleges had in mind. It was difficult to imagine Nick and Trinity swigging back pints, even if it was marginally easier to picture John doing so.

Nick's departing instructions had been brief but specific, "Wait by the telephone box outside the florists," and as Thomas left the room and stepped into the dimly lit landing an addendum was hollered, "And drink plenty of water." By the time he turned to confirm that he understood, Nick, John, and Trinity were no longer in the study and the ornate lamp no longer warmed the room with its rusty tones. All was dark and all was very, very still. They had, Thomas felt, more of a sense of urgency about matters than their collectively calm demeanour might suggest.

Thomas found his way to the phone box. It sat on the south side of the street, growling at the 1960s office block opposite. It was one of the old cast iron, red phone boxes with fluted architrave, domed top, and glass panels on three sides. On the fascia beneath the curve, in bold black letters against a white background, the word *Telephone* pretty much concluded matters, although the lights that should have illuminated it were not working. In an age of mobile phones, red telephone boxes had fallen into redundancy, but some have discovered a new lease of life; converted to house a defibrillator, or repurposed as small community book exchanges where people borrow and donate, eventually resulting in micro-libraries with ad-hoc shelving and hundreds of realities packed into the tiny space. Even with inanimate objects, determinism was having a tough time of it.

Thomas leant against the door, huffed onto his numb fingers before stuffing them into his pockets, and gave a quick glance up and down the road, then up and down again for good measure. After repeating this ritual at least a dozen times within the succeeding minutes, he was finally given cause to perform a double take. He couldn't be certain from that distance, but something appeared to be stirring at the far end of the street and he squinted into the darkness to make it out. Sure enough, just outside the grasp of orange street light, leaf litter at the centre of the road began to eddy. Thomas pushed away from the phone box, watching expectantly. A faint distortion of the air moved into, then out of, the orange light, swiftly morphing into three foggy shapes that moved side by side towards him. The misty outlines entered the orange glow from another street light and as they emerged, resolved into three familiar forms. Thomas smiled at Nick, John, and Trinity with chattering teeth.

"Good man, Thomas," declared John as he stepped up the curb to deliver a firm backslap. This time, after his hand made contact John staggered forwards a step, as if awarded the same potent greeting by an unseen agency. Ignoring the stumble, he carried on.

"Punctual as always."

Thomas pulled back his hood and held out a hand to steady him, "Are you okay?"

"Fine, fine," dismissed John. "Poised for the starting pistol?"

"I'm champing at the bit to know what you want to show me," replied Thomas, his arm still held in readiness.

"Did you drink plenty of water?" asked Nick.

"Yes. Yes I did, but wh—"

"Good good. Right, let's get started shall we?"

"Yes please," replied Thomas. "I'm at a loss as to what you mean by the King Street Run, because I'm guessing it's not what I understand it to be."

Nick looked up at the phone box with a nostalgic smile.

"When a new Keeper is appointed they are shown the location of all the portals that lead to and from grey time, and one of the first was here in King Street. Of course, it's not in the same place because that building was…" and he paused momentarily as if a ghost passed through him, "…demolished over 100 years ago. A sad day. Still, as a mark of respect we retain a portal as close as practicable to the original position, and we always begin what the Keepers dubbed the King Street Run from here."

"Ahhhhhhhhhh," sighed Thomas. "I thought the King Street Run was, well, a pub crawl. At least that's what other students told me in my first week."

"Yes, the undergrads began using it as a turn of phrase back in the 1950s. A group of medical students overheard the then Keepers of St. John's and Pembroke talking about the Run and out of curiosity asked what it was. Back then King Street was well known for its high concentration of public houses and so, in an attempt to cover their tracks they told the students the first thing that sprang to mind, that the King Street Run was a bi-annual pub crawl. They didn't have to embellish it further, student high spirits did the rest."

"But why call it a *run*?" asked Thomas.

"I suppose," returned Nick, slightly evasive, "it's because there are a generous quantity of portals and we tend to whisk the Keepers around them quite…" he gave a single cough "…efficiently."

John awarded Thomas another of his firm backslaps.

"You'll enjoy it old man, and you'll be the first non-Keeper we've taken on the Run."

By this point in their discussion, Trinity had removed four small objects from her coat pocket, no larger than a 10 pence piece. She kept one for herself and now distributed the others around the group.

"Here you go Thomas, fasten this badge to your coat."

Thomas looked at the small object in the palm of his hand and a grey version of The Beatles *Rubber Soul* album cover looked back.

"Awh Trin, you're an old softy at heart," declared John with delight as he fixed the badge to his coat's lapel.

"Revolver! Top drawer!" he added as, with chin on

chest, he admired the noble addition to his attire. He then bounded towards the dark of the florist window, turning the badge to catch the orange street light and admiring it in the reflection.

"Trinity, do not let it be said that you lack a sense of humour," chuckled Nick, looking down at his badge which bore the cover of *A Hard Day's Night*.

Trinity smiled, attaching *Let It Be* to her own coat.

"Our Trin isn't terribly keen on taking the Run," grinned John. He placed a hand on her shoulder and gave a playful shake as he passed by.

She raised her eyebrows indignantly.

"I am perfectly content to take the Run," she refuted. "After all, my Great Court Run is based upon it. I simply consider running to be a rather uncouth activity." She shrugged off the thought and added jovially, "And if you suggest otherwise again I shall take your badge away."

She then turned to Thomas so that she stood directly before him and although now having his undivided attention, she tapped him on the shoulder.

"Thomas, try to walk away from me."

"Sorry?"

"Try to walk away from me," she repeated, moving to one side so that he could step directly into the road.

"Okaaaay."

Thomas took one step, two steps. Easy enough. But the third was laboured, as if he had taken two strides into shallow water and it was now up to his knees. Four steps and it was like trying to wade through wet clay. Unable to manage a fifth he turned and staggered back, partly propelled as if attached to Trinity with a giant elastic band.

"What on Earth?!"

"The badge connects you to us," she explained. "Or, more specifically, to which ever one of us taps you on the shoulder whilst both are wearing one." She gave a gentle tug on his badge and lifted up one side to check it was securely fixed. "It's a little... *trick* we use based on a modified form of quantum entanglement."

"Okay, first of all that's incredible, really, really incredible and I would *love* to discuss that in more detail once this is over," began Thomas, "but also, why?"

Using the cuff of his shirt sleeve, Nick gave a few circular polishes to his badge as he answered.

"We are going to reveal to you the location of every portal in Cambridge and let us be clear, it is only in case you have no recourse but to use one. The badge will enable you to move with us at our speed and ensure we don't… mislay you. Think of it like a safety belt."

"Incredible," responded Thomas, gleefully.

"Before we begin, you have to know that entering a portal isn't the same as with the one I modified for you at the river," clarified Nick.

"If that were the case," added Trinity, "we'd run the hazard of people entering grey time by accident."

Nick nodded in agreement.

"In addition to a key, each portal has its own quirk of entry and that is what you'll need to pay particular attention to throughout the Run. There are no restrictions on egress, simply pass through." He tapped his own badge in readiness. "Because we shall be moving between temporal states in quick succession, there exists the possibility that you will experience slim to moderate disorientation at times – no pun intended – but there is no need for alarm, the effect is transient."

"Got it," responded Thomas, shifting his weight from side to side as if he were about to sprint down the street.

"To conserve our energy, we shall conduct you through the Run in relay. John will accompany you through the first portal, Trinity second, then myself. Each of us will tap you on the shoulder in order to take the wheel, so to speak. We shall proceed in this fashion until you have passed through all 62 portals."

"62!" exclaimed Thomas, suddenly feeling less energetic.

"Yes, 62," confirmed Nick. "There is one portal in every College and each College is responsible for a second elsewhere in the city."

Nick and Trinity stepped back from the phone box and John approached Thomas, tapping him on the shoulder.

"Ready old boy?"

"As I'll ever be," grinned Thomas, his apprehension very much taking a back seat to his curiosity.

John looked up at the phone box.

"This is the location of the King Street portal. It was placed by Peterhouse. It's one of the more convoluted to enter but for that reason it's also easy to recall."

He walked to the door.

"Tap twice on the left side."

Tap tap.

"Before you open the door, check the light has come on," he gestured upwards. Thomas looked at the *Telephone* sign and sure enough the white background had illuminated on all sides.

"In we go."

John held the door open and gestured for Thomas to enter first, leaving the heavy, panelled glass frame to close slowly behind them.

"Badges to manual," began John with a grin. "Would passengers please refrain from raising their hands while the phone box is in motion and when exiting the vehicle, please..." and at this point he pinched his nose to create a tannoy-like effect to his voice, "...*mind the temporal gap.*"

Thomas glanced around the inside of the small box as if expecting something to move.

"Pick up the phone," instructed John in a more serious tone, "hold it to your ear and press the numbers 1, 2, 8, and 4 in that order. Wait for the three pips to finish, replace the receiver, then follow me outside."

Thomas slid his hand around the black receiver and lifted it from the cradle. He held the cold plastic to his ear and pressed the buttons firmly.

1, 2, 8, 4.

Pip.

Pip.

Pip.

No sooner had he replaced the phone than Thomas felt a powerful yet painless pulse knock him from the inside out. It was like being pushed, only without physically moving. Inside the cramped confines of the box the air became almost viscous, as if time were settling like residue rather than passing. He watched his hand move away from the receiver. It left behind a series of ephemeral, ghost-like outlines that traced its previous position, and although transient, each new movement created more visual echoes. The phone box and its details were perfectly clear to Thomas – the grey coin box, the small notice board to its side, a faint reflection in the glass – but he felt detached from it, as if he had been superimposed upon the scene, and his vision seemed to be ahead of his movements, or perhaps it was his movements that lagged behind his thoughts. Somewhere, in this soup of senses, John's instructions pierced through his mind; *follow me outside*. Thomas turned his head and caught the College's eye. John nodded in the direction of the door, an otherwise split-second gesture that seemed to take multiple seconds to complete. He nodded back but it was like trying to communicate underwater, his movements constricted and slow. He could feel himself turn, but his body was still lagging behind his thoughts, and he followed John's exit with a slow, cautious amble. Once outside, he felt an almost instantaneous release and his physical agility was quickly reinstated. He stretched an arm out in front of him and slowly moved his hand from side to side. The echoes around his limbs were fainter and fewer than they had been inside the telephone box, but he continued to wave his hand around, watching the echoes gradually disappear as body and mind synchronised. When the echoes had completely vanished, he turned his palm upwards and rubbed his fingers together, checking his coordination.

"Have you got your sea legs?"

Thomas looked up. There was nothing sardonic in John's countenance, no hefty pats on the back, no quips, just a patient and understanding smile.

"Yeah. Yeah, I'm fine," he responded. "The sci-fi group would *love* this. They'd think me absolutely stark, raving bonkers if I told them, which I wouldn't, and they might be right, but still, they'd *love* this."

Thomas looked along the street. There were no lone cyclists, no clusters of students moving in and out of pubs, no icy blasts of wind, and most conspicuous of all, no voices or clattering glasses. In fact, there was hardly any sound at all, just a distant cracking – like ice sheets breaking – that seemed to come from nowhere and everywhere at the same time. It was the kind of noise Thomas imagined aurora borealis would make. He turned to look along the other end of the street and stillness presided. It was the same strange calm in the same strange monochrome tones that Thomas had experienced by the river the day before. The light emanating from the street lamps was no longer orange but more of a moss green, and the distinct bright red telephone box was now entirely shades of grey. If it were not for the occasional tints of green and red, the scene before him would have resembled a black and white film. Despite its reduced colour palette, there was nothing unpleasant or oppressive in the change, in fact, the atmosphere was akin to walking into one's workplace late at night when everyone else had gone home; that feeling of being out of time, outside the regular flow of life.

"This is the afterglow of consumed time," said John, responding to Thomas' contemplation of the street. He stood still for a few moments, permitting the young man some time, of sorts, to take in the extraordinary surroundings.

"Ready?"

"Incredible," answered Thomas, turning in a circle on the spot. "Utterly incredible."

"I'll take that as a yes." John gave a gentle tug on Thomas' badge just as Trinity had done before, treble checking it was securely fastened.

"Let's go!"

John turned his back to the roundabout and began

walking west, retracing the direction from which he had approached with Nick and Trinity. Within moments he began to jog and Thomas reciprocated, keeping pace but already noticing the pull of the badge, fastening his movements to John's. After a few additional moments John threw a sideways glance, checking Thomas was still okay. He nodded and they quickened into a run. Being both tall and athletically built, Thomas considered he would have little trouble matching John's stride, not yet realising that physical endurance was entirely the wrong kind of stamina required for the Run.

After a few moments more the tempo increased and Thomas was now running at what he considered full tilt. Even though he did not, *could* not, move his legs any faster, the two figures continued to gather speed, darting along the street like protons in a particle accelerator, minus the collision. Hopefully. It was an exhilarating – if disconcerting – sensation at first: the shades of grey that made up every edifice, fixture, and wall bled into one another as they hurtled past, the very shape of structures losing definition until the entire road resembled a thick impasto; long, sweeping brushstrokes smudged by an artist's thumb. As the scenery rushed past his peripheral vision, a few coherent thoughts infiltrated Thomas' mind, foremost of which was the expectation of crashing into a lamp post or the edge of a building. But this was not to be the case. They moved through the streets like a train on a track; sturdy, confident and with him anchored to John's every movement. They sped around the corner of the street, over a small lawn, skimmed through an open gate and into a carpark that Thomas recognised as being at the back of Sidney Sussex College.

Wooooosh.

Out of the car park, into the Master's Garden, through to the Fellows' Garden, and much to Thomas' abject horror, heading straight for a narrow brick archway that leads into Sidney's Cloister Court. For the briefest of moments he closed his eyes, bracing himself for impact, but when he opened them he was standing in the Court, just a few paces past the brick archway. He didn't remember slowing down or telling his legs to stop moving. He was just standing there. And he was standing in *his* time, the technicolour one with alcohol and noisy blackbirds.

John was holding Thomas by the shoulders, looking directly into his eyes.

"How did you enter the King Street portal?"

Not expecting the question and overwhelmed by the journey, Thomas stumbled.

"Er —"

"How did you enter the King Street portal?" repeated John, unflinching.

Thomas found his composure. It must have slipped to the bottom of his feet as they flew across the Fellows' Garden.

"Tap twice on the left side of the phone box," he began hesitantly. "Check the light is on." After every repeated instruction Thomas gave a small nod, as if it somehow stamped it onto his memory. "Pick up the phone and dial 1, 2, 8, 4. Wait for… three pips and replace the receiver."

John smiled and released his grip, but before Thomas could say a word there came a tap on his left shoulder and Trinity beckoned him towards the same archway that John and he had just exited. Thomas turned to say goodbye to John but he had already disappeared.

Trinity stood before the archway.

"Stand with your feet outside of the threshold," she began. Thomas looked down to her feet and observed that the tips of her boots were precisely before the mortar of the flagstone preceding the archway.

"Close the gate." She reached in and pulled it towards her, the black iron frame rattling as the latch fell into the keep.

"On either side of the arch, tap the ninth brick up on both sides simultaneously."

Tap

"Then open it again and walk through."

Trinity did precisely this but before the eager student

could walk through she closed it again. Thomas, his nose mere millimetres from making the acquaintance of the metal bars, smiled meekly back at her.

"*You* do it," she said, pushing the gate open once more and stepping aside so he could stand in front of the arch.

He repeated her actions; closed the gate, tapped the ninth brick up on both sides, and pushed it open. With a deep breath he walked through the archway, Trinity following. Sure enough, the now familiar monochrome backdrop of grey time rushed to greet him, but on this occasion there was no disorientation; no dizziness, no loss of synchronicity, and as he moved his hand about in the air before him, not a trace of a temporal echo. He looked around at the garden, with its brimming flower beds and clusters of scrupulously shaped evergreen trees, all drained of colour but yet somehow more beautiful than he had ever seen them before.

"Jesus Lane," instructed Trinity as she locked sight on a wooden gate set into a long, tall brick wall edging the garden. The badge exerted its pull and Thomas quickly fell into step with her. Before they reached the gate it opened before them and the two passed into the narrow lane beyond.

Unlike his journey with John, where they had risen through the proverbial gears, gradually building speed, Trinity launched into a full-on run with a near immediate sharp right turn. It was like being yanked into a cèilidh mid do-si-do. But Thomas soon found his feet and just as before, the buildings started to blur. The longer they ran, the more he acclimatised, exposing details he had previously been too overwhelmed to pick up on. The most obvious was that despite moving at a phenomenal rate there was no wind against his face. It was like being encased in a bubble.

Thomas was loosely holding onto his bearings but just as he was getting into the stride, he could sense, via the pull of the badge, Trinity's focus on the Round Church, a twelfth century stone building with a striking polygonal bell turret. Before they reached its low brick wall, the hefty wooden door flung open and Trinity and Thomas ran directly inside. Upon entry they came to the same abrupt halt as before, only this time he was better attuned to the experience. It wasn't painful, but in a world where the laws of physics seemed optional, the residue of momentum washed over him like a tsunami and all he could do was stand there, like a human tuning fork, and wait for it to pass.

Thomas had again intuitively closed his eyes and when he opened them he saw they were standing at the centre of the nave, a circular space demarcated by eight enormous Norman columns accompanied by wide round arches. Above the nave, an interior gallery looked down upon them, lined with a further circle of double arches, each one bearing a carved face at its centre. He looked in awe at the high ceiling, almost certain the faces were looking back.

"You're a driving instructor's worst nightmare," jested Thomas, utterly elated but reeling from the finale. "Although you've nailed the emergency stop."

With a rueful smile, Trinity passed into the chancel. In Thomas' world the floor was laid with decorative, earthy-coloured Victorian tiles and although in grey time those tones were absent, their design and construction was every bit as exquisite. Dark wooden pews sat in rows either side of them and Trinity passed to the first one on the left.

"Sit on the right of the bench."

Thomas did as instructed and Trinity sat next to him.

"We push ourselves in one slide to the other end of the stall." And with that Trinity and Thomas simultaneously pushed against the side of the wooden seat, whizzing along its polished surface. He was fully expecting to bump into its left side but instead they moved through a disturbance in the air and arrived back where they had sat down but in *his* time. Before Thomas could comment on the elegance of the portal, Trinity turned to him.

"How did you enter the Sidney Sussex portal?"

Flustered, he responded hesitantly.

"Oh, um —"

"How did you enter the Sidney Sussex portal?" she repeated.

Thomas closed his eyes and rotated his hand in front of him as if winding back his memory.

"Feet before the threshold, close the gate, tap the ninth brick up on both sides at the same time, then open the gate and walk through."

Trinity smiled, saying nothing and phasing as she stood up. In the split second it took her to disappear there came another tap on his shoulder.

"Feeling chipper?" asked Nick with a friendly grin. He was standing behind the pew, his hands resting on its back.

"Incredible!" chortled Thomas, his smile filled to bursting point with sheer delight.

"Good, good, then let us continue."

Thomas stood up and followed Nick back to the centre of the Nave.

"Walk through the centre arch," directed Nick, who had already begun to do just that. They approached the first pew on the left and took a seat on its right side. Before Nick could provide any further instructions Thomas jumped in.

"Push off and slide in one," he grinned, eager to try the portal once more.

Nick laughed.

Each placing a hand on the side of the bench they planed across its surface, reappearing on the same bench in grey time like they were riding the return lever on an old typewriter.

"Still good?" asked Nick.

"*Un*believable! Where next?"

Nick and Thomas made their way out of the Round Church, their footsteps echoing off the stone walls and bouncing around the gallery.

"We're going to take the long way round to the next portal, left out of here, just to give you a trifle more experience with a longer run. Okay?"

"Fine by me," enthused Thomas.

"We're heading back to College, well, just outside, but like I say, we'll take a largely eastern sweep around the city."

As they passed the low brick wall and into the street, Thomas took the opportunity to once again contemplate the calm of grey time. Nick corrected his tie and straightened his waistcoat with a gentle tug, then, standing side by side in the centre of the road, he gave a nod and off they ran. Thomas was becoming increasingly confident with the force of the Run and although the background still blurred and the buildings remained determined to merge, now and again he could make out a distinct road or identify a large structure. It was with great delight that he discerned the Gothic buildings of Sidney's two front Courts, then the unnerving dark path to Martin's Close, but shortly after that they took a sharp left into the extremely narrow – or *bijou* if you're an estate agent – Hobson's Passage. The tempo of the Run coupled with the confined space gave it the feel of a luge course, the tall buildings accentuating their incredible speed. Thomas dealt with the sudden change of direction admirably well, keeping his focus and taking the transition like a seasoned professional.

Although he didn't think it at the time, Thomas would look back on that night and consider the busy streets of Cambridge, with the need to swerve bicycles, circumnavigate shoppers, and politely dodge the sightline of tourists' cameras, to be first class training for the King Street Run.

It didn't take more than a few seconds for the two figures to reach the end of Hobson's Passage, but shortly before turning the corner something flashed into Thomas' peripheral vision, something out of place, something that sent a cold chill slithering down his neck. He flicked his gaze towards it and moving parallel to him at head-height was a pair of small, disembodied blue eyes. For a few brief moments they swam through the grey background in perfect focus, their stare fixed upon him. Then, as quickly as they had appeared, the eyes dissolved into the blur, leaving Thomas with the unnerving feeling that they were somehow still watching. Horror-struck, he turned to Nick but was unable to capture his attention; he was focused on the route and seemed entirely unaware of anything untoward. Thomas tried to shout but couldn't get his muscles to operate; maybe it was a result of his senses being so thoroughly overwhelmed by the Run, but it left him with no other choice than to wait until the next portal in order to inform the Colleges of what he had seen.

When they reached the more spacious environs of the street beyond their pace intensified, hurtling around bends and curves until Thomas recognised they were back in King Street. But they did not stop here; they kept moving until eventually the tall, wavering ash trees lining the perimeter of Midsummer Common came into view. Lying south of the River Cam and peppered with College boat houses, its expansive lawn passed them by in a melange of grey vegetation. Nick and Thomas blazed towards a single-arched bridge in the western corner. In Thomas' time, beneath the bridge, bobbing gently on the water, sat a row of colourful narrowboats tethered to the tow path, the smoke of wood burners lazily drifting from their chimneys and dissipating into the cold night air. Aside from the occasional *slosh* of a fender bumping into the bank, the bridge was quiet and the Common nearly deserted, oblivious to the speeding figures that had passed overhead just a few seconds outside of their own time.

Nick and Thomas raced down the bridge's gentle camber, speeding off in a city-wide curve across lawns, past shops, over car parks and eventually edging back to the town centre. It wasn't long before they were racing down King's Parade and about to pass the front of King's Chapel when Nick came to a sudden stop, and by default so did Thomas. The Colleges had a peculiar way of taking a split second and stretching it like a bungee cord, allowing every movement to be precisely and immaculately timed.

Nick was standing with his hands in his pockets, looking down at the pavement. He was about to speak when, "Eyes!" gasped Thomas, not out of breath but out of panic.

"Later please," responded Nick with an insouciance that fuelled Thomas' already heightened anxiety.

He raised a hand to his forehead and pinched the bridge of his nose in frustration. He tried again, "I really —"

"Please, let us not break with procedure until we have passed through the portal," insisted Nick.

Thomas shook his head in resignation, helping himself to several lungs' worth of grey air to calm himself.

"Okay, okay," he replied, reluctantly examining the pavement that Nick appeared so enamoured with.

The pavement outside of King's is a typical riven-stone path, but there is one slab, smaller and slightly lighter in colour than the others, inscribed with the words *High Maintenance Life* and it is to this that Nick drew Thomas' attention.

"We had to stop before passing through this portal because it's the smallest on the Run." He gestured at the carved stone and Thomas read out the words.

"High maintenance life. What's that?"

"Life."

"But why *high maintenance* life?"

"Why indeed," replied Nick, consulting his pocket watch before turning his attention back to the portal.

"Quite simple. All you need to do is stand on the words and jump. Works both ways."

No sooner had he said it than he jumped on the slab and disappeared. Thomas instantly took up position on the small square and followed him through. He appeared back in his own time, his feet landing flat on the pavement, but before he could repeat his warning about the blue eyes, John tapped him on the shoulder and asked, "How did you enter the Round Church portal?"

Keen to get it over with so he could elaborate upon his observation from Hobson's Passage, Thomas blurted out the instructions without breath or pause.

"Walk through the centre arch go to the first pew on the left and sit on the right hand-side and push yourself with one slide to the left."

Then before Nick could disappear Thomas called out.

"No! Nick! Wait!" holding up both hands as if being held at gunpoint, "Something's in there, in grey time. There was a pair of blue eyes following us, nothing else, just a pair of eyes. As we got to the end of Hobson's Passage. They were in mid-air beside us then they just sort of… dissolved into the background."

John, keen to proceed, placed both hands on his hips and stared towards the night sky, an air of impatience about him.

"I didn't see anything," said Nick. "I don't mean to doubt you, Thomas, but are you absolutely sure?"

"Yes, I'm sure, *absolutely* sure," he affirmed. "What form of Ballardian nightmare *were* they?"

"Form of *what*?" queried John as his head slumped back down, a delighted grin pushing away any trace of frustration.

"John, have you noticed anything like this?" asked Nick.

"No. Not a thing," he replied, still amused at Thomas' turn of phrase. "Thomas old boy, you're starting to sound more than a dash like our dear Nick." He shook his head in delight. "Best get that in check or it'll take you two weeks to say good morning." John chuckled, "*Ballardian nightmare*. I like it. I wouldn't use it but I like it."

"This is most irregular," commented Nick. "I shouldn't like to think we failed to observe an anomaly, that would be most remiss." He pondered the information, flicking out his pocket square and rubbing his spectacles with it. "You must forgive me Thomas, when you raised the matter I was under the impression you were seeing shapes in the clouds as it were, that can happen you know; the Run is a strain on the faculties."

"Are you confident it wasn't simply part of the background?" pressed John. "Perhaps your senses were being mischievous. They can be tricky that way.

Pareidolia does a tremendous job of convincing people they've seen everything from alien statues on Mars to Satan's face in their burnt toast."

Thomas rolled his eyes in frustration.

"I didn't imagine it. Award me with the presence of mind that I know it wasn't pareidolia. Those eyes were as clear to me in Hobson's Passage as your faces are to me now."

Nick nodded but still he was not unduly concerned.

"Your observation is noted. If you catch sight of it again please inform one of us at the earliest opportunity."

Nick was unpretentious and always considered in his responses, but Thomas couldn't help but feel a pervading lack of interest over the occurrence.

"But-but whatever it is, will it know what we're doing?" he queried.

"No," replied Nick. "Well, that is, I have at present no idea what the shapes are or to what they belong —"

"This morning's charred bread stalking your memory," interrupted John.

"No," asserted Thomas confidently. "They were eyes, blue eyes, and they were *definitely* there. Like I said before, they followed us at speed then disappeared."

Nick nodded again, considering the young man's protestations but remaining unperturbed.

"Whatever it is, at the very worst it could only feasibly know you were here on *that* particular part of the Run. That you are taking the Grand Tour is known to us alone."

Thomas, placated to a not insignificant degree by the Colleges' lack of urgency, still felt the need to pursue the matter a little further, "Could this somehow be connected to what's been going on?"

A reassuring countenance took over Nick's face, "Thomas, rest secure that measures have been taken. You will not come to harm, no matter to what insignificantly small oddity these eye shapes might belong."

"Oh, I'm not worried about *that*," Thomas said with a dismissive air regarding his own well-being that almost took Nick by surprise. "I was thinking of you, John, and Trinity and what it might mean in relation to the gargoyle attacks and the temporal drift." He paused, as if he had too many tabs open in his mind and was in the process of closing a couple.

"What measures?"

Nick didn't appear to have heard the question because he phased out of sight as he turned away, leaving just John and Thomas standing in the street outside King's.

"Thomas, we are not the sole occupiers of our time but I have every confidence that the blue mirage is nothing to worry about," said John in a softened, more consolatory tone of voice. "Shall we?" he gestured at the pavement. "Tempus *is* fugiting you know." John walked to the *High Maintenance Life* slab, glancing briefly about to be sure they were not being observed. He then held his nose as if about to leap into a swimming pool and jumped into the air, disappearing before his feet reunited with the pavement. Thomas pressed after him.

"I like that one," remarked Thomas as he reappeared in grey time. "It's classy. It has an understated dignity."

"Don't tell Nick that," replied John.

"Why not?"

"He placed it. Praise risks having to enlarge all the College doorways so he can fit his head through." John laughed and with one hand held high in the air, pointing forward, he declared, "Carpe noctem!"

Shored up by Nick's reassurance and swept up in John's enthusiasm, Thomas put the blue eyes out of mind and with a smile as wide as the arch of Midsummer's western bridge, the pair took off.

If there were a stopwatch capable of tracking discarded time, it would have clocked up at least four hours as Thomas was relayed like a baton between the three Colleges; through arches, between pillars, up staircases, across lawns, and diving into the partially frozen water of a minimalist stone fountain that, with an irony lost on the startled student, resembled a jacuzzi. He kept his nerve, navigated the Run, and correctly repeated the instructions for accessing every portal through which they passed. After the practical and theoretical workings of 59 portals had been satisfactorily covered, Thomas found himself emerging into the aisle between two tall bookcases at the far end of Girton College library, and once again back in his own time. He scanned the vaulted ceiling with an approving nod then turned to John, he no longer required a prompt to repeat the access requirements.

"Push the lion statue to the centre of the plinth and turn the latch 90 degrees anti-clockwise."

"A ripping performance!" John issued a customary smack on Thomas' back and just as before, he staggered back a step, but shook it off immediately.

"Your penultimate portal awaits," declared Trinity as she tapped Thomas on the shoulder. He turned his head towards her then back to where John had been standing. He had already disappeared.

"John will meet us at the final portal," remarked Trinity.

Girton library is a lengthy, welcoming room with the arrangement of furniture demarcating a central walk way. At one end, near the entrance, a row of wide wooden desks sit either side of the centre. At the other, where Trinity and Thomas stood, there are three large wooden bookstacks jutting out from both sides, creating comfortably proportioned reading areas between them, one side having long, leaded windows in the centre of each section. Trinity walked to the nearest window and pushed it open, placing the casement stay on the third hole. She then knelt down and pulled out a very large, dusty book from beneath the bottom shelf, opened it to page 1869 and placed it upon the window sill.

"Any sundries utilised during the Run are monitored and returned to their usual position by the respective Keeper," she explained, seeing the question forming on Thomas' face. Trinity then retraced her steps and placed everything back in its original position, requesting that Thomas repeat the process to enter the portal. Aside from a moment's hesitation regarding the position of the casement stay, Thomas emulated the procedure perfectly.

"The portal is in the aisle between the end bookcases," instructed Trinity.

They walked straight ahead, disappearing as they stepped into the aisle and reappearing at the same position in grey time.

"How do you feel?" she enquired as they walked briskly towards the exit.

Thomas sighed heavily but grinned widely. "If I've lost my grip on reality," he looked about at the grey books upon their grey shelves against the grey walls, "Then I never wish to take hold of it again."

Trinity laughed softly as they departed the library.

They did not run through the buildings of Girton College to reach the grounds; in fact, none of the Colleges ran when inside a building. When Thomas asked why they did not run inside the buildings he received varied but concurring responses; "Bad form old boy" was the response that John had given after sliding down the banister from the Cataloguing Landing in the University Library. "Tawdry" was Trinity's reaction when they had ambled out of the linen cupboard under the stairs in the Master's Lodge at Pembroke. Nick had simply shaken his head at the suggestion when they dropped through the organ loft in Magdalene's Chapel. One does not run inside College buildings. It's as simple as that. It's unbecoming.

Trinity and Thomas made their way, in a suitably composed fashion, from the library and into the Court. Over two miles from the city centre, Girton is located further out of town than any other Cambridge College but rising from its lush and expansive grounds are 150 years of Gothic revivalism that stand as proud as any.

Trinity looked around.

Left.

Then right.

She smiled, staring into the air before her, not focusing on anything but listening intently. It was the first time that night she had paused before launching into a run.

"Enjoy the view, Thomas," she said, still smiling. "Girton is so far out that some people think it's part of Oxford."

A hearty "HA!" came from behind them and Thomas turned to see a woman standing in the doorway with a stylophone clasped in one hand. She was of average height, with large, smiling eyes set into a round, friendly face. Her shoulder length brown hair was clipped back on both sides and her stylish 1940s green jacket, with an asymmetric line of red buttons, was complemented by a matching straight cut skirt and a white blouse.

"My superb powers of deduction tell me this is Thomas," said the woman. "Hello and welcome." She moved forward and shook him by the hand.

"Permit me to introduce Girton," said Trinity.

"It's a pleasure to meet you," he responded, delighted to meet another College.

"Mutual Thomas, mutual. When we heard you were on the Run I know we're supposed to keep out of the way and all that but I couldn't resist saying hello."

"Well," said Trinity, "you get so few visitors all the way out here."

"Thomas," began Girton, "don't listen to what these city-dwellers say, when global warming hits its stride those old Colleges by the river will be first to go."

Trinity cringed.

"I have an ulterior motive for intercepting you," added Girton as she turned towards Trinity. "All the stones have been found." With that, she pulled up her sleeve to reveal a small stone attached to a silver chain around her wrist.

"Splendid!" responded Trinity. "We rid ourselves of a hurdle. You're up to speed?"

"Yes, yes, Peter was here this afternoon." Girton rocked back and forwards on the balls of her feet a few times. "I say though, Michael! Ooof, of all the rotten luck. I've had more amiable rising damp."

"Let's not be too harsh on Michael, he's more or less isolated, outside the sphere of civilised interactions, left to his own insular contemplation. A geographical polyp in a temporal bubble." Trinity cast an eye around the Court.

"*You* know what I mean," she grinned.

Girton laughed, "Unlike the river I shan't rise to you!" She sighed and there were a few moments of quiet before she continued under a more solemn countenance, "Well, as you know, weapons of war are not in my remit but we're all ready. We'll be there."

Trinity nodded with an appreciative smile, and as if there were an unspoken understanding that neither wished to dwell upon the situation, she turned to Thomas, tapping him on the shoulder.

"Shall we?" and the two began to walk away.

Facing the Court exit, Trinity and Thomas stood side by side. Trinity did not turn around, but said over her shoulder, "See you for the main event, Girtie." She turned back to face the Court exit and added, "Providing you remember the way."

Thomas turned quickly to wave goodbye and Girton raised a hand in farewell.

"South to The Backs, that's almost home for you," said Trinity.

"On Dasher, on Dancer…" mumbled Girton as she disappeared through the archway, the electronic buzz of a lone stylophone drifting from the stairwell the moment she was out of sight.

Thomas nodded and without another word, they launched into a run. Across the grounds and into the road, Girton's steeply pitched roofs and red brickwork melting into a terracotta blur behind them like a dusty Sahara sunset. They made their way south across the city, swerving around corners, squeezing down narrow passages, and looping around roundabouts. Having now passed through 60 of the 62 portals, Thomas was modestly skilled at picking out buildings and roads from the blur, and as they hurtled along The Backs he had no trouble identifying the characteristic seventeenth century contours of Trinity's Wren Library.

The Backs, as its name cunningly suggests, is a quaint

area of the river Cam that weaves its way along the back of half a dozen of the most well known riverside Colleges and, having passed the Wren Library, Thomas assumed they were heading directly to King's. However, just as they approached the entrance to Memorial Court of Clare College, Trinity swerved sharply, setting course for a set of small stone steps on the grass verge. She hastened up them, followed closely by Thomas and back in the regular world they both appeared dropping to the ground beneath. Before she could ask the question, Thomas jumped in.

"Put the casement stay into the third hole. Take out the book beneath the shelf, open it to page 1869 and place it on the window sill. The portal is in the aisle between the last two bookcases." He smiled triumphantly.

Trinity did not answer, she merely inclined her head then turned in the direction of King's, strolling casually along the path, whistling *The Lark Ascending* as she disappeared.

"All aboard for number 61," came John's voice, followed by a tap on the shoulder. "This is a simple one to access. It was placed by Queens' and to be frank…" he looked over one shoulder then the other with comical exaggeration, "…it's my favourite."

John stood before the small, well-used stone steps. They were approximately 40cm in width and although their unusual placement was suggestive of them once being part of a much taller staircase, they were in fact mounting steps; in the days when horses were the primary means of transportation, the horse would be held on the far side while the rider ascended. Time had left its signature at their centre, the compact grey stone worn into smooth, shallow cups. It would seem odd to most people but Thomas felt sorry for the steps. Every time he passed them on his way to the University Library, which was almost daily, he was struck by how small and lost they appeared in the thronging setting of the modern Backs, cowering between the long tufts of grass towering over their sides, perhaps hoping no one would notice them. Or paint them white.

"I *knew* there was something unusual about those steps!" proclaimed Thomas.

"I'm sure the feeling is mutual," replied John, pulling his long shirt sleeves straight, first the left, then the right. "Now, no fuss, just straight up and jump. Obviously, narrow steps, so I'll go first and you follow."

"Right, okay."

John trotted up the mounting steps and upon reaching the top, disappeared with an athletic leap. Thomas followed suit and in the fraction of a second following his jump he expected to hear the muffled *thud* of his boots hitting the ground as he made touchdown, but instead he found himself sitting atop some kind of transparent lump. Whatever it was must have been lying low to the ground behind the steps, catching him before he landed. Feeling his weight upon its back, the lump began to move, rising in two swift movements. First the front lifted up, causing Thomas to fall back slightly, then the rear lifted up which seemed to level whatever it was out at its full height. Now perched around two metres from the ground, Thomas' eyes were wide with confusion, looking down at the seemingly empty air on either side of him, trying to fathom the nature of the glass-like mound. His eyes searched for John and they did not have far to travel. The very definition of jubilance, John was sitting upon the back of an identical creature that stood in the middle of the road, not an arm's distance away. With his face aglow, he held in one hand what appeared to be a set of reins, whilst the other gestured a thumb's up.

If something looks like a horse, walks like a horse, and sounds like a horse, then classic problem-solving principles would favour it being a horse. This however, was not a horse as Thomas knew it. The creature had the outline of a horse, but it wasn't the kind you'd see frolicking about a field in *his* time, not least because it was rather difficult to *see*. Standing at what must have been an impressive 19 hands, the horses were solid to the touch, but their bodies were composed of what resembled slow running water, swirls of opaque movement surging like clouds within the confines of a horse's shape. Their large eyes were a sharp, emerald green, standing out like lasers against the monochrome background, and when their hooves hit the ground they did not return the familiar *clip clop,* but rather the sound of crystal upon crystal, like glasses clinking together.

"They're terribly keen to get moving," said John, patting the neck of the diaphanous mare as it pawed the ground with its front hoof. The horse upon which Thomas sat was not wearing a bridle but nevertheless a set of reins lay behind her neck and he grasped them with both hands. Lifting them up he looked underneath, then to each side of the horse's head, trying to fathom where they attached, but they didn't. The reins simply tapered towards the creature's mouth and remained fixed to the air either side of it.

"This is incredible!" exclaimed Thomas, giddy with joy. "Oh please tell me it's a long ride to the final portal!"

"Sorry old boy, just ambling along to King's, but…" he paused as if weighing up the situation. "Oh why not!" he exclaimed. "We'll head back to the top of Queen's Road and take a straight run back to King's. How does that resonate?"

"Yes! That sounds great!"

"And please don't mention this to the others!" John patted the side of his horse once more, "Do we have a deal?"

Thomas was about to repeat his answer, thinking John hadn't heard him the first time but then realised that the question hadn't been directed at *him*. Rather, John was addressing the horses, looking back and forth between the two creatures who not only seemed cognisant of the situation but were impatient to proceed.

"Thomas," began John. "This is Róta." The horse upon which John sat gave a sudden jerk of her head accompanied by a short snort. "And this," gesturing to the horse upon which Thomas sat, "is Kára."

Thomas, still in awe at the magnificent beasts, gently patted the side of Kára's neck.

"Hello Kára, I'm Thomas. Thank you for helping us." Kára shook her head and gave a long neigh. It was similar to the sound of a regular horse, but there was a glass-like tinkle as it faded away, like wind chimes.

Without warning, Róta and Kára prepared to run, both drawing up onto their hind legs. The sudden movement took Thomas by surprise and he leant forward, placing an arm around the horse's neck in fear of falling off. As their hooves reunited with the road the sound of crystal fell about them and they turned deftly about, tails flicking with excitement as they galloped off. At first, the ride was bumpy and Thomas hung on for dear life, but as the pace increased, the rhythm of Kára's gait smoothed out and he was able to slip his arm away from her neck and onto the reins.

The horses ran almost, but not quite, as fast as the Colleges, their powerful limbs moving like pistons as the scenery and buildings on the other side of the river gradually morphed into the now familiar grey blur. And this time, it wasn't only the scenery that blurred; the crystalline sound of the horses' hooves faded from distinct, individual chimes to a single, delicate rush. In years to come Thomas struggled to find a sound beautiful enough to compare it to, but when pushed for an answer he would describe it as being akin to the *whoosh* of the rings of Saturn.

Moving at such incredible speed, Thomas was expecting the horses to gradually slow before turning around, but this was not to be the case. As they reached the end of the street the horses stormed into the air as if they were racing up the camber of an invisible bridge, tracing a wide arch across the sky until gradually descending to rejoin the road and accelerating back towards King's. Thomas' eyes were wide with excitement and when he glanced to his side, that beaming smile was still firmly fixed to John's face. Róta and Kára pelted along the road and Thomas could easily identify the Colleges as they passed:

St. John's.

Woooooooosh
Trinity.
Woooooooosh
Trinity Hall.
Woooooooosh
Clare.
Woooooooosh
Both horses curved onto the opposite verge before making a sharp turn through the back gate of King's. A sudden panic then raced through Thomas' mind; in the monochrome world the bridge had been destroyed in what John would later describe as a "gargoyle-related mishap" and although he remembered Nick saying the structure would effectively self-heal, he was under the impression they might be racing towards a chasm. However, no sooner had the thought entered his head than to his indescribable relief they arrived at a reconstructed bridge, although there was a definite wobble as they coasted over. Róta and Kára sped towards the Gibbs Building, dropping to a canter half way across the Back Lawn, to a trot before reaching the flagstone path, and finally walked calmly to the arch. The two mares then obligingly lowered onto their front legs to enable their visitors to alight before quickly pulling themselves back up.

"Thank you Róta, old girl," said John.

"Yes, thank you," echoed Thomas, still utterly elated. "That was incredible."

Kára lowered her head and placed it over Thomas' shoulder. He was so overwhelmed by the gesture that all he could do was stroke the side of her face.

"Thank you," he managed to squeeze out as she lifted her head a few moments later.

The pair seemed to gesture to each other then turned to the grass, galloping back into the night as soon as their hooves touched the grass.

"Wow," breathed Thomas as he watched them sprint away. "But I thought you said there weren't any animals in this time?"

"There aren't," replied John. "Not exactly. Róta and Kára aren't exactly horses, they're the amalgamation of the consciousness of hundreds, thousands of horses. Just like I'm the amalgamation of the thousands of minds that have graced St. John's." He coughed. "Some more so than others, they don't all exert the same influence. Ask Trin."

"I should have thought of that." Thomas chastised himself. "You know, sometimes I could kick myself for missing the obvious."

"Never shadowbox your insecurities," smiled John, pulling on his long sleeves.

Before he could respond, Thomas' attention was captured by something on the other side of the Court.

"Hold on, what's that?" he asked, pointing in the direction of the river. He retraced a few strides and craned his neck forward, squinting. Sure enough, there was a shape moving slowly but smoothly along the path at the far side. As it turned the corner and headed towards them it quickly came into focus; a tandem bicycle ridden by two gentlemen, both of a similar rotund appearance and both with their light blue trouser legs tucked neatly into black socks pulled half way up their calves. Had Thomas been a little closer he might have seen it was a rather splendid 1939 Sun Wasp tandem. As if conscious of being seen, both men gave a synchronised wave in Thomas' direction, and Thomas, not quite knowing why, waved back.

Aside from a brisk return wave, John afforded the duo no further attention, but he suddenly appeared very keen to move along.

"Gonville and Caius," he remarked, gesturing towards the archway with an urgent but discreet flailing of his arms. "Step to it Thomas old boy, before they propel themselves to this side of the Court." And with that he moved stealthily into the small enclosure.

Thomas followed closely behind, noting how strange the archway looked without the clutter of Fellows' bicycles. There was but one in residence; a Royal

Sunbeam parked perpendicular to the wall, standing upright despite the absence of a rack, and Thomas smiled as he passed it by.

As his foot met the stone on the other side of the arch, Thomas found himself back in his own time. He stood for a few moments, looking out over the lawn and admiring the Gatehouse and Screen, its neo-Gothic pinnacles gently illuminated by the wrought iron lampposts dotted around the path. To his left, the Chapel stood in perfect darkness, slumbering. To his right, the eyes – or if one prefers, the windows – of the Hall flickered with warm yellow candlelight. At that moment, the entrance yawned open, depositing a pair of students onto the path. The gradual closing of the large oak door and subdued chattering from the deposits was the only sound emanating from within the Court. Hidden by shadows, they did not observe John or Thomas emerge from the archway, and as the students disappeared along the path, the sound of their voices tagged closely behind.

"How did you enter the Queen Street portal?" came the gentle, melodic tone of Nick's voice. Nick had appeared beside him and was also looking over the Court.

"That's an easy one," began Thomas, echoing John's words, "straight up and jump."

"If I had a cap I would doff it," laughed John, and no sooner had he administered Thomas with another of his trademark backslaps, than quite unexpectedly he hunched over, as if punched.

"Son of a… physicist," he gasped, clutching his stomach.

Thomas launched himself forward, placing a supportive hand under John's arm.

"Really, are you absolutely *sure* you're okay? Do you need anything?"

John shook a hand dismissively.

"Fine, fine."

Tactfully, Nick fired a round of conversational cover, "It's all those mathematicians," he joked, helping his colleague to straighten up. "It makes the head spin." He smiled, although Thomas couldn't help but feel there was a 'nothing to see here' varnish to it.

"As long as you're okay," yielded Thomas, concerned but confident in the Colleges' assurance that it wasn't anything to worry about.

John, quickly re-possessed of his strength, pulled his long shirt sleeves to order.

"You had better get a shuffle on, old boy." He walked towards the lawn, a chagrined smile slipping away. "Trin will be along soon."

Nick tapped Thomas on the shoulder.

"I do hope this isn't a disappointment, it's a rather easy one."

He turned to face the Gibbs Building arch, which now they were in Thomas' time was packed with Fellows' bicycles.

"I'm not one for ostentatious displays —" began Nick.

A loud cough echoed from John's direction and Thomas looked up to see him rolling his eyes at the gothic Chapel.

"Not when it comes to portals," finished Nick. "Stand inside the centre flagstone before the arch opening. Tap your left toe on the stone three times."

Nick, followed closely by Thomas, then passed over the threshold and into grey time, leaving John to contemplate the Chapel on his own. They walked to the other side of the archway, its grey walls and stone floor once again devoid of all but one bicycle, and an unexpected moment of calm fell upon Thomas.

"It's funny how a black and white photo looks more realistic than a colour one, don't you think?" he mused, drinking in the grisaille landscape.

Nick placed his hands in his pockets, leant against the arch and considered the question while Thomas continued talking.

"It's a bit like that with *this* world. There are things I notice that I'm not sure I'd pay attention to in my own time. Like how vivid the flowers are, the rose garden. They just look so much more vibrant here."

"Perhaps it's the way you look at them," suggested Nick.

Thomas nodded slowly in agreement, "Life's all shades of grey isn't it? People like to think it's black and white, but it never is."

"I appreciate this is a lot for you to take in," Nick paused then corrected himself, "*We* appreciate this is a lot for you take in, but these are unprecedented times and the way you have applied yourself to the situation is something to be proud of."

Gratitude, as ever, never failed to make Thomas feel unworthy of it.

"It's nothing," he replied hurriedly. "So, this is the last portal?"

"Indeed."

"I have to be honest, this isn't something that would've been anywhere *near* entering my head when the Run began, but after the first dozen or so portals I started to wish there were more than 62. What. A. Ride."

Nick laughed.

"How do you feel? Any disorientation?"

"No, none. I do feel thirsty though." Thomas paused, a thought occurred to him. "Is that why you told me to drink plenty of water when I went to dinner?"

"What? No, no." Nick pulled the pocket watch from his waistcoat and glanced at the dial. "I just happen to know the pancakes in the canteen were a little salty today. Right! Back we go!" He held out his arm like a polite butler, gesturing towards the portal. Thomas obliged, walking back through the arch and into the colourful surroundings of his own night-shrouded time.

Trinity had arrived and she and John stood just before the grass, deep in conversation.

"It's an example of how too many factions jostling for power enable a greater evil to take control."

"Quite so," replied John, "And I agree wholeheartedly that a coalition of parties with shared commonalities would have been sensible, but," he threw his head back in frustration, staring towards the night sky before snapping it forward to answer her, "All I said is that he shouldn't have used the Court as a parade ground. I mean, think of the damage to the lawn."

Trinity considered his words. "Well, Cromwell *was* a Sidney man," she said dryly.

Thomas threw a smile in their direction.

"Hello again."

They both turned towards him.

"Thomas!" said Trinity warmly, "How do you feel and what did you make of the Run?"

"I feel amazing and it beats a pub crawl any two days of the year!"

Thomas had completely lost track of time – or perhaps, it was time that had lost track of him – because he had no idea of the hour. Considering they started the Run at not long past 8pm and taking into account the perceived time it had taken to navigate all 62 portals, he was estimating they must now be in the wee small hours of All Hallows' Eve morning. And yet, that conclusion did not tally with the presence of candlelight in the Hall. Even at the most agreeable formal dinners, with several rounds of after dinner coffee, it was unthought-of for candles to be burning at such a late hour. He pushed up his coat sleeve and stared at the watch, its illuminated dial greeting him with a pale blue light.

"Eight-thirty!" Thomas exclaimed with incredulity. "Eight-thirty! It can't be!" He tapped the dial of the watch then held it up to his ear to check if it was still ticking. It was.

"That would appear correct," confirmed Nick. "The Run predominantly takes place in grey time so our temporal footprint, so to speak, was frugal."

"Of course!" said Thomas. "How did I miss that?"

Nick smiled, "Easily overlooked Thomas."

"Your badges please gentlemen," said Trinity as she removed her own and took a step towards Nick. Unpinning *A Hard Day's Night* from his lapel, he dropped the object into Trinity's outstretched hand. Thomas followed suit.

"I really like The Beatles," said Thomas, absentmindedly. "I didn't pay much attention to them until my late teens when George, my friend that runs the veggie café back home, played *Rubber Soul* over the tannoy one Saturday, and it sort of blew me away. I like lots of music: Reverend and the Makers, Pink Floyd, Hack Job, Billy Bragg, and other stuff like that, but that Beatles album really stuck with me." Thomas was lost in musical thoughts. He wasn't musical himself but he listened to a variety of 'real' music, as he termed it.

"Turned out George was a massive Beatles fan and I didn't know until then, so we ended up listening to their entire catalogue over the next few months. We did stuff like that, George and me. He's a bit like the big brother I never had. I mean, I *have* a big brother and he's alright but he doesn't much like me, or The Beatles, and that's okay. I guess we can't like everyone we meet in life, even if we *are* related."

When he was relaxed, Thomas had a tendency to place his inner monologue on loud speaker.

"Well George, at least, has impeccable taste," remarked John. "Come on Trin, let me keep the badge!"

"Badge!" she demanded, her hand waiting impatiently.

John craned his neck to his lapel, slipping the pin out of its hook.

"I note your brief association with the wickedest man in the world wasn't entirely without influence," he sulked.

Trinity shook her head, "Sometimes you behave like you're a hundred years old."

She returned the badges to her trouser pocket with a huff.

"Right, Thomas!" announced Nick before John could rejoin. "Tomorrow is going to be, well, we don't have enough data to reach a defensible conclusion regarding how or what tomorrow is going to be, but we can at least venture to say it's likely to be *eventful*, so may I suggest you head back to your rooms, wind down, and attempt a good night's rest."

Thomas nodded. Very little time had passed in his world since they started the Run and although not physically tired, his mind had been working non-stop for at least four hours of comparative time and he could feel his mental acuity circling the drain.

"Okay. What time should I meet you in the morning?"

Nick tilted his head thoughtfully, then nodded a few times before answering, "I've been considering this." He cast an eye to the others, "It's imperative to assemble our colleagues – ensure everyone is aware of the details of the situation – and to that end we've called an extraordinary meeting in the Senate House tomorrow. While we're occupied with *that*, I wonder if you might be persuaded to collect the stopcock…" he checked himself, "…the Antikythera mechanism and meet us in my study above the Porter's Lodge at…" he took out his pocket watch, then looked up at John and Trinity, "…Noon?"

"Yes."

"Agreed," they concurred respectively.

"Ohhhhh," added John, pointing a finger at Nick first then at Trinity, as if remembering a detail of critical importance, "Bagsy not Gonville and Caius. I am *not* rounding them up. No. Absolutely not."

Trinity stifled a laugh.

"You can mock Trin, but I always get stuck with those two and it's simply not cricket. Do you know what Caius said of me last time we spoke?"

"Desist with the baited questions," she hushed.

John placed his hands on his hips and shook his head in irritation.

"He said I looked *forwallowed.*"

"I say," responded Trinity. "You know they mean it when they unleash the fifteenth century slang."

John flung up his arms then dropped them despondently to his sides.

"Their conversation would be archaic to the ears of Georgian gentlefolk, codebreakers at Bletchley Park would have to think twice before deciphering their side of a chin-wag, and quite frankly, Trin old girl, I'm tired of wading through it." He took a breath, "And for the record, I may be many things but *forwallowed* hardly fits the bill." Agitated by the memory, he fiddled with his cuffs then pulled the sleeves of his shirt straight again, "And better forwallowed than a-a- flapdoodler!"

"John!" admonished Trinity.

"I'm sorry, Trin, but this is a moment for strong words. You can't even excuse it as all those Nobel Prizes going to their collective head because you've had more than anyone else and you're normal. Well, normal for a College with a clock that strikes the hour twice."

John pursued this diversion in a calmer tone.

"I mean, confound it, Trin, to call it loquacious seems kind."

"Do lay off the snuff, John," rejoined Trinity, rolling her eyes.

"No, it's the overwhelming preponderance of theologians," he asserted, continuing with his original point. "They're so accustomed to no one understanding them that they've streamlined the process by conducting both sides of the conversation themselves."

Nick closed his eyes, seemingly in hope of blocking out the exchange. He rubbed his forehead with his thumb and index finger and, ever the ambassador, turned to Thomas.

"Gonville and Caius are perfectly affable. They're…" he stopped for a moment as if weighing up the most diplomatic conclusion to the sentence, "… just a little old fashioned at times." The parallel seemed to elude Nick, but Thomas let it slide.

Before John and Trinity could proceed any further, Nick picked up where he left off.

"*Noon*," he said with a pronounced and forceful clarity. "Thomas, how do you assess the prospect of obtaining the Antikythera mechanism by noon?"

"I'll do my best," he answered, rubbing his eyes then opening and closing them in a few wide, exaggerated blinks. "I can't think clearly right now, my head feels a little foggy, but I've got an idea as to how I can get it. If the curator leaves me alone with the mechanism for ten minutes or so, then it should be pretty straightforward."

"Ten minutes?" responded Nick, taking Thomas at his word. "Good good. I anticipate you'll finish before us, so it will be to your advantage to lunch in Hall tomorrow. Does that dovetail with your thoughts?"

"Yes, yes that's fine. I don't need any encouragement to eat."

"A postscript regarding the extraordinary meeting of the Colleges," added Nick. "These gatherings are rare, but when they take place we cannot sense anything occurring outside of the Senate House." He looked at Thomas sternly, "Fortune is not renowned for its even handedness, so please refrain from offering yourself hostage."

"Keep out of trouble," translated Thomas. "Understood."

"Oh, and it would be preferable if you did not arrive at the Museum prior to eight-thirty in the morning. I must attend to a few details with Rangemen beforehand."

"Right-oh," agreed Thomas. "Actually Nick." A thought had volunteered itself. "May I have a quick chat with you? I might need your help with a… small detail."

"But of course," responded Nick, without a shred of hesitation.

Before they could continue John coughed politely.

"This is an opportune moment for me to bid you fine folks good night." He looked at the sky over the Chapel, the direction of St. John's. "My undergrads have established a Metaphysical Society and it's the inaugural meeting tonight. They'll be fine of course, but one can never be too careful when handling metaphysics." He shook his head sagely. "Best for me to dash back to the homestead, have the old cognitive oven gloves on standby."

"I'll walk with you," said Trinity, as she too turned to leave.

The Colleges politely nodded to Nick and Thomas, and were about to walk away when John suddenly returned and patted Thomas on the arm, "You did well old boy, you were particularly good at the corners." He smiled kindly.

Trinity nodded in agreement, "Rest well, it's been a long night."

"Thank you," replied Thomas. "I'm sure I will, as my dad always says: exhaustion makes a sound pillow." He watched as John and Trinity walked away, their voices barely audible.

"What are your lot up to tonight?" asked John.

"Astro-photography club."

John nodded approvingly.

"Last month," elaborated Trinity, "there were some truly sublime images of Andromeda and…" Her voice melted into the air as the two figures phased out of sight, consumed by the light fog that had now descended.

Following a brief discussion regarding his plan for obtaining the Antikythera mechanism, Nick bade the tired young man goodnight and, finally, Thomas headed back to his rooms.

The walk felt unnaturally long. Thomas always enjoyed the stroll through Front Court, along the side of the elegant Hall and onto Bodley's, and usually he was so preoccupied admiring the architecture that he would have been delighted had it been three or four times the distance. But this time, as he turned down the side of the Gibbs Building and headed along the path, the memory of the Run saturated his mind; image after image, around and around, each portal appearing in turn to his mind's eye – archways and doorways, stairwells and steps, cupboards and benches. They whirled as if someone had spun a mirror ball in his mind, the glare rotating faster and faster, and the images forming ever more coherently. Eventually, the thoughts became so lucid that they seemed to project from his mind and into the night air before him. He blinked into the darkness, certain that wispy strands of fog were contorting into the shape of one portal, dissipating and reforming into a different one, and before too long, dizzy from the illusions, he had to stop walking. He closed his eyes, filled his lungs, and when he had cleared his thoughts as best he could, he opened them again. To be more specific, he opened one eye and when it relayed the message back that the coast was clear, he opened the other.

"This is *not* the kind of hangover I was anticipating when I first heard about the Run," he said to himself as he pushed past the gate, "but nevertheless it's had a regrettable effect upon my senses. I really would benefit from some sleep."

He walked into the Court, his figure obscured by darkness.

"And maybe a nice cup of tea," were his last, lonely words before disappearing through the staircase door.

It was a quiet start to All Hallows' Eve. Even the gate had behaved itself.

The polite sign on both sides reads: *Please close the gate quietly behind you.* If you don't heed its genteel request and instead let it fall shut as you strut casually away, the gate will not only *bang* as it hits the post, but will rejoice in its new found freedom like a Newton's Cradle and rebound and *bang*, rebound and *bang*, until it has exhausted every last shred of energy. It was of no great consequence during the day, but late at night or early in the morning that gate was the murderer of dreams and the slayer of sleep.

Long before the sun had even contemplated donning his hat, Thomas, still dressed in his striped pyjamas, was seated at his shabby pine desk, scribbling away on the faintly lined pages of an A4 notepad. He had been awake since 5am, working studiously. Stacked neatly along the back of the surface sat four pristine piles of papers, predominantly journal articles he had photocopied at the archaeology library – and lived to tell the tale – arranged into subject areas prepared for his first supervision. In front of the papers were a dozen or so books of varying sizes and at the far left, a black metal lamp with a shade so disproportionately wide that it resembled a dog's post-surgery collar. Looming over them all, in a tray of its own, was a large, bloated document with a black and yellow binding comb straining to contain the pages; *Supervisions: The Customer's Journey, volume 1*; preparatory reports that Thomas had thus far managed to half fill out.

"That's it," he announced to himself. "All 62."

He threw his pencil onto the pad and planted his elbows on the desk, cradling his head in his hands. He had spent the early hours detailing the location of each portal on the King Street Run, along with a few scrappy notes about their quirks of entry. Writing details by hand, he would later tell his supervision students, imprints them on the mind in a way that typing falls short of. It is, he would expound with animated hands flicking enthusiastically through excavation reports and bending the pages open in display, similar to processing finds from an archaeological dig; one uses a camera to take photos of stone tools or pottery, but to draw them by hand introduces them to the eye in a more mindful fashion.

Thomas sat up straight and stretched both arms into the air above his head, yawning as he brought them down in a wide, Vitruvian Man arch. He then leant over the desk to flick off the surgery collar lamp and pushed away the chair as he stood up. The first rays of dawn were now adequate to illuminate the little room on their own.

"Time to get going."

He ripped out the carefully written notes from the pad then rifled through the centre drawer of the desk.

"I know you're in here," he mumbled as his hand scrambled amidst the clutter. After a few moments picking up and discarding various pieces of stationery, he picked out a plastic lighter and a small paper bag of grain fastened at the top with yellow wire. He pulled on a long blue dressing gown, slipped on his trainers without tying them, and shuffled out of his rooms.

It was a peaceful, cold morning with a thin layer of frost covering the lawn. Plump, round sparrows decorated the quince tree like Christmas baubles, chattering as Thomas made his way across the grass, a gentle *crunch crunch* beneath his feet. He sat on the wooden bench and slid one of the empty stone flower pots to the slab in front of him, whereupon he placed his morning scribbles inside and set them alight.

"Can't be too careful," he remarked to himself as a slender tail of smoke wagged into the air.

Thomas had read far too many mystery novels that were ruined by written evidence giving the game away, and he wasn't about to make the same blunder. He leant back on the bench and sat in quiet contemplation, now and again throwing a handful of grain to the mallards eyeing him expectantly from the river. The rustle of the bag garnered the attention of an inquisitive blackbird and the boldest of the resident squirrels, and between so many hungry mouths the small pile of feed was soon gone. After returning the flower pot to the mossy circle its base had left on the concrete, Thomas headed back to his rooms, grabbed his towel and braved the cold stone corridor to the communal showers. The hot water, as usual, had little interest in living up to its bill matter and he was subsequently in and out at a speed approaching the previous night's Run.

The doors of the Museum of General and Local Archaeology do not open to the public until 10:00am, but as a member of the Archaeology Department Thomas was permitted access an hour before that. It had just gone 8:00am when he quietly closed Bodley's gate and marched to the Hall, partly mulling over his plan to obtain the mechanism and partly wondering what his parents might make of the situation.

According to his mother, the past was a single event; she was far too concerned with what would happen tomorrow – getting to work, making dinner, and generally keeping a household together – that she had not the time to look back. She came from a long line of hard workers who despite the gruelling days and cracked hands, somehow never managed to accrue much for themselves. Food prices, energy bills, taxes; financially, it took all the running they could do to stay in the same place. And there was never any time. Days were spent at work – a dinner lady – evenings were eroded by travelling from work, and weekends, if they too were not worked, were spent recovering from it. Thomas often considered that had life offered his mother a choice – a woman with a fine head for complex arithmetic – she might have become a mathematician. But the currency of opportunity is time; time to study, time to think, time after time it is the most rationed of resources.

A steel worker at a local factory, his father was a tall,

kindly looking man and although he and Thomas had once been close, the years pulled them in different directions until, by the time he left school, they had become very polite strangers. Thomas often felt that life had beaten the hope out of his father, but he remembered a time when the old man was happy enough; he had a small workshop nestled in the corner of the back garden that only he held a key for. Inside, the walls were lined with shelves, filled to capacity with clocks and watches; some sleeping upon the worktop as if dreaming of the places and people through whose hands they had passed, and others, tick-tocking in conjunction like an orchestra warming up. A solitary wooden workbench, girded with an array of wood cutters, grinders and clamps sat just below a small window overlooking next door's vegetable plot. To the right, an old drawer-filled cabinet, liberated by his father from the local dump, was dotted with tiny white labels indicating 'washers', 'springs', 'small pendulums' and the like. If he wasn't at school, at work or volunteering at the local dog shelter, Thomas would sit with his father in the shed and learn how to fix the myriad ailments of mechanical clocks.

"Morning Mrs Willendorf," chirped Thomas as he placed his tray next to the till and scanned his dining card, his favourite option of daily special pancakes and a strawberry yogurt looking particularly appetising to his rumbling stomach.

"Guten morgen Thomas," greeted Mrs Willendorf in a soft Austrian accent. "You're the first one in today, vell, second, you just missed Rangemen. Vas your bed on fire?"

"Ha!" chortled Thomas. "Don't give me ideas, I'm sure the radiator in my room is only there for the sound effects."

Mrs Willendorf's round, motherly face giggled. Her head was a mass of short, tight red curls and her often blank expression was painted with a wide, rosy smile. Still chuckling, she lowered her head to finish counting out small change for the canteen till.

Thomas found his way to Stratford Canning and slipped his tray onto the end of the long table, checking the time on his watch as he sat down: 8:05am.

"That gives me a 25 minute buffer to enjoy breakfast," he said, addressing the white-haired man in the portrait. Thomas had not made a miscalculation regarding the opening time of the museum; rather, the first part of his scheme relied upon the acquisition of an ashtray, as any good plan of its kind would, and to do that it was necessary to visit the gift shop opposite King's.

The city of Cambridge is lacking in many things: green grocers, hardware shops, places to get electrical equipment fixed, a vintage sci-fi shop – the kind of practical things that are useful to everyday life – but one thing it is categorically *not* short of is gift shops. It was tricky to identify a unique selling point among these establishments, but Thomas had singled this one out because it opened half an hour before any of the others.

Distracted in thought, he wolfed down his breakfast. In fact, he ate it so fast that he did not notice the exceptionally salty pancakes, nor the similarly briny tang to the yogurt. After a leisurely wander around Front Court he headed through the Gatehouse, rucksack clinging to his back like a baby koala. He could see James through the little leaded window at the side of the Lodge and he raised his hand whilst mouthing "Good morning." The Porter returned the greeting with a cheery thumbs up.

Still being fairly early, both the pavement and the road were relatively docile and Thomas' long strides conveyed him effortlessly to the gift shop. He stopped briefly to peer through the window, checking the shop was open and upon seeing a sales assistant stacking objects into a corner cabinet, he pushed on the glass door, an old fashioned brass bell tinkling as he entered. It was a small, dusky interior with widely spaced shelving on both sides and two round display units sitting parallel in the centre, crammed with paraphernalia that no one needed and few wanted, but people bought anyway; King's College

Chapel encased in plastic snow globes, plastic coasters, plastic bookmarks, plastic keyrings, plastic figurines of beefeaters, basically, a lot of differently shaped plastic.

Thomas browsed his way along the shelves until he came across a pile of glass ashtrays stacked on the bottom section of one of the central display stands. He knelt down and picked up the top one, holding it flat on his palm and moving his hand up and down to gauge its weight. Satisfied, he began looking through the ashtrays, *clunking* them into a new pile as he did so. Each one possessed a College crest at its centre and Thomas couldn't help but find it all so very tawdry. Worse than that, there wasn't a King's College ashtray to be disgusted at and so he had to opt for Darwin College.

He placed the obscene object on the counter and the shop keeper gave a broad smile.

"Good morning, how are you?"

"Fine thanks, just picking up a gift for my nan."

"How nice."

Ting went the cash register.

"That will be £26.53 please."

Thomas pulled out a few crumpled 'emergency' ten pound notes from his coat pocket and handed them over.

"Thank you," said the man.

"Thank you," echoed Thomas as he prised up his change from the counter. "No need for a bag thanks," he added as he slipped the ashtray into his rucksack. The shop keeper smiled politely then recommenced arranging fridge magnets of the Baker Street road sign beside the till. Thomas headed out of the shop and back into the street.

The Museum of General and Local Archaeology is a striking neo-Gothic building complete with turret. Tall and proud, it watches over its cosy corner of the world like a grand wizard. Thomas knew it well and would often spend several hours at a time lost in its collections, marvelling at the displays. *Perhaps*, he couldn't help but wonder as he stood outside looking up at the sleepy spire, *that's where Professor Thanatosis is, locked in the tower weaving straw into gold.*

At the bottom of the turreted wall is a large, studded door with hinges so long and twirly that they appear to have crept into place from the surrounding vegetation. Thomas pushed it open, wiping his feet on the coir mat set into the stone floor as he entered. He walked to the end of the small entrance foyer and stopped at the Museum door, peering through the glass and into the Main Hall. He turned the round brass door knob, holding his breath in anticipation that it might be open.

It was locked.

He rapped gently on the glass, hoping the curator might be in earshot but that was equally fruitless.

"Oh well, intercom it is," he remarked under his breath.

When requesting early access to a building, Thomas preferred to avoid using the intercom if at all possible. He felt that if he could catch someone's eye it made the whole situation more informal and people tended to be more amiable to accommodating an early interloper; the intercom seemed to formalise proceedings and because of that, get things off on the wrong foot. It was subtle and fickle, but so is human psychology.

Buzzz went the intercom as Thomas held down the little silver button.

He waited.

No response.

Cringing, he pressed it again.

Buzzzzzzzzzz.

"Yesss?" came a curt response.

"Oh, hello, my name is Thomas Wharton, I'm a grad student in the Archaeology Department. I'm sorry to call so early but I've been asked if I can speak with the curator about taking a few, very quick photos."

An abrupt but indecipherable answer hissed and cracked from the speaker.

"I…zzz d…zzzz."

"You do?" replied Thomas, trying to interpret what the voice had said. "I'm sorry, could you say that again?"

The voice came back in a burst of static, the words

remained muffled but their impatience came through loud and clear.

"*Shhhhhhhhhhh* ou *shhhhhh* ou *shhhhhh*."

"Adieu? Did you say adieu? I-I really *do* need to see the curator if possible, but the intercom isn't very clear, there's a lot of static."

The voice finally clarified, slowly.

"I. D." *Crackle, crackle, hisssss.* "Do. You. Have. Your. Iden-ti-fi-ca-tion badge?"

"Ohhhh, I see, yes, I have it here," and Thomas pulled the small white card from his pocket, waving it in the air for absolutely no one to see.

"Come *straight* to reception," instructed the voice.

There was a loud *buzzzzzzzz* followed by a *click click* as the door unlocked and Thomas pushed through to the Main Hall. As commanded, he walked straight to reception. Admittedly, straight to reception taking the scenic route around a new display of Anglo Saxon metalwork on the opposite side of the room. The Main Hall has a roughly rectangular shape, with high windows and tall Romanesque columns leading up to wide arches that line a charming little gallery. The floorspace is dotted with glass display cases containing objects ranging from Palaeolithic hand axes and Neolithic arrowheads, to Bronze Age swords and Iron Age spears; it's all just a little bit of prehistory repeating.

Mrs Bulbar, the Museum's External to Internal Visitor Experience Navigator, had an irregular face and all the personality of a cold, wet teabag, and as Thomas entered the office she was slumped in her chair with much the same flair; as if freshly squeezed and deposited by a giant spoon. She was a slim, thin-faced lady and her stretchy grey dress was so tight that she resembled the recently consumed meal of a polyester python.

"Hello," grinned Thomas, attempting to inject some affability into his first in-person encounter with the buzzer voice.

"Yesss?" Mrs Bulbar looked up from the computer screen. She had a tendency to extend her S's which, when combined with empty room acoustics, gave the impression that someone was intermittently bleeding the radiator behind her.

"I'm Thomas, we just spoke via the intercom. I'm sorry it's early but I need to speak with the curator about taking a few photos of an object and —"

Mrs Bulbar's expression was as cold as the pennies on a dead man's eyes, and she cut him off half way through his sales pitch.

"ID?"

"Oh yes, yes, here it is." He walked to the opposite side of the desk and held the card in front of her.

Her gaze see-sawed between the photo on the card and the specimen before her.

"You *do* realise that the Museum doesn't open until 10am. *Ten. A. M*? And Dr Seton is *very* busy."

"Yes, I know, and I'm sorry for dropping in early, and although I'm not very good at navigating the SIS:TUM I *did* note in the Museum description that members of the Department are permitted to access the building for research purposes prior to its official opening time."

Mrs Bulbar flinched; this was not an acceptable use of information.

Thomas continued, "And like I say, I *am* very sorry, I wouldn't usually visit so early but it *is* important."

"What exactly do you want?" she snapped. "It's not in my job description to deal with the curator's business and whatever she may or may not have arranged."

"I really do appreciate that, but it's quite urgent you see, I need to speak with Dr Seton about taking some photos. It's very important."

"Maybe if you planned your *ssstudy*," she said, raising her fingers in air quotes, "more carefully then you wouldn't need to disturb *my* work out of hours. I really can't see a reason for me to call the curator. If you wouldn't mind leaving and coming back at 10am when the Museum will be open."

Thomas wasn't a confrontational person by nature – a doctor's plexor would struggle to elicit a knee-jerk reaction from him – but there was something so jarring in Mrs Bulbar's churlish manner, that it struck violently against his sense of propriety.

"I *do* plan my work and —" he said assertively before stopping himself and adding in a softer tone, "Can you *please* tell me where I can find the curator so I can speak with her?"

"You can't speak to Dr —" began Mrs Bulbar, but just at that moment the reception door swung open and in tottered a pile of boxes with a pair of legs poking out beneath them.

The boxes spoke, "Mrs Bulbar can you please help me by taking a couple off the top so I can see to put these down?"

Before Mrs Bulbar could say "Manual handling is not in my job description." Thomas stepped forward to take hold of the top four boxes. Each was the size of a shoe box and judging by the weight, empty.

"Oh thank you!" said the dark-haired woman revealed behind. "They're not heavy, just cumbersome."

She placed the remainder of the boxes in front of a set of grey filling cabinets.

"Just put them on the floor over here please."

"Do *not* obstruct my cabinets!" exclaimed Mrs Bulbar.

"It's only for a short while," soothed the box lady. "As I explained earlier, we're loaning these archive boxes to the Department for their post-excavation work in York. They'll be here soon to collect them."

"If they'd just stop doing these ridiculous excavations then we'd be able to get on with the proper work," snapped Mrs Bulbar, confident she had found a solution to the problem of storing archaeological finds.

Ignoring the comment, Dr Seton – for this is who the boxes had delivered to reception – blew back her long fringe and gave Thomas a quick smile. There was a long, pink scar running along the top left of her forehead, like a silk ribbon. She brushed her hands together to remove the excess dust before extending one in a handshake.

"Hello Dr—," began Thomas.

"Oh, call me Rosetta," she exclaimed.

"Rosetta, thank you," he responded. "My name is Thomas, I'm an archaeology grad…" He paused. "Do I detect an Egyptian note?" he asked inquisitively. He had a good ear for accents and hers was betrayed by a characteristic 'eh' occasionally bridging two words.

"Well heard Thomas, yes – although London has been my home for longer than I can recall. I used to be an interpreter." She pushed a pile of boxes to one side with her foot.

"Aside from a couple of brief sabbaticals in Holborn and Paris, I have spent most of my time in Bloomsbury." Her fringe fell forward and she flicked it back again. "Now, what brings you to us today?"

"Well, as I was saying to Mrs Bulbar." The tea bag shuffled indignantly in its ergonomic dish.

"I'm really sorry to trouble you so early."

"Oh, no matter, we're here, it's fine," replied Rosetta, waving a hand dismissively.

Thomas sighed with gratitude at her hospitality.

'Thank you, thank you very much, that's really kind of you." He then launched seamlessly into phase one of his plan. "Well, my Professor asked if I might be able to take a few photos of the Antikythera mechanism – nothing even remotely invasive, just a few quick snaps of Fragment A. We're working on a public outreach project covering the comprehension of space and time through the ages and he meant to come himself but he was called to a conference at the last minute and he'd really like me to send a shot or two that he can use to get the word out about the project while he's there."

Thomas didn't enjoy lying and it did not come naturally to him, but he had been running through his introductory blurb all night.

Rosetta held up her hands and nodded sympathetically, "I understand the rush of last minute requests." She gestured to the boxes.

"Just this morning, 8 o'clock, I receive a phone call from the Department asking urgently for thirty – thirty! –

archive boxes for delicate excavation finds to loan to a Fellow of King's. So, all this morning I am rummaging in the cupboards and under the desks trying to find the thirty, and this is why you find me waltzing with boxes. But for your request, you are in luck. I can do better than what you ask." The curator smiled enthusiastically as she removed a piece of paper and a pencil from her pocket. "I've already taken some photos of Fragment A. Last night actually. So I can email them to you, what's your email address?"

Thomas, delighted by Rosetta's helpfulness, was utterly dismayed by her efficiency.

"Oh, well, that's really kind of you! But do you think I might be able to take a couple of my own? My Professor wanted a very specific close-up of one side of Fragment A and…" there was no deceit in his concluding plea, "…I admit, I would be absolutely bowled over to see the mechanism for myself."

Rosetta paused for a moment, pressing her lips tightly together as she considered the request.

"Have you handled artefacts of this nature before?"

"Oh yes, from Palaeolithic to Mediaeval. I've excavated delicate objects on a range of archaeological sites, and I've also spent a huge amount of volunteer time cleaning and archiving." On this matter too, Thomas was not burdened to deceive.

She continued to think, tapping the pencil against the paper until finally breaking her contemplation with a sudden inclination of her head.

"Okay, but I will position the mechanism for you and you can take your photos. Does that sound a fair compromise?"

"That would be ideal, thank you," he responded eagerly.

Thomas followed Rosetta out of reception and briskly through the Main Hall to a door marked *Staff Only*. She held her ID card against the electronic reader on the wall and the door obligingly clicked open.

"The Antikythera mechanism is in the archive room,

it's a little stuffy in there but the lighting is *superb* for taking photographs," she informed Thomas as they walked along the grey painted corridor, all the way to the other end.

They stopped outside a door with a small glass window at the centre.

"Here we are."

To its left, side-by-side on the wall, was a card reader and another tannoy. Rosetta held up her card.

Click click.

The door opened.

The archive room was small and pokey, especially when contrasted with the grand vision Thomas had constructed in his mind. It was barely twice the size of his bedroom with a set of dumpy rolling stacks across the far wall, each one with a large rotary handle. The stacks were lined with shelves that were packed with boxes like the ones they had deposited in front of Mrs Bulbar's filing cabinets, and there was indeed an overwhelming stuffiness to the air that made it feel incredibly dry. Rosetta removed two white lab coats from a hook on the back of the door, handed one to Thomas and slipped the other over her black top and trousers. Thomas set his rucksack on the floor at his feet, placed his folded coat on top, then slipped on the lab coat.

A white workbench ran along the wall behind the door, its surface scattered with various silver tools, scale bars, and glass jars. Rosetta walked to the end of the bench where a lone box sat next to an intricately cut foam support. She picked up a pair of white cotton gloves from the other side of the box and pulled them on.

"It's fate," she said smiling. "Look, I have my sorry-looking makeshift support waiting here ready." She laughed.

"It looks pretty good to me," remarked Thomas, noticing the intricate indentations cut into the foam.

Rosetta slid up the top of the box, unravelled the envelope of padding inside, and gently prised up two sturdy cardboard handles atop an inner lining. As she raised the handles, the green corroded shape of the Antikythera mechanism poked up its head and Thomas felt butterflies swarm into his stomach at the thought of having to take it.

"Here we go," said Rosetta, placing the mechanism into the foam support. "Fragment A. What camera are you using?"

"Oh er, a digital one, it's in my bag," said Thomas evasively. "Would you mind if I had a look first?"

"Sure, no problem."

He squatted down in front of the artefact, arms folded on the bench.

"Incredible," he swooned.

Thomas stared with delight at the ancient orrery. It was around 13cm square, a giant of astronomical importance, and he became so engrossed marvelling at its construction and age that he almost forgot why he was there. It took a sudden, unexpected *buzz* from the intercom to wake him from his reverie. Almost immediately there came a second *buzzzzzzzzzz,* followed by a third more impatient *buzzzzzzzzzzzzzzzzzz.*

Rosetta raised her eyes to the ceiling as if calling upon some kind of ethereal intervention then walked to the intercom set beside the door. She removed her gloves, threw them onto the bench and pressed the silver button.

"Hello Mrs Bulbar. Is everything okay?"

The receptionist's voice oozed out of the wall, "There's another one!"

"Another *what* Mrs Bulbar?"

"Another ssstudent!"

"Well, Mrs Bulbar," Rosetta responded in a monotone voice, "this *is* a museum, and sometimes the tricky little scamps manage to get through the doors." She closed her eyes and Thomas took the chance to surreptitiously see what his watch had to say about the time: 8:57am.

"Well, it's not in my job description to deal with them."

"I think you'll find that greeting visitors to the Museum is given passing mention in your job description Mrs Bulbar," contended Rosetta.

"It is *not* in my job description to field questions about boxes or to be subjected to ssstudents swarming all over my office, disrupting my work. This one says a person called Rangemen sent him to collect thirty boxes or some such nonsense. I refuse to know anything about it."

"Are we calling *one* student a swarm?"

"Come to deal with him please," finalised Mrs Bulbar, her voice receding into the brickwork.

After mumbling what sounded like a prayer, or perhaps an anatomically correct rundown of locations from which one cannot smoke a pipe, Rosetta turned to Thomas.

"I better investigate what act of carnage is taking place up there. But I will first assist with your photographs."

Seizing his moment, Thomas promptly responded.

"Oh no, no, please don't worry about *me*. I'll probably be a good ten minutes so feel free to see if Mrs Bulbar is okay, I don't like the thought of her struggling."

"It is *not* Mrs Bulbar I am concerned about," responded Rosetta, "But you are very kind Thomas. Are you sure you don't mind being alone while I deal with this? The climate control creates a still atmosphere that not everyone finds agreeable."

I've experienced stiller, Thomas thought to himself. "It's absolutely fine, really, I don't mind at all."

"Very well, I won't be too long." Rosetta pressed the large, red *Door Release* button beneath the intercom and exited the room, her white lab coat flicking around the wall as she left.

Thomas waited a few seconds then sprinted to the door, pressing his ear against it. As soon as he heard the *thud* of the outer door he knew Rosetta would be in the Main Hall. He picked up the cotton gloves and scurried back to the bench. Kneeling on the floor, he grabbed his rucksack and pulled out the glass ashtray along with a square shortbread tin, the type of slightly twee, ornate affair that one gives grandparents at Christmas. This one was navy blue with an embossed cityscape of Seville on the lid and up until last night had served as Thomas' filing cabinet.

"Okay smokers of Darwin College, it's time for you to take the stage."

Wiping his forehead with the back of his hand he briefly closed his eyes in an attempt to push away the guilt of the impending theft.

"But don't feel bad about it." He gave the ashtray a sympathetic tap, then forcing a wide smile added in a more upbeat tone, "As they say, you are the truth in masquerade." The smile faded as quickly as it had appeared and he shook his head as if predicting an answer.

"No, that doesn't convince me either."

Swiftly moving on, he placed the ashtray and the biscuit tin side by side on the bench and after removing the lid transferred to it several layers of padding from the archive box. He then slipped on the white gloves and repeatedly clenched and released both hands as if about to crack a safe. Wrapping his fingers around the sides of the mechanism he gently lifted it into the tin, laying it down as tenderly as if he were putting a baby to sleep. He was just about to position a layer of padding over the top when, out of the corner of his eye, he thought he saw someone looking through the glass panel of the door. His heart jumped and he raised his head towards it but there was no one there.

"Must have been a reflection," he said, taking a few deep breaths to calm himself.

He resumed packing the mechanism and several long minutes passed as layer after layer of soft padding was scrupulously tucked and moulded around the delicate object before finally replacing the lid and sliding the tin into his rucksack. Throughout the whole process he would occasionally raise his head, holding his breath while listening for the *thud* of the outer door that would signal Rosetta's return. All remained clear and he continued with his task, swaddling the glass ashtray in a long piece of padding then wiggling it into the archive box.

Suddenly, the telltale *thud* of the outer door bounded up

the corridor. Thomas' heart sunk and his fingers lost their dexterity. He snatched up a piece of spare padding from the back of the bench and, replicating the mechanism's original packing, folded it neatly into an envelope at the top of the box. He pulled off the gloves and flung them onto the bench just as the door made a *click click* and Rosetta walked back in.

"Ohhhh, Thomas I am very sorry to have left you for so long, but peace has been restored to reception. Mrs Bulbar has once again unfettered access to her filing cabinets and the office is student-free, but I have bad news…" She picked up the cotton gloves from the bench and threw them from one hand to the other.

"…the Fellow who requested the boxes now requires them to be taken to York as a matter of urgency."

She rubbed her brow.

"York!"

Still in good humour she smiled wearily.

"I don't mind the journey, it's a pretty one, but this means I can only give you ten further minutes before I must leave. I am sorry, but there is no other option if I am to make it to York in time.

Thomas, almost shaking with panic, picked up the lid of the archive box and swiftly slid it back on, sealing in the ashtray's duplicitous role.

"Of course," added Rosetta, gesturing with her gloves towards the box, "if you need any additional photos you are welcome to visit again tomorrow, but alas, I shall not return to the Museum today."

"I-I'm all done!" stammered Thomas as he pushed the box containing the ashtray further back on the bench. "And I re-packed the mechanism." Which, he told himself, was not technically a lie, he just happened to have re-packed it in a biscuit tin that was now sitting in his rucksack. "All safe and sound," he added, which was an unknown variable and therefore also not technically a lie.

"Excellent! Did you get all the shots you need? I don't want to rush you. You *are* welcome to return tomorrow."

"Yes, yes, I have absolutely everything I need. Thank you."

He began to slide off the lab coat, walking towards the door as he did so.

"You're very welcome Thomas, it was good to meet you."

"And you too. Really appreciate your help thank you, thank you very much."

His heart was pounding so hard that he was sure Rosetta must be able to see it thumping through his t-shirt.

Just when things seemed to be bubbling along acceptably and Thomas could almost envisage getting away with the whole ghastly affair, Rosetta said the one thing he had not anticipated.

"I'll have just enough time to check the mechanism before leaving for York."

His face dropped, a split tea bag of an expression, and noting this she smiled reassuringly.

"Nothing personal, don't worry! I have every confidence in your care. It's just a matter of protocol. Would you like to stay while I do it?"

Thomas jolted as if receiving an electric shock. He had expected – no, he had relied upon – the curator accompanying him back to the Main Hall to complete the heist. Flustered, he spat out a puny cover story so he could leave as fast as possible.

"Oh, um, actually, I have to give my first supervision in ten minutes, I can't believe I forgot, so I'd best head off sharpish. Thank you. Thank you again."

He backed his way to the door, pulling his rucksack gently onto his shoulder and desperately hoping that Rosetta would not immediately open the archive box.

"Okay Thomas, good luck."

His hand stopped in mid-air before the *Door Release* button, his mind rattled.

"Good luck? With what?" he asked skittishly.

He was certain she knew what he had done and was making a reference to his feeble attempt to get away with it.

"With your first supervision!" she laughed.

"Oh yes, yes of course. Thank you, yes. Well, I'm sure I need all the help I can get. Thank you. Thank you very much." And with that articulate farewell ringing in her ears, Thomas turned back to the door, his hand now resting on the *Release* button.

"Are you heading back to reception?" he asked nervously, desperately hoping it might induce her to leave the room.

"No, no," answered Rosetta. "I'll put the Antikythera mechanism to bed first."

Thomas shot a glance at the archive box sitting atop the counter.

"Right. O-okay," he stuttered, frantically wondering how to encourage her elsewhere. "Do you think you could show me how to get out of the corridor?"

He turned to face the door, closing his eyes in embarrassment at the absurd question and wishing the moment away.

Rosetta raised an eyebrow in amusement.

"Thomas, you are kidding me? It's a corridor. You cannot get lost. Press the red button and the door will open. But I like your humour very much." She laughed and turned towards the bench.

Thomas felt numb with panic but short of hurling himself on the archive box and begging her not to open it, there was little he could do to prevent the theft being discovered and so he took his leave, walking as fast as he could along the corridor without actually running. *Maybe* he thought to himself, *I should wait in the corridor for her to discover that the mechanism is missing and when she comes running after me I will say it was just a joke or that I was testing security.* Just as he reached the outer door and almost dared to let himself believe that he had devised a workable safety net, Rosetta came shouting after him.

"Thomas! Thomas! Stop!"

He stopped but he did not turn around. He stood motionless, his fingers resting on the *Door Release* button. He listened to Rosetta's approaching footsteps and closed his eyes, the dread building inside of him, aghast at how his reputation could possibly recover from the dishonour when it became known that *he,* a once trusted, punctilious, reliable student, had stolen an irreplaceable artefact.

"You forgot this," she said cheerily.

Thomas opened his eyes and turned rigidly to face her. Rosetta stood about a metre away with a broad smile, holding his parka in her outstretched hand.

"You'll catch your death without it."

His heart popped back up from where it had sunk to hide between his kidneys, and a wave of relief washed over him.

"Thank you." His eyes lit up. Never did he imagine being so deliriously happy to see that battered old parka. "Can't believe I forgot this."

"You clearly can't wait to get to that supervision!"

Thomas gave a nervous chuckle.

"Yep, it'll be a show stealer." He looked away, rolling his eyes so hard that he feared they might get stuck. "Thanks again!" he said, gesturing to the coat and turning to leave.

"Pleasure, Thomas. Have a good day."

With a friendly smile, Rosetta turned to walk back down the corridor.

"So polite," she said to herself as she reached the door to the Archive Room.

What both Rosetta and Thomas had been unaware of as they stood talking in the corridor, was that the lights had flicked off in the Archive Room and a small figure had phased into its darkened hold. The form moved swiftly towards the door and placed a hand upon the release button whereupon a low *click click* signalled the mechanism had locked. The figure patted the door handle with what seemed like a sense of satisfaction then turned back into the room as it phased out of sight.

Thomas hit the red exit button and as the door jolted open he walked energetically through the Main Hall and back into the foyer. He felt so weighted with shame that he couldn't bring himself to look into a single glass display cabinet.

In fact, so furtive was Thomas' exit that as he passed reception, the door of which was now propped open with surplus archive boxes, he did not hear the restrained voice buzzing out of the tannoy:

"Yes, Mrs Bulbar, I appreciate it's not in your job description to fix doors and I wouldn't dream to suppose otherwise." It was Rosetta. "I'm only requesting that you contact maintenance to take a look at the Archive Room door. It's jammed and I cannot get in. I will ask one of the post-docs to be on hand, but I can't wait any longer, I must leave now to make it to York on time."

When he reached the external door Thomas pulled upon it so eagerly that he had to immediately catch it to prevent it striking the internal wall. As he stepped outside, the cold light of day fell upon him like a spotlight and he kept his eyes to the ground, paranoid they might betray his crime. He took a deep breath then strode away from the Museum and into the street beyond, devoured by bobbing crowds and weaving bicycles. After a few minutes, his mind dripping with remorseful sweat, he stopped suddenly, deep in thought at the practical consequences of his action.

"I'll get sent down," he said to himself as he tightened his grip on the bag's strap.

"I'll get sent down so hard I'll be able to take samples from Earth's core."

For the remainder of his walk, Thomas was so wrought with guilt that he was convinced everyone he passed was looking at him with an accusatory glare. The wind-blown trees seemed to whisper to each other about it. Even the call of blackbirds bobbing along the College forecourt sounded like *tut tut tut tut tut* to his ears. Of course, *no one* looked at Thomas with an accusatory glare and had the blackbirds been conscious of the situation, they no doubt would have told him that he had done the right thing. And as for the trees, well, aside from Rangemen, who *knows* what they might be thinking.

Although his actions were justly driven, Thomas found the mechanism's acquisition a heavy burden, anticipating the Museum curator rugby tackling him to the ground at any moment. But she didn't, and as he stole through King's Gatehouse a free man, a matter of habit diverted him into the North Lodge to check his pigeonhole. A single sheet of paper awaited him; a note from the Director of Studies of St. Catharine's College asking if he were able to supervise three additional undergraduates. Although he had yet to give his first supervision, Thomas was momentarily so delighted at being asked to do more that he almost forgot what he was anxious about.

"I'll have to book another room," he said to himself with buoyant optimism as he stepped out of the North Lodge.

"I'll have to book another room," he repeated, stopping in his tracks at the thought of reuniting with Mr T. Pyrone and his sidekick. His optimism crumbled like a sea stack into raging waters. He pushed up his coat sleeve to check the time: 10:00am.

Leaning with his back against the wall he contemplated his options.

"I have a long wait before I'm to meet Nick and the others... so I *could* easily run along to submit the room forms *now*..."

Thomas was fidgety at the best of times, so the thought of lying at anchor for several hours was most unappealing.

"If I'm going to accept these extra supervisions then I need to get that room booked *now*. If I wait until next week, even later today, there might not be a room available and after all, it'd be a shame for me to sit around twiddling my thumbs when I could actually *achieve* something.

He rubbed his chin thoughtfully.

"I mean, I haven't done any work since all this began and I don't want to waste time."

Torn, he stared back down at the supervision request.

Was *now* really an appropriate moment to worry about this? To give time to mundane matters when there was so much wonder about him?

In a trice, snatches of his conversation with Dr Watt burst into his head, bouncing off the face of his every doubt like a ping-pong ball thrown into an empty room.

"Yes," declared Thomas, suddenly seeing the answer was strikingly obvious. "This is *precisely* the time to do it."

With that, he pushed himself from the wall, crumpling the letter into his pocket. He dashed into the Porter's Lodge to collect the necessary paperwork and James was more than happy to whisk off the requisite number of point 5Cs. He then strode out of the Gatehouse, over the road, and into St. Edward's Passage.

Thomas was all too aware of his precious cargo and the need to keep it safe, and he briefly entertained hiding the mechanism in his rooms. But what if the Bedder, one of those wonderful, well-meaning housekeepers were to accidentally move it? Or what if whoever is controlling the gargoyles gained access to his rooms and stole it? Or, the ultimate indignity, what if the Curator raised the alarm at the missing artefact and the powers that be searched his room and found it? No, without knowing if the last part of his plan had been executed, Thomas' internal judge and jury considered the mechanism to be more secure in his personal custody.

Perhaps it was the act of tasking himself with such a run-of-the-mill errand, but as he walked through the narrow street, the simple goal rested his nerves. He followed the curve of the path as it twisted by the front of St. Edward's church, admiring the west tower as he went. The tall building presided over the street, its ochre stucco and brick parapet beautifully complimented by the Autumn leaves carpeting its small churchyard. He was about to look away when something caught his eye and this time it stopped him dead in his tracks.

"Do you mind!" came an annoyed voice from a man

who had been walking several strides behind him and was forced to perform an emergency stop. If there's one thing Thomas had discovered about the natives of Cambridge, it's that a cavalier approach to pedestrian etiquette is heavily frowned upon.

"Oh, I'm terribly sorry," replied Thomas in a distracted, half-hearted apology. His attention had been arrested by one of the tower's little arched windows and he now stood with narrowing eyes, trying to pierce the darkness behind the glass. He wasn't confident, but he thought, just for a second, that he saw the same blue eyes that had appeared alongside him in Hobson's Passage when on the King Street Run.

"It *can't* be!" he said to himself, his gaze abseiling down the side of the tower, but just when he was about to chalk it up to imagination, there they were again! But this time they were looking out of the small window above the doorway. Two small blue eyes leering out of the shadows, and worst of all, they were looking directly at *him*. Thomas felt a cold chill run through him and all other thoughts crumbled from his mind. He tightened his grip on the strap of his rucksack and walked on, keeping his focus on the glowering eyes. As he passed the side of the heavily buttressed church the little blue orbs blinked then vanished from the window. Thomas slowed his pace but carried on walking, scrutinising the church and its grounds, searching for anywhere they might reappear, but there was no sign of them. He reached the open space of Peas Hill and with a sigh of relief turned to look at the east front, his eyes foraging about the large arched windows. Nothing.

After a last, drawn-out glance he hastened towards the Market Square, now and again looking over his shoulder, but still the blue eyes were nowhere to be seen.

The farther he walked from the church, the more relaxed he felt, and as he dodged his way past groups of chatting shoppers his worry was sufficiently quelled by the sight of the bakery window that he stopped to peruse its pastries. Croissants, sausage rolls, gingerbread men, everything looked and smelled delicious and Thomas was contemplating whether or not he could justify treating himself when all of a sudden two blue eyes appeared in the reflection of the glass. He swung around expecting to see someone or something standing behind him but there was nothing. He turned back to the window and the eyes were still there, a ghostly visage hovering over his right shoulder, staring at him then at his rucksack.

He backed away from the window, panic-stricken. An elderly lady standing next to the bakery doorway noticed Thomas' discomfort and turned to address him. In defiance of the Autumn weather she was wearing a dark green summer dress with little white cap sleeves, a dainty straw sun hat trimmed with green berries, and her hands were concealed within a pair of wrist-length white gloves.

"Oooh I *know* dear," she said with a bright smile and laughing eyes. "It all looks so tempting doesn't it, but you're doing the right thing, *get away* before those cream cakes lure you in!"

Thomas threw her a quick smile but then made a double take. The lady seemed familiar and her appearance was so vivid against the rest of the street that at first he thought he knew her, but he didn't. When he turned back to the reflection, the eyes had disappeared.

"They're following me," he mumbled under his breath but it appeared the lady heard him.

"Oooh I know, they sit on the hips for months!" she giggled.

Thomas, a gnawing disquiet growing in his stomach, smiled again at the lady.

"Yes, yes they do," was his distracted response and staring back into the reflection, he once again tightened his grip on the rucksack, fearful the blue eyes might know he had the mechanism.

"Thomas?" said the elderly lady. He turned to face her, an almost tangible sense of urgency had taken over her expression.

"Run! Run Thomas!"

Before he could ask how the lady knew his name, he saw the blue eyes ripple back into the reflection in the window and almost simultaneously thought he felt a tug on his rucksack which sent him spinning around. When he turned back the elderly lady had disappeared, but her voice returned to whisper in his ear.

"Run!"

He couldn't explain it, but something instinctive told him to heed her advice. Not wishing to look conspicuous he started off with a brisk walk, reaching around to his rucksack and pulling the loose handle onto his other shoulder so that the bag was now strapped firmly across his back. His pace quickly increased, with the walk turning into a trot, and the trot turning into running as fast as his legs could carry him to the other end of the street. As he passed the shop windows he glanced intermittently towards them and in every reflection the blue eyes stared back, disappearing only as the glass gave way to the dividing brickwork between shop faces. He turned left when he reached the end of the street and it wasn't until he made it to the first café that he realised he was running in the opposite direction of Mill Lane. Oddly, it may have been the wrong direction, but he couldn't help but feel he was going the right way. The street was busy with pedestrian traffic and the road heaved with cars and bicycles, a constant stream of life that Thomas was beginning to feel increasingly isolated from. He glanced into a hairdresser's window and among the clutter of shampoos, conditioners, and hairspray, the reflection of two blue eyes stared back.

Suddenly and without the shadow of a warning, an industrial waste bin careered out of a narrow passageway directly ahead of him. Rather than keep on rolling and bump down the curb, as would have been the natural course of its motion, the bin came to a distinctly *unnatural* halt, as if it had been intentionally positioned into his path. Thomas was powerless to avoid crashing into it and the collision would have been decidedly unwholesome had it not been for the fortuitous arrival of a passerby. A stylish man wearing a blue suit, yellow shirt and a long grey coat, had not moments before strolled casually into the road. His footsteps were perfectly timed between the traffic and upon reaching the other side he effortlessly pulled the bin from Thomas' course.

What Thomas did *not* see as he rushed by, was that after returning the object to its rightful place beside the hairdressers, the man in blue had continued walking up the deserted alleyway, whistling calmly as he phased out of sight, the soft notes of *The Phantom of The Opera* bouncing about the walls long after he had disappeared.

Thomas did not stop running until he approached the front of Sidney Sussex, turning towards the road and bobbing around on the spot, anxious to cross. Behind him, the buzz of building work drifted down from scaffolding outside a shop and he tried to focus his mind while he waited for a gap in the traffic. Staring one way then the other along the road, he could not possibly have known that a short lead pipe had just been pushed by an invisible force from atop the scaffolding; a short lead pipe that was now falling with a guided trajectory towards his head. Even Thomas' thick curls would offer little buffering against such an impact. However, just before the object could test the durability of his unsuspecting cranium, it was intercepted by an outstretched hand. Feeling the rush of air above his head, Thomas turned sharply and was confronted with the smile of a distinguished man in what appeared to be his early twenties, walnut skin and onyx eyes. One may have expected his striking red suit, which featured a prominent line of alternating gold and white buttons down the waistcoat, to draw the attention of onlookers, but people barely appeared to notice him. Thomas glanced at the pipe in the man's hand then up to the scaffolding, and back down to the pipe. He did not require an introductory workshop and breakout session to realise he had just been pardoned from certain discombobulation. He raised a hand to his head, as if comforting himself from the thought, then looked intently at the young man.

"Wolfson?" he whispered. The man gave a confident wink at the recognition, then walked away, nonchalantly rotating the pipe like a majorette's baton as he disappeared, quite literally, into the throng of shoppers.

Filled with a new sense of determination, Thomas turned his attention back to the traffic. There was something urging him on. He looked up and down the road, still waiting for a gap in the congestion and he ran across at the first opportunity, sliding between two bicycles and earning himself a disgruntled set of *ting ting tings* from the riders. He jogged up the road, bowling distrustful looks into darkened corners, but aside from snagging his coat on a clump of wild *Nemophila menziesii* growing out of a wall, there were no more unsolicited tugs upon his bag and the eyes, if they were still in pursuit, remained hidden.

Ahead, the tower of the Round Church was just visible in the distance but Thomas swung a sharp right instead, heading for the little wooden gate in the brick wall of Sidney Sussex. Before his hand could touch the latch, the gate swung open before him and he sped into Cloister Court, completely missing the tall, bespectacled man who had so obligingly opened it for him. The man, dressed in a pair of dark red cord trousers and a navy blue shirt, watched the fleeting figure with a kind but concerned expression.

Thomas paused as he reached the archway that leads to the Fellows' Garden. Doubled over, he rested his hands on his knees and gasped sharply. Once he had drawn half a dozen deep breaths, he closed his eyes and squared his shoulders, moving his hands to rest on the small of his back as he let his head fall skywards.

"You know what they say," came a well-spoken voice from behind him. "What doesn't kill you makes you linger." Thomas turned to see the tall man exiting through the gate, phasing out of sight as he did so.

"Sidney," Thomas nodded with a grin. "That was Sidney. I'm sure of it."

By coincidence 'lingering' is precisely how, at a far

away symposium in the not-too-distant future, Dr Watt would politely summarise human existence.

Thomas glanced around the Court, searching for any sign of the blue eyes, but there were none. All was still. He turned to the gate and positioned his feet before the threshold, reaching inside and pulling it shut, *clink*. He tapped the ninth brick up on both sides and opened the gate, walking straight through. As if someone had ripped off a piece of wallpaper to reveal a faint imprint of the pattern on the lining paper, so the monochrome garden appeared before him. Thomas raised his hands to his face, sliding them down his cheeks in relief that the portal had worked, and after pausing for a few moments he sauntered through the Fellows' Garden, in the direction of the car park beyond.

"And that man by the scaffolding *was* Wolfson, I'm sure of it," he affirmed to himself, thinking about the man that had caught the lead pipe. "He just…" and he shrugged his shoulders "…*looked* like Wolfson." He pulled the straps of his rucksack forward, realigning the bag across his back. "But I'm not sure about the man in blue. I didn't see him for long enough to be able to tell. And the elderly lady, I don't think I was ready, I wasn't paying enough attention. Flippin' 'eck Thomas you can be such a dim wit."

With this simple rumination the panic that had pursued him through the city began to subside, giving way to a calmer, more measured frame of mind.

"I wonder if the Colleges would permit me do some writing in here," he laughed. "Time doesn't pass as such and it's so quiet. Perhaps that's how old Monty managed it."

But the calm was not to last for long. Before he could reach the car park Thomas developed the disagreeable sensation that he was no longer alone and something in his gut told him that it was not a benign presence. He turned around, his gaze rootling about the garden for anything unusual, relatively speaking, darting over lawn and trees, scanning the grounds from left to right.

Suddenly, he saw it!

Around three metres off the ground in front of a copse of silver birch in the centre of the garden; a distortion of the air, semi-transparent like a soap bubble but with wispy grey swirls moving around inside of it. It was roughly spherical, around a metre in diameter and it was hovering in mid-air. Thomas was standing approximately 30 metres away and he narrowed his eyes, squinting into the area around the trees, trying to make sense of it. At first, the amorphous globule seemed to be making minor fluctuations in shape, pulsing one way and the other, turning and moving back, but the longer he stared, the more he realised that it wasn't changing shape at all, rather, it was changing colour, or more accurately, it was *acquiring* colour. The grey swirls were developing into lengthier, ribbon-like strands, angry tendrils that surged around the confines of the shape and everywhere they passed they deposited a layer of grey, colouring the object like someone blowing smoke into a port glass, each movement adding more definition.

For all he could move, Thomas may as well have been cast in bronze, but after nearly three minutes of gawping in disbelief, he flinched when the two largest trees behind the strange entity bowed over to opposite sides, as if something very large had pushed them out of its way while walking through. Unfortunately for Thomas, that is precisely what had happened. As the trees sprang back, rebounding side to side like two recently opened Jack-in-the-boxes, he was met with the dawning realisation that the spherical shape was in fact the head of a creature that had been looking through the trees at him; a giant head that had now been joined by its giant body. His eyes widened as the rest of the semi-transparent being stepped out from the cover of the trees and pulled itself up to full height. It stood around ten metres tall, three metres wide, and its entire frame was seething with the same grey tendrils as its head, churning in a circular motion, each rotation providing more depth and clarity to its identity.

Thomas, frozen in horrible fascination, could only

watch as the petrifying creature took a step towards him, its enormous foot pounding onto the grass with a *thud* that vibrated through the ground and into his bones.

Another step.

Thud.

The creature was now around 20 metres away and still it lumbered closer, and with every slow step, the grey swirls filled more of the void, surging in ever decreasing circles towards the centre of its chest until eventually it was revealed in all its horrific, Gothic detail; a gargoyle of immense proportions with two tiny, bright blue eyes. There was no doubt; these were the same piercing eyes that he had observed in Hobson's Passage while on the Run, and the very same eyes that had stalked him through the town.

Thomas stared at the gargoyle, ten metres of solid trouble with an expression that looked like a stomach ulcer feels. Breathing used to seem so easy, but looking up at that snarling grey face, he had to remind himself how it was done. Unlike the smaller gargoyle he had encountered by the river, this gargantuan beast was bipedal with more-or-less human limb proportions, but that is where the physical similarities ended. Its powerful limbs, both arms and legs, bulged with muscles beneath its ostensibly cold, stone surface. Its hands seemed disproportionately small but this was compensated by each having four long fingers tipped with a sharp, triangular talon. Its feet more closely resembled cloven hooves, but instead of being split in half, these had three webbed toes, and like its fingers each was finished with a sharp, hooked claw. Its chunky torso was similarly well-built but the ribs and collar bone were strikingly prominent, so much so that the protrusions resembled a breastplate. Its short neck was considerably thicker at the bottom with a series of muscles straining under the pressure of the large head. Enormous brow ridges arched over its eyes and above that, sitting either side of its head, were two long horns that curved around its pointed ears and stopped just short of piercing its own cheeks. Its nose was wide and flat, with four deep-set furrows carved into the bridge and small nostrils flaring rapidly as it breathed in and out. Its mouth hung half open, revealing a jaw full of small, razor sharp teeth augmented by two lower canines that were so large they almost reached its stumpy little nose. As if not already formidable enough, the nightmarish vision was framed by a pair of enormous griffin-like wings arching out from its back and as it moved forwards they stretched out, temporarily blocking the grey sunlight.

"The time lice," Thomas babbled to himself, dumbfounded. "This is what the time lice have morphed into."

"Run!" came a voice into his ear. "Run, Thomas!"

The voice, which sounded very much like the elderly lady from outside the bakery, was just enough to rouse him from his catatonic state and without wasting another moment he turned towards the car park, running as if the hounds of hell were at his heels. He could hear the sound of giant footsteps pounding the ground behind him, but he kept focused, thinking of the nearest portal he could take back to his own time; the circular lawn in First Court of Christ's College.

It was at least two full minutes before Thomas began to decelerate and as he did, he strained his ears for the sound of the gargoyle but there was neither sight nor sound of it. He eventually slowed to a jog but didn't yet feel confident enough to come to a complete stop. The further he ran, the more his mind flooded with thoughts. He already knew from his Run along Hobson's Passage that the gargoyle's eyes could travel at speed, and despite its body appearing extremely powerful and strong, its movements had been laboured and slow; clearly his pursuer could not run in the same way as the Colleges. He was also prepared to speculate that the creature was unable to take corporeal form in *his* time, which would explain why only its eyes appeared to him. It could however exert a very clear influence over objects in his time, or at least, Thomas strongly suspected that to be the case; the self-propelled industrial bin and the guided lead pipe gave him great cause for concern. He turned the corner of another road and with it more questions piled upon him; why hadn't the gargoyle flown after him? Surely that would have made for a swifter chase? He swung a sharp left through the Great Gate of Christ's College, past the Porter's Lodge, and directly to the centre of its fine circular lawn.

Wooooooosh.

Thomas jogged out of the portal and appeared back in his own time on the pristine lawn. The timing of his arrival was most providential; between the end of one set of lectures and the beginning of another, the upshot being that there were very few people in the Court. A notable exception was the Head Porter of Christ's who happened to be walking around the flagstone path and who nodded in acknowledgment to Thomas without so much as raising an eyebrow at the sight. On the other side of the Court, nestled within a neatly pruned wisteria, a staircase door opened and two students walked out, just missing his arrival.

"Excuse me!" one of them shouted to Thomas, "You're not supposed to walk on the grass!"

Thomas looked up. It was Graham Wakes.

"You shameless anarchist, Mr. Wharton," shouted a very amused Graham. He turned to the other student, a tall woman wearing a long green coat, "It's okay, that's my friend Thomas, there'll be a good reason why he's doing whatever he's doing." He frowned. "And I have absolutely no idea what he's doing." He then continued shouting at Thomas in feigned outrage, "Just because you're from King's doesn't give you the right to go traipsing over other folks' grass. Have a care will you!"

Thomas raised a hand by means of apology and obligingly crept off the lawn in long strides.

"You see..." Graham explained further to his companion, "...Thomas is a sort of academic uncertainty principle; the more we know *what* he's doing the less certain we are *why*."

Thomas reached the path and stood still for a few seconds, gathering his thoughts before jogging around the Court to where Graham and the other student were standing.

"Graham, I know it looks bad but I, er, I thought I saw an injured blackbird on the lawn but when I got to it, it flew off." Being a notoriously poor liar it was the best excuse he could improvise.

Graham raised an eyebrow.

"You must be careful, Thomas," he said in a serious tone. "Christ's blackbirds are *notorious* for leading outsiders astray." He laughed and shook his head. He didn't believe Thomas for one moment, but was so amused by the encounter – and so laid back in temperament – that he didn't much care what the real explanation was.

"I'm really sorry Graham but I have to run, I'm late for a meeting." Thomas started to move towards the Gatehouse but then turned, "I'll see you next week and we'll make a start on those ideas for the sci-fi group!" He walked a few steps further and turned again, "And if you think your blackbirds are tricksy, wait until you meet our sentry squirrels."

With that, Thomas sped off, leaving Graham chuckling on the other side of the Court.

"Okay," said Thomas to himself as he walked away, re-focusing and attempting to coax meaning from what he had observed. "Okay. It's big. It's very, *very* big. On a scale of one to apocalypse it's three riders and death saddling up."

He ran his hand through his hair, his thoughts trained on the gargoyle.

"But it seems it can't run like the Colleges, or indeed move very fast at all in physical form in grey time, and it can't materialise physically in *this* time." He nodded his head.

"That's good. Surely that's good for us. But it *does* appear capable of manipulating objects here. That's bad for us." He walked back past the Porter's Lodge and into the street. With hypotheses reverberating around his mind, it wasn't long before he found himself at the end of Pembroke Street with a new look of confidence about him.

"So, let's get a better look at you," he said, determined.

Thomas looked wistfully up and down the street, contemplating his next move. He decided to press on to his original destination of Mill Lane, which by this point in his journey presented the closest portal, and return to grey time from there.

With courage fortified by his findings regarding the limitations of the time lice – or rather, the giant gargoyle they had morphed into – Thomas breezed along the street, casting an occasional look into shop windows to see if the blue eyes were lurking within.

They weren't.

He arrived at the busy crossroads before Mill Lane and came to a stop by the traffic lights, glancing at the illuminated *Wait* light and the red figure beneath it. He placed his hands in his pockets as he stood at the curb, mulling over the gargoyle's behaviour and committing to memory the salient facts he would present to the Colleges.

The light change usually took no more than around 30 seconds but at least a minute passed and still the *Wait* light and its little red cheerleader remained lit. With suspicion building at the long wait, Thomas started to feel uneasy. He looked back down at the signal box and there, staring back with a fierce, narrow glare, were two blue eyes set into the head of the red figure. The sight hammered a chip into his new found confidence, tightening his chest and fusing his spine, and he looked away. His mouth suddenly felt dry and his throat constricted, and he swallowed hard to clear it.

"It's just trying to slow me down," he told himself. "Be patient. Stay focused."

A further minute passed and still the lights remained red. An impatient crowd was now swelling on both sides of the road and Thomas could feel himself being nudged forward by it, but he stood firm, looking straight ahead. The traffic was typically heavy for the time of day and it was far too dangerous for him to attempt running across, especially when the lights were in the pay of his enemy.

Another minute passed and on the other side of the road Thomas noticed the crowd had started to part, like a bow wave from a ship, and there emerged a smart, besuited woman who came to a stop at the side of the signal box. Despite granting her pole position in such amiable fashion, the crowding people didn't afford her any particular attention. She wore a vintage style navy blue suit with wide-flared trousers and a plain black shirt with a large pointed collar. Her shoulder length blonde hair was unfastened but largely hidden by a floppy black sun hat with the image of a white deer head on the front. She smiled at Thomas as she placed her hand atop the signal box and suddenly the *Wait* sign changed to *Walk,* the little green figure illuminated, and the steady *beep beep beep* that tells pedestrians they have right of way began to sound.

"Lucy," said Thomas as he returned the smile, stepping into the road, "Lucy Cavendish."

Lucy raised a graceful hand and tipped her hat discreetly as they passed. When he reached the other side of the road he turned to see her again, elated to have encountered another College, but she had already vanished.

Thomas sprang up the curb and ran down Mill Lane until the long line of shiny black doors with their brass letterboxes and hexagonal door knobs came into view. He walked towards the building beneath the large elm tree, but stopped before it, looking for something on the ground.

"Now, when Nick brought me here on the Run I had to have a leaf from the elm tree on my person. Ah! Here we go." He bent down to pick up a dry yellow leaf from the path and tucked it into the top buttonhole of his coat. He then pushed open the door and entered the foyer that would conduct him, reluctantly, to the office of Mr T. Pyrone.

"Thomas! Hello again," came a familiar accent accompanied by a bouquet of incense. He lifted his head to see Petra, the helpful lady he encountered on his previous visit. She must have just left her office because she stood statuesque in the doorway, as if half-carved into the wall, as she turned to greet him.

"Oh hello!" he replied. "Wow, you've got a good memory remembering my name!"

"You are very polite Thomas, this I always remember." She smiled, "So, what task returns you to our secluded basin so soon?"

"Same task," said Thomas grimacing. "I have another Room Booking form to submit. Can't say I'm looking forward to it, although I do…" and from his coat pocket he pulled out the form along with its two photocopies and waved them in the air, "…have the duplicates this time!"

"Bravo Thomas, this will save you from unspeakable wrath for sure!" She laughed and Thomas couldn't help but laugh too; Petra had an infectious giggle that seemed to make the cavernous corridor just a little less sterile.

"I will take that for you." She held out her hand to take the forms.

"Oh no I couldn't, I don't want to put upon you."

"I am up and down these mountainous stairs all day long," she laughed. "I will take the papers, they are not boulders, so I do not mind the weight."

With a relieved laugh Thomas handed her the forms, "If you're absolutely sure then thank you again, very much. I really appreciate it."

"You are welcome." And she turned to enter her office, the scented air disappearing with her.

Thomas, overjoyed by this fortuitous turn of events, waited for the door to click shut then tip-toed past Petra's office and along the anaemic corridor to check no one else was in the foyer area.

All was deserted.

He walked back to the base of the wide stone staircase and took a couple of deep breaths.

"Now… remember what Nick said about entering this portal; tap the bottom step twice with my left foot."

Tap.

Tap.

"Keep my hands *off* the balustrade and walk in the centre of every other step."

He proceeded up the stairs, keeping his focus straight ahead so that he didn't stumble. As he reached the middle of the staircase, the stale, white painted walls morphed to the familiar grey of the monochrome world and Thomas revelled in the sight of it. Back in his own time, Petra reappeared in the office doorway.

"Thomas?" she called out, craning her neck up the staircase. "Strange, I thought I heard him going up the stairs." She shrugged and went back inside.

In grey time Thomas gave a victory jump on the small half landing.

"Yes!"

Then, placing his hand on the balustrade, he skipped down to the foyer, turning to look up the stairs when he reached the bottom. He recalled the first time he walked up that staircase, just a few days before, and the moment he thought he saw water on the steps. When on the King Street Run, Nick had explained that the water-like effect was time distortion and that by tapping his boot on the stair to remove a leaf, Thomas had inadvertently instigated the opening of the portal; there must have been another leaf stuck to his sole that went unnoticed. Had it not been for him putting his hand on the balustrade he might have passed through by accident. Thomas turned away with a sense of satisfaction and almost danced his way into the monochrome Mill Lane.

"Where are you?" He looked up and down the street as he mused upon the whereabouts of the gargoyle. As much as he didn't want to encounter the malevolent carving again, he knew that any information regarding its strengths, weaknesses, and general disposition could be critical for defeating it, and with the knowledge that he could at the very least outrun the creature, he was determined to find out more.

Thomas wandered around the streets, bereft of colour

but not of atmosphere. He looked in shop windows, stared up at rooftops, and listened for any tell-tale sign that his quarry might be close by. Had there been such a thing as a monochrome mouse and had it been stirring, Thomas would have heard it. But everything appeared orderly and quiet, the sound of his footsteps accompanied only by that peculiar distant cracking. After a long yet unproductive search, he meandered his way back through the city centre until he found himself walking through the entrance to the New Museums Site, a shrinking refugium for science-based buildings located between Pembroke and Corpus Christi.

Architecturally speaking the area is something of a pick-and-mix. There are several ranges of Victorian buildings in the Gothic revival style and a scattering of more utilitarian but still handsome yellow brick buildings from the 1930s, but like so many areas it suffers from an infestation of glass and concrete carbuncles from the 1960s onwards, including the old metallurgy tower where Thomas would – point 5C permitting – be booked to give his first supervisions the following week. He rounded the corner and as he passed the abandoned tower he looked up, rolling his eyes.

"Looks awful with or without colour," he mumbled.

To the untrained eye, the square into which Thomas had just turned was a lacklustre effort lined with 1960s buildings cosplaying as east Berlin. It looks the same to the trained eye. These particular buildings once housed examination rooms and lecture halls for the material sciences, but were now used as administrative offices. Thomas stared into their dull, dark windows, then paused for a moment to listen for any unusual noises, but all remained silent.

Despite an absence of good taste and purpose, the square has one redeeming feature, it contains one of the most useful student cut-throughs in Cambridge; a short, narrow path known as *Dead Man's Alley* that runs alongside the former materials science building. The alley, hopefully not about to live up to its name, opens out into a tiny courtyard at the back of one of the city's theatres, not far from the Market Square. This small area of black tarmac is encased by a tall, red brick wall and is predominantly used to store the industrial wheelie bins used by the theatre. More importantly for Thomas, the opening to the alleyway has a black iron gate which coincides with a portal and its secluded location made it the discreet choice to reunite with his own world at this busy time of day. However, just when his foray into grey time seemed to be drawing to an uneventful conclusion, he caught sight of something in the reflection of the metallurgy building.

He stopped and turned to face it.

The blue eyes! They were looking out from the glassy darkness of a third floor window, scowling directly at him. He swung around expecting to see the gargoyle forming behind him but only the brutalist buildings stared back. Thomas turned again, his eyes flicking one way and the other, skimming the buildings for the creature.

Still nothing.

All was quiet, until suddenly there was a hungry, desolate wail then, *WHOOOOOOSH!*

The gargoyle jumped down from the rooftop behind him, its enormous wings spread out to their full width, but doing little to mitigate the force of the impact as its large feet met with the concrete. It had been hiding, its eyes merely reflecting in the glass, waiting in ambush for the moment Thomas walked into the square and it could corner him. It landed in a crouched position, its muscle-bound arms stretched out to either side. The impact sent shockwaves through the ground, rattling windows and knocking Thomas down like a skittle. The gargoyle hauled itself to its feet, a mere 15 metres distant and immediately tramped towards him. Thomas tried desperately to scramble to his feet but every time he made an effort to stand the vibrations from the creature's footfall knocked him back over.

With its mammoth strides and Thomas being bounced around like a pea in a whistle, it didn't take long before the gargoyle was looming over him, staring straight down and forming two stony fists.

Thomas stared up in horror as the gargoyle brought down one of the stone cudgels. He fell to his knees and raised his hands over his head, waiting for the inevitable impact, his life flashing before his closed eyes; he wasn't too fussed by the first 18 years and the following five were something of a disappointment, but he felt a deep sense of injustice at being snuffed out in view of his academic achievements.

But nothing happened.

The film of his life had played out and the reel was still spinning as the colossal being emitted a sharp banshee-like cry.

Thomas opened his eyes.

The gargoyle was incandescent with rage and it soon became clear why: there was a sparkling blue light arching over the student, like an upturned glass bowl, creating a barrier between him and his would-be assassin. Thomas had no indication where the light had come from but under the circumstances he didn't greatly care. It was beautiful, a flickering blue shield cascading over him. The gargoyle raised a fist and Thomas flattened himself to the pavement, eyes scrunched tight and once more placing his hands over his head.

"Ffff…lippin' 'eck," he gasped to himself. "There was no mention of this in the application form."

Thud!

The gargoyle's fist collided with the top of the sparkling arch.

"By accepting this offer from the University of Cambridge you accept that you might be hammered flat by possessed architecture."

Thud!

The creature rained down another heavy hit upon the light, but it had no effect.

"What am I saying?" panted Thomas, momentarily putting his fear aside and looking up from between the cover of his hands. "It would have been in the small print."

Again the gargoyle pummelled the light, but it remained impenetrable. It was stalemate.

Thomas, gathering his senses, noticed how the ground beneath the shield did not shake as the gargoyle pounded furiously about him, and he slowly dragged himself to his feet. He reached out a hand and tentatively touched the light. It was soft and cool, and felt like running water but without being wet, and he was able to push his hand straight through. Emboldened, he looked around him, assessing his options and the distance to the portal.

Frustrated, the creature continued pacing around the dome of light and every time it completed a circuit it raised its head to the sky and let out a long, piercing scream. This chilling but reliably repetitive behaviour is just what Thomas needed to tip the odds in his favour.

The young man watched intently as the gargoyle once again circled his position and when it snapped its head back to let out another howl he seized the moment, sprinting through the blue light and towards the alleyway. He could feel the impact of the gargoyle's footsteps clambering behind him, but his modest head start kept him just a few strides ahead of the strongest shockwaves.

Thomas reached the gate that leads into Dead Man's Alley and without looking back, launched himself through in a flying jump, trusting to luck there was no one on the other side to crash into. He landed face-first on the black-sacked avalanche from an over-filled industrial bin. As lacking in elegance as his re-entry may have been, he had at least made it back to his own time in one, non-tenderised piece. He pushed himself up to rest on his forearms and his head dropped forward as he took a few deep breaths; it may not have been the freshest of air, but it was better than no air at all. Just.

Suddenly the thought struck him. The mechanism!

Thomas put breathing aside and quickly sat up, pulling the rucksack around to his chest. He unzipped the centre pocket and pulled out the metal tin. He then gently raised the lid, screwing up his forehead with trepidation as he peered under the top layer of padding.

"Oh! Thank goodness!" he exclaimed.

Thanks to his careful packing, the mechanism was unaffected by his adventures. In fact, it hadn't so much as shifted position.

"I'm a squirrel with a peanut," he laughed, his hand shaking as he tapped the top of the Christmas tin in relief. "Let's get you back to College."

He slid the box back into his rucksack and after giving his jeans and parka a quick brush down, marched off in the direction of King's, his head nearly bursting at the seams to tell the Colleges all that he had discovered.

Chapter 8: The Mediaeval Phase

It was a tough deliberation, but after much soul-searching Thomas concluded he had earned a sausage roll. The clincher was, when staring up at the gargoyle's enormous stone fist descending towards him, his stomach had rumbled. The thought of being pounded into oblivion was one thing, but accepting his fate on an empty stomach was quite another. The moment had pushed him impolitely close to his own mortality and this was one small indulgence he now felt wholly justified in claiming. In fact, to hell with the expense; Thomas bought himself *two* sausage rolls and ate both before stepping through the Gatehouse. As he finished the last succulent morsels, he screwed up the paper bag, crammed it into his coat pocket, then checked the time on his watch: 11:55am. He was ahead of schedule and with a smile of quiet self-congratulation, breezed into the Porter's Lodge.

"Good morning, and what another fine day it is," greeted James, standing behind the desk, hands folded neatly atop the counter.

"Morning James," returned Thomas. Not for the first time, the sound of his own voice surprised him. It was subdued and shaky. "I think I might have picked up a cold," he said meekly, excusing himself with a cough.

James responded with an understanding nod.

"Nice pot of hot tea upstairs. Nothing that can't cure."

"Thanks James, really appreciate it," rasped Thomas.

He grinned self-consciously and headed through the narrow doorway in the corner. When he reached the landing he could see Nick's study was open but no one was inside. He placed his rucksack on the desk and removed the old biscuit tin, carrying it to the mustard chair with the striped throw, whereupon he collapsed into what was left of its worn out comfort. With the tin on his lap and an arm dangling either side of the chair, he let his head fall back. He closed his eyes, desiring nothing more than the peace and quiet of the little room. The calm remained with him for at least ten minutes, after which he was roused by someone addressing him.

"Apologies for our tardiness, Thomas." It was Nick. He, John, and Trinity were seated in the other chairs. They must have phased into position because there had been no sound or movement prior to the arrival of Nick's voice.

"The proceedings of the extraordinary meeting have only recently concluded." He was in the process of tucking away his pocket watch.

"Gonville and Caius was there," added John, rolling his eyes. "Although with Magdalene in attendance they didn't hold the monopoly on obscure soliloquies."

"John!" rebuked Trinity.

"I mean, Pepys was all very well of a type," he carried on regardless, irreverently waving a hand about. "Plague and fire, yes yes, all jolly interesting from a raw historical perspective." He shook his head slowly side to side, "But by jove the chap was a tricky one."

John put his musings aside and with a look of approval, leant forward, firmly shaking Thomas by the hand.

"Good work, Raffles. Stout of heart and all that." He then lounged back comfortably into his chair.

"My heart is stout," laughed Thomas. "It's my legs that are easily scared. I feel a bit of an idiot."

"Thomas," began Trinity, "strength works a different way in different minds – the wise it enlightens and the fool it blinds." She paused, considering him sagely, "And a fool you are not." She leant sideways against the arm of the chair, placing a hand on the brass whistle as she did so. The subtle flash of blue light that Thomas had dismissed as a reflection the previous night appeared beneath her hand once more, but this time he observed how the object seemed to absorb the energy.

Before he could enquire after it, Nick leant forward to conclude the handshakes.

"Splendid work." He beamed with pride at the exhausted pile of Thomas – who by now had a half melted look about him – then threw a satisfied glance to the other Colleges at this gold standard of studentship.

Trinity smiled and poured the tea, offering the first cup to the weary grad.

"We know but *few* details of your morning's expedition," she said with a raised eyebrow that was trying to be displeased but couldn't quite manage it.

Retracting limbs and shaping himself into something approaching three dimensions, Thomas sat up to take the saucer.

"Thank you."

"You caused quite a stir prior to the meeting," she cast an eye to the others. "Early this morning, Nick requested Queens' presence at the museum."

"All credit to Thomas," insisted Nick, picking up his cup. "It was *his* suggestion to seal the Archive Room."

Clink.

Thomas nodded in appreciation but added, "Although when I left the museum I didn't *know* the Archive Room had been sealed. When the curator didn't walk me back to reception as we'd expected, I was worried the plan had been abandoned. I suppose I was hoping for some sort of confirmation and when it didn't come I suspected the worst."

He smiled, laughing at himself, "I'd never have taken the mechanism sight-seeing if I'd have known. I was expecting the curator to launch a manhunt for me."

Nick accepted the comment with a 'point well made' inclination of his head and continued, "And as for Queens', it was assistance provided with equal measures of discretion and efficacy."

"Quite so," agreed Trinity. She picked up the silver sugar tongs and dropped two lumps into her own cup before continuing. "Thomas, prior to the meeting Queens' trailed your journey back to College and was somewhat dismayed when she found herself following you back out again. After advising you at the bakery, she put out the word for those closest at hand to guide you to the portal at Sidney, that being the most expedient route for your return to College."

"They also thought it would remind dear coal-powered Sidney to get a shuffle on," added John.

"Queens'?" queried Thomas. "That was Queens' at the bakery? The elderly lady with the straw hat?"

"Yes," she confirmed.

"I can hardly thank her enough. I recognised Wolfson and Lucy straight away, but who was the gentleman in blue?"

"Robinson," replied John, already topping up his cup. "Nice chap, very progressive, and a thoroughly good egg." He rocked his head side to side. "But," he added in a quieter, more serious tone, "He *does* have a tendency to walk on the grass. Herschel knows I'm all for progress but that's borderline nihilism."

"Of course! Yes, Robinson. I can see it now. Impeccable timing."

"That's the fellow," said Trinity.

Rejuvenated by the warmth of the tea, Thomas straightened himself up in the chair, or at least, as straight as could be achieved against its hillocked surface.

"How much do you know about what happened while you were in the meeting?" he asked, pushing his shoulder against one particularly enthusiastic spring.

"We know you were successful in appropriating the stopco… the *mechanism*," replied Nick, now accepting a second cup as John made the rounds. "And we know from the Keepers there was an incident of not insignificant magnitude, but we remain woefully ill-informed as to the detail." He frowned, "Dash it, Thomas, the last we knew of your whereabouts was from Lucy who reported that she'd expedited your journey to Mill Lane, we had no reason to suspect you'd return to *our* time."

"Well," said Thomas, "if there's more tea on the go then make mine a double because I have *a lot* to tell you."

Thomas spent the next hour in animated narration, detailing every aspect of his misadventure, and the Colleges listened intently, without a single utterance or interruption, save to offer him another cup of tea. The first thing he established was that the tiny blue eyes he observed on the King Street Run did *not* belong to a tiny creature as Nick and John had assumed but rather, to the uncontrolled proliferation of time lice that had taken form as an enormous gargoyle. He then recounted how the appearance of the gargoyle morphed from opaque distortion to stony giant, its size and its features, its strength and its power. He explained how, because of attempting an ambush next to Dead Man's Alley, it appeared ignorant of practicalities, including student knowledge and the location of portals, and finally, he described the strange light that saved him from becoming as flat as one of the mushroom pancakes he so keenly devours every morning.

At this, John perked up, "That was my little welcome gift."

"What was?" frowned Thomas.

"Keeping you un-pancaked."

"You mean you made the light appear? How did you do that?"

"*You* made the light appear, Thomas," interjected Trinity. She then raised her tea cup to John in a subtle toast. "But John gave you the energy to do so."

"I don't follow. I didn't make the light appear. It was just there when I opened my eyes."

"You willed it there unconsciously, as a defence mechanism," explained John. "Hinc lucem et pocula sacra; it's more than just a motto, old boy. Light and tea."

Thomas furrowed his brow, trying to comprehend what he meant.

Nick turned his teacup in its saucer and fussed with the spoon. "It seems a little bad form on our part and for that I apologise unreservedly," he confessed. "But we couldn't inform you beforehand because we were undecided as to whether you would have reason to use it, and, well, we didn't wish to alarm you with extraneous variables."

"Extraneous," John smiled at Thomas with a look of

friendly camaraderie, "The most alarming of *all* the variables."

"Use *what*?" Thomas asked with complete bewilderment.

"All those times John slapped you on the back," said Trinity, her usually impenetrable expression had a vague look of embarrassment to it. "He wasn't being a childish irritation, although I appreciate why you, or indeed anyone else, may have thought that."

"Bit harsh," laughed John.

"He was giving you a little of his energy. In case you required it at some point. To protect yourself."

Thomas fell quiet, his memory running a stock check on all the occasions John had gone out of his way to impart a firm backslap.

"And those times when John doubled over? What was happening *there*?" he asked.

John shuffled in his chair as if reliving the experience, "The more energy one donates, the more the process acquires a short but strong backward momentum."

The full context of the morning was only now beginning to sink in and although Thomas' body felt like an empty husk, his mind was awash with both surprise and gratitude.

"Nick, that's what you meant when you said measures had been taken, isn't it?"

Nick nodded, also raising his tea cup appreciatively at John.

"I should have seen that coming," continued Thomas, shaking his head in slow appreciation. "I hardly know what to say. Thank you John. Thank you very much. I'd almost started to think you were being a bit public schoolboy-like with all the back-slapping – and in my defence it *did* happen a lot – but I guess not. Thank you. Thank you very much."

"Oh, don't make excuses for him Thomas," laughed Trinity. "If you'd spent the best part of 200 years listening to him quote Wordsworth as if no other poet had put quill to parchment, you'd know he really *is* quite insufferable."

"And waxing lyrical about nature being red in tooth and claw would be an improvement?" rebutted John.

"I am more than familiar with your oeuvre and I confirm that it would. Or you could try a little Byron. After all, you attire yourself like him."

There was a slim pause and Thomas was quick to interpose, "I prefer Rupert Brooke." He grinned, casually sipping his tea.

John and Trinity, unaccustomed to guest commentators, paused for a split second before the whole room erupted into laughter and for a few lighthearted moments all the sherry in the city could not have created a more congenial atmosphere. And that's *a lot* of sherry.

After a few seconds more, a smiling Nick reluctantly intervened, "My good friends." He held up his hands as a request for order. "I must return us to the matter at hand."

John and Trinity nodded, each one looking at the other as if they had won the exchange.

"I'm sure it's because they were founded so close together," jested Nick, gesturing with his eyes towards the others. "Please carry on, Thomas."

Thomas leant back in his chair, shaking his head in amusement, "Where did I get to?"

"You were about to elaborate upon the inadequacies of a plus-sized waterspout," clarified John, raising his cup and taking a deep drink.

"Oh yes. Well, there are two obvious flaws in the gargoyle's capabilities. One is that it's slow, it doesn't appear to be able to move its limbs efficiently at all, it's almost as if the left side of its body doesn't know what the right side is about to do. As I said before, I outran it with just my regular human speed, which means that as Colleges you'd be able to run circles around it."

"And the other flaw?" prompted Nick.

"Well, for all its size and apparent power, its wings appear to be more-or-less redundant, so I reckon it either has to walk to where it wants to go, which, given its inefficient locomotion seems indiscreet and therefore unlikely, or it has to dematerialise then re-form when it gets there, which, based upon my experience at Sidney, would take at least a few minutes. If I were casting the runes, I'd predict it to remain non-corporeal in order to conceal itself and move about at speed."

The Colleges nodded in agreement.

"What leads you to suggest its wings are vestigial?" enquired John.

Thomas returned his cup and saucer to the tray.

Clink.

"Two reasons." He leant back, crossing his legs and resting an elbow on the arm of the chair. "First of all, when I ran away from it at Sidney —"

"Tactically retreated," corrected Nick.

"Ha! Yes, when I *tactically retreated* at Sidney it didn't fly after me. Why not? I should have been easy prey if it were flying. Second, when it jumped down from the building behind me at the New Museums Site, at the most generous its wings acted more like a parachute to cushion the impact. It didn't *fly* down from the building."

Nick nodded thoughtfully at Thomas as he pulled the watch from his waistcoat pocket, "Three o'clock."

He then looked around the room, an expression of confidence illuminating his face, "My friends, we have much to discuss. May I suggest we ask James if he would very much mind fixing another pot of his most excellent hot tea, and, running with the good Dr. Watt's metaphor, see if we might construct a plunger with which to unburden ourselves from this stony blockage?"

"Agreed," replied John and Trinity in unison.

That impish grin returned to Thomas' face, "Maybe we could give it a room booking form to submit."

The Colleges and Thomas remained fixed to their tattered armchairs, lost to time as they talked and planned, drank tea and planned some more until eventually, late afternoon light gave way to early evening dusk. Tea cups empty and their minds full, everyone sat back in their chairs, imbued with the kind of energy that goes hand-in-hand with a new idea.

"Thomas, you're comfortable with what has been asked of you?" enquired Nick.

"Yes," he replied adamantly. "Meet the other Colleges on Midsummer Common at 11:30pm tonight. Wait for Michael to be called then deliver him the mechanism."

"Good good. In order to maintain the link with Michael, the Colleges cannot break the circle and so your expedient delivery of the stop… the mechanism, is imperative. It's also of vital importance that you don't arrive at the Common earlier than 11:30pm —"

"Because you, John, and Trinity are going to set up a diversion at St. Edward's church to draw out the gargoyle." Thomas finished Nick's sentence with a smile.

"Precisely, and not only do we wish to avoid testing the friability of your physical composition, but it would be to our advantage to take this confrontation to the church. Keep the gargoyles concentrated in one discreet area."

"Quite so," concurred Trinity. "From what we can ascertain the gargoyles are little more than stones waiting to be thrown, a delay tactic to prevent us reaching Midsummer Common in time."

"And if we don't confront them on *our* terms then we risk being followed and jeopardising the call," continued Nick.

"And if we don't make the call…" began John, but no one wished to finish the sentence and the study fell silent.

Nick looked around the room with enough gravity to keep a solar system in check.

"Never before have we fought the gargoyles en masse." He sighed thoughtfully, "We would be ill-advised to expect their behaviour to tally with any of nature's creatures. The wolf pack cooperates and the flock overwhelms but, unlike our grey foes, they are not driven by malice or by cruelty. Negative thoughts are unprincipled and selfish; towards us, towards each other. Let us keep in mind that their greatest strength is their most obvious weakness; brute force and numbers. If we keep focused, this should be relatively straightforward."

"Nick old boy," grinned John, "Are you trying to convince *us*, or yourself?"

"Both," smiled Nick. "What's that catchy saying about rainbows and rain?"

"That a rainbow is produced by light reflecting from water droplets at an angle of 42 degrees?"

"42," nodded Nick, "Yes, John, that's the one."

Thomas consulted his watch, "It's eight-thirty."

Nick rose from his chair, followed by John and Trinity. They stood looking at each other for a moment, each with an air of firm resolve.

"Thomas," began Nick, "I must reiterate how important it is for you to remain out of harm's way. This creature cannot be reasoned with. I should prefer that you leave College at 11:15pm and use the Gibbs Building portal, that way you won't have to leave College grounds in *this* time. Does this sound acceptable?"

"It does, but are you sure there's nothing else I can do to help?"

"Absolutely nothing, you've already done and are doing so much. We need you to keep the mechanism safe and bring it to Midsummer Common on time."

"Understood," replied Thomas.

"Shall we?" said Nick, looking at John and Trinity and gesturing towards the doorway.

Thomas stood up. "Oh!" he exclaimed. "One question that's been itching in my mind; the more I've thought about it, the more I realised that in *this* time the blue eyes only seem to appear in glass, at least, that's the only way I've observed them. Is there a reason for that?"

Nick answered in his usual matter-of-fact way, "Glass is a medium of clarity. Look from the inside of any window in our time and it reveals what is happening on the other side in *this* time."

Thomas smiled with an impressed nod, "That's a neat trick."

Nick added, "You may have noticed me in the bakery window a few days back and —"

"And in the window in the Student Facilitation Building," finished Thomas. "Yes!"

Then with a sudden realisation he added, "And in the window at Bodley's?"

"Yes," confirmed Nick. "I was tracking your movements as you approached the river. I apologise for the clandestine measures but it was imperative to ensure our first meeting."

Thomas reflected on the occasions, smiling, "I really did think I might be going full uncle Erasmus for a few moments back then."

Nick raised an eyebrow then proceeded to the doorway, stopping briefly to tap the glass of the little barometer. The measuring hand dropped to 'Stormy' and he nodded in quiet understanding.

"Good luck," said Thomas. "Really… Good luck." His earnest tone betrayed his concern and Nick returned to the room, placing a hand on Thomas' shoulder. Thinking that he was about to say something moving or profound, Thomas was slightly taken aback by what came next.

"If I should lie, think only this of me…" Nick paused to straighten his tie and there came to his face a look of mild embarrassment, "…it was done with the finest of intentions but nevertheless I must apologise for having Rangemen lace the vegan options in our fine canteen – which ordinarily offers a gastronomical feast for the discerning palette – with copious levels of salt."

Thomas stared back blankly and couldn't help but smack his lips as if retrospectively detecting a briny twang to the pancakes.

"Regardless of the short chronological distance, travelling back and forth in time is a strain upon your body's natural level of sodium chloride," clarified Nick. "But summoning a shield – I refer to your encounter with the time lice gargoyle – even more so. Thus, you were in need of precautionary dosing."

Nick patted Thomas on the shoulder and leaving the young man standing in front of his chair, the Colleges departed. Thomas turned just in time to see the three of them phase out of sight, Nick raising a hand of farewell as they disappeared.

"See you soon," said Thomas with an uneasy sense of foreboding. "And take care."

Despite his concerns, Thomas consoled himself with a single, fragile thought; if there was one thing his short acquaintance with the Colleges had shown him, it's that they were not adept at expressing urgency; it is not a word they freely engaged with owing to its devil-may-care relationship with thinking things through. But that they were aware of the stakes could not be gainsaid, and Thomas had no doubt they would confront those stakes in the only way they knew how; after tea and with decorum.

Thomas stared through the doorway and into the empty hall for a few short moments more, then slumped into the chair, burying his head in his hands as he landed.

"Flippin' 'eck."

Chapter 9: The Post-Mediaeval Phase

Peas Hill is a stumpy little road, but what it lacks in size it makes up for in character; a charming nook of the city centre encased by a pleasing, almost organic architectural ensemble that ranges from sixteenth to twentieth century. Here, the east face of St. Edward's church stares fondly at the Guildhall, from which it is separated by a wide pedestrian walkway. The latter, an imposing edifice in the neo-Georgian style, is very much the Admiral of the Fleet. Out of its five tall storeys, several first floor windows display striking bronze balconies, the ground floor is ashlar stonework and its upper brickwork is laid in bond, Flemish bond. Nothing was stirring, but it was soon to be a little shaken.

It was at the other end of this diminutive street that three figures phased into grey time. Nick, John, and Trinity walked towards the church and came to a stop, side by side, outside the east front, looking up at the roof.

"45," announced John.

"That's 15 each," replied Trinity. "The dust will linger for days."

"And what about the main blockage?" asked John. "Can we be certain it will disgrace us with its presence if we start smiting its minions?"

"Without doubt," answered Nick. "If negative thinking has one defining feature, it's misplaced confidence." He angled his neck to peer down the passage. "And I'll wager it has some form of sentry, so if you see one sneaking off, leave it be. We want to secure the attention of its master." He took a deep breath and continued in an almost incensed tone.

"I am *not* prepared to risk my Chapel being carved up into a series of upswanning… upturning… upwhatever offices…" He stopped abruptly, his own words having taken him by surprise.

Trinity turned to him, intrigued, "Extraordinary. A

silversmith I am not but I recognise the hallmark of Thomas.”

Nick raised his eyebrows, “Yes. I-I rather think it is.” He nodded slowly, as if a thought were slotting into place. There was something suddenly different about him. Not in his appearance or how he moved, but a renewed strength behind the eyes, and it looked suspiciously like candour.

“Well, this was unexpected,” he said, tilting his head to one side as if admiring a new outfit. “It suits me!”

He stood thinking for a few moments then with another deep breath, promptly reunited his attention with the church, unclipping his baton; the unspoken signal that John and Trinity should take up positions at either side of the church. For several minutes the three figures stood silhouetted against the moss green glow of a nearby street light, staring up at the crouching gargoyles, each one searching for signs of movement, but all remained still. For now.

“Oxford is empty,” quipped John, examining the stone faces, “All the devils are here.”

Trinity unclipped the whistle and held it in her hand, considering the object as if expecting it to talk.

“Nick?” she shook her head in mild frustration as she returned it to the clip. “I shall require a little longer. I’ve expelled more energy than I’ve been able to save, but it’s almost there.”

“Understood,” replied Nick. “Regardless, it is first necessary to shake the tree and see what flies up.” He tightened his grip on the baton then cast it to the floor. The sound of metal striking metal echoed around the quiet street and it jumped into the air, extended, for him to catch. John and Trinity followed suit. With a glance either side to check his colleagues were ready, Nick hurled the weapon at one of the gargoyles and it exploded upon impact, raining debris onto the churchyard.

There was no going back now.

The baton curved in mid-air and returned to Nick’s hand. Without hesitation, John and Trinity did the same, each aiming for stationary gargoyles which subsequently exploded upon impact. But these were to be the only free shots. With an eye opening here and a clawed foot shuffling there, the gargoyles began to wake, fixing their eyes upon those whose inverted names were inscribed into the fabric of the church, carvings that identified them for attack as clearly as if they were Old Harry himself.

"Be swift my friends, time is slipping." Nick took aim again while Trinity's and John's batons returned to them.

Crassssh

One more fell victim to Nick's baton, prompting at least a dozen to rise from the north side of the building, swarming into the sky and circling the bell tower before coming to rest on the high Guildhall roof behind them. Another cluster took shelter behind the steeply pitched roofs to the west and yet more behind the scattered chimney pots, from where they now peeked around the sides like snipers. Just as Nick had predicted, the smallest gargoyle, the beady-eyed critter from atop the church entrance, retreated into the darkness of St. Edward's Passage, off to find its master.

Trinity spied a gargoyle peering out from between two yew trees in the churchyard and she cast her baton through the narrow gap, striking it between the eyes and cleaving it like a log. The two fragments fell apart with a muted *thud* onto the soil. Another of the creatures – watched with great interest by its peers – made an opportunistic dive from the far end of the road and Trinity ducked out of its way, waiting for her baton to curve around the church. John swiped the gargoyle as it flew past, sending it hurtling into the Market Square. The plump ball skipped along the wide, open space like a stone skimming the surface of a pond, bouncing several times before tumbling onto the slabs and shattering.

Two further gargoyles launched themselves from the Guildhall roof, their wings arched tightly behind their backs, while two more swooped from the bell tower. With a quick glance either way, Nick took aim at the largest of the pair approaching from the church, knocking it sideways into the other and smashing both into the wall of the Arts Theatre. A small mound of bricks crumbled to the street, leaving behind a jagged gash with a plume of rising dust. It looked as if someone had taken a bite out of a hot pie.

At the same time, John and Trinity had hurled their batons at the gargoyles descending from the Guildhall roof; John's met its target but the other abruptly re-routed to avoid Trinity's, and it continued plummeting towards her. Unperturbed, she remained in place, staring calmly at the descending grey mass; when it approached touching distance she dived out of the way, rolling towards the Guildhall then standing to catch her baton upon its return. The gargoyle could do little else than meet the road at full speed, smashing upon impact and leaving a small crater in the tarmac.

"Messy, Trin," spluttered John, waving the dust out of his face as he scrutinised the eaves of one of the smaller, timber framed buildings. "We're not trying to wipe out the dinosaurs."

"If you could throw in a straight line, that would be jolly helpful," she rejoined, scanning the sky for more incomers.

"Stay alert," interrupted Nick, "We have their attention."

With that, he moved into the centre of the pedestrian walkway, closely flanked by John and Trinity. Laying his baton on the ground he removed his pocket watch, holding it before him. A purple glow emanated from his palm, flickering around the base like gas flames beneath a saucepan.

The three looked about them, waiting with uneasy vigilance.

As intended, the gargoyles had not only recovered from the surprise wake-up call but seemed emboldened by the Colleges' apparent withdrawal and it wasn't long before there was a wholesale charge towards them; four dropped from the Guildhall roof, several swooped in from the Market Square, a small flurry arose from the bell tower and shot forwards, and from further away, more raised their heads and joined the flow. Nick looked up, his face a picture of concentration as he gauged the speed and trajectory of each stony missile. With his finger hovering above the left winding crown he waited for the first gargoyle to arrive within three metres before pressing it. A purple and white light erupted from the dial, surging like a geyser into the air before cascading over the Colleges, encasing them like a gift shop snow globe. The vanguard had no time to take evasive action and one after the other they slammed into the light with a series of thunderous bangs.

The gargoyles shattered on contact, each one reduced to a pile of crumbling masonry that slid down the curve of the arc, a series of dusty mushroom clouds rising from the impact points. Those further back in the advance veered off at a steep incline, avoiding the light altogether and surging up to various hiding points where they now sat on their haunches, mingled within the niches and cavities of the surrounding buildings.

Trinity turned in a circle, assessing the retreating figures, "They may have charged together but you are quite correct Nick, they're not working in concert."

"And they're as sharp as the corners on a farthing," added John, his baton resting casually over his shoulder.

"Negative thoughts," replied Nick paying particular attention to the church roof. "Insidious and imprudent, they lack the capacity for cooperation. *That* at least is in our favour."

There was a sound of a high voltage short circuit and the light from the pocket watch flickered then blinked from existence. While Nick returned the time piece to his pocket and stooped to reclaim his baton, Trinity unclipped the brass whistle from her tunic, held it firmly in her hand and closed her eyes. When she opened them again she smiled at Nick.

"Ready." And she gently blew upon the whistle.

Two large gargoyles atop the church watched intently as she did this, perhaps expecting the object to emit a high pitch noise that would render them immobile, but as they waited, their necks craned forward in anticipation, no sound emerged and they exchanged a fleeting, almost conceited look, the kind of look that suggested they considered the Colleges were running out of tricks.

However, had those gargoyles been a part of Trinity College, and had they, at the moment the whistle was blown, been inside its monochrome walls, then they would have felt the whistle's silent echo vibrate around every court and along every corridor, its whisper twisting around every staircase and through every window, as the College announced a call to arms.

— ∞ —

In Thomas' time, two Fellows of Trinity College – gowns blowing in the wind – were walking around Great Court, their arms animated and their voices loud in discussion. Out of the blue, as if an invisible force had passed through them, their conversation ceased and they stopped walking. All of the lights in Trinity College went out. Even the lamp posts lighting the path of the Court fell into darkness, as if their energy had been momentarily siphoned elsewhere. The two figures stood motionless, scanning the stillness. Suddenly, a bright, navy-tinted light shone out from the window to the right of the Great Gate. It remained lit for a few seconds before going out and reappearing in the adjacent window. That in turn remained visible for a few seconds before similarly disappearing and illuminating the next window. This chain reaction continued around the Court, up and down the various sized buildings, even along each of the stained glass windows of the Chapel, maintaining a rough horizontal line until the first window to the right of the Great Gate was alight again. It was as if someone was running into each room and turning the lights on then off so that only one window were lit at a time. But this was not a student prank; the lights began to flick on and off with increasing speed until from inside the Court it produced the effect of standing inside a spinning zoetrope, the flash of light moving faster and faster, around and around the top line of the buildings until suddenly it stopped. A few, silent seconds later the College returned to normal. The lamp posts buzzed back on and the two Fellows could see they shared the same uneasy expression. Slowly, they walked on, not uttering another word.

— ∞ —

Back in the Trinity College of grey time there were signs of movement in the Chapel, where the sound of rustling masonry tumbled gently out of the Victorian porch. Inside the ante-chapel are six life-size marble statues of noted alumni: As one enters, Isaac Newton – clasping a prism – is to the left, opposite the organ screen, then Thomas Babington Macaulay, Alfred Tennyson, and William Whewell on one side, Francis Bacon and Isaac Barrow on the other. Each of the statues began to shudder, as if shivering from the cold, then they fell still for a short moment before shuddering once more. At first, their movements were subtle and staggered, made up of a series of staccato jolts of the kind a robot might make, small jerks of the head and twitches on the eyelids, but as their efforts continued the motion became more fluid. Eventually, with a sound of fracturing stone, the statue of Isaac Newton opened its eyes and surveyed the room, then one by one the other statues turned their heads towards it. The figures began to lift their feet, the sinews of mortar binding them to their bases stubbornly stretching, long strands of masonry extending like tendons until finally snapping with a puff of marble dust as the statues jumped from their pedestals and walked out of the Chapel.

In the heart of the Wren Library, a statue of George Gordon Byron, book in one hand and pencil in the other, stood from its pensive pose and it too strode out, leaving nothing but a light cloud of dust falling through the air above its now empty base.

In a niche above the door of Trinity's Great Gate, the eyes of Henry VIII's statue blinked into life. With an orb and cross in one hand and a sword in the other, it jumped from the wall, landing on the ground with a loud *thud* before walking into the road, its sword hand raised in the air. As the statues began to filter their way through College grounds, Isaac Newton led them towards the Market Square.

Back in the throng at Peas Hill, John and Trinity threw themselves to the ground as gargoyles swooped at them from all directions. Nick, attempting to curb their movement, threw his baton down once more and its edges took on a luminous purple hue. He raised it above his head, spinning the javelin between his fingers until it rotated like the blades of a helicopter and when it was turning so fast that its shape began to blur, he launched it towards a pack of gargoyles hovering over the church. The baton whirled amidst them and in the confusion dispatched three with ease, showering fragments of stone over the churchyard before arcing back to Nick's side.

By now, John and Trinity had stood up and each was engaged with a gargoyle that had boldly landed on the pavement before them.

"Above you!" John warned; two further gargoyles had locked onto Trinity's position, one soaring from the Guildhall roof and another from the Market Square. Without delay she propelled her baton downwards and it sprang back with a dark blue glow. Before the gargoyle on the pavement could work out what was happening, she leapt onto its back, using it as a platform to jump at least three metres into the air and pitching her baton sideways at the gargoyle approaching from the Square. It struck the creature in the chest, carving its torso into thick shards and as the weapon rebounded sideways it met with the second incomer, releasing a flurry of fast-falling grey confetti. Trinity caught the baton as it hurtled back towards her and, grasping it firmly with both hands, spun it vertically before thrusting it into the neck of the foe beneath her. The stone collapsed to blackened dust.

John meanwhile appeared nearly over-powered by his own pointy-eared adversary. He was lying on his back, holding the creature at bay with his baton wedged under its chin. Given the jeopardy of the situation he was inappropriately yet characteristically blasé, clutching the baton with just one hand, while his other struggled towards his waistcoat.

"John!" said Trinity curtly. "Refrain from cuddling that gargoyle and cut along." To give him cover she manoeuvred to tackle another of the creatures sweeping in stealthily from the far side of the church.

"Just…a…little…further," mumbled John, jostled from one side to the other, fighting the toothy sculpture.

"Ah! Gotcha!" he exclaimed as he tore a single brass button from the front of his waistcoat. He quickly slid the item between his lips then placed his other hand on the baton in order to better repel the creature. Once its otherwise impressively sharp teeth were at a more agreeable distance, John spat the button towards it. By good fortune, although John would later maintain it was virtuoso aiming, it landed flat on the creature's ridged forehead. The gargoyle looked up, its dopey expression betraying a moment of confusion before reigniting its attempts to remove John's face. What the creature could not see was that the button had fixed itself in place, and upon doing this it had taken on the same grey colour and texture as its host. The button dissolved into the ashen surface, leaving behind what looked like a tattooed outline on its forehead. All of a sudden, four grey tendrils shot out from the button holes, wrapping around the gargoyle's head like the arms of a giant leviathan encompassing an unsuspecting ship. The creature leapt back, clawing at the strange vines but to no avail; they wound denser and stronger around its head, moving rapidly to engulf its entire body, pulling tighter and tighter until finally it imploded under the pressure. The tendrils disappeared instantly and all that was left of the gargoyle was a small hill of black rubble where it had previously stood.

"Buttons are great," said John looking at the dusty pile with satisfaction. "They do things up."

— ∞ —

Thomas paced the length of his study like a caged cockatoo, stopping now and again to peer out the leaded windows in the same fashion. He cupped his hands around his eyes, forehead leaning against the glass, and bobbed his head one way and the other as he scoured the darkness. He had no idea what he was looking for, but his mind was a heady cocktail of worry and anxiety and the compulsion to look for it gave him some minor purpose while waiting for 11:15pm.

He had long since visited the Hall for dinner. Mrs Willendorf also worked the occasional nightshift as waiting staff and upon seeing Thomas' hungry expression, let him slip in during that night's Formal; thoughtfully, she had pulled the tray racks to one side so that Thomas, with his less than formal jeans and parka, could sit obscured behind them at a small table usually reserved for stacking water pitchers.

Vegan carbonara with chickpeas and aubergine bacon, served with a side of fried rice and root vegetables. It was delicious and ordinarily the fine spread wouldn't have stood a chance against Thomas' healthy appetite, but on this occasion he ate uncharacteristically slow, so slow in fact that he was almost saddened to note the distinct lack of salt in the meal. For a moment he smiled, thinking how sheepish Nick had been when confessing Rangemen's culinary meddling. The memory unlatched other lighthearted thoughts, such as John's flippant remarks and how he and Trinity quarrelled like siblings. He also reflected on the incredible sights and insights shared with him; the Colleges, the portals, Nick's bicycle, and of course Kára, but just when he found himself in good humour, his mind wandered to what might be taking place in grey time, after dark in the playing fields, to what danger the Colleges might be facing as he sat there eating his carbonara, and he could eat no more. Even a seductive berry compote was initially returned untouched to the tray collection point before he made a run back to grab it – after all, it did look *very* good.

In the knowledge that he had several hours to burn before leaving for Midsummer Common, Thomas forced himself, for as long as possible, to remain in Hall looking for distractions, but the last straw arrived in the form of Richard Wilberforce-Owen.

"Hello Thomas, good day?" enquired Richard groggily as he plonked down opposite at the little table. He deposited his wine glass with a heavy *clunk,* the deep red contents sloshing over the rim and spattering the table top. In his current frame of mind Thomas was not remotely interested in holding a conversation with anyone, least of all Wilberforce-Owen, inebriated or otherwise. Although with Richard, it was sometimes tricky to tell the difference.

Thomas had to break the glass on his emergency enthusiasm to respond, "Yes, yes, just reading mostly. How's the thesis? Almost finished?"

Wilberforce-Owen had such dark, dense eyes that they looked as if they might collapse into black holes at any moment and they stared back at Thomas, utterly perplexed, as if neither he or his giddiest aunt had a clue what he was referring to, but then he cottoned on.

"Oh *that.* Oh you know, I'll cobble the last bit together over the weekend. Should have submitted last week but had an absolute blinder of a Formal at Clare. Threw up in the rose bushes. Bloody fantastic night."

Wilberforce-Owen, with an intellect as fierce as a cheetah's roar, was a final year PhD student carrying out research into an episode of cathedral history, specifically the Palaeolithic foundations of Norwich Cathedral. The only snag to his otherwise superlative proposal was that in a show of unity with every other cathedral on Earth, Norwich cathedral does not possess Palaeolithic foundations and the idea that it would is so utterly absurd that it turned out to be just the kind of blue sky thinking, synergy, taking it forward, boiling with the potatoes, you can't polish a coprolite but you can roll it in ochre idea that the SIS:TUM's approved research boards were looking for. A more credible proposal would have been to carry out a topographical survey of Narnia, but Wilberforce-Owen had pitched the idea with such élan that he acquired more grants than he knew what to do with.

Suave, sophisticated, and born knowing which way around the dinner table to pass the port, Wilberforce-Owen was the kind of man who walked into a room like he was walking onto a stage; his long, confident stride accompanied by the heavy, purposeful footsteps of good breeding. He knew the menu of every restaurant within a 20 mile radius of the city and his role as representative for the Committee Board for Removing Unnecessary Tautology in Communication Transmissions left very little time, or requirement, for academic pursuits.

"You still planning to stay on for the PhD?" slurred Wilberforce-Owen.

"Yes, yes, hopefully. I guess it all depends on how my Master's pans out." Thomas nodded, disinclined to size up his chances right now.

"Don't worry about it. Just look at what your Supervisor does, tell them how fantastic you think their work is and how inspired you are by them and they'll accept any old rope."

Wilberforce-Owen had a knack of unintentionally pressing every one of Thomas' buttons, one after the other, like a child in a lift. What was worse on this occasion is that Thomas couldn't work out if he was annoyed about the vacuous nature of the comment, surprised that Wilberforce-Owen was trying to help – albeit in a way that was anathema to Thomas – or whether deep down he suspected there might be an element of truth to it. Ultimately, he didn't want the ball to be under *any* of those cups.

Thomas smiled as best he could and his next comment was intended to provide a natural end to the conversation, whereupon he expected Wilberforce-Owen to politely laugh and take his leave. But as tends to be the case with well-laid plans, this one was feeling contrary.

"I'm hoping to make William Stukeley proud," said Thomas, preparing to depart.

"Who? Is that your Supervisor?"

Thomas frowned. "William Stukeley?" he repeated.

Blank stare.

"The father of archaeology?"

Blank stare.

"Eighteenth century. The first person to systematically investigate Stonehenge and Avebury?"

"You really take all this seriously don't you?" laughed Wilberforce-Owen, picking up his wine glass and rotating the last of the contents.

The question rankled.

Thomas took a deep breath, "I'm studying archaeology because I think it's important and I'd like to make a contribution to the field. So, yes, I suppose I do."

Wilberforce-Owen stared back in what almost looked like wonder, as if he had chanced upon a faun.

"You know?" continued Thomas, "Contribute towards a shared global knowledge of mankind's place in time and space?"

Wilberforce-Owen had no interest in answering. "Did you go to the Formal at St. Ed's last night?" he asked instead.

Thomas rose from his seat, smiling politely, "I'm very sorry Richard, really, but I have an appointment to keep." Wilberforce-Owen, none the wiser, raised his glass in acknowledgment and stood to lean upon the little table, swaying as he did so.

Thomas picked up his tray, deposited it at the collection point, and aside from running back to swipe the berry compote, wandered straight back to Bodley's Court, bolstering his spirits by admiring the architecture. As soon as he reached his rooms he placed his rucksack gently on the sofa and toppled rigidly, like a felled tree, onto the adjacent cushion, his feet bouncing up like thick roots. He craned his neck to his wrist: 9.45pm.

"Arrrrgh an hour and a half? I've got another *hour and a half*!" he exclaimed in frustration. He sat pinching his lip, staring thoughtfully at the wall and tapping his fingers on the cushion.

— ∞ —

The Colleges surveyed the roofscape; composed and alert, their eyes scrutinising every crevice and cornice. The remaining gargoyles were learning, albeit slowly, from the mistakes of their predecessors and becoming sneakier as a result.

"Why aren't they attacking?" said John, his baton held before him, poised for the next strafing, "What are they waiting for?"

They were hiding amidst the rooftops, prowling the dark places, looking down but not swooping upon the Colleges, and now and again their wrinkled, stony faces would look towards the empty Market Square. Suddenly a loud *BANG BANG* vibrated around them, shaking the ground and sending the gargoyles into the air like a flock of startled birds.

"I rather think our blockage has arrived," said Nick.

The smaller combatants circled over the buildings, their wings pushing down great pulses of air. The Colleges turned to face the large, open Square and the imposing shape of the giant gargoyle lumbered out of the shadows, its beady-eyed lackey nestled on its shoulder like a pirate's parrot.

"Would you like to take this one, Trin?" joked John, looking up at the Brobdingnagian nightmare with its grimacing, fanged mouth hanging half open.

The three moved to stand at the edge of the Square, the wide space permitting some much needed room to manoeuvre.

"May I suggest two of us dispatch the outstanding church gargoyles whilst the other keeps this one suitably occupied until… the appropriate time," proposed Nick.

"Agreed."

"Affirmative, old boy."

In an instant, John dashed into the Square, the giant gargoyle howling as he passed, unable to move quick enough to pound him with one of its wrecking ball fists. John easily outran the creature, becoming little more than a blur as he circled the beast before coming to a halt at the other side of the Square.

"Come on old chap, do make an effort to keep up," he shouted to the gargoyle, which now lolloped clumsily towards him.

With the monolith distracted, Nick and Trinity turned their attention to what was left of the church gargoyles. They both tapped their batons on the ground whereupon they sprung back with illuminated edges. Nick spun his above his head and Trinity turned hers at her side. They scanned the formation of gargoyles overhead then, exchanging a glance, simultaneously cast the rotating weapons upwards. The two spun in opposite directions, Nick's felling two over the church and Trinity's slicing through three directly above them. The resulting debris crashed about them, layering their coats with dust. The spinning batons stilled then curved back to Earth, each finding the hand of its owner.

"I make that about a dozen of these wilier ones to go, including the little perisher on our truculent friend's shoulder," summarised Nick.

"Agreed."

John was darting one way and the other around the giant gargoyle, which intermittently threw back its head and screeched with frustration. For the time being, given that he could not deploy his baton accurately on the move, all John could do was to keep running in circles, stopping now and again to recapture the stone behemoth's attention. This was a highly effective strategy for five, perhaps ten minutes, during which time Nick and Trinity were able to further thin the gargoyle ranks, but suddenly the creature emitted a different howl, a long shrill scream, whereupon its remaining courtiers ceased their attacks on Nick and Trinity and soared to their master. A further piercing call and the collective swarm turned their attention to John, now stationary and waving his arms at the giant, oblivious to his newly attained bullseye status. Seeing the danger, Nick and Trinity ran towards him, blurring from the creature's view. One gargoyle had already begun a dive, plunging towards John with claws outstretched and wings folded tightly behind its back. They could see the potentially tragic scene unravelling before them but were powerless to alert John any faster.

Just as the gargoyle was about to reach him, the sharp points of its claws almost within grasping distance of his back, a sword shot out from the darkness, boring a hole through the creature's centre. The impact sent the gargoyle hurtling to the ground beside John, knocking him backwards as it bumped his shoulder, and showering him in debris. John, now lying on the ground, stunned but unhurt, raised his head to look in the direction from which the sword was cast. Nick and Trinity arrived at his side just in time to see the stone feet of Henry VIII and the rest of the unlikely cavalry emerge from the gloom. The statues bowed their heads to Trinity and she inclined hers.

"Better late than out of sync, ay Trin?" said John as Trinity pulled him to his feet. He patted some of the dust from his shoulders and gave a nod to the statues that now walked either side of him, fanning out around the Market Square. Only the statue of Byron paused, regarding John with an air of suspicion. It gave his outfit a cursory glance up and down then, placing a hand on either side of its own lapels, marched away with a clear sense of superiority.

Before anyone had a chance to collect Henry VIII's sword from the mass of blackening rubble, the small, round figure of the beady-eyed gargoyle swept across the pavement, skimming the air close to the ground and scooping up the weapon into its little clawed hands, waving it in the air triumphantly as it returned to perch on its master's shoulder.

The giant gargoyle began stomping about, attempting to crush the statues as they moved along the pavement, but it was indecisive and easily distracted, unable to decide on a course of action, and so even the comparatively slow moving marble figures were able to outmanoeuvre it with well-judged strides. The Byron statue patrolled the west side of the Square, its cool, white eyes flowing in crests and troughs along the rooftops, smooth as a light wave – no doubt something fashionably ultraviolet – twisting the marble pencil thoughtfully between its fingers. A gargoyle swooped in from the direction of the church and Byron seized its chance, throwing the pencil upwards as the creature passed overhead. The point passed into its neck, throwing it off course and introducing it face-first to a shop front on the north side. The impact demolished the lower half the building, sending a cloud of dust and rubble into the air and garnering the attention of the giant which now lumbered towards the statue, fists clenched in readiness.

At the centre of the Market Square, Henry VIII took the orb in one hand and pulled the cross from the top as one would the pin of a hand grenade. It then paused for a few seconds, looking up at the remaining gargoyles, waiting for several to accumulate before propelling the orb into their midst. With a crack of air and a sudden flash that resembled cloud-to-cloud lightning, the orb exploded, tearing two apart. The giant snapped its head around but was first intent on smashing the tiny statue in its focus. It brought down its fist upon the pavement, missing Byron by little more than a metre.

Macaulay, carrying a book, and Tennyson, carrying a pipe, were jointly tracking another gargoyle flying in circles close to the ground, its movements as predictable as a fly buzzing around a ceiling light. Both statues retreated into the shadows and the next time the gargoyle approached, Tennyson blew a thick plume of smoke into the air, while Macaulay thrust the book into its flight path. The plan was effective but sadly the impact was so great that the statue of Macaulay also shattered, leaving behind a mound of powdered marble glistening like fresh snow amidst the gargoyle coal.

Back on the western front, the giant had only just

realised that it had missed its intended target. It lifted up its feet, one then the other, gormlessly looking beneath before searching the pavement and finally spying Byron on its way to join Tennyson. The creature lurched forward, raised its fist and smashed it sideways into the preoccupied figure, swiping it off its feet and unintentionally, though to the giant's delight, driving it into Tennyson. The two figures broke apart and Byron's marble head rolled along the path, eventually coming to rest beside John's feet, a self-satisfied look on its face.

"Do *not* say it." Trinity scowled at John, predicting his response. "Do *NOT* say it."

John looked down to the marble head, then to the shattered remains of Tennyson, the gargoyle still mindlessly pounding the ground around it.

"Two bards with one stone," he grinned.

While the statues worked to eliminate the remaining church gargoyles, the Colleges had gathered on the south side, exchanging hurried words whilst intermittently blurring out of view to distract the erratic boulder and keep it within the confines of the Square.

John had taken one such circuit and stopped on the east side to distract it from bringing down a fist upon Newton when, out of the corner of his eye, he spotted a gargoyle hurtling towards him; he dropped to the ground just in time to avoid a collision but the limestone lump vectored sharply and before he could regain his composure, it was on top of him. The gargoyle's sharp fangs pushed gradually closer as he struggled to position his baton low enough under its thick neck to more effectively push it back. Just when John had started to entertain the thought that his aggressor might actually succeed in taking a bite, the smooth pearly face of William Whewell's statue appeared behind its shoulder. Like a seasoned wrestler, Whewell locked its hands around the centre of the gargoyle's torso and prised it away, stumbling backwards against a lamppost with the sedimentary mass wriggling in its arms. Despite contending with the sheer power of the creature's bulky frame, Whewell's statue did not waver in its vice-like hold. Seeing no other viable option, the marble figure gave a calm nod of farewell to John, then jumped into the air. It wasn't the kind of jump that allows a swift get away, nor the kind to navigate an obstacle. Rather, it was the kind of jump intended to provide enough force to smash both itself and the gargoyle onto the concrete pavement. The statue achieved its goal; the two figures hit the ground with a resounding *smash*, the black and white remains scattering like an upturned game of chess.

— ∞ —

Tired of pacing his rooms, Thomas sank into his desk chair and rested an elbow on the table. He had tried reading, but all he could do was look at the words. He had tried listening to the little radio that sat on one of his bookshelves, but it was just noise. He twisted his wrist to check the time: 9.45pm.

"What?!" he exclaimed, straightening up like a sentinel meerkat. He tapped the dial then held it up to his ear. It had stopped working.

"What? No! No!" he pleaded as he tapped it again, gaping in dismay as the second hand wavered to and fro before reluctantly picking up where it had left off.

"You cheap load of cr…" Thomas stared into the air before him then suddenly roused himself.

"The time, what's the time!" He stood motionless, looking around the room. Then he remembered his alarm clock and nearly tripped over his own feet scrambling to the bedroom. He slammed into the bed as he picked up the little clock and stared into its face: 11:23pm. "It has to be wrong. It *has* to be wrong." He dropped the clock on the bed and ran back to the study, unzipped the bag and pulled out his old mobile phone: 11:23pm. The bedside clock, had it a sense of pride, would have felt rather smug by this point.

Thomas threw the phone back into his rucksack, slung it over his shoulder and bolted out of his bedroom, leaving the door to bang shut behind him. He hared out of Bodley's Court and similarly left the gate to go to town with its kinetic energy. *Bang,* rebound, *bang,* was all he could hear as he raced over the bridge towards The Backs. This was, of course, the opposite direction to the Gibbs Building, the location of the portal that Nick had instructed him to use and which was itself a half-hearted stone's throw from Thomas' rooms, but the young man had decided he needed a leg up to reach Midsummer Common on time. He ran with all his might until reaching the little stone mounting steps and pounced upon them with as much agility as his glorified monkey physique would permit. The familiar colours of his world drained away and Thomas landed in grey time atop a sleeping Kára.

"Yes!" he exclaimed, patting the side of her head. Kára turned her eyes upwards, looking with surprise at the unexpected visit.

"I'm sorry to come back so soon," he declared. "Really, really sorry but I need your help. My watch stopped working and I have to get to Midsummer Common by 11:30 to help the Colleges. Please Kára, will you take me there?"

With a snort, the gallant horse pulled herself up to full height, shook her head as if casting all thought of sleep away and after pawing the ground in preparation, stampeded into the night.

— ∞ —

Throughout the melee, the giant had lurched indecisively about, confused by the Colleges' swift movements and the strange stone beings that so infuriated it. It was angry and without conscience, and as its blue eyes scanned the street below, it clasped its fists tightly, bringing one down on the unsuspecting statue of Isaac Barrow and hammering it to dust.

"The throat!" shouted Nick.

"Got it," replied Trinity. "John?" she chimed again to make sure he had heard, "The throat."

"Affirmative old girl."

Another gargoyle plunged towards John and he crouched down to avoid its outstretched talons.

"Why me?!" he exclaimed with irritation, "Why do they keep swooping at *me*?"

"Well, you *are* very annoying," Trinity smiled.

"Where are you? Where are you?" said John under his breath, looking for where the diving gargoyle had gone.

"John!" shouted Trinity. "The roof behind you!" She rested her baton on her shoulder, ready to assist.

John turned to see the gargoyle staring down at him, sneering with the kind of scorn that only angry stone can muster. He felt the weight of his baton and raised it at an angle.

"Don't fail me now old friend."

With that, he sent the metallic bar darting upwards. Having had ample time to witness the College take aim and seeing the projectile heading towards it, the creature slouched lazily to one side, assuming it had outmanoeuvred the attack with ease and watching with disdain as the missile whizzed past its head. The time lice had leached such hubris into the gargoyles that even if one of its brethren had urged it to look behind, it would not have heeded. Little did it know but John had intended for the baton to make its strike on the way *back*, thus avoiding the debris raining down on himself. The baton curved through the air behind the gargoyle and passed straight through its dumpy torso. So efficient was the hit that John caught the weapon before the first remnants of coal-black debris hailed into the gutter.

John looked with pride to his left at Nick and to his right at Trinity.

"And *that*, dear colleagues, is how we do things on *my* part of the river."

"A triumph of luck over skill," dismissed Trinity, smiling.

The Colleges and remaining statues began to spread out around the giant gargoyle. Trinity nodded to the statue of Newton and it took a step forward. The creature screeched in vexation, raised a fist in the air and brought it crashing down on the nearest statue, Francis Bacon.

Trinity closed her eyes in dismay. "He was my first Keeper," she said sadly, unable to watch the gratuitous pounding.

"Trinity?" Nick shouted, looking up at the gargoyle then to the statue of Newton. "It's time!"

She nodded and the statue took another step forward, holding the prism in both hands and raising it above its head.

"Excuse me!" shouted Trinity, trying to draw the gargoyle's attention in Newton's direction. "I say up there, hello!"

The creature swung around, its nose wrinkling as it snarled, looking down and preparing to pummel the offending statue. Before the gargoyle could bring down its bludgeon, a small white light appeared at the top of the prism. At first it was just a speck, a tiny ember, but very quickly it grew brighter and more intense before suddenly splitting into its constituent colours and blasting a rainbow towards the giant. Recoiling, it raised its ridged hands to cover its eyes, taking a step backwards that inadvertently led to it crushing Henry VIII. The creature wailed at the sky, the vibration echoing around the Square. It stomped the ground with its chunky, clawed feet and its head shuddered as if trying to shake the colours from its eyes.

"One chance. Make it count," shouted Nick. "GO!"

Nick, John, and Trinity thrust their batons towards the ground for extra charge and each acquired a radiant shimmer. They then thrust them down again and the colours intensified, pulsing with a low electrical hum. The creature lowered its hands to reveal an expression contorted with anger, but its eyes were no longer blue; they were the same stony grey as the rest of its face and it seemed blinded by the loss. As if suspecting what was about to happen, the small, beady-eyed minion abandoned its master's shoulder and slunk away to the Guildhall roof, from where it now observed the scene with low, deprecating growls.

Simultaneously the Colleges threw their batons at the giant's throat and it let out an agonised howl as each one met its target, the luminosity growing on contact; purple and white for Nick; dark blue, light blue and red for John; dark blue, yellow and red for Trinity. As the strength of the lights increased, the Colleges withdrew to the relative safety of Peas Hill, watching as the beast stomped and writhed, smacking its fists into the ground and along the face of the buildings.

Knowing it had served its purpose, the statue of Isaac Newton quietly withdrew through the Crescent at the opposite side of the Square, returning to its marble plinth in the ante-chapel of Trinity College.

The giant screeched, unable to navigate and increasingly weak as the lights intensified. Dazzled by the sun-like glare, the beady-eyed gargoyle had long since averted its gaze, but the Colleges looked on unaffected. The colours gradually blended together, producing a shining blue collar that grew in power until it released a bolt of piercing white light that shot into the sky, ripping the giant's head from its neck and carrying it high into the air. The body tottered sidewards, falling into the north face of the Guildhall, the facade crumbling in a twisted heap of bronze balconies and former Flemish bond brickwork. As the bolt of light dissipated into the clouds, the gargoyle's head plummeted to terra firma, smashing into the centre of the Market Square with all the ferocity of a modest-sized meteorite. Unlike the church gargoyles, the giant's physical form did not turn black and crumble, rather, upon contact with the ground it exploded into thousands, millions of tiny, transient dark sparks that spread out just a short distance before vanishing.

— ∞ —

In Thomas' time there was no *visible* sign of the skirmish that had taken place just a few seconds out of sync in that very location. Indeed, in Thomas' time the Square was relatively peaceful. The market stalls were closed up for the night, stacked in neat rows along the centre, and two mobile food vans were catering to the city's nightlife, a queue of a dozen or more people stretching out from each counter. Groups of club-goers walked around the pavement, chatting and laughing, and the only thing cutting through the air was the smell of fried onions. In the monochrome world, the gargoyle's head had hit the ground with such an immense impact that echoes were sent both backward and forward in time, and the people of the Market Square felt a tremor run through the ground.

"Must be an earthquake," said one voice.

"We don't get earthquakes *here* do we?" asked another.

"Probably just a heavy lorry in the next street," responded one more.

Then the people turned their attention back to the menu boards and the moment was forgotten.

— ∞ —

Kára galloped at full and focused velocity, darting around curves, over lawns, and speeding along streets, her long, graceful strides making short work of the twists and turns that led to Midsummer Common. Thomas, his eyes more accomplished than ever at picking out details from the blur, recognised the phone box in King Street and the sight filled him with renewed optimism. They barrelled across the roundabout at the top of the street, over the path, and finally Kára's hooves touched down on the soft grass of Midsummer Common. She began to slow and Thomas could see a gathering of people ahead of him. It was the Colleges – or, at least, 28 of them – standing in an enormous circle that encompassed the majority of the Common. As Kára slowed to a trot, he could hear the chatter of voices as the Colleges shouted to each other in brisk conversations. He dismounted the translucent horse and patted her gently on the neck.

"Thank you. Thank you very much. You'll have to let me know, or tell one of the Colleges if I can bring you something to say thank you. Maybe some sugar lumps? Or an apple?"

She snorted.

"Maybe I should just promise not to make anymore unannounced visits," he smiled, stroking her soft face.

Kára shook her head, turned, and cantered back over the Common. For a few moments Thomas watched her gallop away, then walked around the circle until he arrived at the northernmost point, and to the College he intuitively identified as Peterhouse.

— ∞ —

Nick, John, and Trinity walked side by side, back into the Market Square. Dusty, and with a torn coat tail here and there, but otherwise unscathed.

"How are we?" asked Nick.

"Cock-a-hoop old boy, positively cock-a-hoop," replied John, dusting himself down.

They were preparing to make a cursory search of the rubble; if any gargoyles survived then the Colleges wanted to be certain they were no longer under the negative influence of the accumulated time lice. Nick pulled out his pocket watch, which now only possessed a single winding crown, and stared at the dial, "11:31pm."

John and Trinity nodded in acknowledgment. Time frame considered, it was judicious to err on the side of caution and the three set about their task with appropriate zeal. It was the only kind of zeal they knew.

The black stone of smashed gargoyles had nearly all dissolved, with just a few oil slicks scattered here and there, slowly evaporating. As they searched the wreckage it soon became clear that only one creature had survived the final explosion and remained roughly intact; the diminutive gargoyle that had so brazenly stolen Henry VIII's sword. When the giant crashed into the Guildhall, this lone escapee was the first thing to tumble and that is precisely what saved it from being crushed; no sooner had it been blown from its perch and glided to the ground than an L-shaped section of moulding from one of the tall, narrow windows fell over it, providing an impromptu shelter. Now, after pulling itself free of the rubble, it sat with a forlorn look upon its face, turning one way then the other as if running a diagnostic test. But it was not without damage; the lower quarter of its left wing had been shattered and it now terminated in an uneven, jagged edge.

The confused creature scrambled upright onto its four stumpy legs, small pieces of stone rolling down the concrete mound as it did so, each sending up a little plume of dust as it disturbed the rubble. The creature's wings moved ever so slowly. The sound of smooth, sliding concrete that usually accompanies a gargoyle's beating wings was instead staggered and slow. Noting its disorientation, the Colleges were satisfied that the giant's influence over the gargoyles of St. Edward's church was untethered.

Trinity walked purposefully towards the debris. She had no intention of harming the creature but instinctively it started into the air, still brandishing the short sword in its long, human-like fingers. Its take-off was understandably awkward, like that of a particularly well-fed wood pigeon. Indeed, the injury proved such an impediment that it could only lift itself as high as the second floor of the Guildhall and even then it flew at a slight angle, looking as if it were struggling to keep airborne. Regardless, the creature flapped onwards, edging back to its rightful place atop the entrance to St. Edward's church.

"Go home. Rest. And recover little fellow," said Trinity under her breath as she watched its dumpy shape limp away. She then turned to locate the position of her companions, walking into the surreal green light that fanned its way into the Market Square from one of the few remaining lampposts.

Nick and John stood in the middle of the Square. The sound of small pieces of rubble falling from the battered buildings had all but ceased and the once thick blanket of dust had settled to a smoky mire around their ankles. John's body was angled towards Nick as if in conversation, but his head was turned towards Trinity.

Nick had just returned the baton to his belt, his hand still on the brass clip and he too was looking towards her.

Seemingly, something had caught their collective attention mid-discussion.

Trinity stared back, tilting her head quizzically. After such a rumpus one may be excused for expecting their countenance to betray notions of victory or – if not wishing to be too showy about things – mild triumph, but Nick and John did not register so much as clement relief. Rather, they were anguished, and for a split second, for the first time in her near 500 years of existence, Trinity felt the cold, unpleasant rush of confusion.

What Trinity could not have known, what she could not have seen as she walked from the mound of rubble, was that in an act of hapless discard, in an attempt to gain more height, the last gargoyle had thrown the sword of Henry VIII's statue to the ground behind it. The creature had not aimed for Trinity, it was simply chance that the sword fell through the air, over just the right distance and at just the right angle, to pierce through her back and come to a stop protruding through her chest.

Chapter 10: The Modern Phase

Slowly lowering her head, Trinity studied the dull stone blade jutting out before her. With a furrowed brow, almost in disbelief, she lifted a hand to its cold surface. Already there was a dark blue patch around the wound, signalling the onset of decay. A few knocks from a malevolent gargoyle is one thing, but being run through with a sword from one's own College has its own, very particular consequences.

"Inconvenient," she whispered, raising her eyes as Nick and John ran forwards.

"Trinity!"

"Trin!"

Nick arrived at her side, threading his arm through hers for support. John had pulled a pewter button from his waistcoat as he ran and now held it carefully between thumb and forefinger. He knelt down to better examine the sword, then gently placed the little disc on its tip. The button jumped into the air, no higher than a mis-fired tiddlywink and landed flat on the surface. No sooner had it sunk into the stone than grey tendrils shot out from its centre and into the blade, winding around the length of the sword, along the section that passed through Trinity's torso, and all the way to the hilt. Within seconds, the weapon turned navy blue and crumbled.

"Can you walk?" asked Nick. Trinity was weak and the three instinctively knew the decay could not be stopped. It would spread outwards from the injury, growing darker and deeper, until eventually she would be consumed.

"It's barely a scratch," she replied defiantly.

Raising his head in the direction of King's, Nick gave a short, sharp whistle. For anyone in the other time who may have been in the vicinity of the Gibbs Building at that moment, so expeditious was the bicycle's response that they may have detected the faint, inexplicable sound of rattling metal echoing around Front Court as it swept out of the arch, across the lawn and rocketed through the grey time Gatehouse. Buttressing maintained, Nick reached his other hand into his waistcoat pocket and removed the fob watch. Its shiny brass surface glinted under the light from the lamppost and pressing the winding crown, its cover flicked open: "11:56pm."

"Plenty of time," responded John. "In fact, we could stop off for a spot of tea before the main show if you like, Trin." He smiled, trying to raise her spirits.

Within a moment there came a rattle, a screech and a faint smell of burning rubber, as the Royal Sunbeam appeared around the corner of Peas Hill, careering into the Market Square as if fitted with a steam turbine. It came to an abrupt stop at Nick's side and he helped steady Trinity as she climbed side saddle onto the seat, both hands gripping the centre of the handlebars then resting her head upon them.

"Please board the vehicle," said Nick, gesturing John to the back of the bicycle. He promptly took up position, standing upon two protruding metal plates either side of the back wheel.

Nick placed a foot onto the left pedal, his other held out to the side and reaching past Trinity, took hold of the handlebars.

"Ready?"

"Yes, yes," she responded hurriedly, struggling to lift her head.

"Midsummer Common," Nick instructed the bicycle. Looking down at the rapid spread of the wound he tapped the handle bars with encouragement, "Make it fast old girl."

The bicycle gave a rattle, then a shake. Despite its three College cargo it rose effortlessly off the ground, no more than a few centimetres, and turned in mid-air until it faced in the direction of the Common whereupon it trailed off like a comet, a tail of bright white energy flowing behind it.

— ∞ —

The night air on Midsummer Common was chilly but not unseasonably cold and the sky was uncluttered by clouds. Thomas had complied with Nick's instruction to remain beside Peterhouse but he was filled with equal measures of impatience, optimism, and impending doom. He had already adjusted his wristwatch to the correct hour and repeatedly held it to his ear to check it was still breathing. Once again he pulled up his sleeve and the illuminated dial shone back, soothing his brow with cool blue light: 11:57pm. He dropped his wrist like a sledgehammer, placed his other hand on his forehead as if warding off a migraine, and began scanning the Common for the missing Colleges.

"They'll be here. Don't fret," chirped Peter, calmly puffing on his pipe, the smoke meandering around him in forms that closely resembled algebraic formulae. Also in compliance with Nick's instructions, Thomas stood outside of the Collegiate circle; Peter would be the last to call and Michaelhouse would likely orientate the gatehouse to face that final voice – Thomas, therefore, could walk directly inside. He turned in the direction of the roundabout, looking for any sign of Nick, John, and Trinity, but all remained frustratingly still.

"We're going to start the call," announced Peter.

"Can we do that without Nick and the others?" panicked Thomas, conscious that Trinity would be the first of the missing Colleges to call.

"Oh yes, don't worry, Trinity will be here before it's her turn and by deuce, we have to start now or we won't finish by midnight."

Peter clapped twice to capture everyone's attention and once all was quiet and the Colleges each faced the circle, he nodded to Robinson, signalling that he should commence. The young College did not delay.

"*Robinson!*" he affirmed towards the circle, followed with a raised voice thereafter by each College in ascending age.

"*Clare Hall!*"

"*Lucy Cavendish!*"

Thomas felt a warm rush pass over him, as if the very air was being pulled into the circle.

— ∞ —

As the bicycle turned sharply into another street, its wheels flickered with specks of white energy, tiny flames flying from the spokes like the ephemeral light of a handheld sparkler.

— ∞ —

"Wolfson!"
  "Darwin!"
  "Churchill!"
Thomas held his face in his hands. "Please, *please* come on!" he begged the night as the call progressed.
  "Murray Edwards!"
  "St. Edmund's!"
By this point, a thin funnel of air had started to rotate at the centre of the circle. Outside of the boundary Thomas held up a hand, attempting to feel the effect of the motion, but there was nothing. Indeed, outside of the circle, grey time was as still as it ever was. Except for the very clear sound of its movement, the wind was entirely contained within the area demarcated by the Colleges. The call continued, each voice adding to the strength of the spinning air.
  "Hughes Hall!"
  "Selwyn!"
  "Newnham!"

— ∞ —

The Royal Sunbeam charged up King Street, its wheels turning faster and with more sense of purpose than they had ever turned before. Past the telephone box, over the roundabout, wheels sparking all the way.

— ∞ —

"Fitzwilliam!"
  "Girton!"

The thin funnel of air had developed into something more substantial, a wispy vortex that more closely resembled a dust devil, and as each College called it became slightly wider, taller, and spun with more energy.

"Downing!"

"Homerton!"

The call ticked on, retracing the years, stepping through the grooves of the metaphorical stone steps, each name winding back their collective history just a little further.

"Sidney Sussex!"

Just as Thomas was about to roll up his sleeve to hurl another insult at his cheap wristwatch, the sound of the Royal Sunbeam clattered into earshot and he looked up to see the bicycle speeding across the green. It came to an abrupt halt at Trinity's space in the circle, faint swirls of smoke rising from its frame and a few residual white sparks dripping like condensation from its tyres. Nick and John immediately jumped off and helped Trinity to stand. Thomas stared in horror at the sight of her wound and was about to run towards them when Peter put a hand on his shoulder.

"Thomas, your solicitude is to your eternal credit, but please remain where you are."

The daunted student gaped helplessly towards the trio. Nick raised a hand in salutation and Thomas, glancing back to Trinity, did the same. Once she was standing Nick and John were reluctant to leave but she was insistent.

"Go! Be quick!"

John occupied the space in the circle next to Trinity, and although some wide distance apart he kept a concerned eye upon her. She was unsteady and holding one arm around her centre, but she stood straight and in line with the others. The dark blue decay had spread as far as her shoulders and it was clear she did not have much energy remaining.

"Emmanuel!"

By now, the dust devil had grown so strong that

Colleges were calling their names with a shout in order to be heard over the increasingly turbulent wind, and with each call the formation grew wider and more energetic. Spinning like a top, faster and faster, an unseen hand powering it on.

"Trinity!"

A new energy entered the maelstrom. It began jolting backwards and forwards, tracing a series of large geometric shapes in the soft ground.

"St. John's!"

At the sound of John's voice the force began moving around the perimeter of the circle, brushing close to the face of each College and leaving a shallow trench in its wake. Unlike the other Colleges, gazes anchored to the inner turmoil of the circle, John shared his attention with Trinity; powerless to assist but determined she would not suffer alone, smiling to her with as much comradeship as he could muster. Trinity responded with the kind of expression that was half thankful and half chiding him for not focusing on the task at hand.

"Jesus!"

"St. Catharine's!"

The dust devil had grown into something so large and so powerful that it approximated a tornado; a long, wild funnel stretching into the night sky with ferocious speed and energy, carving the circular ditch deeper into the ground until there was a clearly defined henge.

"Queens'!"

Once again it moved wildly about, scoring shapes of various sizes and at different locations, each movement creating more pronounced furrows. Outside of the circle Thomas stood in perfect calm and he watched the proceedings unfold with both fascination and disquiet. The Colleges were shouting louder, competing with the increased power of the tempest.

"King's!"

With Nick's call the storm accumulated so much extra depth that it now resembled a supercell, a raging wall of thick, rotating clouds that filled the entire circle. The flat base was flanked either side with puffy grey-white clouds that undulated skywards to a giant overshooting top that resembled a frothy head of beer. Thomas could no longer see the full circle, his vision obscured by the dense mass. For the same reason, Nick could no longer see Trinity but as she stood, wavering in place, a single white petal fell from the sky and landed on her hand. She did her best not to smile, but stood all the firmer nonetheless.

"Christ's!"

"Magdalene!"

"Corpus Christi!"

"Trinity Hall!"

Thomas knelt down and removed the old biscuit tin from his rucksack. He then dropped the bag and stood behind and to the side of Peter, clutching the box so tightly that the rosy tips of his fingers turned alabaster.

"Gonville and Caius!"

"Pembroke!"

"Clare!"

Thomas held his breath.

"Peterhouse."

Peter did not shout his name, rather, he spoke it gently, but the word resonated around the Common with such force that it appeared to collide with the supercell, sending a bolt of light from the base all the way to the top. The energy then fell back to Earth and crashed about like lightning inside the funnel, flashing in one place then another, lighting up the dense interior for brief moments before a flare appeared elsewhere.

The Colleges were unmoving, undaunted, looking always towards the centre of the storm. Thomas gawked at the spectacle, clutching ever tighter to the small box. The giant cumulus clouds started to rise, the lightning still pulsing within them, but underneath it was revealed to be clear and calm. At the centre of the circle he observed what looked like the tip of a tower poking through the grass and the higher the clouds rose, the further the tower emerged. It wasn't tearing through the soil like one would expect with the exhumation of a large object, rather, it was akin to a hologram, albeit one that was very well defined. Thomas blinked hard; as the clouds ascended, the clearer it became that there was not only a tower rising from the ground, but the tips of other buildings too, including turrets and parapets, a cloister, and a three sided court lined with broad arches. These were the earthworks carved out by the storm.

"Michaelhouse!" declared Thomas in quiet awe.

The clouds continued to retreat, pulling Michaelhouse from the depths of time, until eventually the entire College stood within the giant earthwork. Before his very eyes, the buildings slowly changed from spectral translucence to solid brick and mortar. Humble in size but elegant in style, Michaelhouse stood before the astounded Thomas. Dominated by thick stone walls and large traceried windows, the College had a controlled grandeur, and not simply because it had risen out of the ground; it was an architectural lesson in the beauty of the Decorated Style.

As the last of the clouds dissipated, an encouraging nod from Peter prompted Thomas forward and he took a step inside the circle, initially hesitant at what might occur. When all appeared safe, he ventured slowly along a narrow path that led to the Gatehouse, its large wooden door set within two enormous stone pillars. The face of the door was dotted with lines of hand-forged iron nails and two long, sturdy hinges reached almost to its centre. He held the box firmly in his left hand and with the other took hold of the large, round knocker, tapping it down on the metal plate beneath. The resulting sound boomed around the circle.

Baaaaaaaaaang

Baaaaaaaaaang

He let go of the iron ring and stood stock-still, listening intently for any trace of movement within the building.

Shuffle

Shuffle

His ears pricked at what sounded like a pair of loose-fitting slippers approaching the entrance and before his mind could race ahead thinking who or what might be wearing them, the large door creaked ajar and he was confronted by an elderly gentleman. Atop his head was a dark blue smoking cap embroidered with fine, delicate flowers and a plush gold tassel at the centre that draped to one side.

"What trouble have they got themselves into now?" He rolled his eyes.

A warm orange light crept out of the doorway, illuminating the man. He was shorter than Thomas, around 1.6 metres in height. His smoking cap was complemented by similarly embroidered slippers – who had already introduced themselves – and a pair of wide navy trousers could be seen beneath the thick hem of a long and luxurious dressing gown. Heavily quilted and silky in appearance, the flamboyant robe had a paisley decoration in shades of dark blue, red, gold and white. It gave him a theatrical, slightly druidical appearance.

Thomas was momentarily lost for words.

"Come on, come on, get in," said the man, pulling back the door and waving Thomas inside. "The quicker you move, the quicker I can get back to my work."

The elderly man stood aside and as Thomas walked into the Gatehouse the door fell shut behind him. It was a small but welcoming area with a classic stone floor and a simple, solid construction that Thomas found incredibly charming. On the opposite wall was another large gate which he assumed must lead into a courtyard. The warm orange light emanated from the bouncy flames of two torches held in metal sconces on the west wall, and set into fine linear moulding across from those was a smaller wooden door. It was to this entryway that the man beckoned him.

"Come through, come through. Excuse the mess, I wasn't expecting visitors so take me as you find me."

Thomas stepped up the low threshold and his mouth dropped open as he entered the chamber. It was the size of a large, stately drawing room. On the far wall was a small cast iron fireplace with a roaring fire and a marble hearth that curved out in a graceful semi circle. Although narrow, the surround was beautifully constructed. There was a line of art nouveau tiles on either side of the grate decorated with green heart-shaped leaves on winding, linear stalks and the hood was adorned with delicate leafy tendrils. The mantelpiece was similarly narrow, but it accommodated an array of carefully placed clutter that Thomas couldn't quite make out from the tangled shadows.

To one side of the fireplace sat a large wingback chair with an upturned book on the arm, and at the centre of the room, its surface covered in metal springs, levers, boxes, pendulums and other small paraphernalia, was a large wooden desk with square chunky legs. But the feature that had made Thomas' mouth fall open was the clocks. Every centimetre of every wall, and the one long shelf that ran around it, was occupied by clocks: banjo clocks, skeleton clocks, anniversary clocks, cuckoo clocks, wall and mantel clocks of every age and every style ticking and tocking inside the tiny room, and every one displayed a different time. Even the space behind the door was occupied, for there stood a tall, mahogany grandfather clock, like a guard on sentry duty. The face was as handsome as a clock face could feasibly be; black Roman numerals on a crisp white background, autumnal scenes between delicately hand painted spandrels, separate second and calendar dials set vertically either side, and two discrete winding holes for time and strike, staring out like eyes.

"My dad would *love* this!" was the only thing Thomas could say as he took in the time soaked atmosphere. The man, who had pottered over to the fire to reposition a log with the poker, turned with a smile.

"Likes clocks, your father?"

"Oh yes!" replied Thomas, scanning the room, his eyes greedy with wonder and suddenly feeling entirely in his element. "I sometimes used to help him repair them. Nothing too difficult because I was just learning, or trying to at least."

"Do tell, do tell," said the man, suddenly amenable as he placed his hands on his hips and gave the young man his undivided attention.

"It was silly really, you'll think it ridiculously easy compared with what you probably do, but the first one I repaired was a granddaughter clock, 1930s, so not terribly old as these things go but it was beautifully carved, ornate pillars on each side."

"Oak?" asked the man.

"No, mahogany. Which isn't my favourite when it comes to clocks..." Thomas edged towards the grandfather clock, marvelling at the craftsmanship, "...I think oak has a superior finish, but this particular one was terribly good quality, very intricate carving."

Thomas felt so comfortable in the room and so happy with the question that for a few moments he quite forgot himself, and the whole time he spoke his eyes were rummaging about the walls admiringly. "Anyway, it was a common problem; it hadn't been oiled for years and so the workings were rubbing together. All I had to do was take the mechanism apart, clean it – which took *forever* because it was absolutely filthy and I didn't have proper brushes so I had to cut down cotton buds to different sizes – then I put it back together, oiled it, and it worked like a charm."

"Oh well done Thomas, well done. Smartly improvised."

"Ah, it was nothing, anyone could have done it," he shrugged, his eyes still applauding the array of time pieces.

The elderly man, satisfied with the cut of his visitor's jib, shuffled forward with his hand held out.

"How do you do."

"You have the advantage of me," said Thomas, shaking his hand. "Would I be correct in thinking that you're Michael?"

"Yes indeed I am, yes indeed."

Michael walked back to the fireplace and picked up something from amidst the shadows on the mantelpiece.

He tucked the object under his arm, carrying it to the desk at the centre of the room and waved the student over as he set it down. Thomas placed the old biscuit tin on the surface next to it then picked up the item.

"An Enfield clock case?" he queried, examining the small oak shell with its domed top. It measured around 30cm in width, the same in height, but was empty; faceless and without the life of inner workings.

"Indeed it is, but very soon it will become a temporary home for that stopcock you've brought me," said Michael, gesturing to the biscuit tin. "Tell me. What *have* they done this time?"

Before Thomas could answer, Michael continued, "Or should I say, what *haven't* they done this time?"

"Who?"

"The Colleges! The Colleges! Academically brilliant? Yes. Not half bad. But only horses should wear blinkers!" Agitated, Michael fussed about the desk, picking up pieces of rolled up paper and oily rags, pendulums and springs, and holding them up to his eye and placing them back down again. "Then they come to me! Interrupting my work with the problems *they* have nurtured into existence." He stopped abruptly and looked up at Thomas.

"No offence to *you* dear boy, no offence directed at you *at all*."

"None taken, really."

Michael busied himself walking around the desk, his nimble fingers ferreting through a small pile of springs.

"Ah! Here we are," he said, picking up a brass winding key and holding it aloft as he headed back to the empty clock case.

"What did you mean when you asked what the College's *hadn't* done?" asked Thomas.

"They don't want to be troubled by anything that doesn't tickle their immediate fancy. It's always been the same. And no good will come of it. Did you take a good look at my buildings before you entered?"

"Yes I did, very beautiful. I've always been an admirer

of Mediaeval buildings that can be relatively square and simple but yet the quality of the craftsmanship bestows an elegance on even the most utilitarian."

"Indeed! Well observed! Though I *had* started to add a few nice curves around the windows, but nevertheless, not an ivory tower in sight!"

Thomas paused for a moment, "It's funny, but the whole square and simple approach doesn't work as you get closer to my time. Trust me, you're better off not seeing the depths to which concrete can plummet a town."

Michael nodded sympathetically, patting Thomas consolingly on the back. He then picked up the biscuit tin and moved it to a space on the desk in front of him.

"Of course, I *did* want to do more with the place but I was young, impetuous, and pre-occupied with acquiring land. It seemed important at the time and I suppose I got so wrapped up in it that I lost myself. Too late." He looked down at the table with a haunted melancholy.

"I would have at least liked a few more turrets with twirly bits," he added remorsefully.

"Well, I think your buildings are tremendous as they are," said Thomas, trying his best to cheer him up. "And I have *never* seen such an incredible collection of time pieces. No other College has something like this!"

"And nor will they dear boy. Nor will they. They spend too much energy wasting time for it to be on their side. Looking away from your problems does *not* make them disappear." He sighed. "I should know."

Michael turned his attention to the biscuit tin and gently removed the lid. He peeled apart the padding and nodded at the oxidised gear.

"Let's get you into place," he said to the fragment as he opened the back of the former clock. Plucking the Antikythera mechanism from its soft bed, he gave it a cursory look over before sliding it onto a single rod inside the case. He then closed the little wooden door and turned the chimera to face them, the mechanism now staring out from where a clock face would usually be.

Michael rested his hands on his hips and stared down at the object as if waiting.

"Hmm, why aren't you working?" he said to himself. "Oh! Of course! You need a drink don't you!" And he tottered back to the mantelpiece, swiftly returning with a triumphant look and a small oil can, the latter of which he placed on the desk. After administering the mechanism with a few drops, a soft yellow glow began to emanate from within, presently sending out small shards of golden light from its central spokes. Within moments it was so bright that Thomas had to look away, covering his eyes. When he opened them again the light was gone and he turned back to the table. Upon the desk sat the same Enfield clock case, but where the corroded remains of the Antikythera mechanism had rested was now a set of immaculate, gleaming bronze gears. At the front was a round disc that resembled the face of a barometer, but with a complex display that consisted of seven circular bands, the outer two of which were lined with scale marks like those of a ruler. There were seven gold hands of varying lengths, each one corresponding to a specific band on the disc. Two of the arms carried an embellishment: a sun on one and a crescent moon on the other. At the centre of the disc was a small hollow, identical in appearance to the winding hole of a clock. Behind, there was a series of interlocking layers made up of different sized gears, all slotted neatly together with pins and springs, and many bearing fine inscriptions and illustrations of planets and stars.

"Magnificent!" gasped Thomas, bending down to look directly into the mechanism. "It's a masterpiece! Utterly incredible!"

Michael, standing to his side, looked down at the young man, then to the Enfield clock case and back to Thomas. He raised an eyebrow. "It's a stopcock," he said dismissively.

Thomas appeared mortified; as if his porcelain expression had been dropped, shattered and clumsily glued back together.

"But it's a very nice one," he added with a smile, not wishing to offend the young man's admiration for the device.

"Now to wind it up." Michael picked up the little brass key that he had excavated from the pile of springs and slotted it into the hole at the centre of the front disc. He turned it firmly but carefully, each turn clicking with the sound of the mainspring. Once wound, he removed the key and stood back, looking down at the face. The seven circles of the front disc began to move, each rotating in a different direction to the one before, the hands gradually moving backwards and the gears behind turning seamlessly.

"The trick is to align all the hands with this section," explained Michael, using the tip of the key to point to a set of wavy lines at the top of the outermost circle. "Once all seven hands reach this point, we can turn the stopco… um, the mechanism off."

Thomas knelt in front of the desk, his eyes wide with fascination at both the object and its remarkable transformation. He watched as the hands ticked around the dial, each one keeping a different pace. One by one they neared the set of wavy lines and as the slowest hand pointed towards it, Michael gently inserted the key in readiness. The second, third, fourth and fifth hands reached the wavy lines, then the faster moving sixth, and the moment the energetic seventh ticked into place, he turned the key counter clockwise. A loud, low hum engulfed the room, like the noise of a ship's engine slowing down before coming to a stop, then silence. Michael waited a few moments, nodded to himself then removed the key.

"Is that it?" asked Thomas, surprised at the simplicity.

"Yes, yes, until the irresponsible bunch repeat the same mistake."

"Will the Colleges' time be back where it should be? And the river – will the river be flowing the correct way again?"

Michael opened the clock case and pulled out what was

once again the green corroded gear of the Antikythera mechanism. "Yes, yes. There'll be some *minor* temporal residue but the chronophage will mop that up." Gesticulating as he spoke, Michael held the mechanism nonchalantly in one hand, waving it about like a conductor's baton. Thomas' panic-stricken eyes tracked its every movement, his hands making involuntary catching motions. "It's of no use for larger spills but it'll take care of the dregs perfectly well. Of course, what they *really* need is a kairosphage, but what do I know?" He tutted.

Thomas gave a quiet sigh of relief as Michael placed the mechanism back into the padded tin. He then looked at the student with an intense, almost exhausted concern.

"The Colleges. They are charming and they are idealistic. They are collections of ideas, aspirations, embodiments of unbridled brilliance, but," he sighed, "the little twinkly lampposts, the ones that look so picturesque when you walk the Court at night, are twinkling a little less these days. And the Colleges won't look long enough to notice."

He smiled and put a hand on Thomas' shoulder.

"You should leave now dear boy, I must get back to my work. But please do not think it has been anything other than a pleasure to meet with you."

Thomas picked up the tin in one hand and held out the other to shake Michael's.

"So polite," remarked Michael, taking his hand.

"Thank you for your help," said Thomas as he walked towards the door. "I know everyone is really sorry to have bothered you. And your clocks, I really do admire your collection and the way you've looked after them. I only wish I could visit again."

"Be careful what you wish for, Thomas; wishes have a Jinn-like way of being granted!"

So heavy was the door that Thomas had to use both hands to prise it open and stepping outside he turned, raising a hand in farewell. The wide aperture shrank slowly, like the final stages of an eclipse.

"Take care young Thomas!" Michael shouted through the crack. "And keep the twinkly lights twinkling!" he added just before it slammed shut.

Thomas walked back to the Gatehouse door, pulling it open and staring into the night air. He stopped for a moment, his arm outstretched behind him, still grasping the large ring, lost in thought. He looked up, casting his gaze along the quarter circle of Colleges that were visible from his viewpoint. Those he could see turned expectantly towards him but all he could do was stare back. Perhaps it was the fatigue brought on by the physical and mental exhaustion of the past few days, or perhaps it was the extraordinary and repeated leaps of faith he had been forced to take, or perhaps there was a more profound enlightenment that was only now beginning to crystallise, but he felt different, like a spring had snapped.

He walked the path away from Michaelhouse, back past Peter and to the outside of the circle. Still he said nothing, his face unwilling to commit to an expression. As soon as he reached his rucksack he knelt down and carefully returned the tin to the centre pocket, leaving the bag to rest on the grass as he stood to watch Michaelhouse disappear. The tumultuous clouds did not descend as Thomas thought they might, in fact, there was no grand exit of any kind. Rather, with the Colleges still in place, Michaelhouse became fainter and fainter, until finally it vanished with a whimper and he could once again see the entire circle of Colleges.

Except one.

Trinity's place in the circle was now empty.

The Common erupted into cheers and claps as the Colleges rejoiced in a good job well done. They began to gather and talk in groups and Thomas' ears were filled with thanks and congratulations, but he felt unable to respond. He began to make his way around the former configuration of the circle, all the while receiving pats on the back and hand shakes from those he passed. But still, he could not speak. He rushed past groups of Colleges, ignoring requests to engage him in conversation; his focus was solely on trying to find Trinity and eventually he broke into a run to reach the space that she had occupied during the call. Nick and John were already there and both greeted Thomas with handshakes and a *gentle* pat on the back.

"Michael was really nice," began Thomas in a subdued tone. "The clocks. You should see the clocks he has in there. It's incredible. He took an empty Enfield clock case and put the Antikythera mechanism into…" his voiced trailed off, he was looking over their shoulders.

"Where's Trinity?" he asked plaintively, the last reserve of enthusiasm draining from his face.

John's expression fell to the ground. Nick closed his eyes then, opening them slowly, placed a hand on Thomas' shoulder.

"She *isn't* dead," he said with a soft, empathetic tone. "Not in the sense you might think. She was wounded by one of her own swords. None of us could hope to make an expedient recovery from such damage. But she… she *will* recover." He stumbled as if uncertain of himself.

Thomas was crestfallen, his expression competing in a tug of war between remorse and anger, "Will she be back? As she was?"

"Yes, of course," replied Nick. "Trinity is still with us, but she's weak, too weak to even stand in grey time. And it goes without saying that John and I will watch over her students and Fellows until she's back to full strength. But it's going to take time."

"How long is *time*?" Thomas was, very slowly, tiring of the endemic aloofness.

There came a remorseful look to Nick's face. "In all likelihood," he shook his head as he scrambled to guess the unguessable, "a couple of years, perhaps. This situation is unprecedented."

"What?! A couple of years!" declared Thomas, animating his hands in the air and raising his voice. "A couple of years?!" He looked around at the other Colleges who were still busy congratulating one another, patting each other on the back amidst raucous laughter.

"Why does no one else seem bothered by this?" He turned around in a circle, his outstretched arms gesturing at the other Colleges. Although Thomas was relieved the plan had come to fruition, he felt wretched and it confused him. The more he looked about him, the more uncomfortable he felt; the more erudite conversations he overheard, the more pithy quotes proffered, the more obscure works of art that were referenced, the more his discomfort grew. His mood was darkening. His mouth felt dry and his breath became short. Again he looked around at the laughing and the congratulations and he felt suffocated by it.

"Thomas," began Nick, stepping towards him with a look of concern. "It's okay —"

"No!" Thomas cut him off. "It's *not* okay." He began to walk away, turning briefly, "And Nick, it's okay to say it's not okay."

Thomas walked further into the throng of Colleges then turned once more, "And it's *really* not okay."

The disparity between his own grief at losing Trinity and the ease with which it seemed to be accepted by those around him, had twisted that nagging feeling in the pit of his stomach into focus.

"Hello!" he shouted to the Colleges. Nick attempted to calm Thomas by placing a friendly hand on his shoulder but it was too late, he pulled away and bored into where the centre of the circle had been.

"Thomas, please talk to me, tell me what's wrong. What's not okay?"

"It's just wallpapering over the cracks isn't it?" he replied without slowing his pace.

"What is?" asked Nick, earnestly confused.

"All of this! The hag stones around your necks, calling Michael, the Run, the Antikythera mechanism. Woodchip flippin' wallpaper. The *real* problem was the giant gargoyle, and I don't see how that's been addressed."

Nick gave a flustered smile then said in a placating tone, "But we did, we destroyed the gargoyle, it's gone."

"No! You're just not looking at it!" He burrowed still further into the crowd.

"HELLO! Everyone!"

The loud voices and widespread conversations evaporated into pockets of quiet chatter as one by one the Colleges turned to face Thomas and drew closer to hear him.

"Look at you," he began, his voice calm but exasperated, "You're brilliant. You're *all so brilliant*, so gifted, and so utterly preoccupied with being brilliant that you don't see what's going wrong." He turned in a complete circle, staring into the face of each College and as their bewildered expressions stared back, a lifetime of doubt ripened to something approaching certainty.

"Because what's going wrong is *not* brilliant and it's not about *being* brilliant." Their blank stares exhausted the very last of his once inexhaustible patience.

"Maybe I'm naive," he shrugged and let out a thin laugh, "fair enough, I'll admit to that, lots of empirical evidence to support it." He raised a hand in the air, accepting his own charge. "But *you* have a problem! You'll have to bear with me on this." He placed his hands behind his back and clenched them together, as if about to address a lecture hall full of undergraduates.

"I've fallen in cow crap less full of cow crap than some of the paperwork I've had to fill out over the past few months. The paperwork itself isn't the problem..." he paused, "well, it *is* a problem but the scale of it is a symptom of a much *bigger* problem."

He shoved his hands into his pockets and stared into the distance. The Colleges remained quiet, poker faces all round.

"You have a malady. It's an affliction wrapped up in a breed of bureaucracy that equivocates over the vagaries of what it does because it *doesn't do anything*. But it's convinced you that it's indispensable. And *you* fall for it. Or if you haven't fallen for it you consider it too irksome to challenge." He paused, as if disappointed at the banality of it all. "*That* is its raison d'etre."

Thomas rubbed his temples then held his head for a moment before continuing, "I mean, who *are* the pernicious overlords who slid this SIS:TUM into place?" He returned his gaze to the crowd. "Its entourage has been given the shelter of committees and guidelines, written into the infrastructure, made untouchable behind a moat of processes and conventions." He shook his head wearily. "You're becoming superfluous to your own existence."

He began walking one way then the other, "It's about administrative tails wagging the academic dog. It's about entire ecosystems of forms, processes, and project management software that doesn't give a damn if this is a university or a *fucking sweet shop.* But you *don't* see it. Do you? And what the problem *really* is, is that you don't *want* to see it."

He looked around at the faces of the Colleges. Some remained looking straight at him but others averted their eyes to the grass or to exchanging uncomfortable glances. Undeterred, Thomas muddled on.

"You know *why* the SIS:TUM exists?" He raised his hands in the air before him, "The same reason *any* system like that exists. Because whoever controls the system, controls those who are forced to use it. Stone me! It can't have academics running unchecked all over the place, doing research and teaching people stuff! Where would it all end! No, best stick a muzzle on it and a very long leash."

He took a deep breath.

"Like I said, no doubt I'm a bit naive, and I can't ever hope to see what *you* do, but this thing looks like it has long, *long* tendrils to me. The consequences are seismic. Despite what the SIS:TUM implies, not *everything* is a business. Not *everything* is for sale. There are swathes of potential students with first class minds who can't meet the Faustian deal passed off as tuition fees, so instead of formulating scientific hypotheses or writing the next great masterpiece, they're on zero hour contracts stacking the shelves in supermarkets or working for hardware wholesalers watching their fucking lives tick away. The system you pretend not to be responsible for is rotting this world from the inside out."

Frustrated, he raised his hands in the air then brought them down on the top of his head.

"And as for pimping yourselves out to uptrading workshops." He ran a slow hand across his brow and rolled his eyes. "Good grief! The concept boggles what's left of my clearly unhinged mind. All the wisteria in the world won't make that a good look."

He turned in a circle, scanning the Colleges. He had so much ingrained respect for their existence that it shattered him to speak harshly, but he knew he had to persevere. He ran both hands down the sides of his face.

"I'm not saying you need to bother your brains with every little thing that goes on in your world, and I'm not saying that you can fix the entire system, because you can't do that. The problem stretches beyond each of you, beyond the University, beyond academia, and you shouldn't preoccupy yourself with trying to fix that because *your* role, *your* purpose, *is* to be brilliant, that's obvious, I *know* that. But if you would apply just a *little* of that brilliance, a milligram of that perspicacity, a *soupçon* of your stupendous hive mind to the wider picture, look up from your self-obsessed pursuits for just a moment and *push back* when you're able, then maybe, just *maybe*, it won't one day turn into a ten metre tall gargoyle and kick you up the collective *arse!*"

Dejected, Thomas grabbed the coin that hung from his belt and tore it off, throwing it into the grass at his feet. He strode calmly but purposefully out of the circle, picked up his rucksack and headed off in the direction of King Street.

After a brief silence, he heard footsteps padding the grass behind him and Nick caught him on the elbow.

"Thomas! Please wait."

He stopped immediately and turned, "I'm sorry Nick. I'm sorry to let you down. I don't mean to insult anyone. I'm sorry to disappoint you."

Nick stared back, his eyes remorseful, almost fragile. He held out his hand and offered back the coin but Thomas shook a hand in refusal. His rage had abated but his stance had not.

"I have enormous respect for you. For *all* of you, but you're like a cancer patient that keeps on smoking." His voice had returned to its usual understated tone.

"I'm really happy that your world is back where it should be and despite the headaches and the salty food I've loved every moment conversing with you, John, and Trinity." He laughed, "Weirdly, it's been the happiest few days of my life. But maybe that's why it has to be balanced out by me making a fool of myself. I apologise for my incautious words and my intemperate language, but I can't take it back, Nick. I'm sorry."

Nick looked down at the coin in his hand then back to his student. He didn't utter a word but rather just patted him understandingly on the shoulder. Thomas gave a weak smile and took his departure. For a moment Nick stood looking after him but turned as John came running up behind.

"The right person at the right time," said Nick proudly.

"He's going to go far," added John.

Almost in unison they turned towards the other Colleges who were still standing on the Common. They had not resumed their conversations and a sombre mood hung in the air.

"We have work to do," said Nick quietly, tucking the coin into his pocket as they walked back to the centre of the Common.

Thomas didn't know how the Antikythera mechanism found its way back to the Museum but no one was more relieved than he, when sitting in Hall at breakfast, to watch Richard Wilberforce-Owen flick through photos of it on his mobile phone, whilst declaring from the opposite side of the table that it was "a piece of grim looking scrap."

When he awoke that morning and wandered bleary-eyed into his study, he had found his rucksack open, the old biscuit tin sitting atop his desk, and a glass ashtray nestled inside. He could only assume that – with Rangemen's discreet assistance – the mechanism had been quietly reinstated to the Archive Room by Nick.

Thanks to Wilberforce-Owen's vocal curation, Thomas quickly discovered that prior to the opening of its latest exhibition, the Museum of General and Local Archaeology had revealed the star of its show by posting a few images of the mechanism on social media, majestic in its new glass case. The corroded Fragment A, forever known to Thomas as *The Stopcock*, was now sitting in the centre of the Main Hall.

Back in his rooms and without the need to devise a plan to return it himself, Thomas set about preparing for his upcoming supervisions, or at least, he tried. He made a desultory attempt at reading; books, journal articles, revision notes, essays, but his mind refused to focus and he couldn't shake the familiar feeling that he ought to be somewhere else.

Rising from his desk, he wandered to the little leaded window and leant on the sill, looking across the Back Lawn. His eyes hovered over the river and he laughed as he remembered Gonville and Caius on their tandem bicycle and John's eagerness to elude them. He considered the arch in the Gibbs Building and thought of galloping over the wobbly bridge with Kára, his eyes tracing the route until it led him back to the riverbank, at which point he dwelt upon the first time he met the Colleges. Then he thought of his monologue from the previous night and he winced, dropping his head into his hands.

"God, I'm an idiot."

Thomas maintained that uncomfortable pose for at least half an hour, his mind re-playing the events of the past few days, contemplating what it meant for his future, wondering how on Earth he had ended up in this position in the first place, and that in turn dragged his mind all the way back to his childhood.

It was certainly against the odds that Thomas should have grown up with such a fascination for archaeology, all the more so because the successive councils of Baulkwall had done sterling work in expunging it. Many years ago, his father had possessed a small, thin book entitled 'Baulkwall in the 1930s' and Thomas would spend hours staring at photos of the once grand high street. It was like staring into a different world, yet in the same place. He marvelled at the charm of the pretty architecture and the sense of pride it seemed to instil in people. Perhaps that's why it was torn down. The once quaint town centre had been virtually demolished in the 1960s in order to march in a battalion of square brutalist buildings. All that survived of the old town was a small sixteenth century church and an art deco cinema, the latter of which was turned into a nightclub on one side and a set of boutique shops on the other.

"Probably would've preferred to be pulled down," remarked his mother upon reading about it in the newspaper.

"Saruman in charge of planning again," returned his father, shaking his head.

The cinema's colourful history was given brief lip service by a plaque set high above the main door and as a child Thomas often stood before it looking up, trying to understand. He *saw* the words but to him they *meant* something very different. To him, it was a betrayal of the past; here is the ground where something beautiful once stood, now obliterated for your retail pleasure. Here are the remains of something worth knowing about, buried beneath 20% off summer shirts. The moral of the story, he guessed, was that there are no morals; they get in the way of turning a profit.

It took Thomas a good few hours to stir himself from the depressive mood that followed him about that morning. Even the ducks had to bide their time before their first feed and the squirrel was most indignant at being kept waiting. He felt embarrassed by his speech the night before, but he fell short of regretting it. He wished he had been more eloquent in his delivery and that in itself annoyed him, and he tortured himself over not having quoted any Latin or perhaps some poetry that cleverly summed up the moment, but no, he did not regret it. He had gone from feeling the most at home he had ever felt in his life to feeling he had thrown a bucket of water in the face of everything he most respected. Wallowing in contrition, he pushed himself up from the window sill, still staring over the lawn; in a confined circle at the centre, the morning fog seemed to rise up in very faint, smoky wisps, giving the impression that someone had recently extinguished a small bonfire.

"I bet Wilberforce-Owen would have quoted some poetry," he said despondently. "It probably would have been the catchphrase from a supermarket advert but it would have been delivered in iambic pentameter, so that's okay," he huffed.

By mid-day, Thomas was still unable to settle, his mood as black as Newgate's knocker. He loved to walk and whether he was clearing a mind blank, window shopping at bakeries, or just strolling about the city enjoying the views, he needed little encouragement to get out. But he was worried. Ever since he took up residence at King's he had been greeted with such a warm sense of belonging that he feared, after his outburst, it might feel different, like he didn't belong. The spectre at the feast. Persona non grata. Passport a'la Porlock.

Thomas had never really belonged or felt welcome anywhere before, not even in his family home, but to receive the disapproval of 900 years of collective history was more than he wanted to face up to. On the other hand he knew that remaining in his room and dashing out solely to visit the canteen was not tenable as a long term strategy and he wandered back to the window, resuming his position against the sill.

"I wish I could have said goodbye," he said, thinking of Trinity. "But Nick said she's not dead, just…" and he stumbled to find a condition that made any sort of sense, "…under the weather. But I would have at least liked to wish her well." He shifted his weight as he continued to think.

"I do a good job of messing things up. Charging in when I'm not prepared. Story of my life." He wrote his name in a thin layer of dust at the back of the window sill.

"But I never meant to insult anyone, I just don't always have the same clever words as-as- Wilberforce-Owen." Frustrated at the thought, he scratched through his name and stood up straight.

"Well, Thomas H. Wharton," he addressed himself in a stricter tone of voice. "Slayer of grammar, imbecile of the moment, it's time you stopped feeling sorry for yourself, got dressed, and did the decent thing. Whether you're wanted or not!"

Thomas walked with a sense of purpose to his bedroom wardrobe and pulled out a wire hanger displaying his smartest outfit; a grey suit with matching tie, a white shirt, and on the bottom of the wardrobe floor, a pair of smart black shoes. This was the outfit he kept solely for Formal Hall, but on this occasion, it was an emergency. Thomas wanted to pay his respects to Trinity and intuitively felt the best way to do that was to visit her Chapel, even if it were just for a few minutes. He combed his hair as best as his unruly locks would permit then picked up his coat from the back of the door and pulled it on. Looking in the mirror he groaned at how the battered green parka undermined his very best effort to look respectable.

He closed Bodley's gate with a gentle *tap* and trooped off in the direction of the Gatehouse. The sharp Autumn wind clung about his face like icy spiderwebs and he narrowed his eyes into pillbox slits, blinking at the neo-Gothic buildings and their ornate flourishes, smiling at the angelic faces that looked down from beneath several of the arched windows. He was compelled to give a double take to one of the faces because he thought, fleetingly, that it winked at him. He stopped, looking up at the small cherubic face and fought against the wind to keep his focus, but it did not move. Disappointed, he pulled the hood of his coat forward and held it tight around his chin as he pressed on.

"Thomas! Thomas!" came a high-pitched voice from behind him, followed by the characteristic *bang* of Bodley's gate slamming shut. He turned to see Helena Troi sallying forth.

"I've joined a madrigal choir! I'm crazy aren't I!" she squealed, but before Thomas could make his excuses and get away, she launched into what vaguely resembled *Early One Morning* and which, unhampered by melody, left him almost lost for words.

"Well," interrupted Thomas, bringing her showcase to an abrupt intermission. "I can see why you're so keen for dinner and a show in London."

"I know!" she squawked, her exuberance entering the stratosphere. "Of course I'm now in an *unbearable* situation where I don't know whether to finish my PhD or become a singer."

Thomas, who was overwhelmed by the scale of his desperation to retain his position at College, couldn't help but feel angered by Helena's indifference to the same.

"I'm sure Cecil Sharp would be keen for you to finish the PhD," was his clipped response. He turned on his heel and started to walk away but before his mind could pat itself on the back for finally cutting short a seemingly frivolous conversation, he was instead struck with remorse for it and by the third stride he turned abruptly.

"Helena," he shouted, trotting back with a repentant expression, "That was unfair of me. I apologise. It's no excuse, no excuse *at all*, but it's been a challenging week. I'm sorry."

She laughed it off, "Forget it, we all have weeks like that."

"No, no, I can't. It was wrong of me." Thomas stared up at the buildings then back to Helena's placid face. "Look, I don't know much about zoology but I do know that everything I've heard about your research is superb. You've clearly got a talent for it, why set that adrift?"

She did not answer. The gravity of his response was disproportionate to the question, but for precisely that reason, she seemed moved by it.

"Just..." he smiled, "give it a chance, you might miss your research if it were gone. I'm sure it'd miss *you*."

And with that Thomas continued on his way. By the time he reached the Gatehouse he half expected to hear Helena's distinctive voice sing out to another target, but it never came.

"Going for a walk, Thomas?" asked James. He was standing in the doorway of the Lodge with a warm smile and a calming cup of tea. Or perhaps it was the other way around.

"Oh, I'm sorry James, didn't see you there, I was trying to keep the wind out of my eyes." He still had the hood of his coat pulled tight around his face and was now busy pushing back the sides so that he could better see the Porter.

"As much as I don't want to give their ego any additional muscle, Trinity Chapel has a special service shortly and you might like to go," suggested James. "I know you like that sort of thing."

"That's exactly where I'm off to," replied Thomas. "I didn't realise there was a special service though, d'you think I'll be allowed in?"

"I do. In fact, I think it'll be right up your street."

For a brief moment Thomas toyed with the idea of

asking James if he knew what had happened to Trinity, but feeling it didn't seem appropriate and was probably a matter for the Colleges to deal with, he simply smiled in appreciation.

"Great, thank you, James."

"One thing though, Thomas." James smiled as he raised a finger behind each ear and pushed them forward, giving himself a most comical appearance as he flapped them back and forth. "Tell the Trinity Porters to take their bowlers off, it pushes their ears out and in this wind they'll get stuck like it."

Thomas laughed and suddenly a part of the weight he was carrying fell away.

"Thank you," he repeated earnestly. James' unerring good nature was just the buoying up he needed and with a lighter mood about him, he wended his way out of the Gatehouse.

Despite the time of day, the short walk was not impeded by pushchairs or large groups of tourists. In fact, the streets were extraordinarily well behaved, so much so that Thomas didn't have to take evasive action to avoid a single bicycle. In very little time he found himself at the Great Gate of Trinity, but as he rummaged around in his coat pocket for his student ID, he noticed the 'College Closed' sign on the forecourt.

"Morning," said Thomas as he presented his ID card to a Porter standing beside the gate. "I see the College is closed. I'm from King's, I just wanted to pop into the Chapel for a couple of minutes, would that be possible?"

"Good morning, Thomas. Yes, of course. We can forgive you being from King's," said the Porter without looking at his ID. Thomas had long since stopped wondering how so many people knew his name and he now took it as part-and-parcel of recent events. The Porter was wearing a smart black suit and College tie, and an immaculate bowler hat. Thomas couldn't help but feel slightly disappointed that it failed to push the man's ears forward, but nonetheless he smiled again at James' words.

"Our Head Porter mentioned that there's a special service at the Chapel this morning. Are you sure it's okay for me to go in?"

The Porter frowned as if surprised Thomas had to ask.

"Of course, of course." He looked over his shoulder towards the Chapel then back to Thomas, regarding him sympathetically. "But as it *is* a special service make sure that you sit on one of the far benches closest to the altar." And with that he opened an arm towards the Court.

"Tremendous, thank you for the advice. I would have remained in the ante-chapel if you hadn't said, but I'll make sure to do as you say," promised Thomas as he walked through the arch.

"So very polite," said the Porter as the young man ambled off.

The moment Thomas entered Great Court he was struck by an overwhelming feeling of absence. He knew Trinity would recover, eventually, but knowing she wasn't fully present made for a strange, displaced atmosphere. He wandered towards the Chapel, its Perpendicular tracery draped like fine lace doilies over its large windows, and as the grey sunlight fell upon the stained glass it brought out a surreal vibrancy in the colours. The chunky wooden door was held open with a short iron hook fixed to the wall and from inside the sound of 'O Holy Night' drifted out through the small porch.

Thomas removed his coat and hung it over one arm, straightened his tie and shuffled nervously into the ante-chapel. Sharp beams of light broke through the windows, tiny specks of dust dancing about inside of them. He looked around, smiling at the statues and admiring their intricate carving. Then, bobbing his head one way and the other, he searched for a place to leave his coat and being nowhere else, folded it up and placed it beside the plinth upon which Isaac Newton stood.

"Sorry," said Thomas, looking up at the statue. "It's only for a moment," and he patted the parka as if he were leaving his dog outside a shop while he went in.

A magnificent oak screen divides the ante-chapel from the Chapel proper, and as Thomas walked through its open doors he paused in order to identify the correct seating to aim at. It may not be what many would expect a combination of stone and tiles to create, but the atmosphere was warm and peaceful, almost cosy, and Thomas felt very much at home, as if he could curl up on one of the wooden stalls and close his eyes.

The benches in question are arranged along the sides of the Chapel, facing the aisle, and the choir stalls are at the centre, but strangely, no choir stood within them. Without giving it too much thought, Thomas assumed the choir must be in the gallery behind him. Upon the seats no more than 30 figures were scattered about both sides, all wearing black academic gowns and with heads bowed. Heads bowed or not, Thomas was so very embarrassed at having to walk past an assembled mass while the choir was singing that he kept his eyes down, staring at the black and white floor tiles until, as instructed, he reached the bench nearest the altar. He quickly sat down, folding his hands in his lap.

Outside, the sky had darkened but the grey light it cast inside the Chapel merely added to its peaceful disposition. Thomas sat still, his eyes gazing up to the exquisite carved canopy, along the panelled walls, over the stained glass windows, and back down to the tiled floor at his feet. He closed his eyes, mesmerised by the beauty of the choir's voices and for several minutes fell into an almost hypnotic peace. He remained in that position, unflinching, until the last note of the hymn echoed through the Chapel and at that point, very quietly under his breath, he spoke.

"Get well soon, Trinity." He smiled at the stained glass window opposite, hoping wherever she was that she might have heard.

Thinking another hymn would commence in a moment and that his departure would cause minimal disruption if he left beforehand, Thomas looked about him, expecting at least one other person to stand or perhaps hear a cough, but no one moved and the Chapel remained curiously silent. Already considering himself an interloper at this, a special service of all things, and not feeling entitled to remain for the entire event, Thomas stood as discreetly as he could, side-stepping out from the stall and pulling his suit jacket straight as he slunk into the aisle. He was about to start walking when something gently pushed him back on the shoulder and as he looked down he thought he saw the slender, ghost-like hand of Trinity disappear before him.

Just then, a man sitting on one of the back benches stood up, looked directly at Thomas and began to clap. The sharp noise bounded boisterously around the otherwise quiet Chapel and Thomas racked his brains to think if he had made a terrible faux pas by standing when he should have remained seated and was now being reproached. Before he could ruminate further, someone on the opposite benches began clapping and he turned to see that they too were standing and looking directly at him.

Baffled, Thomas edged further along the aisle and as he did, one by one the congregation raised their heads, standing to clap as he passed. Irresolute and at the centre of an increasingly loud ovation, he looked shyly into the crowd for an explanation. All of a sudden he recognised someone, then another, and another. It dawned on him that the congregation was made up entirely of Colleges. He paused, uncertain what to think, his eyes making the journey all the way to the organ screen, whereupon he saw Nick and John standing either side of the doors, smiling; Nick with hands in his pockets and John leaning casually against the frame.

Reassured, Thomas beamed into the crowd and continued slowly along the aisle. The further he walked, the more of the Colleges stood and clapped until the entire Chapel reverberated with applause. Some nodded in acknowledgment, others smiled warmly, and the more he looked amongst them and the more the sound filled his ears, the more it overwhelmed him. Amongst the familiar faces he noted Wolfson who, along with Lucy, briefly stopped clapping to give a thumb's up – a gesture disapproved of by nearby Sidney who shook his head at the young Colleges' informality. There was Emma who never stopped clapping but did lean sideways to give Sidney a playful nudge. Girton sat on a front stall smiling, and in the row behind her was Robinson whose wide grin never faded from his face. He saw Queens', minus the straw hat, applauding faster than anyone else, her sparkling eyes thoroughly enjoying proceedings, and finally he spied Peter on a back bench; stately and dignified but nodding in approval.

Thomas' jaw ached with happiness, his muscles locked in a crescent grin as he looked from one side of the aisle to the other and back again, the sound of friendly thanks falling about his ears like roses thrown onto a stage, and it took every fibre of his being to keep his watery eyes in check. He approached the doors under the organ screen where Nick stood one side and John on the other, both now clapping. Thomas stopped briefly as he stood before them. Nothing was said. He nodded, and Nick and John smiled in return. They then each took a step backwards and faced either side of the doorway, still clapping as he passed through.

The sound of applause rang into the ante-chapel, pulsing through the stone floor until Thomas had walked as far as the statue of Isaac Newton. He stood motionless in front of the marble plinth, his eyes closed, listening to the final echo dissolve into the air. When he opened them just a few seconds later the ante-chapel was in silence. He turned to look through the doors and the Chapel was empty. Or, more precisely, there was no one inside. He sniffed, looking up at the statue as he choked back a tear and as he admired the near translucent quality of the marble, something hanging from Newton's hand caught his attention. Something small and shiny. Thomas reached up and gently lifted the item from the carved fingers. It was his coin; the one that George had given him, the portal key he had thrown onto the grass of

Midsummer Common. He wrapped his fingers tightly around the clasp and lowered his forehead to rest against it. Nick must have placed it for him to find. He sniffed again, wiped the side of his face with his sleeve and clipped the coin onto his belt.

After folding himself back into his coat, Thomas stepped outside, an ineffable sense of well-being settled upon him.

"We haven't had a service like that for over fifty years," came a voice from beside the door. It was the Porter he had spoken to at the Great Gate.

"It was beautiful," croaked Thomas, unable to elaborate. Once again he wiped his cheek with his coat sleeve then smiled meekly. "This wind really stings the eyes doesn't it."

"It does. It does indeed," agreed the Porter, tactfully gazing about the Court.

"You might like to admire the front of the Great Gate as you leave, sixteenth century, a lot of people miss the beauty of it because they're too busy rushing in and out beneath, but it's worth a moment of your time."

"Thank you... thank you, yes, I will."

The Porter tipped his hat politely and carried on his way. Thomas walked slowly towards the Great Gate and as he rounded its wall and glanced outside he could see a group of people standing in the street, looking up at the Gatehouse. People in the street staring at College buildings is not in itself a strange occurrence in Cambridge, but the number of people – combined with the mixture of laughing and pointing – hurried Thomas through the arch and to a position just in front of the crowd where he could observe the source of their amusement. The statue of Henry VIII stood characteristically sombre in its usual place in the niche above the doorway, the orb and cross in one hand and in his other hand... a wooden chair leg. The sword was nowhere to be seen, and it never would be again. No one knew who placed the chair leg into Henry's hand but Thomas suspected it would have been Trinity's Keeper.

Trinity had a dry sense of humour and as soon as he saw the ridiculous sight, he knew she would be amused.

For a few seconds Thomas simply stared at the statue and its irregular weaponry, then he chuckled and the chuckle gave way to a snigger, and the snigger developed into a full-on belly laugh. Very soon he was doubled over laughing at the beautiful absurdity of it and wiping away a couple of stray tears from his eyes. Well, the Autumnal winds that blow in from the Fens can be *very* cold indeed.

Thomas *did* do well enough in his Masters to stay on and read for the PhD. Indeed, he won a generous scholarship to do so. And the housekeeping? The wheels of large institutions turn slowly and the wheels of large, old institutions turn even slower, but some of the smaller gears in the mechanism showed signs of movement; when Mr T. Pyrone insisted that his office assistant required an assistant of his own, his request was denied and the funds diverted to King's for the establishment of a new post-doctoral Fellowship in ancient Greek archaeology. More good fortune arrived in the reappearance of Professor Thanatosis, who, in the early hours of Halloween morning, finally cleared his pre-term paperwork by setting fire to it on the middle of the Back Lawn.

St. John's led a coalition of Colleges requesting the old Metallurgy building be reinstated as a lecture hall, and Peterhouse was instrumental in blocking a University level decision to double the size of the Office of Data Service Transmission and Inter-Communication for Alumni Smelting and External Opportunity Quantification, or at least, until someone could explain what it did. But perhaps most exciting of all, lecture timetables were added to the SIS:TUM.

In a first known to the Colleges, the gargoyles of St. Edward's church never reassembled in grey time, even the beady-eyed one from above the door disappeared. Stranger still, they vanished from Thomas' time too. The disappearance of such prominent architectural features caused quite a stir in the city, with the local newspaper describing the apparent theft as an unprecedented act of cultural vandalism. Whether it was theft or whether their sustained damage, both physical and ideological, was so great that their destruction echoed forward in time, Thomas could only guess, but even today St. Edward's church stands a little architecturally naked without its spirited protectors.

— ∞ —

Seven years later, on another cold and crisp All Hallows' Eve, three semi-transparent figures materialised from the night air and swept silently over Front Court of King's College, heading towards the Hall. Inside, five long tables were dressed for dinner, each one lined with bright-eyed undergraduates eagerly chatting and exchanging anecdotes over after dinner coffee. It was a small, private gathering for the students of one of the College's post-doctoral Fellows, Dr Thomas H. Wharton. A quarter of the large Hall was aglow with candlelight, the flames casting tall and distorted shadows on the oak panelled walls, and a lighthearted anticipation hung in the air. At the other end of the Hall, which was shrouded in darkness, a table had been laid with a silver tea service and three China cups and saucers, though for the time being these chairs remained unoccupied.

In his spare time, Thomas wrote ghost stories for his students and it had become tradition for him to read them at his yearly All Hallows' Eve dinner in the Hall. For dramatic effect, he told the students that it was necessary to lay spaces for three of the royal Colleges because for one night every year, when their spirits walked the streets of Cambridge in corporeal form, they might be invited to sit among them. It was a tradition the students embraced wholeheartedly.

As the clock struck 9pm the undergrads began to tap their tea spoons on the side of their wine glasses and a low chatter circled the room. At the head of the centre table Thomas stood, coughed to clear his throat and held up his hands in appreciation. The sound of *clinking* glasses faded and the students shuffled in their seats to get comfortable. No one spoke, no one made a noise; all eyes were upon Thomas. He paused for a few seconds, looking about at the keen faces. When he chanced to look up, towards the unlit end of the Hall, he detected a faint, spectre-like movement and he squinted into the darkness. For the first time there were three figures, not just two, seated at the table, one of them pouring tea. The candlelight was discreet, obscuring the sudden watery sheen to his eyes and he acknowledged the figures with a subtle nod. He coughed again and evoking the spirit of M.R. James, commenced reading from a short manuscript on the table before him.

"Have you seen Michaelhouse?" He looked questioningly along the tables. "Be present on Midsummer Common at midnight on All Hallows' Eve and it might be the *last* thing you see."

Sitting at the end of the Hall, veiled by shadows, the three Colleges raised their cups in approval.

Acknowledgments

The most valuable thing you can give anyone is your time, so thank you: Adrian Boutel; Alison, Peter and Sofia; Jim Evans; D. Ling; J. Ling; Alan Marshall; Gemma Thorp; and Bert Vaux.

Elsewhen Press

delivering outstanding new talents in speculative fiction

Visit the Elsewhen Press website at elsewhen.press for the latest information on all of our titles, authors and events; to read our blog; find out where to buy our books and ebooks; or to place an order.

Sign up for the Elsewhen Press InFlight Newsletter at elsewhen.press/newsletter

HOWUL
A LIFE'S JOURNEY

DAVID SHANNON

"Un-put-down-able! A classic hero's journey, deftly handled. I was surprised by every twist and turn, the plotting was superb, and the engagement of all the senses – I could smell those flowers and herbs. A tour de force"

– LINDSAY NICHOLSON MBE

Books are dangerous

People in Blanow think that books are dangerous: they fill your head with drivel, make poor firewood and cannot be eaten (even in an emergency).

This book is about Howul. He sees things differently: fires are dangerous; people are dangerous; books are just books.

Howul secretly writes down what goes on around him in Blanow. How its people treat foreigners, treat his daughter, treat him. None of it is pretty. Worse still, everything here keeps trying to kill him: rats, snakes, diseases, roof slates, the weather, the sea. That he survives must mean something. He wants to find out what. By trying to do this, he gets himself thrown out of Blanow… and so his journey begins.

Like all gripping stories, *HOWUL* is about the bad things people do to each other and what to do if they happen to you. Some people use sticks to stay safe. Some use guns. Words are the weapons that Howul uses most. He makes them sharp. He makes them hurt.

Of course books are dangerous.

ISBN: 9781911409908 (epub, kindle) / 9781911409809 (200pp paperback)

Visit bit.ly/HOWUL

LACUNA
CHIMERA
Part One

Erin Hosfield

**You can abandon your past…
but your secrets won't abandon you.**

As a tattooist, it's easy keeping people at arm's length. Distract them with questions, and when they inevitably ask their own, reply vaguely. Lie. When the lies pile up, disappear.

It's a cycle Lynna's all too familiar with. Staying guarded is a necessity, but what keeps her safe is also what keeps her lonely. It's an empty existence, hiding behind lies, and she wishes she was someone else. Someone not burdened with a secret.

A year into her most recent move, the loneliness bleeds into her work, and she admits a few truths. At the insistence of a client, she explores the city's night scene, where she meets the enigmatic Rhys. As the months progress, so do her feelings for him, despite the risks of getting too close. When a dangerous encounter leads her straight into his arms, she abandons her past in exchange for a new beginning, only her secret refuses to be abandoned. With her life hanging by a thread, she's forced to confess, but the secret that will change everything isn't hers.

Set in an alternate present, *LACUNA* opens with Lynna's transition to an atmospheric northwestern city. Derailed from what she's built, she finds herself immersed in the lush world of medicinal horticulture, enveloped in the kind of close-knit relationships she always craved. Her fantasy has become reality, but not without caveat. As she plunges further into this new life, she begins to expose the conflicting threads holding it together, and what she discovers will bring more questions than answers.

ISBN: 9781915304537 (epub, kindle) / 97819153041438 (386pp paperback)

Visit bit.ly/Chimera-Lacuna

About V.R. Ling

V.R. Ling (Victoria) has a life-long love for science fiction and fantasy, and by coincidence science and fiction have separately shaped her life; the science part came in the form of a degree in archaeology, a Masters in biological anthropology, and then a PhD in biological anthropology from King's College, Cambridge. On the fiction front she is influenced by the likes of H.G Wells, Jules Verne, M.R James, Douglas Adams, Charles Dickens, Wilkie Collins, and many others. She also has a life-long fascination with the 19th century (literature, scientific advances, architecture); Victoria by name, Victorian by nature. She is an animal lover, vegan, likes sixties music, adores classic *Doctor Who*, and has an antique book collection that smells as good as it looks.

www.ingramcontent.com/pod-product-compliance
Lightning Source LLC
Chambersburg PA
CBHW051242210726

48287CB00002B/355

*9 781915 304414 *